Jim,

A Stone Island Sea Story

I finally got to sign one for you!

Beyond the Ocean's Edge

Watch for typo on pg 19

Dave Andrew McChesney

D. Andrew McChesney

outskirtspress
DENVER, COLORADO

Beyond the Ocean's Edge
A Stone Island Sea Story

v3.0

Cover image provided by D. Andrew McChesney

Outskirts Press, Inc.
http://www.outskirtspress.com

ISBN: 978-1-4327-8037-1

Library of Congress Control Number: 2012903259

PRINTED IN THE UNITED STATES OF AMERICA

Chapter One

A French Surprise

In February 1801, off the French coast, His Britannic Majesty's Frigate *Theadora* intercepted four French merchantmen attempting to evade the British blockade. After a short chase, and as she prepared to fire a warning shot, the four came about and hove to. The frigate lowered boats and sent one to seize each of the enemy vessels.

The launch, *Theadora's* largest boat, crept steadily toward the waiting barkentine. Edward Pierce, the third lieutenant, nudged the tiller to keep the boat on course, making the slight changes in heading without conscious thought or effort.

"A routine operation, do you think, sir?" asked Midshipman Thomas Morgan. His oldest uniform, purchased before a final growth spurt, fit snugly. The midshipman's white collar patches were stained and dirty.

"One would think," answered Pierce. "Still, something about it doesn't set well."

The launch topped a crest and the Frenchman appeared to be noticeably closer. The forty British seamen in the launch would board the apparently surrendered merchantman, place the crew under guard, and search the ship. Once certain that none of the crew was hiding and that the cargo posed no risk to a prize crew, the majority would return to *Theadora*. Morgan and eight hands would remain onboard, with orders to sail to any English port.

"How is that, sir?" questioned Morgan, continuing the conversation.

"Do consider the ease with which we have reached this point," replied Pierce.

As they drew nearer, Pierce sensed strongly with each passing moment that something wasn't as it should be. He felt uneasy and his suspicions deepened. It gnawed at him, distinct from the nervousness he had when facing danger. He had learned to accept that, although he wished he could face deadly peril with the same nonchalance that everybody else seemed to exhibit. His stomach would knot, he would urgently need to move his bowels, and a seasickness-like wave of nausea would wash over him. But it was perfectly normal for him, he recalled. Once action was joined, the symptoms would disappear.

"We sight them after dinner, just into the afternoon watch. Do they panic and flee in separate directions? *Theadora* is but one ship. Surely two or three could escape while we take one or two. Did you observe, Mr. Morgan, their quickness and precision in coming about? No disorder and confusion, as expected of undermanned and panicked merchant seamen."

"Aye, it did have a smart look to it. Many an admiral would be proud, did his fleet maneuver that well."

"I expected a longer and more intense chase," said Pierce. "Surely *Theadora* is handier and faster in these seas, but it should have lasted further into the night. Amazingly, we caught them in less than four hours!"

As they waited for the English boarding parties, the French crews maintained a rigid sense of order. Sails were constantly trimmed. No one seemed to spend their last moments of freedom raiding the spirit lockers and getting cannon-kissing drunk. Not all merchant crews awaiting capture did that, but it was known to happen. It was strange that they kept their ships in such perfect order, even if they were sober.

"They did not wait for the warning shot to be fired," commented the midshipman.

"And the bow chaser cleared away and ready to fire when they hove to. The barkentine led, but the others swiftly followed. Again, that strangely precise seamanship," added Pierce.

"Perhaps they want to be taken."

"Aye, they might be refugees, *émigrés* seeking safety from the guillotine. But why did they run? And now they don't signal or send a boat. They simply wait to be boarded."

Pierce looked across the water. A hundred yards away, Sollars, the second lieutenant, was in the first cutter as it headed toward the second Frenchman. Beyond him, Mr. Forrest, the first lieutenant, commanded the second cutter, and Mr. Small, the senior midshipman, the gig, as they pulled toward their assigned prizes.

The seamanship haunted Pierce. It hadn't been typical of merchant seamen, French or otherwise. It had been more disciplined, more precise in its execution, like well-trained and well-led naval crews. French merchantmen sailed by naval crews who were apparently surrendering. But why? Were the French up to something beyond giving themselves up? Or was his imagination playing havoc with the reality of the situation? It would be best not to take chances and be prepared for any ruse the French might offer.

"Mr. Morgan!" Pierce said.

"Aye, sir?" replied the sandy-haired midshipman.

"When we board, your prize crew to cover all access below. No one on deck without permission!"

"Aye aye, sir!"

"Simmons!"

"Aye, sir?" The grizzled seaman looked up. His graying pigtail bobbed with the motion.

"Ensure the carronade is ready! Fire at my word, or should the situation demand it! It will warn the others, if the Frogs are up to something."

Normally Pierce would not have explained in such detail, but with Simmons it was best to do so. The man was a superb seaman and an expert gun captain, but years of hard drinking, fighting, and whoring had deprived him of his common sense.

"For all of us," began Pierce. "We board as if under fire. Do not wait for myself or Mr. Morgan to board first. All hands on deck, rapidly as can be, and ready for a fight!"

That brought a chorus of cheerful "aye aye, sirs!" several grins, and even some winks as the boarding party reacted excitedly to the prospect of combat. Voices rose; men jostled and nudged their shipmates. An oarsman missed his stroke, caught a crab, and threw the starboard side oars out of rhythm. The launch veered drunkenly.

"Silence!" roared Pierce. "Damn your eyes!" He leaned into the tiller to correct the course. "You whoresons row like drunken Spaniards! Together now!"

Morgan rechecked the priming in his pistols.

"Don't let the Frogs know we suspect them. Act as before! You'll lose your spirit ration, all of you, does anyone's actions warn them!"

Promise of the cat would deter most and be brutally painful for the unlucky soul who might disregard the order. Pierce couldn't threaten to flog them all, and would struggle to flog even one. But the prospect of dancing at the gratings was not a guarantee of total obedience. Some sailors seemed nonchalantly oblivious to the cat. But if he threatened the sacred right to a daily grog ration, the men would enforce the order themselves. None would want to lose the time-honored privilege.

The barkentine was yards away now. "Pull hard, lads!" he said quietly, and a moment later, he ordered, "In Oars!"

With steerageway still on the launch, Pierce put the helm hard over and swung neatly alongside the Frenchman. The barkentine and launch were bow to stern, port side to port side. The bow hook caught hold of the main chains.

"Board!" he yelled and scrambled up the barkentine's side. He had a cutlass in one hand, but found a hold with the other. One foot gained purchase on a wale. He lunged upward, grasping the rail with his cutlass-holding hand. He found footing on the aft portion of the fore channels. Pierce tensed, leapt, and landed on deck.

The prize crew already stood over the hatches leading below, with their cutlasses and pistols at the ready. A dozen forlorn and bewildered Frenchmen stood near the helm. One wore an old fashioned tri-cornered hat and what had once been a fashionable coat. The hat was crushed and battered. The coat was dirty, threadbare, and patched in many places.

Its wearer spotted Pierce. "M'sieur lieutenant, why you board like this? We are surrendered! We are given up! You board not like gentlemen? Capture and sail for England?"

"We have new hands," Pierce said, as convincingly as possible. "This gives them practice boarding a hostile and combative enemy vessel. Even though, Captain ... you are the captain, are you not?"

"Oui, M'sieur." He bowed resignedly.

"While we are aware you have surrendered, it is safer for all that we take every precaution." He would not admit he suspected something.

He heard a metallic rasping, scraping noise from below deck: a sword or cutlass being drawn from a scabbard. A "clang" followed. Somebody had dropped something.

"Theadorans! Look alive!" Pierce shouted.

A seaman guarding the fore hatch crumpled to the deck, his midsection wet and red with blood. Three Frenchmen pressed up the ladder and hacked at the English with cutlasses and boarding axes. Two of the enemy went down, but more came behind them. Another Theadoran went down, and more French crowded out of the hatch. These weren't the barkentine's usual crew, but French Navy seamen, marines, and even infantrymen.

"Simmons!" roared Pierce. "Fire!"

Simmons obeyed instantly. The small carronade boomed. Pointed at the Frenchman's hull, its round shot and load of canister struck devastatingly. The blast tore through the thin scantlings. A chorus of screams, moans, groans, and curses followed from below.

"Lofton! Keep an eye on these Frogs!" Pierce pointed his cutlass at the small group that had been on deck when they first boarded. There was no fight in them, but Pierce would not chance them to flee and later cause trouble for Morgan's prize crew.

French seamen, marines, and infantry fought their way through the hatches and spilled on deck in an unending tide. Nearly dark, the deck was illuminated by lanterns and flashes of musket and pistol fire.

Pierce leaned over the rail and shouted at Simmons. "Keep firing!" The small boat carronade could not match the guns on the barkentine, had they been in use. Still, its fire served to distract and disable any enemy remaining below deck.

The British were hard pressed. Against two to one odds, they fell back to the after deck. A French marine lunged at Pierce, bayonet fixed and glinting dangerously. He deflected the attack, slapping the musket barrel away with his cutlass. He swept his foot and tripped the unbalanced Frenchman. As he fell past, Pierce brought the cutlass hilt down on his head. The enemy marine fell heavily to the deck.

Another Frenchman came at him. Pierce swung the cutlass viciously and felt it bite into flesh and bone.

"Theadorans!" he rasped. "Regroup aft!"

The British fell back and formed a small impenetrable knot around the wheel. The carronade boomed again. There were more screams from below deck.

"Another one, Simmons!" hollered Pierce.

As Pierce swung his cutlass again, he bumped one of four swivel guns mounted on the barkentine's after deck. Pierce pulled a pistol from his waistband. He opened the pan and let some of the priming fall into the swivel's touch hole. He closed the pan and held the pistol parallel to the small cannon. He aimed into the mass of Frenchmen that pressed aft and pulled the trigger.

The pistol discharged and the spark caught in the swivel's priming. It went off an instant later. The blast tore through the enemy.

He dodged a bayonet attack by a French infantryman. A quick push and the soldier went over the rail and into the launch. Simmons would see the Frenchman properly restrained.

Pierce pushed forward to the other swivel. He used his other pistol to prime and fire the small gun. The pistol ball struck the swivel's muzzle and ricocheted into the rigging. The pistol ball deflected the muzzle downward, and when the swivel went off, it viciously cut the legs out from under several attackers.

The carronade boomed again. Simmons and the two hands with him loaded and fired as quickly as they could. Smoke from the short-barreled gun drifted around them, caught in the wind, and blew aft.

During a momentary lull, Pierce heard sounds of battle echoing across the water. Evidently Sollars had run into much the same situation aboard his prize. Had Forrest and Small also met resistance?

Another Frenchman loomed menacingly through the evening gloom and powder smoke. Pierce swung his cutlass, and that assailant fell to the deck. An instant later he felt a stinging, slicing blow to his upper arm.

A young French naval officer readied his sword for another thrust. A real fencing expert, thought Pierce. No slash-and-gash lad. He had studied fencing years earlier but was never proficient at it. Still, when facing an adversary fighting in a trained and traditional manner, he instinctively tried to match it.

The cutlass grew heavier with each parry, thrust, or swing. His left arm ached, seeping blood.

Exhaustion and pain caused him to wonder if he would finish this opponent. Would he be the one vanquished? Desperate and in sudden fear of his life, he attacked with renewed vigor, causing the Frenchman to reel back. Pierce prepared to deliver the final blow, but the Frenchman froze and gazed past him with a look of astonishment. Deciding quickly, he swung the flat of his blade against the Frenchman's head, rendering him unconscious. The sharpened edge would have killed him, but he might be of some value alive.

Pierce turned to see what had distracted his opponent. *Theadora* loomed out of the night. Jackson had not lain idle after the boat's carronade had fired. *Theadora* passed along the barkentine's starboard side. Her fo'c'sle loomed over Pierce, and Jackson shouted, "Any of you below?"

The evening's first stars and a rising moon illuminated Jackson perched in the frigate's starboard fore chains. Winded and hoarse, Pierce doubted his voice would carry the twenty-five yards to his captain. He shook his head violently.

Jackson waved his hat in acknowledgement and turned around. A short moment later the first four double-shotted guns of *Theadora's* starboard battery roared out. Eight twelve-pound iron cannonballs smashed into the Frenchman's lower hull. The barkentine shook and trembled from the impact. The next four guns thundered, and again the prize quivered violently. The final four fired, completing the broadside. When *Theadora's* quarterdeck drew abreast the barkentine's waist, her four starboard eighteen-pounder carronades erupted and belched canister shot through the crowds of Frenchmen.

Theadora sailed past to gain room, turned to starboard, and headed into the wind. The momentum of her turn forced her past the wind and she fell off on a port tack. She passed across the stern of the Frenchman. The port battery of twelve-pounders crashed and roared, shattering the stern. Then *Theadora* moved on to deal with the other hostile prizes.

The surprise and the devastation caused by the frigate's broadsides quickly turned the tide in favor of Lieutenant Pierce's boarding party. With many of their comrades wounded or killed, the remaining Frenchmen fought half-heartedly. Cheering, the British seamen pressed the attack. More Frenchmen threw down their weapons and dejectedly held their hands up. With long-practiced drill, the British placed them under guard, forward of the mainmast.

"Men!" Pierce's voice sounded harsh and distant in his ears.

"Starboard watch stand down, but stay alert. Port watch, a dozen to watch the prisoners. Another five put this vessel to rights. The rest, with me! Mr. Morgan, you as well!"

Pierce stopped momentarily. He sighed and took a couple of deep breaths, glad the fight was over. There was no feeling of glorious triumph at having taken the barkentine. He felt merely relief. He was also very tired and had a very sore arm. No longer did the anxiety of coming battle tie his stomach into knots.

For the first time, British sailors went below deck. Pierce went aft to the cabin. If the enemy had failed to destroy sensitive documents, their recovery could prove invaluable to England.

Theadora's second broadside had totally devastated the barkentine's cabin. Pierce sifted through the wreckage. In a small and miraculously undamaged wooden chest, he found unsealed and opened orders. He also discovered a coded signal book. What a tremendous find! Perhaps these documents would give Great Britain the edge to end the long-lasting savage war! They lay amongst other correspondence, perhaps the personal letters of the chest's owner? Pierce replaced everything in the chest, closed it, and tested it for weight. It was not heavy, and for the time it would be safe in the cabin. He left it and went along with Morgan.

Pierce, Morgan, and five seamen worked their way forward. They peered suspiciously into every place where a desperate enemy might hide, kicking open the doors to the small cabins along the companionway and lighting the interiors with Morgan's lantern. No one was alive, even though many hapless individuals had been below when *Theadora's* broadsides smashed through the hull. Their unseeing eyes and silenced voices could not, did not protest British intrusion into their final rest. In places, the seamen looked through jagged shot holes and saw the stars' gleam reflected on the water.

Aft of the mainmast, a solid bulkhead divided the lower deck. Both doors that led forward were shut. Suspicious and wary, an able seaman kicked the port door open. The other hands stepped through, ready for any surprise assault. Morgan followed with the lantern, and Pierce entered the forward compartment, expecting to find chests, crates, kegs, bales, and barrels of cargo and provisions. Certainly, there would be more in the hold. As the lantern's light slowly filtered into the recesses, an amazing sight appeared to their eyes.

"Oh my Lord!" exclaimed Morgan.

"What the devil?" said one of the seamen. Another loosed a string of obscenities that Pierce wished had come from his own lips instead.

"Damn my eyes!" he exclaimed. "I've never seen the likes of these before!"

None of them had ever seen such heavy armament on a merchantman! Commercial vessels were commonly armed for protection against pirates and privateers. A typical merchantman would carry a few small cannon -- four-pounders perhaps -- on the open main deck. There would also be a few swivel guns to help repel boarders. But here sat huge hulking twenty-four-pounder long guns, four to a side. They were not cargo, secured for transport somewhere, but mounted in carriages and ready along each side.

"They'd have to blast through their own hull to use them," Pierce said. "But a dammed nasty surprise for anyone alongside."

Morgan was there with the lantern. "Look, sir!" He pointed and moved the light for better effect. "They've cut ports for 'em inboard. Not sure about outboard. See, they've strengthened the frames to take the strain, sir. Wager there're extra timbers in the hold as well."

"I fancy as much, Mr. Morgan. Someone open a port!"

A brawny young seaman tugged strongly at the nearest port lid tackle. Pierce stood at the muzzle of the huge gun and looked out at the lid. Across the outside portion of the small door, thin pieces of sheathing ran in random lengths, giving the appearance of an entire section of hull planking. The entire outer hull was covered with a thin layer of extra wood. When the ports were shut, the bulwarks appeared smooth and unpierced by any openings. No one alongside would suspect the presence of the huge guns behind the seemingly solid hull.

Why did a typical French merchantman have such an armament? Why was it carrying such a large crew of naval personnel? Was his earlier imagining just the beginning of what the French had planned? The papers in the chest might hold the answer. Since he did not understand French, he would return it to *Theadora* so that Jackson might read its contents.

"Mr. Morgan, continue your search! If we are taking on water, put the prisoners at the pumps!"

"Aye aye, sir," replied Morgan.

Pierce went aft and retrieved the chest. He hefted it to his shoulder, wincing because of his wounded upper arm. Topside, he set the chest down and winced again.

On deck, a sense of order had been established. The French merchant crew was on the fo'c'sle, guarded by pistol- and cutlass-armed seamen. The prisoners were despondent, but accepting of their fate. Meek as lambs, thought Pierce. They'll not be any bother.

The French seamen, marines, and infantry were gathered aft, guarded by eight British seamen. The swivels had been reloaded and trained on the defeated French. The small cannon reinforced the seamen's personal weapons.

Other Englishmen knotted and spliced as they repaired damage done by *Theadora's* murderous broadsides. Captain Jackson had aimed to hull the merchantman, but a few shots had missed and had torn through the top hamper. Pierce wanted to take no chances, either with the material condition of the vessel, or the slight chance that one or more Frenchmen had so far evaded capture. With the full boarding party available, it was best to effect repairs now. Later, with only a few hands, Morgan would not have a chance at it.

"Starboards, on your feet!" he hollered. "Go Below! Stuff what you can into any shot holes! Be alert for any Frog a-hiding!"

Those who had been granted a few minutes' rest groaned, but set about their assigned duties.

Midshipman Morgan returned to the upper deck. "We've been all through her, sir, stem to stern, keel to weather deck. No Frogs! Not holed below the waterline! No specific cargo, aside from those damned twenty-four-pounders!"

"No other cargo, Mr. Morgan? Very strange!"

"Aye, sir."

"I have the starboards at shot holes and a final search for hidden Frenchmen. When they're done, we'll stand down to a degree. Give the hands a bit of rest, other than watching the prisoners. When *Theadora* finishes with the other prizes, I'll return and you can have charge here."

"Aye aye, sir," Morgan replied as he set about implementing Pierce's latest instructions.

"Prudent of the captain to have prizes remain in sight for the night. You will keep young Mr. Hadley and that little brig under your lee?" suggested Pierce.

"Aye, sir! This evening vindicates your insistence on larger boarding parties, does it not?"

"It does, Mr. Morgan, although I never thought to see it be proven in such dramatic fashion. I sought to prevent incidents as befell Mr. Hadley this past November. A thorough search of that Frenchman would have prevented them retaking his prize."

"Nor could he be expected to retake her again, along with another Frog as well."

"If that scuttlebutt is even true. Never mind that Mr. Forrest asserts that it is."

"Hadley would be in a French prison had *Minerva* not recaptured the Frenchman," said Morgan. "With the crap he takes about the lost prize money, perhaps he wishes he was."

"Most of it is good-natured and quite sympathetic."

"It's only Mr. Sollars that says anything harsh against Hadley, sir. Damn upset about the prize money, he was. Still is, it seems."

"I do agree, but ask that you watch your words about a senior officer. We have our opinions of him, but best they remain unsaid," cautioned Pierce. "Now, kindly send up a blue light, that *Theadora* knows this prize is secure."

Moments later a rocket hissed into the night sky. At the peak of its trajectory it burst and bathed the dark sea in a harsh blue light that diminished quickly as it fell back to the surface. Within the next half hour, three other colored lights soared into the heavens, each one indicating that a prize had been taken. After a short pause, a gun boomed aboard *Theadora*, acknowledging the captures and signaling boarding parties and boats to return.

"I shall return to *Theadora* then, Mr. Morgan. The French Navy officers will accompany me, as Captain Jackson would entertain them, I'll wager. They would welcome a bite to eat, some drink, and an evening's conversation, although the captain may send them back for transport to England. Of the others, lock both groups below. Separate them and maintain a steady watch! Don't give them the chance to plot and retake the damn thing."

"Aye aye, sir. No need to end up like young Hadley," remarked Morgan.

"Indeed not, Mr. Morgan!" Pierce said.

With full darkness now descended upon the sea, the French Navy officers were herded into the launch. The Englishmen not a part of the prize crew joined them, their menacing looks and threatening gestures keeping the prisoners controlled and docile. Pierce climbed down with the chest and grunted an order. They shoved off and headed back to *Theadora*.

Chapter Two

To Our Advantage

Pierce was wet, miserable, and chilled through. An after-midnight mist sifted through the rigging, condensed on the top hamper, and fell in large cold drops to the deck. He could not escape the stinging drops of ice-cold water. His body ached from the exertions of boarding and capturing the French barkentine the evening before. His wound had been stitched and bandaged, but now his arm ached and throbbed.

Upon his return to *Theadora,* he had found secure quarters for the French officers and reported to the captain. When he finished those tasks and managed a bite to eat, he had fallen asleep in a wardroom chair. The nap had lasted only minutes before he was awakened to assume duty as officer of the watch.

He shifted the glass, strode to the helm, and glanced at the binnacle. The course shown on the compass was the same as Captain Jackson had ordered the evening before. Pierce felt the cold wind against his face. It had not veered, backed, nor varied in strength during his duty stint.

The midshipman of the watch stood by, ready to turn the glass. The last grains of sand fell through and he turned it over. Now in the upper compartment, the sand began another half hour's descent to the lower chamber. The young gentleman nodded, and forward a marine gently rang the ship's bell. Seven bells, three double "dings" and a lone final "ding" told all that the current watch was nearly over. Early in the commission, Captain Jackson had ordered the bell muffled or struck easily during the night. He knew sleep was often interrupted at sea, and sought to eliminate at least one thing that could awaken tired, sleeping, and deserving tars.

"A half hour more, sir," the midshipman said quietly and conversationally to Pierce.

"Yes," Pierce answered.

Midshipman Andrews was tired. He had not taken a direct part in the boarding the night before, but with so many hands involved, he had assumed a double watch, which had followed his duties during the chase and in launching the ship's boats.

The helmsman, who had been a member of Lieutenant Forrest's boarding party, was also exhausted. "A while longer," Pierce said encouragingly. "We'll all get a little rest soon."

"Thankee, sir. Thankee," replied the helmsman. "Beg pardon, sir, but what was it about? I mean, sir, the Frogs? Never seen 'em do that sort o' thing before."

"Nor have I," mused Pierce.

He wondered what might be found in the small chest he had brought back from the barkentine. But it was inappropriate to discuss such matters with even a trusted and dependable hand such as Hopkins. Should he do so, and even should Hopkins swear his silence, the forenoon watch would find the ship swamped with scuttlebutt.

He merely said, "We will know soon enough."

He kept moving, afraid he would fall asleep if he remained still for very long. While Pierce eagerly awaited the chance for some well-deserved sleep, he also dreaded the arrival of the one who was to relieve him. Lieutenant John Sollars had already voiced his displeasure with Pierce's being given the largest boat and being sent to the largest and potentially richest prize. However, it was the captain's policy to rotate boats and prizes amongst the ship's officers. Seniority did not dictate which boat or which prize. Nevertheless, Sollars blamed him for being assigned a smaller boat and smaller prize, his missed supper, his missed rum and wine, and the drunken stupor he invariably achieved if duty did not soon beckon.

In the next minute, Sollars was on deck. "Well, Pierce, I hope you're satisfied, keeping us up until all hours! Missing supper! Up at such an ungodly hour to stand watch in such god-awful conditions! It's bad enough without your ideas for larger boarding parties! Keep kissin' the captain's arse, and see what it gets you! Now, give me the damn glass!"

Pierce handed him the telescope, and said, hoping to mask the irritation in his voice, "Course nor' nor' west. Wind's not changed. Haven't shortened sail. Prizes ahead and keeping station." Then daringly he added, "Which they would not be, had this been done the old way!"

"Regardless, a simple boarding now disrupts the entire ship's routine."

Pierce, anxious for relief, patiently repeated, "Course nor' nor' west...."

"Course nor' nor' west. Wind's the same. Same sail. Prizes keeping station. I relieve you," Sollars repeated, in the time-honored tradition that ensured understanding.

"I stand relieved," answered Pierce. He headed for the relative warmth below and chuckled at the relative mildness of Sollars' remarks. He was too exhausted to be bothered by the second lieutenant's insinuations. Sollars was always contemptuous of anyone's ideas to better *Theadora's* efficiency. That he was did not surprise Pierce at all.

The noises of a ship coming to life shook Pierce out of a deep, dreamless sleep. A mere two hours was not enough, but in service tradition, all hands were expected to start the day. He would not be the only one lacking sleep. The hands were lucky to get even four hours of uninterrupted sleep. Many officers got even less.

It was an effort to move. His arm throbbed. Every muscle ached and resented the call to action. He washed his face, combed his hair, tied it, and dressed. He chose to wear the better of his two undress uniforms. He would wear it while the other, the everyday one, was cleaned and repaired. Had he a little more to his name, he would have had more uniforms made the last time ashore.

The chill wind across the deck revived him. He yawned twice, and that helped to further awaken him. The sun was not yet up, but a lighter, brighter spot on the horizon showed where it would soon appear. He mustered his division and reported its status to the first lieutenant.

"...and three in sick bay, sir, injured in last night's action."

"None killed?" queried Forrest.

"No sir, none from my division. But two are in a bad way, and one is not sure to make it."

"Not such a bad butcher's bill for last night's work. Four killed, fourteen wounded. Of those, five are serious," said Forrest.

"Gentlemen," said Captain Jackson, joining them from the hallowed windward quarterdeck. "Be so kind as to join me below! Mr. Sollars may leave the deck to Mr. Small."

"Aye aye, sir!" they replied.

"Fifteen minutes, gentlemen!"

"Aye aye, sir!" they answered. Pierce turned and headed below.

Ten minutes later the captain, the lieutenants with the exception of Sollars, and the master were in the cabin. Sollars arrived, scowled, and sat down. He scowled a second time at Pierce, who ignored it.

"Good morning, gentlemen. I trust all are as rested as possible following last night's adventures. So good of you to join us, Mr. Sollars."

The captain went on. "We must commend Mr. Pierce. While the effort required to provide well-armed and larger boarding parties taxes us all, it was proven useful last night. Had he not suspected something amiss enroute to his prize and prepared those under his command, the outcome might have been quite different. We surely would have prevailed, but damage to all ships might have been extensive. There would have been a much larger casualty count, both amongst our own and the enemy."

"He should have seen it sooner," said Sollars with an accusing air.

"You are indeed correct, sir. I should have seen it sooner," responded Pierce.

"Point taken, Mr. Sollars, Mr. Pierce. But are we not all at fault for failing to see it? We should have seen it, well before launching boats! Were we blinded by a routine operation and the prospect of prize money?

"The question throughout the ship is 'What are the French up to?' I have read through the papers Mr. Pierce brought off last night. While my French is not that good, I comprehend it well enough to know we may have uncovered something that could greatly influence the war."

"May we know, sir?" asked Forrest.

"Indeed," answered Jackson. "The Frogs have a vessel at Le Havre that needs to get to sea. It's so important to them that they won't risk its capture in a normal attempt to run the blockade. Instead, they would have it escorted by an English man-of-war; an English vessel manned by Frenchmen! Once through the blockade, that ship can continue to its destination and the frigate can attack British shipping."

"The merchantmen, sir? The guns?" asked Phelps, the master.

"Of course, they first needed to obtain a British frigate. The merchantmen were bait, a lure to bring us close. Depending upon how we had approached them, they had several options as to how to take us. Had they chosen to engage, the heavy guns aboard those ships could have overwhelmed us. Had they closed and boarded, they had enough men to overpower nearly any frigate crew.

"Had their plans been realized, those four would have gone after our shipping. Disguised as captured prizes, they would have had access to any English port. With those hidden guns they could destroy and disrupt vast concentrations of shipping."

"I see," said Pierce. "No doubt the guns would have played havoc with any vessels coming alongside."

"Indeed!" agreed Mr. Phelps the master.

"Naturally I'll notify Admiral Tompkins of this. He may use the knowledge to formulate plans for individual ships or the entire squadron. Surely he would pass it on to the Admiralty and His Majesty's Government."

"As of now, sir, the French don't know we have disrupted and discovered those plans," said Pierce. "Could we not take advantage of that?"

"Before we notify Admiral Tompkins?" asked the captain.

"Sir, might we say, 'while we notify flag'? We have four prizes. Let one carry reports while we make use of our advantage."

"I would think it enough, sir, having that vessel bottled up. They won't send it to sea without a captured frigate. We have eliminated that possibility." Sollars genuinely saw no need for further action, or was opposed simply because Pierce seemed to advocate it.

"Mr. Sollars?" Jackson asked

"We have done enough in this matter, sir. The admiral should determine any further action."

"Mr. Pierce?"

"I say we have not done all we can! That ship must be vitally important if they devise such a scheme to get it through the blockade. If we can capture it, that ship we might turn the war in our favor!" Pierce was fully awake, and his mind raced with possibilities. "Why settle for a little when there's the opportunity for even more? But we must act quickly, before they discover their scheme has been sunk!"

"Excellent," mused Jackson.

"How would you accomplish this, Mr. Pierce?" asked Sollars with a nearly undetectable sneer.

"Quite simple, really," Pierce stated. "We only need convince them we are French. They send out that ship so we may 'escort' it through the blockade. Far enough to sea, we reveal our true nature and take it!"

"A stroke of luck if it could be done." Forrest seemed in favor. "To convince them we are French? Do we stand in under the tri-color, they would not believe it. Such ruses are very common."

"A good point, Mr. Forrest. I will read deeper into the captured papers. They may hold the answers to that and other questions. For the time, I have it to follow upon Mr. Pierce's suggestion. We must use every opportunity to strike at the enemy. Mr. Sollars, when you resume your duties, alter course to return us to the French coast."

"Aye aye, sir!"

"Gentlemen, I will expect you for supper, when we shall continue discussion of pending actions. Until this evening, then?"

Pierce stumbled as he left. The alertness brought on by zeal for further action had worn off. Perhaps he could get an hour of sleep before Sollars tried to do the same. He fell asleep immediately, but tired though he was, he awoke when the forenoon watch was called. He was still awake some minutes later when Sollars came into the cabin and made ready to crawl into his cot.

"Pierce, you're the damn third lieutenant! The damn junior lieutenant! That you decide a course of action? That's for Jackson! Does he need advice, he'll ask it. I've told you before about kissin' up."

"He didn't directly ask for suggestions, but he did lead the conversation to where they could be made."

"You asinine scrub. He was merely being civil. No doubt he already had it in mind. He wasn't looking for suggestions, but you stuck your head in unasked. He enjoys your boot-licking enough that he puts up with it."

Pierce grew more frustrated with Sollars. "I may be junior, but I am a lieutenant. Do not begrudge me my efforts at my duty, sir!"

"Duty!" Sollars snorted. "You wish only to make a name for yourself. Your family, your father is nothing. Coachman for the village squire, he is! Think yourself a King's man? You can't even purchase decent uniforms. Took an old half-crazed yellow admiral to get you appointed midshipman. That, or you'd likely be pressed and on the lower decks. You're after the glory, the rank, and the prize money!"

"Sir! I protest!"

"'Sir! I protest!' Whatever for? It's true and you know it. Now get out and let me sleep!"

Even though the cabin was also his, Pierce was tired and did not want to continue the argument. On his way forward he met Midshipman Small. "Should anyone look for me," he said wearily, "I'll be in the cable tier."

"The cable tier?"

"Yes, the damn cable tier!"

"The cable tier, aye, sir! Mr. Sollars?"

"Yes! Damn his eyes!"

"Aye aye, sir." Small knew not to make any further comment about a senior officer.

In the cable tier, Pierce found a semi-comfortable position. He closed his eyes, and his breathing slowed. But as sleep rapidly overtook him, he began to wonder about Sollars' bitter antagonism. With the questions now running through his mind, he became aware of the rats scurrying about the heavy cables. The varied noises and assorted odors of a ship at sea filled his senses, and he found himself unable to sleep at all.

Sollars had been right about his background and his entering the Royal Navy. His father was a squire's coachman, an honorable profession. The family had always had a home, and food on the table. The squire was a kindly and fair man. Pierce and the squire's son had grown up together and were the best of friends. The squire had not discouraged the friendship and had treated Pierce as his son's equal.

Pierce had always thought he would take over as the squire's coachman. But if one of his older brothers gained that position, he would have been content as a storekeeper or tradesman in the village. The question of serving in the King's Forces never arose. His family did not have the money to purchase an army commission, had he thought to pursue such a career. While the squire surely would have helped, it was possible that even he did not have the resources or connections for such a thing. Pierce had given even less consideration to a naval career. He did know that no one of reasonable sanity volunteered to serve as a common soldier or seaman.

Just after his sixteenth birthday, two older brothers and three friends were pressed to serve in His Majesty's ships. He had felt an actual hatred for the Service, that it could snatch men out of their homes, away from family and friends, even out of the arms and the beds of wives or lovers, send them to sea with poor food, brutal discipline, and the ever-present chance of death or injury. The squire tried to get the five released, but he did not have the influence required.

One of his father's fellow coachmen was employed by a retired admiral living nearby. The elder Pierce had lamented the impressments of his sons and their friends to him. He in turn had spoken to the admiral. When the old sea officer had visited the squire, he had asked to see the squire's son and his friend, Edward Pierce.

"Lads," he had begun, "I know you are distraught by the press gangs. Yet, your brothers and friends serve King and Country. If the Navy did not force men into service but could rely upon them to volunteer and serve willingly, the world would be a better place. You can remain and risk further incursions of press gangs. With war, they will only become more common. Will you succeed? Some do and some don't. Why not the two of you obtain appointments as midshipmen? Become King's Officers and beat them at their game! It would be easier for you to find your brothers and your friends. You may not see them released, but you could ensure that their service is fair and just as possible."

Edward Pierce and Isaac Hotchkiss had been dead set against it. Both wanted nothing to do with an institution that could steal men away from home, family, and their everyday lives. The admiral pointed out that both were younger sons and not guaranteed to inherit their fathers' positions or titles. They both needed careers.

After many weeks' persuasion, Edward and Isaac had reluctantly allowed the old admiral to find them appointments. Luckily they were able to begin their naval careers together as midshipmen in His Majesty's Sloop-of-War *Ferret*. Neither had been quite ready for the rough realities of the service, and it had taken many weeks to find themselves. Both had endured endless hazing and seemingly confusing and conflicting rules and orders. Eventually they had established themselves as competent "young gentlemen."

Pierce had found that way of life to be second nature to him and he had prospered in it. He was not the perfect midshipman and more than once had *kissed the gunner's daughter*. To be caned while bent over the breech end of a gun had painfully caused a certain loss of dignity. More often, his indiscretions had caused him to spend time aloft *mast-headed*. In nice weather this had been a rather pleasant form of punishment. Pierce had known of others who had secured themselves in the rigging and slept through their mandatory time aloft.

Pierce had come to see that some abused power and used their rank to extort obedience and service from others. There were those that had catered to these demands and in turn coerced their juniors. For some time he had thought that he would need to become such a tyrant if he were to be successful. But that did not set well with him. He had been raised in circumstances where rank and class were blurred by genuine friendship and common concern. Instead, he chose to follow the example of those who led -- rather than drove -- the men under them.

He understood the need for rank and privilege to foster and preserve good order and discipline. Still, a senior should respect his juniors, listen to them, be concerned of their welfare, and most importantly, trust them. As time wore on, he found that he had to modify his idyllic beliefs to fit the realities of the service and basic human nature.

He would never order the last man on deck flogged. Pierce had seen that and it never made any sense, because there would always be a last man. He had seen men push, shove, fall, and suffer injury or even death, simply to avoid a threatened flogging.

Yet he understood that if an officer promised a flogging, the captain was obligated to back his subordinate. There was a certain loyalty that needed to be maintained, both up and down the chain of command.

Pierce abhorred the very idea of such brutal punishment. The first time he witnessed a flogging, he had ended up weak, dizzy, and pale. He had been shocked and sickened by the brutal sound of the cat landing on the miscreant's back, his obvious agony, his stifled screams, and the huge amounts of blood and torn flesh. He had to focus on some far distant spot and entertain thoughts quite removed from the ghastly spectacle, if he were to witness it without hinting at his aversion.

Aboard HMS *Ferret,* Pierce gained a reputation as a daring and resourceful young officer-to-be. He was quick to spot an advantage and to act upon it immediately. He was also able to note any disadvantage and act decisively to overcome it. He had learned to suggest a course of action so that his superiors believed it their own idea. If they credited themselves, it was fine, as he knew where the idea had originated. If they credited him, he was thankful.

In the fall of 1795, prior to his nineteenth birthday, Pierce had transferred to the even smaller *Mariner*. Although a midshipman, he was ranked as acting lieutenant and was very near the top of the chain of command. He was junior only to the captain, a master and commander, and the first lieutenant, the only other commissioned officer on board. The three had worked well together and *Mariner* had gained a reputation for bold and innovative actions against the French Republic.

His commission brought with it another transfer. He went from the small *Mariner* to the hulking seventy-four *Orion*. He served as her fifth lieutenant under Captain Sir James Saumarez, and saw fleet action at the Battle of the Nile.

As Pierce waited for sleep to come in the comparative solitude of *Theadora's* cable tier, he knew he was already more successful than he had ever hoped to be.

John Sollars had been commissioned five months earlier than Pierce, and yet he was nearly eight years older. He had served since before his twelfth birthday and apparently had stood the examination for lieutenant several times. Did his repeated failures make him envious of Pierce's successes and emerging capabilities? Did Sollars value social position and hereditary influence over ability and skill? Did he view his commission and position as a right, rather than an earned reward?

As he contemplated all this, his fatigue won out and Pierce fell asleep. Nevertheless, when four bells sounded, marking the middle of the afternoon watch, Pierce awoke and gingerly got up. Sollars or not, he would return to the cabin and clean up. He was scheduled to have the first dog watch and would be on deck and on duty in another two hours.

Sollars was already gone. Slowly, as he was still stiff and sore, he pulled off his clothes. He used a flannel soaked in the tiniest amount of fresh water to wipe the dirt and sweat from his body. Fresh water was precious and he used only enough to maintain a minimum standard of cleanliness.

He found the shaving soap, made what lather he could, and set about removing two days' growth of beard. He worked slowly, stropping the razor from time to time. It was an agonizing shave. The soap and cool water did not soften his whiskers. Every one of them fought against the blade. When he finished, he had amazingly cut himself only twice. Clean-shaven, he felt more like a ship's officer.

Then he donned fresh underclothes, a clean pair of stockings, and a pair of seaman's cotton duck trousers. His one good pair of breeches would so remain unless he wore them often. At sea he usually wore the long trousers more commonly associated with the hands. He had bought a few pairs at the start of the commission, but they had since worn into rags. Now he supplemented his wardrobe by purchasing replacements from the slop chest.

His second-best shirt was clean, and he was glad to wear it with its patched elbows and frayed cuffs. Unfortunately he had been wearing his best shirt to board the French barkentine. Now, one arm was cut through by the Frenchman's sword, and the entire sleeve was soaked and stained with his blood. Pierce's third-best shirt, the only other one he had that he might consider wearing, was decidedly more worn than his second-best.

Sollars was right. He couldn't even afford decent uniforms. He brushed off his best undress uniform, remembering that he needed to get the other cleaned and mended. If he didn't, he would not have best and second-best uniforms. Pierce brushed his hat and tried to mold it into normal form.

He glanced at his shoes. If a midshipman reported for duty with shoes that disgraceful, he would be soundly chastised and perhaps mast-headed. He found his shoe black and soon had them shining. He did not want to go on watch looking like an errant, snot-nosed midshipman.

Having some time before he assumed the watch, Pierce stepped out into the wardroom. Did something remain from dinner? He had not eaten breakfast and had missed dinner, attempting to sleep, but actually, brooding in the cable tier. He found a small plate of salt pork and peas. He was suddenly very hungry and fervently hoped no one had saved it for a later meal. He never considered that someone might have left it for him.

Sollars was the exception to the rule of share and share alike. It was commonly held that he counted every crumb on his plate, and if he could not account for eating each one, he would complain loud and long about his thieving mess mates.

Pierce took his mug from the hook and filled it from the pitcher on the table. The beer was stale, but it was wet, and he was thirsty.

Before he went on watch, he would visit the surgeon, have his arm looked at, and see what the doctor recommended for cleaning the blood from his other uniform. When his watch was over he would normally return to the wardroom, to have supper and an evening of conversation with his fellow officers. Tonight, however, he would join them and the captain for the evening meal and a discussion of their upcoming venture.

Chapter Three

Man Overboard

The first dog watch was nearly over. Pierce was glad for a two-hour rather a four-hour round of duty. Duties were split in the late afternoon and early evening to allow all hands a chance at supper and other evening activities. It also allowed an odd number of watches each day and a variance in when each watch was on deck. Pierce's duty as officer of the watch came in rotation and its frequency depended upon the number qualified to stand the watch. Currently, the three ship's lieutenants and the master shared the duty. The senior midshipman took a turn when it would not interfere with his duties as midshipman of the watch. On most King's ships, the first lieutenant did not stand watch in rotation, but alternated time on deck with the captain. Aboard *Theadora*, however, Lieutenant Forrest had a better feel for the ship if he stood watch regularly, and had inserted himself into the rotation. Captain Jackson had not faulted the idea and occasionally took the duty for a surprised and grateful junior. He once said he needed to occasionally refresh his memory of being a watch-standing officer.

Sollars and Andrews arrived to assume their duties as officer and midshipman of the watch. The turnovers were complete and as Pierce turned to leave, he heard the captain call out, "Mr. Andrews!"

"Sir?"

"I shall require Mr. Sollars' presence below. You are qualified to have the deck?"

Taken aback, Andrews stammered, "Y-Yes sir!"

"Your opinion, Mr. Sollars?" asked the captain.

"As any of the midshipmen, sir." Sollars was noncommittal.

"Mr. Pierce?"

"Undoubtedly, sir. Indeed more than many of the young gentlemen."

"Very well then," said Jackson. "Mr. Sollars, pass on to Mr. Andrews any instructions you would have for him, and join us below."

"Aye aye, sir!"

"Mr. Andrews," continued the captain, "You know the standing orders. I am to be called should you need to alter course or shorten sail. I do tend to overlook that requirement if you must act hastily to prevent loss or damage to the ship."

"Aye aye, sir!" responded Midshipman Andrews.

"Now gentlemen," he said to Pierce and Sollars. "My cabin in ten minutes."

"Aye aye, sir!"

Pierce went below, glad at last to be out of the biting cold wind. He hung up his muffler and pea jacket and ensured his good gloves were safely tucked in the pockets. He made a final unsuccessful attempt to put his cocked hat in decent form, and left for the captain's cabin.

Jackson welcomed and bade him be seated. Shortly the other officers, as well as Midshipman Small, arrived. He was the senior midshipman, and for many weeks had been assigned duties and responsibilities more suited to a lieutenant. He was in all ways, except actual pronouncement of the fact, an acting lieutenant.

"I hope you do not expect a great feast at the captain's table tonight," began Jackson. "My cabin stores are quite depleted, and I make do, as does the rest of the ship's company."

"Quite all right, sir," said Phelps. Here they could dine in more comfort than in *Theadora's* wardroom, eat from better china, drink from finer glasses, and sit in more comfortable chairs. The captain's steward had the first pick when a cask of salt beef or pork was opened. He knew for whom he prepared meals and took special care with them. The wardroom steward had several to provide for and could not or would not give as much attention to the meal's quality. In the wardroom, it was questioned whether or not the steward even cared.

After supper and the Toast to the King, Captain Jackson ensured that everyone had a full glass. "Gentlemen, an announcement before we discuss that French ship in Le Havre.

"Mr. Midshipman Small has fulfilled many duties normally assigned to a lieutenant. I cannot provide him a commission. However, I can designate him as Acting Lieutenant Small. From this time onward he shall be considered as fourth lieutenant in *Theadora.* Congratulations, lad." The captain reached across the table to shake Small's hand.

Small was slightly red-faced, either from embarrassment or the just-finished meal and wine and could manage only a weak but heart-felt, "Thank you, sir!"

The others, even Sollars, shook his hand or patted him approvingly on the back. Pierce raised his glass of Madeira. "A toast to the new fourth lieutenant!" Perhaps he celebrated that he was no longer the junior lieutenant, but Edward Pierce was a kind-hearted soul and he offered the toast and the congratulations purely for Small's accomplishment.

Finally Jackson said, "It's time we work. I have sent copies of my report with two prize crews. Ideally both, assuredly one, will find and deliver it to Admiral Tompkins. He would no doubt prefer I had forwarded the documents recovered from the barkentine, but we may have use of them. When we are done with them, they too will be sent on.

"I have spent the day studying the French codes. They are a cunning, resourceful, and untrusting lot. As Mr. Forrest surmised, to have approached under French colors would not have fooled them. For this operation at least, they use signals similar to ours. Ten flags, from 'zero' through 'nine' which alone or in combination can represent every letter. They also use certain combinations to indicate specific orders or messages."

"The same that the signal 'one, six' is 'Q' or 'engage the enemy more closely'?" asked Forrest.

"Precisely! But they've thrown a twist into it. Which flag represents which numeral changes from day to day, apparently at random. The codes for specific messages change from day to day as well. If today, 'one, six' is 'engage the enemy more closely,' tomorrow, 'three, seven' might indicate the same thing. The 'three, seven,' would be as specified in the day's code."

"Rather complicated, I must say," remarked Pierce.

"Indeed!" For once Sollars agreed with Pierce.

"Why such complications?" puzzled Phelps.

"It must be because of the importance of that ship's mission. Only those directly involved have the codes. Only if all signals are correct will they consider things shipshape," answered Jackson.

"There are also recognition codes. We are most interested in these, for if correct we will be identified as an English ship with a French crew."

"Simple enough, I would think."

"There are challenge queries, and standard or obvious answers may not be correct."

"Are we able to pull this off?" asked Sollars.

"It will take effort, of course. Answers needed are in the code books." Jackson went on again. "They have thrown one more loop in to it. The recognition signal also depends upon the course we sail when sighted, and the time of day."

"Damn! What suspicious bastards!" exclaimed Forrest.

"Indeed! Mr. Small, you are conversant in French?" asked the captain.

"Aye, sir."

"And you also read it?"

"Aye, sir."

"You will be our special signals officer. I give you full access to the

French codes. Copy anything you need, but they must remain here. Mr. Pierce will help devise a method of using their signals such that it doesn't confuse us."

"Aye aye, sir!"

"Mr. Pierce?"

"Aye aye, sir!" Pierce already had ideas about the changes in flags and codes, and how to implement them. "Sir, do they use the same flags?

"Good point, Mr. Pierce! They use the same, plus two we do not. But we found several complete sets aboard two of the vessels taken last night."

Jackson stood, indicating the evening was over. "We have two, perhaps three days before we put this into effect. We shall meet tomorrow at dinner for further discussion. Now, I must bid you all goodnight."

In spite of the chill night air, Pierce went on deck. Six men in the cabin for the past hour or more had made it rather stuffy. He was full, and perhaps had drunk a glass or two more of Madeira than he should have.

He had no qualms about drinking, even drinking too much at times, but he wanted to do so as he chose. If he had no duties or responsibilities in the near future and could sleep it off, he had no problem with it. When he had solutions to consider at the captain's request and duty in the small hours of the morning, he preferred his head be clear.

Sollars was on deck as well, having the last half-hour of his watch to complete. Andrews updated him on what had transpired while he had been below. He looked up, glanced at Pierce with a touch of scorn in his expression, and turned back to Andrews.

Pierce wondered at Sollars' attitude. Was Sollars upset at having agreed with Pierce on a minor point of the discussion? Was he upset at having to return and complete the remainder of his watch? He had spent over three-quarters of it at the captain's table, while Pierce had spent all of his on deck.

Pierce moved aft to the signal flag lockers. Each had several compartments that were labeled for and held several copies of a particular signal flag. Mentally Pierce took all the number *one* flags from their compartment and set them aside. Then he transferred the *seven* flags out of that compartment and put them where the *ones* had been. He continued until he imagined all the flags to be in different locations from where they had been.

That would allow them to send the French signals properly. If directed to hoist number *six*, one would hoist whatever was in the number *six* compartment. But the signalmen knew the flags by sight. Unless alerted to the plan, they would find and hoist the actual number *six* signal flag.

Pierce felt chilled as the warmth of food and wine wore off. It was time to go below for a little rest. He would be up again in the wee hours of morning.

Theadora rolled noticeably as the wind gusted or a larger-than-usual sea passed under her. Pierce pondered the sensation. The weather had been remarkably calm for the past two weeks and quite warm for February. The west winds had been steady and moderate. *Theadora* had been between Le Havre and Calais when they had encountered the four French merchantmen. Following that action, they had sailed northwest to bring the English coast just in sight. There, they would wear ship and head south. That would bring them back to the French coast and the Bay of Seine, off Le Havre, and place them back in their assigned patrol area.

In order to expedite capture of a particular French ship, they had headed south a day earlier. To approach as directly as possible, they were on a starboard tack, heading to the southwest. If the weather held, they would reach the Bay of Seine in a day or less. Then they could approach Le Havre and appear to be under French control. Should the wind veer or stay westerly and significantly increase its strength, it would be too dangerous to approach the coast. Too much wind, regardless of direction, would prohibit the French ship from coming out.

If the wind backed, *Theadora* would be delayed in arriving. She would have to tack, stand away from the coast, and get far enough westward that a starboard tack would take her into the Le Havre area.

Thoughts about the weather and its implications lasted only a moment in Pierce's mind. It was colder than when he had assumed the first dog watch four hours earlier.

Forrest was on deck, having just relieved Sollars. He spotted Pierce. "A bit cold unless required, I'd say."

"Aye, sir, it is." Pierce broke out of his reflections. "It was warm following supper. I needed some air, but I fear the chill has overcome the heat. I am on my way below."

"Thoughts on the weather, Mr. Pierce?"

"Colder for sure. Changing, I think, sir," Pierce answered. "But to what, I can't say."

"Nor can I," continued Forrest. "Now below with you! Warm yourself before required to be here!"

"Aye, sir!"

Pierce shivered and hastened below. He should have the cabin to himself, as Sollars would be in the wardroom, enjoying his spirits. He would not have to endure Sollars' biting comments, and could get a decent rest before the midshipman of the watch called him to duty. If Sollars returned to the cabin and found Pierce asleep, even he had the decency to avoid waking him.

It was neither Sollars in a fit of relinquished decency, nor the midshipman of the watch that awakened Pierce. Calls shrieked from the bo'sun's mate's pipes, and shouts and yells roused out all hands to shorten sail and 'bout ship. Instinctively, in the utter blackness that pervaded the cabin, Pierce found his clothes and threw them on. He remembered the cold and slipped into his pea jacket. He wrapped his muffler about his neck, and hastily found his tarpaulin and sou'wester. Shoes on, he headed for the deck.

The wind took his breath away. Large cold drops of rain flew horizontally and stung his face raw. Small snowflakes and pellets of sleet beat against him. He heard the loud tattoo they made, rattling against his foul-weather clothing. He shivered.

Theadora was still on the starboard tack. The stronger wind heeled her farther to port. The portside gun ports were often underwater. Spray exploded about her bows, and a steady procession of seas washed over the fo'c'sle and disappeared into the waist. Pierce staggered to the quarterdeck and let those there know he was on deck. He grabbed a speaking trumpet and made his way to the fo'c'sle, his station for making or shortening sail. He would need the trumpet to communicate with the quarterdeck or the hands in his charge.

The last hands arrived and Pierce hoped they appreciated that Jackson did not flog the last to muster. They quickly took their places aloft or on deck.

The bows dropped suddenly and Pierce instinctively grabbed a hammock netting stanchion. The port bow shouldered it way into a huge sea, and the water rose over the rail in a fury of spray and foam. The dark icy cold water swept aft.

Faintly Pierce heard the captain from the quarterdeck. "Shorten sail! Triple reef topsails!"

Triple reef? Pierce could not remember *Theadora* ever being triple reefed in his two years aboard. Surely, double reefed would be sufficient. But he was not the captain.

He repeated the captain's order. "Triple reef topsails!" The pipes screeched eerily over the wind's roar as they relayed the order to the hands aloft. He barely heard Jackson's order to haul on the weather braces. He repeated that order as well, and checked that it was being done. The yards were brought around and the shrieking wind struck the sails from both sides. They shivered with indecision. The strain on the canvas eased, allowing those on the slippery and precarious foot-ropes to fist it up and secure reef points about the excess canvas.

With topsails triple reefed, yards were braced around, the wind struck the after sides of the sails again, and *Theadora* regained steerage-way. She ceased the wallowing that she had begun when the sails had been set a-shiver. The heel was less and she rode easier.

Pierce wondered if the wind had shifted as well as gaining in velocity. Had it backed southerly, they would need to come about soon to avoid being blown onto a lee shore. As he pondered the question, Pierce heard Jackson give orders to make such a change of course happen.

The helm was put up and *Theadora* fell off her close-hauled starboard tack. On a starboard reach she gained speed. Jackson ordered, "Helm alee!" and she swung her bows back into the wind. "Head sail sheets! Weather braces!" The momentum gained by the short run on the starboard reach carried her head through the eye of the wind. The storm jib was shifted over and caught the wind over the port bow. The jib exerted tremendous leverage and forced the bow further around. Hands feverishly brought the yards around and the wind again caught the after side of the sails.

Pierce wondered why Jackson had tacked instead of wearing ship. Perhaps he did not want to put the stern to the seas that were running. Was it better to be caught in irons than to be pooped by a following sea? There had been some risk with *Theadora* on a reach and broadside to wind and waves rolling dangerously in the troughs. Still, in the just-completed maneuver, she had been placed in such jeopardy once. Had they wore, she would have been there twice.

Still learning, Pierce questioned his ship-handling instincts and compared his probable actions to those taken by the captain. Someday he would ask the captain his reasoning and Jackson, always one to teach his juniors, would tell him.

Theadora plunged through the raw stormy night. On the port tack she ran with triple- reefed topsails, a storm jib, and the barest scrap of a fully reefed spanker. The heel to starboard was moderate and bearable. From time to time white water flashed over the starboard bow and cascaded aft. Soaked to the skin, Pierce checked to see that all tasks were completed.

On the huge foreyard, fifty feet over his head, three skilled hands rechecked the gaskets securing the furled forecourse. As they moved inboard, their task completed, a gigantic sea thudded solidly against *Theadora's* bows. The frigate staggered from the impact. A shudder passed through the frigate that was magnified aloft. One of the three men on the foreyard slipped, his feet losing traction on the slippery horse. Pierce heard his shriek of terror, and helplessly watched the hapless man fall into the sea, yards from the ship.

Instantly Pierce shouted, "Back the main topsail! Man overboard! Man overboard!" He grabbed a line and heaved it to the man in the water.

"Grab the line!" Pierce shouted. "Grab that line!" The man struggled to stay afloat, but didn't hear or comprehend Pierce's pleas to clap on to the line.

Way was off the ship and she tossed and rolled in the stormy sea. Pierce found another line and knotted it about his waist. "Mitchell, tend this! I'll go for him."

"Aye aye, sir!" Mitchell grabbed the line from Pierce. "Dobbs! Hogan! Bear a hand here!"

Pierce clambered into the port fore channels. As the bows dipped into the sea, he stepped off. "Where? Where is he?" he asked. Men along the side shouted, but Pierce could not distinguish an answer.

"Silence there!" roared Jackson. "One man only! You, Mitchell! Tell him where!"

Mitchell scanned the surface of the water. "Mr. Pierce! He's aft, sir! He's aft!" Pierce began swimming aft along the port side of the ship. "Farther out, sir!"

It was desperate work swimming in the cold water. His clothing, already soaked through from the rain and snow, threatened to drag him under. He struggled on, guided by Mitchell's calls. He felt the line he had earlier tossed to the luckless individual. He kept hold of it as he swam. He might need to tie it about the man so others could pull him aboard. Very possibly he would not have the strength to keep himself afloat while aiding the seaman to return to the ship.

Pierce heard feeble splashes ahead. "Nearly there, Mr. Pierce!" Mitchell's voice came from the rail. Pierce's next stroke struck the man's shoulder. "You got him, sir!"

"Hang on, man! I have you!" was all that Pierce could manage. He rested briefly, treading water. "You'll soon be back aboard. Get this line about you!" Pierce secured the line under the man's arms and about his chest.

"On deck! Haul away! Both lines!"

Pierce let the hands on the fo'c'sle return them both to *Theadora*. He concentrated on keeping both his and the seaman's head above water. Finally they were alongside, and eager hands reached down to haul them from the sea.

"Take him first!" Pierce urged. Then other helping hands reached for him and he was on deck.

Phelps ordered the main topsail braced around and the ship resumed her course.

"He should be all right!" said Jackson. "Not often a man falls in this weather and lives. That he struck the water and not the deck is surely miraculous. He will be most grateful for that, Mr. Pierce. For your aid as well, I'll wager."

"I'm glad he survived," said Pierce, shivering. "Who was it?"

"Thomas, foretopman," answered Forrest.

"I debate charging him with carelessness," said Jackson. "Perhaps stop his grog a day or so. But in sickbay, he'll not be entitled to any spirit ration, and that would suffice for any penalty, should I so decide."

"Punished for surviving, sir?" Pierce somewhat daringly asked.

"Oh no, Mr. Pierce," replied Jackson. "I am extremely grateful for his survival, and I commend you for making it so. Rather, should I follow my intentions it would serve others as a lesson in caution."

"Aye, sir."

"Mr. Pierce, are you able to stand to your duty now?" asked Forrest. "Or do I make other arrangements for the morning watch?"

"That time already?" asked Pierce. "If I might shift to dryer clothing, I'll assume the watch."

"Very well. Get below and warm yourself. Mr. Phelps will keep a few moments more."

"Thank you, sir! The wind shifted?"

"Aye, it did. Backed! Near southerly now. Come up strong, in a matter of moments. We had no chance to shorten sail gradually."

"We've seen that before," said Pierce. His teeth chattered. "Tell Mr. Phelps I'll relieve him shortly." He made for the companionway and went below.

Chapter Four

No Rest for the Weary

Theadora plunged through the storm. On a port tack, she heeled to starboard and occasionally drove her bows into a larger-than-usual sea. Cold dark water exploded over her bow, turned white as it whipped full of air, and streamed, black and icy, off the fo'c'sle. Her decks rose and fell, twisted and lurched as the seas thrashed around and under her.

Those unfortunate enough to be on watch took shelter the best they could. Hands not actively engaged sought the lee of the weather rail, which provided a small break from the wind. Others stood by on the gun deck, where the gangways offered a minimum of shelter from the driving rain and snow. Two helmsmen stood shivering and numb at the wheel. From time to time, one departed for the dubious shelter of the rail or gangway and attempted to warm up. At the same instant, another left that miserable sanctuary and took his place at the helm. When the one who remained could no longer grasp the wheel, he too sought the meager protection offered and in turn was replaced. The lookouts operated in similar fashion. The midshipman of the watch sat huddled against the mizzenmast.

Pierce paced the deck, trying to stay warm, while wondering if the midshipman of the watch was awake. Sleeping on duty was a serious offense, but if he needed the young gentleman, he could nudge him. In spite of the wretched weather, *Theadora* rode steady and did not fight the helmsmen. Keeping on the set course was simple enough, so he said nothing about the rotation that had evolved entirely amongst them. The hands had also devised the rotation and relief of the lookouts.

He credited the hands because they covered their duties and made provisions for their comfort and well-being. At the same time, he berated himself for not devising and putting such a plan into effect. It was his duty to ensure the performance and the well-being of the hands on watch.

Sollars would have refused any request by the hands to undertake such an arrangement. Nor would the hands ever have developed such a pattern on their own, had Sollars been on duty. They would not have dared ask for or initiate such a routine, knowing Sollars as they did. They also knew Pierce and that he would not object to their attempts at comfort, provided all vital stations and duties were manned. Like him, they were merely trying to stay warm and awake.

Pierce timed his movements to *Theadora's*. He heard the wind play amongst the taut straining rigging and drum against the tight stretched canvas. He sensed the very pulse of *Theadora* as she reacted like a living creature to the forces of the wind and sea. He was acutely aware of the sounds, motions, and vibrations of the frigate, even though his mind wandered and was currently on other matters. Should the tune of the gale singing through her masts change, or should the rhythm of her movements alter, he would know instantly.

While the weather had seemed cold a day ago, the wind had not been an icy wild beast that sucked the warmth out of him. A day earlier, it had been a benevolent force of nature that gently propelled *Theadora* through the water. The mist that condensed on the rigging to fall like rain had been the most uncomfortable aspect of that previous watch.

Now he was tired and sore again. Earlier he had been roused from his sleep, along with the whole of *Theadora's* crew, in order to reef sail and 'bout ship. That was exhausting in itself, but as that evolution ended, a foretopman fell into the sea, and Pierce had gone into the frigid water to save the doomed man.

The knowledge that he had succeeded and a double shot of brandy had warmed him. He had changed into drier clothing and assumed the watch. Although Lieutenant Forrest had offered to have someone else stand the duty, it never occurred to Pierce to beg relief from duty after his unplanned frigid swim.

Thomas, whom he had rescued, rested warmly in sickbay as he recovered from his ordeal. All but the most cold-hearted of officers would grant him some time to regain his strength. Pierce, while also having gone into the sea, hadn't slipped and fallen from aloft. He had waited until the ship plunged into a sea and had stepped off into the water.

The wind and rain cut through his clothing, chilling him to his core. His teeth chattered. He wrapped his sodden garments more tightly about him, and quickened his pace, hoping the increased activity would warm him.

The sound of the pumps changed. They had been going all the while, but their clanging and banging had faded into the background of normal shipboard noises. Now, with new strong hands working them, Pierce noticed that the rhythm became faster and stronger. Another failure on his part, he thought. As with relief for the helmsmen and lookouts, he had not made provisions for keeping the pumps manned.

The wind gusted. Chilled by the increased blast, Pierce shivered. What was he doing on deck during a winter storm? Better to be below, out of the wind and rain and snow. Best, he thought, to be ashore and indoors, seated before a huge roaring fire.

The answer, which he knew, even as he asked the question, lay in his sense of duty, his feelings of loyalty, and his conception of honor. It was in response to all three that he faced the elements and strove to ensure the safety of *Theadora* and the well being of her crew. Beyond that, it was his immediate responsibility to preserve the frigate as a fighting machine that defended King and Country. Pierce and the others fought to protect and defend not only a nation, but a way of life.

He believed that the fight would eventually cleanse the world of war itself. Once the conflict was over, Englishmen would no longer worry about press gangs and cruel dangerous sea service. He despised obtaining crews by such means, although he knew that it was often the only way to man the ships. Would these damnable wars end so the Navy wouldn't require more men than it could find? Would that service to King and Country before the mast be a rewarding and worthwhile vocation, something desired and sought-after, rather than despised and avoided?

The real end of the war would also mean that the French, Germans, Italians, Poles, Spanish, and others throughout Europe would not need to worry about conscription into the various armies. Nor would they have to worry about goods or property being summarily commandeered for military use.

The war, a result of the French Revolution, had gone on for years, and appeared that it would go on for many more. Pierce did not blame the French for their original tries at liberty, but they had wanted too much. The process had exploded into chaos. The Reign of Terror, with its unreasoning slaughter, had led to governments that, while pledged to liberty and justice, were as corrupt as the deposed French monarchy. After arbitrarily redrawing the internal map of their nation, the French had embarked on a conquest of all of Europe.

If only the French had followed the United States in their Revolution! The British colonists in North America had declared their independence from England just three months before Pierce was born. That war had lasted long enough for him to have heard it discussed as he grew older. At first he had thought the colonists misguided, but later evaluation caused him to alter his thinking.

In the beginning, the colonists had fought to preserve their rights and status as British subjects. It was only when these grievances were not satisfactorily addressed that they had declared themselves free of the Crown. When freedom was won, they had not silenced opposing factions or sought to bloodily conquer new lands. The new nation had remained relatively weak and vulnerable, such was its fear of strong government and large standing armies.

However, the Americans had realized the flaws inherent in their original government and had adopted a written constitution. Pierce had studied it several years earlier and admired the balance that had been achieved among the three separate branches of government. Compromises balancing the state's power with the rights of individual citizens, and provisions for an orderly transfer of power at regular intervals impressed him. He had been astounded when Washington had stepped down after two terms as president. Washington had the power, charisma, and public adoration to have continued in office and to have by fact or declaration become a king.

Pierce indeed admired the United States, although he struggled with the concept of a nation without a designated sovereign. He often admitted to himself that he would not want to go to war with that new nation. He was not worried about their tiny navy and any minuscule threat it posed to the mighty British fleet. He simply would not want to fight a people that were so after his own heart.

The blackness of the night started to gray a little. Dawn would arrive soon, and not long after, his cold wet stint as officer of the watch would end. Had the wind slackened? Had the rain eased as well? He watched the hands trying to stay dry as they went about their rotations at the helm, on lookout, and at other required duties.

He felt fortunate to serve in *Theadora*. She was a good ship, although one of the smallest frigates in the Royal Navy. Rated at twenty-eight-guns, she mounted a dozen twelve-pounders along each side of her main deck -- an upgrade, due to her stout construction, from the nine pounders normally carried by ships of her rate. She mounted two long nines as bow chasers, and two more as stern chasers. Four eighteen-pound-carronades were set evenly spaced along each side of the quarter deck.

Theadora's crew was well-trained after more than a year in commission. Most hands got along well with each other. The officers and warrant officers recognized each other's rank, seniority, and professional abilities.

They were for the most part good and true friends. There was a common respectful bond between the officers and crew. They had taken many prizes during the commission, and when it ended, all would profit.

Pierce was lucky to serve under Captain Granville Jackson. Like Pierce and many of the officers aboard, he was not a man of class or social distinction. He had earned his commission and post rank solely by his efforts and accomplishments. He trusted his officers and readily sought their opinions and advice. When suggestions were made he accepted them gratefully, and if acted upon gave proper credit.

Pierce had served with others who would not accept anyone's ideas or suggestions. To make a suggestion then, he had had to be subtle and indirect. He had to stealthily guide those individuals so that they arrived at the same conclusion and thought it their original idea. He found it refreshing to be direct and to the point when suggesting alternative courses of action.

Pierce knew that Jackson often sought suggestions in order to confirm his own plans and ideas. Still, the captain was open to those that differed from his. Perhaps differing opinions allowed him to see the situation from other angles. By seeking their opinions and suggestions, Jackson was, in reality, training them. He had once said that he was constantly training his replacement. Someday Jackson would have the seniority to captain a larger frigate or a ship-of- the-line. By then one of his lieutenants might have made post and been placed in command of *Theadora* or a similarly rated ship.

Jackson was also quite an enlightened disciplinarian. Floggings were rare and usually occurred when a less humane junior officer promised one. There were also certain offenses that regulations and tradition directed to be punished in such a manner. Jackson preferred that miscreants perform extra and often distasteful duties. Watch and watch was common for any errant officer or midshipman. A misbehaving seaman could expect to clean heads or polish bright work.

Sometimes an offending individual stood back-to-back watches. For many, it was punishment enough that the captain knew of the offense.

Forrest would probably remain a lieutenant. He was an excellent officer and fit perfectly into his role as the captain's assistant. But he lacked imagination and a flair for innovation. Routines he knew posed no problem, but a couple of twists or a situation that he had not seen before completely baffled him. He was a good, true, honest officer, and an excellent seaman. Pierce felt fortunate to serve with him.

The only person aboard ship that Pierce had any problems with was his immediate senior. Sollars, the second lieutenant, evidently felt that he was of a higher class than even the captain. He resented that the others, especially Pierce, constantly made suggestions. He seemed not to care about their success or winning the war. Yet should a chance for prize money slip away, he groused about it for days. Sollars had been deeply bitter about the loss of prize money when the French crew had overpowered Midshipman Hadley's prize crew and recaptured their ship. He had said some very vile and nasty things about Hadley in the months that had followed.

Lord help the crew of any ship that Sollars ever commanded! He was cruel, heartless, and saw the average seaman as a cogwheel in the machinery of the ship. He continuously threatened floggings in spite of extra watches ordered by the captain. Most of the discipline problems were in his division, or amongst those assigned special details or duties under him. Midshipman, now Acting Lieutenant Small, was inventive, adventurous, loyal, and courageous. Pierce held him in high esteem. He could be counted on in battle, or as a shipmate and friend.

The black morning lightened and became more of a dismal gray. A dark form mounted the ladder to the quarterdeck. The figure, dressed in a tarpaulin and sou'wester, was difficult to identify. As the individual neared, Pierce saw that it was the captain.

The captain! The midshipman of the watch slept not more than six feet away! Should the captain find it a sufficiently grave offense, he could come down hard on the hapless young gentleman as well as on the officer of the watch. It was Pierce's duty to ensure young Mr. Townsend remained awake. Again he chastised himself for failing to do his duty.

Pierce made a subtle move toward the sleeping figure. He hoped to kick it awake, unnoticed by the captain. "Never mind, Mr. Pierce!" said the captain. "Lad can sleep through anything, I'll wager. He's here should you need him."

"Aye aye, sir!" Relief at the captain's understanding washed over him.

"The weather eases, would you say?"

"Indeed it does. I had determined that should it lessen more, to have sent below for permission to shake out a reef."

"About at that point. But let it wait until the day begins. Hands need their rest."

"Aye, sir."

The helmsman at the wheel the longest started to head for the lee of the weather rail. He noticed the captain, halted, and resumed his duties. "Mr. Pierce?" he called quietly, "Beggin' your pardon, sir, but can we still…?"

"Aye, carry on as before," answered Pierce.

"Excellent move, Mr. Pierce! If he can't grasp the wheel, he isn't of much use."

"Aye, sir. But credit the hands for it. I saw sense in it and allowed it."

"Wager you'll make a fine captain, Mr. Pierce. Never underestimate the resourcefulness, the loyalty, and dedication of the hands."

"Aye, sir."

"Now that Mr. Small is acting fourth, he has been inserted into the officer of the watch rotation. He'll relieve Mr. Sollars at noon. I suggest the two of you smooth your plans for the French signals. We want it all finalized this evening."

"I have part of it in mind, sir. To do so properly we will need the carpenter and the sail maker," Pierce said. "It would do to have separate stowage for the French flags."

"Splendid!" replied the captain. "When you and Mr. Small reach final agreement, have Mr. Cook and Mr. Nielson provide."

"Aye aye, sir."

One helmsman glanced knowingly at the other and nodded. His partner momentarily left the wheel and prodded the midshipman of the watch. "Mr. Townsend! Sand's about outta the glass, sir!"

Townsend stirred and rubbed his eyes with cold, chapped hands. He got to his feet and instinctively caught his balance as the deck heaved under him. He spotted the captain and nearly lost his balance a second time. He had been sleeping on watch, and the captain knew it. Surely he would be severely punished. His mouth opened and shut silently as he tried to speak and could not.

Pierce saw his alarm. "You need not worry, Mr. Townsend. We have both been excused for your nap. Please attend your duties."

"Aye aye, sir!" His relief was evident. He watched the last grains of sand run out and deftly turned the glass. "Three bells, sir."

"Thank you, Mr. Townsend," said Pierce. It was only an hour and a half into the watch, and in another thirty minutes the day would begin for *Theadora.* Four bells would be struck vigorously. The bo'sun's mates would start the caterwauling of their pipes and run through the berth deck ensuring that every last man jack was up.

Pierce preferred that his relief, the unpleasant Lieutenant Sollars, not be on deck any sooner than required. But as the morning watch lasted two hours into the official day, Sollars would be up and about well ahead of time. Pierce did not look forward to Sollars' presence. He merely wanted to get out of the weather and into some dry clothes, and get a minimum of sleep.

Sollars arrived soon after three bells sounded. He was freshly shaven and dressed in relatively clean and dry clothes. His eyes were slightly bloodshot, and he rubbed at them vigorously. "Well, Pierce," he said. "I suppose 'congratulations' are in order. It's not every man that falls from aloft and lives to tell it. That is one lucky topman!

"But if I were captain, you would be under arrest and confined to quarters. The nerve, I say, countermanding the captain's orders! Risking your life, the life of a King's Officer, to save someone! Christ, Pierce, men die all the time! It's a dangerous occupation we subscribe to. And you, gone for a swim to save a common seaman."

"Mr. Sollars!" the captain said forcefully from the weather quarterdeck. The second lieutenant had not noticed the captain's presence, or had not realized the volume of his speech. "Most fortunate you are not captain!"

"Sir?"

"I fully supported Mr. Pierce's actions. Had I not, his orders would have been overridden at once. Never forget, Mr. Sollars, the real backbone of this ship, any ship, are those who are skilled in working her, the hands for which you have so much disdain. Good topmen are worth their weight in gold, and we cannot afford to lose even one. We have enough hands away in prizes that we are short throughout the ship. Mr. Pierce's actions met the ideal of service to the ship, to his shipmates, to the Navy, and to the nation itself. Think of his performance as you desire. But do you not come on *my* quarterdeck and presume to tell me that such performance of duty is wrong!

"Until otherwise informed, you will relieve Mr. Phelps as well as Mr. Pierce. See to it you properly relieve Mr. Pierce when time!"

"Aye aye, sir!" answered Sollars with a trace of resentment in his voice and a glare of defiance in his eyes. If Jackson observed it, he didn't respond. However, Pierce noticed, and would lay odds that Jackson had seen and would remember it.

Pierce seethed, angry with himself for what he saw as omissions in his duty. He was irate at Lieutenant Sollars' remarks and because he had not spoken to defend himself. He was ashamed that Jackson had had to defend his actions. Still, it was better that the captain should do it. He was junior to Sollars and needed to watch his words. With rancor already between them, an inappropriate remark could spell the end of his career. At present, he was nearly mad and tired enough to cross the fine line of self-control and do something that would land him in real trouble. He actually thought to plant his fist firmly on Sollars' nose and flatten it.

Self-control and reason took over as Pierce gradually calmed himself.

The now-awake midshipman of the watch turned the glass. "Four bells!" he hollered. Forward, a seaman rang the bell in two pairs of "dings." Pipes squealed and the ship came to life. Those hands lucky enough to have been asleep tumbled from their hammocks and hurriedly dressed.

Forward, Pierce mustered his division. All were present or accounted for. He was uncomfortable when they greeted him as a hero and were determined to give him three cheers. "Belay that!" he growled at them. "I did my duty and that is all. Any of you would have done the same had you the chance."

Their faces fell and their mood became somber at his words of rebuke. They were crestfallen. These men appreciated their division officer, had tried to tell him so, and he had refused to accept their accolades.

"I do appreciate your sentiment," he added. "It is just not proper that it should be so displayed."

Pierce struggled to keep the distance between himself as an officer and the hands that tradition and the rigors of discipline demanded. He would much rather accept their congratulations and be a hero and a friend in their eyes. He would step amongst them, shake their proffered hands, allow them to pat his back and make a big to-do over it. But that would not be for the best. He would become too familiar with the hands, and the illusion that officers existed on a slightly higher plane would be lost. Amongst these men he would not lose any respect or authority, but it could cause problems with other divisions and their officers. Other officers, especially Sollars, would see it as a breakdown of the Navy's class system, which to many was the reason for its success.

"We understand, sir," said Hopkins. "Just wanted you to know, sir, that we and all hands aboard, sir, want to say 'Thankee, sir' for it. Sure as 'ell, Thomas is sayin' so, sir."

"If he is, I'm grateful. And, we are not short a topman. Now, let's get about your duties."

"Aye aye, sir!"

At eight bells, Sollars relieved him and Pierce went below to sickbay. Thomas was awake and as Hopkins had predicted, tried to thank Pierce profusely. Pierce shrugged off the gratitude, again alluding to the fact that *Theadora* had not lost a skilled topman. "...that is, Thomas, when you are out of here and back to your duties. Has the surgeon said?"

"Maybe tomorrow, sir. Says I got stunned, sir, what when I smacked into the water, and wants to make sure nothin' else ails me."

"You'll be back in no time. You realize your spirit ration is stopped while you're here?"

"Aye, sir." Thomas grinned. "Doctor says I need medicatin' now and then. That what he calls medicine's got a bit o' kick to it, sir." Pierce remembered the fire in his throat and belly after a double shot of medicinal brandy earlier that morning.

"The captain says he may charge you with carelessness, endangering your life, and stop your grog as punishment. As it stops while you're in sickbay, he allowed that that would suffice." Pierce grinned slightly.

"Sure he did, sir! No doubt grinning as well. Tell 'im, sir, I'm guilty as charged. Sometimes just luck is all it is sir, what keeps a man from losin' his step, sir."

"Very true. Thomas, can you read?"

"Some. Don't get much chance to."

"I'll bring a book by later for you. It'll make the time go quicker."

"Aye, sir. Thankee, sir."

Pierce found Small in the wardroom. They discussed the French signal codes and how best to implement them. Small agreed to separate flag bags for the French signals. He also agreed that those involved would need to know to hoist the flag from the specified bag and not what they knew to be correct. The sail maker and carpenter were there as well, having coffee and a bit of toast. Pierce approached them about preparing the needed rack and bags. Neilson agreed immediately. Cook, who contrary to his nature, could not equate the work with some aspect of carnal activity, went through his entire list of projects before reluctantly agreeing. He did so only when told that the request had the captain's support.

The wardroom steward arrived bearing a fresh pot of coffee. Pierce nodded in the affirmative, and the man poured him a cup. Savoring the warmth of the beverage, he sat in silent thought for several moments, debating whether or not to wait for breakfast or to go straight away for a little rest. Eventually, the overriding desire to sleep overcame any slight pangs of hunger, and Pierce made his way to his cabin. Pulling off his shoes and outer garments, he hung them up, unrealistically hoping that they might eventually dry. He yawned several times, sprawled across his cot, and immediately fell asleep.

Chapter Five

A British Surprise

Two days had passed since the storm engulfed *Theadora.* It was still cold, but the rain had ceased. The wind had died to a stiff breeze, veered, and was now out of the west southwest. The small frigate ran southeast on a broad starboard reach, topgallants set. The sun occasionally peaked out from the multitude of white clouds, while whitecaps dotted the sea's surface. The occasional wave crashed against her bows, resulting in icy spray whipping across her deck.

The evening after the storm, *Theadora's* officers gathered once again in the captain's cabin and made final plans to capture a very important French ship. The French dared not risk its capture by the blockading English fleet and had developed an elaborate plan to spirit this particular vessel to open waters. Edward Pierce and *Theadora* had thwarted the first part of the complex scheme: the capture of an English frigate. Now His Majesty's man-of-war had the French plans and signal codes and would use that knowledge to lure the ship out and capture it.

They discussed disguising *Theadora's* crew. Posing as a British frigate manned by the French, they wanted to look like Frenchmen attempting to be British. Captain Jackson directed that all hands relax standards of grooming and dress. He encouraged the normally forbidden practice of exchanging clothing and uniforms to give the appearance of appropriated, ill-fitting clothing. Marines were told to cease their spit and polish, allowing their red uniforms to look soiled and unkempt.

The temporary flag bags and rack had been completed earlier. Small had consulted his lists of the daily French signal codes and had filled the bags accordingly. Pierce had briefed all the hands who would work with the signals. They knew to use the flag from the bag that was called out, regardless of what flag was actually there. This morning, Small had changed flags to match the French code of the day. He also had both French recognition signals bent on the signal halyards, ready to be run up if needed. Now, at noon, he supervised the readying of the afternoon's recognition signals.

Pierce was on the fo'c'sle, teaching a small group of midshipmen, master's mates, and ship's boys the finer points of navigation. Mathematics did not come naturally to him, and he had worked many long hours to hone his navigational skills. He had persevered and now did a very respectable job of determining the ship's position. Perhaps because of his earlier difficulties, Jackson had requested he teach the others. He knew the problems they faced and had the insight they needed to learn and understand the science of navigation.

It was expected that midshipmen should learn to determine the ship's position, plot a course, and account for wind, tide, and underwater abnormalities. Master's mates needed those abilities as well, for should they ever be warranted as sailing master; their primary duty would be as navigator. In *Theadora,* others were included, as they might find themselves navigating a small boat or prize vessel. Jackson also included those ship's boys who demonstrated an aptitude for navigation. If possible, he would see the most promising lads appointed midshipmen.

Earlier, Pierce and each class member took noon sightings, tracking the sun until it reached its highest point in the sky. They recorded the elevation reading in degrees, marked the time when noon occurred, and calculated the difference between this time and noon on the ship's chronometer. Because that precise instrument was set to Greenwich Time, the difference determined longitude, or their distance east or west of Greenwich. The angle of the sun at its zenith helped establish latitude, or their location between the equator and the poles.

Pierce finished working his solution, waited an extra minute, and called time. "Now, what have you come up with?" He walked through the group and eyed the results written on their slates. "Some have placed us within sight of my position. Good! You may be as correct as or even more correct than I. Some of you still have trouble taking accurate readings. Keep practicing! The fix is only as good as your sightings. Now let us determine a position from a set of arbitrary readings."

"Sail ho, off the starboard bow!" The cry from the main topmast lookout interrupted Pierce as he read the problem's particulars.

"Where away?" shouted Lieutenant Forrest, officer of the watch.

"Two, no, three points off the starboard bow. Looks English, sir! I can just see topsails!"

Sighting another ship, the class forgot about their lesson, and they tried to see what was happening. "Sit! All of you!" snarled Pierce. "We will finish today's session. There has been no call to stations." Reluctantly, the group returned and began work on the problem that Pierce quickly provided.

Forrest hailed the lookout again. "What course?"

"Making for us, sir. She's hull up now."

Forrest turned to the signal midshipman. "Send up our number and inquire as to hers!" Then to the midshipman of the watch he said, "Mr. Andrews, my compliments to the captain -- and what appears to be an English ship is making for us!"

Both young gentlemen replied with an "Aye aye, sir!" and set about their assigned tasks.

Forward, Pierce kept the navigation class at task. "Five minutes more and you should be done. Concentrate! Shut out everything else. Forget the sail on the horizon. We'll soon know who she is."

Captain Jackson arrived on the quarterdeck. "What of her now?" he asked the lookout.

"Close hauled, port tack! Heading straight for us, sir! Can't make her number, sir!" The lookout studied the approaching ship with his glass. "Deck there! 'Nother sail, more off the starboard bow! Hull down! Same course as the first, sir!"

Pierce called time and checked the results obtained by each of the class. "Some of you still need work at this. The figures I provided should have placed you here." He pointed out the location on the chart spread over the starboard nine-pounder bow chaser. "Amazingly, some of you determined that we were well in the interior of Greenland. But does it ease your mind, I once found the ship's position to be the potential source of the Amazon. It takes patience, practice, and a thorough understanding of the process."

The lookout passed down the identifying number flown by the approaching vessel. Her topsails were visible from deck now. "*Acorn*, sir, of twenty-guns. Captain Douglas is in command," said Midshipman Townsend, consulting the ships recognition book. The lookout called down another set of signals flying from *Acorn*. Townsend pored over the recognition book again. "Vessel astern is the brig-sloop *Hound* of sixteen-guns. Commander White."

"Very well," said Jackson. "Signal them, 'Rendezvous on me! Captains repair on board!'"

"Aye aye, sir!"

The flags were bent on the signal halyards, soared aloft, and broke out into the wind. Soon the acknowledgement flew from the *Acorn*.

Pierce continued with the navigation lesson. "The solution is easier when you know where you were the day before. A ship can move only so far in a single day, so you will have an idea of where you currently are. Arbitrary readings, such as we just attempted to solve, can be more difficult and may place you anywhere. You must be able to solve these as well. Those among you who had difficulties, continue to practice with the sextant and look to the mathematics involved. Do you require help, please see me. Class dismissed!"

Theadora shortened sail, taking in her topgallants, as the two smaller English warships approached. When they passed to port, she came around onto the same heading. "Heave to!" fluttered from *Theadora's* signal halyards, and when it was hauled down, all three backed topsails and rested on the whitecapped sea.

From the fo'c'sle Pierce watched as the two vessels hoisted out captains' gigs. The boats were quickly and smartly manned. Their respective captains embarked and made their way across the narrow expanse of water separating the vessels.

Pierce moved toward the quarterdeck. He knew both the approaching captains, or had been acquainted with officers having the same names. Douglas had been first lieutenant in *Ferret* when Pierce was a midshipman. He remembered White as third lieutenant aboard *Orion*. As now, Pierce had been the most junior lieutenant, then the fifth, during his rather brief tour aboard that ship-of-the-line.

The first of the gigs approached *Theadora's* lee main chains and the bowman hooked on. The gig came abreast the entry port and the captain scrambled up the outer ladder-like steps. As his hat appeared, the bo'sun's mate's pipes squealed. The marines presented arms, and the side boys tugged at their forelocks. Captain Jackson and the other officers raised their hats in salute. Pierce, now on the quarterdeck, did the same.

Jackson introduced himself to the visitor. "Wait for Captain White, and I'll introduce my officers."

"I'll abide by that," agreed Douglas.

The second gig hooked on, and her passenger mounted to the quarterdeck with the same fanfare. There were two fewer side boys because Master and Commander White was not a post captain.

With the captains of both vessels now on board, Jackson introduced *Theadora's* officers. "May I present Mr. Forrest, first lieutenant; Mr. Sollars, second; and Mr. Pierce, third. This is Mr. Small, acting fourth; and Mr. Phelps, the master. Captain Northcutt of the Marines."

"We both have served with Lieutenant Pierce," said White. If he hasn't changed since *Orion*, sir, he is no doubt a trial for you." He smiled briefly. "But a most valued subordinate."

"I would say more of the latter," said Jackson. "You will soon discover his value to this ship."

"Quite!" Douglas spoke. "Pierce, you've come a long way since *Ferret*. No doubt you'll go farther as well."

Pierce had difficulty phrasing a reply. These were old acquaintances, old shipmates, but still they were senior to him. Both had command of Royal Navy ships, and Douglas was a post captain. "It is good to see you again, sir. Both of you, sir. I do hope to advance as far as my abilities allow."

"You mustn't forget Lady Luck!" chuckled Douglas. He was a large rotund man, and Pierce remembered him as having a normally jovial disposition. Still, cross him and he could turn into a raging bull.

"Enough small talk, gentlemen! Let us go below and attend to business. If time allows, we will dine and my officers will join us." Jackson led the way below. "My apologies for *Theadora's* unkempt appearance. You shall soon understand why, I believe."

"I hadn't noticed," remarked White, but Pierce knew that wasn't true. He remembered White as having an eye for detail that would have noticed the slightest deviation from perfect.

With the captains below, the officers on the quarterdeck relaxed. Forrest sent the midshipman of the watch to see if the cook could spare something for the gigs' crews. Small and Pierce stood at the lee rail and treasured the sun's warmth whenever it broke through the clouds. Sollars scowled at Pierce. Forrest caught the hostile glance and in turn scowled at Sollars. Sollars went below, and nobody on the quarterdeck was sorry that he did.

"What could they be up to?" asked Small.

"I'll wager it has to do with our upcoming enterprise," Pierce responded. After a moment's thought, he continued. "*Acorn* and *Hound* are newly arrived and are probably keeping a close watch on Le Havre. The captain, I surmise, would ensure our arrival doesn't interfere with their routine. More important is that our arrival does not cause the French to notice any disruption in the routine."

"And we may need their support, if that ship comes out. But how would the French deal with them if they actually had command of *Theadora*?"

"They seemed to have had all angles figured, so surely they had something in mind. And surely that ship will come out. The Frogs have invested heavily in getting it through the blockade. To them, it must be imperative that this ship sail," mused Pierce.

"Quite so!" continued Small. "Hopefully they will be bent on its sailing and readily accept us as being under French command."

The three captains returned to the quarterdeck a half-hour later. "Shame you won't stay to dinner," said Captain Jackson. "But I do agree with your reasoning. After our endeavor is complete?"

Douglas, being senior, left first. As soon as he was seated in his gig, the cox'n gave the order and the small boat shoved off. Immediately afterward, White's gig came alongside and he departed as well.

"Alter course now, Mr. Forrest, for Le Havre! Northeast by east. Set royals as well, if it please you!"

"Aye aye, sir!"

Forrest shouted orders. Bos'un's pipes shrilled and hands jumped to their stations. Strong backs braced the topsail yards around, the sails filled, and *Theadora* gained steerageway. Those at the wheel put the helm up and the bow swung to port. They passed through the wind, and soon it came at them from the starboard beam. Moments later it was from nearly astern. As the assigned course crept nearer, the helmsmen eased off on the turn and *Theadora* settled onto the new heading. Aloft, men unfastened the gaskets that held the tightly furled royals to their yards. Others manned the halyards, the yards rose, and the sails were sheeted home. Then they manned the braces, adjusting the yards to make the sails draw most efficiently. Jackson ordered courses set as well, not to waste any time in arriving off Le Havre.

At dawn the next morning, Le Havre was in sight from the masthead. Small had the morning watch. As the sky lightened and the watch drew to an end, he consulted the French codes and switched flag bags to agree with the day's codes. Moving the entire bag was more efficient that swapping out the flags contained in each bag. Agreeing with Small's suggestion, Pierce had directed the carpenter and sail maker to make the rack and bags accordingly. Pierce, already on deck, thought to help Small with the signal flags, but decided he might be in the way and interfere with Small's routine.

Pierce did not feel it beneath his station to help anyone. He often lent a hand to the most junior crewman, readily tailing onto a line to help straining seamen hoist a heavy load. Yet as *Theadora's* third lieutenant, he would help only if others were not readily available. Pierce gladly helped his seniors and peers as well, having learned that a junior was expected to assist before his aid was requested. It earned him recognition as an attentive subordinate, and if this appeared to be *bootlicking*, the thought never occurred to him. He had been raised to follow the *golden rule*, and if obedience to that basic tenet aided his superiors and earned him a bit of favor, that was the way it was. Amongst those of similar rank, willingness to help each other promoted comradeship and teamwork. Aboard *Theadora*, this interdependence was evident daily. All officers, including the captain, willingly came to each other's aid. Like Pierce, most of them freely helped anyone who needed it.

The one exception to this rule of help and be helped was the ship's second lieutenant. Sollars helped Jackson and Forrest only when required, or if such action was in his own best interest. Extremely conscious of seniority, it normally took a direct order for him to aid Pierce, the midshipmen, or the warrant officers. Help for any of the hands was, for Sollars, a journey into uncharted waters. He would sooner watch a seaman rupture himself while encouraging the struggling crewman with curses, vile oaths, and threats of punishment. In turn, all aboard were reluctant to help Sollars, unless such aid contributed to the ship's success, or was demanded by direct or implied orders.

Theadora stood in as close as she dared, leadsmen in the chains testing the depth of the water, and lookouts watching for hostile shore activity. As she headed northwest with the town to starboard, she flew the day's recognition signal from her starboard main yardarm. Abreast of Sainte Adresse, the frigate wore and retraced her route past Le Havre and the correct recognition signal now flew from the port fore yardarm. When in sight of the coast adjacent to Honfleur, she wore again and started the process over.

Each time she came about, the position and composition of the recognition signal changed. The constant shift in signals, controlled by the date, their heading, and the time were part of the French scheme. Compliance with the complicated sequence would verify that the English frigate off Le Havre was really under French command.

When *Theadora's* lookouts had first spied the coast line adjacent to Le Havre, Captain Jackson brought the ship to a higher degree of readiness. He doubled the lookouts and detailed additional helmsmen in case they were needed. Hands stood by, ready to maneuver the ship at a moment's notice. They abandoned the regular officer of the watch rotation, and half of the officers stood duty at any one time. The captain and the first lieutenant alternated their time on deck, and in effect, the entire officer cadre of *Theadora* was now on watch and watch.

For the first two days, nothing happened. Each time they passed Le Havre, men stationed aloft trained glasses on the ships in the harbor. One ship appeared ready to sail, but it made no move to do so. There were no signals or challenges from shore, although the semaphore station's arms often moved excitedly as it communicated with the next station inland.

On the second afternoon, as they passed just out of range of a shore battery, a flurry of signal flags flew from a recently erected flag pole. With the aid of his glass, Pierce saw the signals from deck. He wrote the numbers down and consulted the day's code sheet. "Mr. Forrest," he said, "the signal is, 'English frigate, name your captain!'"

"A pre-arranged challenge?"

"Believe so, sir," Pierce replied as he bent over Small's signal notes. "Aye, it's a challenge. Reply is to be, 'John Bull and Tom Roast Beef.' Shall we answer, sir?"

"By all means, Mr. Pierce. Do not keep them waiting. Mr. Andrews, please inform the captain that we have communication with shore!"

"Aye, sir!"

Pierce consulted the signal sheets and had what he hoped was the proper response bent on. They soared up the halyards and broke free, flapping vigorously in the wind.

"There is a new signal from shore, sir," said Pierce again. "It's 'Enemy in sight,' sir."

"Our reply?"

"According to Mr. Small, sir, we are to send, 'Engage the enemy more closely,' using our own codes."

"Very well. Attend to it, will you, Mr. Pierce"

"Aye aye, sir!"

"Finally recognized our presence, have they?" said Jackson as he arrived on the quarterdeck. Apparently he had been asleep, as his uniform was rumpled, his features puffy, and his hair tousled. "What has transpired?"

Forrest told the captain about the exchange of signals that had occurred prior to his arrival.

"Another signal sir," said Pierce. "'Captain, come ashore!'"

"That's not expected!" declared Forrest.

"Indeed not!" remarked Jackson. "Throws a kink, I'd say."

"Perhaps not," interjected Pierce. "We should defer on the possibility of English ships appearing and questioning an English frigate communicating with shore."

"You are quite right, Mr. Pierce. I don't believe such a response is in the codes. You would be advised to send for Mr. Small to help with the phrasing. His French is better than mine," Jackson stated.

Small arrived moments later. He and Pierce composed a reply that was soon hoisted aloft.

"Understood," came back from the battery.

"What took them so long, sir?" asked Forrest. "We've been in sight two days."

"Consulting with Paris, Mr. Forrest. We saw the semaphore station."

"Aye, sir, we did. Boney has a hand in it, sir?"

"Indeed! Mr. Forrest."

"New signal, sir!" said Small. "It says, 'Sailing with morning tide. Be at point specified for departure!'"

"Mr. Small, the correct acknowledgement, if you would."

The next morning, well before the tide would change, Captain Jackson sent the hands to breakfast, following the tradition of ensuring a crew had full bellies when going into action. Then the ship cleared for action. The carpenter and his mates took the captain's furniture and other effects below for safekeeping. There they were not only out of harm's way, but their absence allowed access to the guns in the cabin, and reduced the chances of enemy shot producing a deadly hail of splinters. Guns were loaded but were not run out.

Theadora moved to her assigned position. Minutes after the tide changed, those on deck saw activity on the ship that had her yards crossed. The fore topmast staysail and spanker were hoisted, and the main topsail was set aback. The ship gathered sternway. The yards were braced around, her head came around, and she moved forward. Slowly, almost majestically, she came out of Le Havre and headed south on a starboard tack.

In accordance with the captured French instructions, the frigate remained directly off Le Havre. When the French ship, a large East Indiaman, settled on a port tack, *Theadora* ran out her guns, set all the sail she could, and came tearing down on a starboard reach. *Theadora* passed inshore and cut off any return to safety. If other English ships appeared, it was supposed to look like she was capturing the Indiaman.

As the two ships passed, *Theadora* shortened sail and came about onto a port tack. The timing was perfect and she settled off the Frenchman's starboard quarter.

"Mr. Pierce, there is no shot in the port bow chaser?" queried Captain Jackson.

"Aye, sir."

"Then you may fire the warning shot!" The nine-pounder banged sharply and the report echoed across the water. The Indiaman feigned panic and came into the wind. Taken aback, she drifted and finally came around and settled again on the port tack. While aback, the French colors at the stern came down. To all appearances she had surrendered, and was a prize of the English frigate that had daringly cut off her return to Le Havre and had so terrorized her crew that she had surrendered after the firing of a single shot.

"Well done, lads!" said Jackson with a sigh of relief. "Better than expected! Need more open waters before we actually take her."

"Aye, sir! We need be careful to not give them cause for alarm."

"French are signaling, sir," said Small. They want the captain to come aboard."

"Damn!" Jackson was perplexed.

"Remind them again of other British ships?" suggested Pierce.

"See to it!"

"Aye aye, sir!"

The ships continued on the port tack, *Theadora* astern of the other by half a cable's length. *Perpignan* was carved and painted across her stern, although the paint was faded and some of the carvings broken and missing.

Perpignan set more sail. "Mr. Forrest, topgallants!" ordered Jackson.

"Aye aye, sir!"

"Match her!"

"Aye!"

The coast line grew fainter as both vessels continued to the northwest. Sainte Adresse faded from sight and now they were for practical purposes on the open sea.

"Douglas and White should appear about now," said Jackson.

"How's that, sir?" questioned Sollars. "I thought we were in this alone?"

"Worried for prize money, are we, Mr. Sollars?" Jackson read the greed in Sollars' query. "It is a small exchange that they help. Capturing *Perpignan* is more pressing than any division of shares. She is a well-armed Indiaman, and might fight, should we try to take her alone. They will do as insurance."

"Aye, sir," said Sollars discontentedly.

Once more the French requested that the frigate captain come aboard. As *Theadora's* officers decided how to refuse again, further enemy signals announced that two sail were in sight to the west. *Theadora's* lookouts saw them at the same time.

"Mr. Small!" barked Captain Jackson. "Signal our friend, 'Submit we heave to! Will appear to have boarded you!'"

"Aye aye, sir!" replied Small. "It will take a bit to translate into today's code."

"Quite all right. That will give time for our help to close in."

The two sail on the western horizon were on a starboard broad reach, headed directly for the frigate and the East Indiaman. As Jackson had surmised, the two were *Acorn* and *Hound*.

"Signal from *Perpignan,* sir. 'Sound advice! Heave to on my lead!'"

"Acknowledge, Mr. Small."

When *Theadora* acknowledged the signal, the Frenchman put her helm to starboard and came into the wind. Hands manned the braces and backed the topsails, effectively holding her in place. *Theadora* did likewise, and the two lay upon the water, rolling with the swells.

"Mr. Forrest, hoist out my gig, the launch, and the first cutter. Mr. Pierce, take the cutter and a boarding party! Mr. Sollars, take the launch! Neither of you need hurry! Remember, we are French! Our friends need be close so they may be of value."

The three boats were hoisted out slowly, with a great deal of fuss and ineptitude. Pierce imagined that the evolution had never been done slower than during the entire commission. Boarding parties were selected and issued arms. At Pierce's suggestion, Jackson signaled the French to tell them the boarding parties were a show for the approaching English ships.

As the boats neared *Perpignan*, two more sets of signals rose up *Theadora's* signal halyards. The first requested *Acorn* and *Hound* remain to windward and be ready to engage if needed. The second was to the East Indiaman, demanding her immediate surrender.

Jackson's gig came along the Frenchman's port side. Pierce and Sollars both came along the starboard. The boarding parties swarmed aboard while Jackson proceeded directly to the quarterdeck. As he reached it, the French realized the meaning of *Theadora's* latest signals, and a torrent of curses gushed from the French captain's throat. Although Pierce did not understand the words, he easily guessed their meaning. A pale and dapper-looking young man, dressed in the latest civilian attire, hung his head.

"What? Where is…? Who?" The French captain switched to English. "You are not Captain Dubois! Where is he?"

"Be calm, Captain," said Jackson. "Dubois is alive, well, and in England by now. You will join him soon. Speak French if it is easier."

Upon boarding the Frenchman, Sollars and Pierce worked to ensure the safety of the prize. Sollars' boarding party quickly went through the ship and rounded up crew and passengers. They herded the captives into the waist and placed guards over them. Pierce and his men conducted a thorough search to determine what cargo and supplies the ship carried.

Pierce returned to the upper deck and reported to Jackson. "We found a lot of military stores aboard, sir. Several thousand muskets, powder, ball, cartridge cases. There are also two dozen four-pounder field pieces, broken down for shipment, as well as uniforms, shoes, and blankets."

"Very well, Mr. Pierce. I see why they wanted this through the blockade," replied Jackson. "But I'll be dammed if I know where they were bound. Neither Captain Mirebeau nor Special Envoy Clion will admit anything." He nodded toward the two Frenchmen, perhaps as a means of introduction. "Dammed Frogs are as tight-lipped as … oh, never mind, Pierce. I have, however, concluded that Mirebeau devised this elaborate attempt to beat the blockade."

"Indeed, sir?"

"Its failure certainly explains his temper."

"Did you know they were prepared to destroy the ship, rather than see it captured?" asked Pierce.

"How's that?"

"Fuses laid to all the powder stores, sir. Hopkins smelled burning slow match. We were able to put it out before…."

"Before?"

"Before it reached the junction with the quick match. The explosion would have destroyed *Perpignan* and possibly *Theadora* as well. There is a great deal of powder on board, sir."

"Congratulate Hopkins! Great sense of smell."

"I already have, sir, but more recognition surely would be appropriate," opined Pierce.

Minister Clion interrupted. "The ship was to explode and you prevented it?"

"Yes," answered Pierce.

"Alas! Our lives are spared, but the wrath of First Consul Bonaparte will remain. I almost would not return to France if I could." While despondent over his failed mission, the young man breathed easier.

"You knew?" Jackson asked incredulously. "You knew fuses were laid? Lit?"

"Oui, I knew. I ordered them lit when it was apparent you were indeed English. I had orders that this mission not fail … or else."

"Of all the.... Most cold-blooded thing to expect! Yes, give one's life for country or a great cause! But to purposely blow one's self up! There's a limit, Mr. Pierce! A limit, Minister! A limit! Damn you! Damn Bonaparte! This goes far beyond that limit!" Jackson was livid. "Get him away from me!"

After his rage burned out, Jackson, now joined by Captain Douglas and Commander White, toured the prize vessel. Acting on previously made plans, Midshipman Andrews was left on board in charge of a prize crew. *Acorn* supplied a junior midshipman, six hands, and two marines to augment those from *Theadora*. Commander White detailed a quartermaster, three hands, and two marines to round out the prize crew. The three captains believed that would be enough men to sail the ship and guard against any recapture.

Pierce felt tired and weak as the cutter returned to *Theadora*. His heart pounded, and he grasped the tiller tightly to steady his shaking hands. In spite of the late afternoon coolness, he was damp with sweat.

"Cool as ice, he was!" said Hopkins to no one in particular. "Sez, 'We gotta find that slow match!' We looked and looked and I thought we was goners. But he just keeps looking. Then he finds it and cuts it and stomps it out. Had this much to spare! Before the quick match caught!" Hopkins indicated the quarter inch of remaining slow match between thumb and forefinger. "Quick match was laid to all the powder aboard. Woulda been nuthin' left! Woulda sunk the Frogs! Coulda sunk us!"

Pierce had not been cool as ice. He had been terrified. He had feared they would not find the burning fuse in time, and that the next instant would bring injury or death. He knew how close they all had come to being blown into oblivion. When they had smelled the burning match and had realized what it implied, the fear had risen in his throat. A cold numbness had spread throughout his entire body. It had taken great effort not to run screaming to the upper deck and leap wildly into the sea. With unimaginable effort he had forced himself to stay calm, to ignore the panic that had threatened to overpower him, and to instigate a systematic search for the burning match.

Had Hopkins realized the match's purpose? If so, had he been as close to panic as Pierce had been? Now with the danger passed, did prattling on about it allow Hopkins to calm himself?

"Ease up, mate!" whispered Mitchell, seated on the thwart beside Hopkins. "Look at 'im. It was a close one and about to have done 'im in!" Mitchell pointed aft at Pierce with his chin.

Hopkins thought a moment. "Aye, it was close at that." Then he was silent and left Pierce to recover from the terror on his own.

Chapter Six

Peace at Hand

The early October day was warm, with only a few clouds marring the blue sky. The moderate wind stirred up an occasional white-cap and urged the frigate swiftly onward. *Theadora* scudded along under all plain sail as she stood out to sea.

Pierce was officer of the watch. In spite of fair weather and a break away from the dangers of the French coast, he was in a foul temper as the last half of the forenoon watch approached. Yesterday as Sollars had relieved him, the remarks and criticisms had been unusually grating and insulting. At dinner, Pierce had found the salt beef unpalatable. Even well-experienced with the bad food common aboard ship, he could not eat it. The boiled peas were just as awful, and the ship's biscuit more weevils than bread. He tried to wash the meal down with slime optimistically called water. He had been aboard *Theadora* a year ago to the day, and if things didn't change, he would be aboard next October as well.

"Mr. Hadley!" he roared at the midshipman of the watch. "Four bells were off three minutes by my watch. I'll trouble you to turn the glass more promptly in the future. See we are on time!"

"Aye aye, sir!" was all the ship's junior most midshipman could say. It was usually a pleasure to have duty with Lieutenant Pierce; however, today it was pure agony. The lieutenant had jumped the hapless young gentleman when he had arrived on deck with his uniform incorrectly buttoned. He had criticized the midshipman's every duty and task, and it looked as if he would do so for the two hours of the watch that remained. He had complained about the shine on his shoes and the fact that he wasn't properly shaven. Never mind that Hadley wasn't old enough to grow any real whiskers.

Nor did others escape Pierce's wrath. He constantly harangued the helmsmen to keep to the exact course set by the captain. To him, it seemed the hands responded slowly to his demands to correct the sail's trim.

Presently he found that he had nothing more to complain about. That itself irritated him. His logical, congenial side told him to enjoy the day. But his emotional, irrational dark side reveled in a storm of anger, despair, and hate that churned deep within him. He silently wished that Sollars would relieve him late, giving him an excuse to make a caustic and biting remark to the ship's second lieutenant. That he was junior didn't matter. He would say what he wanted and be damned for saying it to a senior officer. He might even take a swing at him. He had listened to Sollars' remarks and insinuations for well over a year and could not endure them much longer. Pierce did find solace knowing that all aboard junior to him also suffered the sting of Sollars' biting tongue.

There was the matter of the ship's stores. Supper had been inedible in the wardroom and presumably at the cabin's table for the past three days. Lord knows what was served on the lower deck. *Theadora* would need to return home soon to replenish, or fresh stores would need to be brought out to them. They had last replenished six months ago, when after capturing *Perpignan, Theadora* had returned to Portsmouth. She had remained only long enough to load provisions. No one, other than the captain, had left the ship. He had left only on official business, to fire up the victualling yard and get their stores aboard as soon as possible. The officers and crew had worked around the clock while in port, loading and stowing those precious supplies. Hands were not allowed off ship other than as part of a working party under the strictest supervision, lest they desert.

There was no worry about the ship's manning level. All the prize crews had returned recently, and new hands assigned to replace those killed in combat or by the sea itself.

Today might give them new direction and insight. Two days ago they had exchanged signals with His Majesty's Brig *Hound.* The small warship had relayed orders for *Theadora* to rendezvous with HMS *Bristol*, the flagship of the North Channel Squadron.

"Deck there!" the lookout at the main topmast head roared. "Sail off the port bow!"

The hail shook Pierce out of his introspective stupor. It also raised his ire to a new level, interrupting his black thoughts and private rage. "What can you make of her?" he hollered back.

"Topsails! Opposite course to us, sir!"

"Very well! Watch her!" Pierce turned toward the midshipman of the watch, who was half-prepared to run from the unusually grumpy third lieutenant. "Mr. Hadley, respects to the captain and that a sail is sighted off the port bow!"

"Aye aye, sir!"

"Deck there! Another sail, same bearing. Both 'ave altered course towards us, sir!"

"Thank you! Can you identify either?"

"No, sir! Not yet!"

When Jackson came on deck, Pierce told him that the two sail sighted had altered course toward *Theadora*.

"Mr. Pierce, we would alter course as to close them!"

"Aye aye, sir! Starboard your helm!"

"Aye aye, sir!" replied the helmsmen.

"Hands to the braces!"

Theadora slowly and easily swung her bows to the south. "Deck there! Sails dead on the bow, sir!"

"Very well! Ease your helm. Hold her there!"

Theadora headed directly for the two unidentified ships. She was on a broad starboard reach, and the others were on a port tack. Should they prove to be enemy vessels, *Theadora* had the desired weather gage and would be in complete control of any fight. The other ships were in the situation most preferred by the French, who would rather be to leeward and have an avenue of escape.

"Masthead!" hailed Jackson. "Anything yet?"

"No signals, sir! Nearly hull up! Look English, sir!"

"Our number please, Mr. Hadley!" said Captain Jackson. "If it is the flagship, we sha'n't be caught short answering."

"Aye aye, sir!"

Six bells sounded. Pierce checked his watch. Still three minutes off. Hadley hadn't lost more time with his half-hourly turning of the glass. Pierce was disappointed that the disparity hadn't increased, depriving him the chance to again ruin Mr. Midshipman Hadley's already awful day.

When the lookout reported the two ships hull up, one was identified as *Bristol,* the sixty-four-gun flagship of the North Channel Squadron. The other vessel was *Druid,* a thirty-two-gun frigate.

"Signal from flag, sir. 'Upon arrival, heave to! Captain and third lieutenant repair on board,'" said Morgan, acting as signal midshipman.

"Very well, Mr. Morgan. Acknowledge!"

"Aye aye, sir!"

"Mr. Pierce, your presence is requested aboard the flagship," remarked Jackson.

"Aye, sir!" said Pierce. Perhaps he would chance to meet with Isaac, who at last word was fourth lieutenant in *Bristol*.

"Have Mr. Sollars relieve you early. Before we depart, do make yourself presentable."

"Aye aye, sir!" Pierce could not report aboard the flagship in worn slop-chest trousers and an old undress uniform with blood stains on the obviously mended sleeve. "Mr. Hadley, respects to Mr. Sollars and that he is to relieve me soonest!"

"Aye aye, sir!" said Hadley, as he left on the run. Pierce did not envy him the task of telling Sollars to relieve the watch early. Yet, in his present temper, he enjoyed the thought of the young midshipman catching the full measure of Sollars' wrath. He also felt small measure of satisfaction at Sollars' annoyance in reporting early. Sollars seemed dedicated to making Pierce's life miserable. It was only fair that he have the occasional opportunity to return the favor.

Sollars arrived, grumbled at Pierce for the request to be relieved early, and complained even more when told that it was due to the admiral's order and the captain's suggestion, which for all practical purposes was an order. Nonetheless, he assumed the duty. Forrest also arrived on deck, as he would be in command while Jackson and Pierce were aboard the flagship.

Below, Pierce quickly changed into the best uniform that he could assemble. He exchanged his well-worn seaman's trousers for his one good pair of breeches. His second-best shirt would do, as now it was really his best. His dress uniform would hide the shirt's patched elbows. Hopefully the frayed cuffs would not be noticeable. He put on clean stockings -- his last good pair -- blacked his shoes, and was ready to go.

He arrived on deck just as *Theadora* settled on the same course as the flagship and the accompanying frigate. The three ships were line abreast, with *Bristol* to windward and *Theadora* in the leewardmost position. "Heave to" broke out on the flagship. When both of the other vessels acknowledged, it was hauled down. That was the signal to execute. Soon all three lay resting upon the water, topsails backed against the masts.

Even before that evolution was complete, the captain's gig was hoisted out. It waited alongside, the crew neatly dressed in the flat-topped straw hats, white frocks, and short blue jackets that Jackson had provided for them. Pierce thought that if he were captain, he would outfit his gig's crew in similar but better fashion. Indeed, it would look sharp to have the entire crew in a uniform rig. But even for the gig's crew, the funds came out of the captain's pocket. One could often judge a captain's personal wealth, whether from family or success in prize money, simply by how his boat's crew was decked out. At present rate of his success with prize money, however, Pierce thought he might be content to do as Jackson had done. He also knew that many of the furnishings and special stores that a captain enjoyed were paid for out of his private funds.

"Let's not keep him, Mr. Pierce," hinted Jackson. In the tradition of the sea service that decreed that a senior officer was never kept waiting in a small boat, Pierce went down into the gig. On deck, the side boys formed up at the entry way, officers saluted, and the bo'sun's mate's pipes squealed. As Jackson's cocked hat descended past the deck edge, the ceremonial raucous ended. "Shove off!" barked Jackson as he took his seat. Perhaps someday, Pierce thought, he would have the privilege of arriving or departing with such fanfare and ceremony. Someday!

His foul black mood had nearly disappeared with the bustle of getting ready to visit the flagship. Now it returned and he sat in the gig, brooding. He was curious and a bit apprehensive as to why he should be ordered to report to the admiral. He could see the squadron commander sending for the first lieutenant. But the third lieutenant? True, his old friend, Isaac Hotchkiss was aboard *Bristol*, but it was not a junior officer's prerogative to request a friend's visit. Why on earth would he be needed aboard the flagship? Had he done something for which Jackson had reported his behavior to the admiral? Was he now enroute to a flag-level rebuke, reprimand, or worse?

"God, Mr. Pierce! Not so glum!" said Jackson. "Not every junior lieutenant is requested to report to flag. We'll be asked to dine. As 'Britannia rules the waves,' their stores will be much fresher."

"Yes, sir," replied Pierce. "I'm quite sure they are."

"Indeed, Mr. Pierce, every ship has fresher and more palatable." Jackson was silent for a moment. "If you fear that are summoned for punitive action, put such thoughts out of mind. Nothing in my reports could be anything but positive."

"I admit that such had crossed my mind, sir," Pierce said with a tone that indicated he wasn't yet totally convinced.

"Lad, I know Tompkins well. Served under him as lieutenant years ago. What I am as captain, as an officer, is from him. Fair, just, and recognizes a deed well-done. Wager he waits to pass along accolades. Your friend is aboard as well?"

"Aye aye, sir!" Pierce felt more at ease, but he still had doubts in the back of his mind. If he wasn't summoned to be admonished, what could he have done that would warrant recognition from the admiral? But regardless of the reason he had been summoned, he would have a chance to see his boyhood friend.

"Boat ahoy!" The challenge from *Bristol* sounded strongly across the water.

"*Theadora*!" answered Lofton the cox'n, indicating that that particular ship's captain was aboard. The gig came alongside and the bow hook and the cox'n held it fast at the accommodation ladder. Jackson mounted the side of the small two-decked ship-of-the-line. As his hat appeared over the edge of the deck, the pipes started. Once they had finished and Jackson was fully aboard, Pierce climbed the steep side. Through the entry port, Pierce saluted the quarterdeck. "Come aboard, sir!" he said to the officer of the watch.

A young lieutenant wearing a perfect uniform and carrying a brass spy glass polished mirror-bright under his arm returned his salute. "Very well, sir! Welcome aboard!"

Jackson beckoned him to join the group of officers standing under the break of the poop. There Pierce met Captain Wyndham, flag captain; Captain Hope, fleet captain; and Captain Stanfell of the *Druid*.

"Gentlemen, Admiral Tompkins will meet with the two frigate captains first," said Captain Hope. "Lieutenant, you may wait in the wardroom should you choose. The flag lieutenant will see you are entertained."

"Most gracious of you, sir," said Pierce. It was no surprise the admiral would see the captains first. Becalmed by the wait, he felt the old self-doubt return. His foul mood threatened to return in stronger form than before. And where was his old friend? "I would be obliged for the flag lieutenant's company."

The rest of the group, all gold lace, gold bullion, blue broadcloth, and cocked hats, disappeared aft into "flag country." A familiar-looking lieutenant approached. "Edward, it really is you!" he exclaimed.

Pierce looked in astonishment. The flag lieutenant was his childhood friend, Isaac Hotchkiss.

"Yes, Isaac, it's me! And you, the flag lieutenant? I thought you fourth in *Bristol*!"

"Until recently, yes. I've not had the chance to pass the news. Come! We can have a drink and fill in the missing years. It will be a while before he sees you."

In the wardroom, Hotchkiss reached into a small locker and brought out two glasses and an unopened bottle of wine.

"I hope this is to your liking. It's one of several that *Hound* took off a French coaster. White gave some to the admiral, and he passed it along to his staff. This is the last I have."

"I'm sure it's excellent," said Pierce. "But you know I've never been a connoisseur."

"I also remember you watch your drink, especially if duty or action follows."

"I should watch myself now. I shouldn't be in less than full control when I see Admiral Tompkins."

"Just as well," said Hotchkiss. "Although from what I see of him, he would not use one meeting to form an opinion. I warrant he has already done that."

"A good one, do you think?"

"I would warrant that as well."

"Well then, old friend," asked Pierce, "can you tell me why I am to see him? Do you know?"

"Aye, I do. The flag lieutenant knows everything!" Hotchkiss laughed. "But I would not steal his thunder." He poured each of them a half glass of wine and sat down. "I was somewhat in jest about the flag lieutenant knowing everything. Truth is, I do know of much that happens, both in the squadron and in the service as a whole. I stay in my present position because I keep what I know to myself."

"You were always good at that."

Pierce told him of being an acting and then a commissioned lieutenant aboard *Mariner*. He remarked on the strangeness of going from that small sloop-of-war to *Orion,* a seventy-four- gun ship-of-the-line, one much larger than *Bristol*, where they now found themselves. He described the changes he had experienced reporting aboard *Theadora*, and his satisfaction in serving aboard the small frigate. He even related his ongoing problems with the second lieutenant.

Hotchkiss remarked that there was that sort of individual in everyone's life, and allowed that he had had his share of them as well. He had remained onboard *Ferret* after Pierce had transferred, and had been commissioned on his second try. It never occurred to them to determine who was senior. Should they ever serve in the same ship, the question of seniority would not come into play unless it was crucial to their duty status.

Hotchkiss had remained in *Ferret* another year, and had transferred to *Bristol* as fourth lieutenant. When the previous flag lieutenant had taken ill, the admiral, impressed with the ship's young lieutenant, had had him transferred to his staff.

"Have you any recent news of my brothers?" asked Pierce as he sipped his glass of wine. It was the one question he wanted to ask but had been unable to bring to the fore until this second serving.

"Indeed I have," answered Hotchkiss. "In my present duties, I've found it easier to track their whereabouts. You knew they were with Nelson aboard *Captain* at Cape St. Vincent? Now I believe they serve under a Captain Palmer in *Atlas*, presently in the Mediterranean."

"Indeed, I knew of their service with Nelson but had lost track over the intervening years. Now perhaps I will be able to get word to them. *Atlas* is a good ship, I'm told, although I don't know much of Palmer."

"Nor I," replied the flag lieutenant. "I've heard stories, but as he is post captain, and quite naturally my … our … superior, I think it best to not elaborate."

"That does not bode well for them, I fear," lamented Pierce.

"I shouldn't be concerned for them. I understand his problems lie elsewhere."

"The ship's officers? Family?"

"Only in his mind, I should think." Hotchkiss was silent for a moment. "Perhaps I have said too much. The wine? An old friend? Nonetheless they have as much sea time as we do. They know the ropes. *Atlas's* fourth lieutenant is one who will make a name for himself. From what I've heard, he'll see to the well-being of the entire crew."

"Do we know him?"

"Name's Rowley, and there are quite a few tales circulating about him. You've heard of the prize retaken by another Frenchman with the original English prize crew recapturing both? He was the midshipman in command."

"I've heard the story but never believed it. Forrest swears it's true but couldn't remember the name. Perhaps he never knew. I do recall seeing something about a Rowley in the *Gazette*."

A sharply uniformed midshipman knocked and stuck his head in the wardroom. "Mr. Hotchkiss, sir, the admiral will see Lieutenant Pierce."

"Thank you, Mr. Elliot."

Following his friend to the admiral's cabin, Pierce's mood was much brighter than it had been earlier that morning. He resolved that could he maintain his dignity as a lieutenant, he would apologize to Hadley and the others for having made the forenoon watch such a torment. He debated but rejected the idea of offering any amends to Sollars.

As they approached the flag suite, Pierce heard the squeal of pipes. "That would be Captain Stanfell, returning to *Druid*," remarked Hotchkiss.

Outside the admiral's cabin the marine sentry sprang to attention. Hotchkiss knocked twice. "Enter!" a voice said from within. The tone was authoritarian, yet it conveyed a sense of warmth and friendship, or so it seemed to Pierce, in good spirits for the first time in many days.

The flag lieutenant opened the door, stepped in, and announced, "Lieutenant Pierce, sir."

Admiral Tompkins hoisted his bulk out of his chair and came around from behind his desk. "Come in, lad! Come in! Both of you! I know you are old friends and shipmates." He offered his hand to Pierce, who clasped and shook it firmly. The returned grip was strong, the fingers and palm callused and rough. The desk and office duties of a flag officer had not yet physically softened the man. "Here, sit and relax, Mr. Pierce! You too, Mr. Hotchkiss!"

Pierce hesitated, not considering it proper to sit and relax, especially in the presence of a rear admiral and a post captain. Jackson sat in a large overstuffed chair; his legs crossed and a glass of Madeira in his hand. Reluctantly Pierce moved toward the chair the admiral indicated. "Go ahead, lad, have a seat!" the admiral insisted. Pierce sat. Hotchkiss, somewhat less reluctantly, took the other chair. There were only the four of them in the cabin. Stanfell of *Druid* had departed. Captains Hope and Wyndham were elsewhere aboard *Bristol*.

After an offer of a glass of wine, which Pierce politely refused, Admiral Tompkins began. "Mr. Pierce, over the past months, I have eagerly looked forward to reports from His Majesty's Frigate *Theadora*. Not only do I rejoice in the actions she had taken against the enemy, but I also look forward to the latest exploits of her third lieutenant. If they weren't portions of official reports, they would make very enjoyable reading."

Pierce felt warm, slightly embarrassed by this praise from the squadron commander. "Sir?"

"Don't be so reluctant to accept praise that is due, Mr. Pierce. Surely you realize that much of *Theadora's* success during her present commission is due to your actions and suggestions?"

"Merely my duty, sir," said Pierce humbly.

"Not merely your duty, Lieutenant, but your duty far above and beyond what is expected of a third. You suggested bigger boarding parties to prevent crews from retaking prizes or the cargo itself from causing harm. Instinct and experience warned you last February as *Theadora* took those four French merchantmen. You insisted *Theadora* act immediately upon the information obtained. You risked your life to save a member of *Theadora's* crew. You also risked your life to prevent destruction of a captured French East Indiaman, no doubt saving many, many lives. You and indeed all in *Theadora* have done your duty. You have all done your duty to the point of not having a duty to perform."

"Sir, I don't follow...."

"It's peace, lad!" interrupted Jackson. "Hostilities ceased two days ago!"

"Peace?" asked Pierce incredulously.

Hotchkiss nodded smugly. He had known.

"You are aware, Mr. Pierce, that peace negotiations have been ongoing. They had been at an impasse, until the French received word a certain ship had been taken," said Tompkins.

"The Indiaman, sir? *Perpignan?*"

"Yes, Mr. Pierce," answered Jackson. "We found those military stores on board?"

"Aye, we did."

"Yet we knew neither mission nor destination, and no one would tell us," added Jackson.

"Captain Mirebeau and Minister Clion, I'm sure, revealed nothing," suggested Pierce.

"When the prize reached England," said Admiral Tompkins, taking up the story, "the Admiralty was at a loss regarding the ship's specific mission. The shipwrights and carpenters surveying her found what appeared to be an unsound timber. It rang hollow. A void caused by rot, or poor French workmanship? Closer inspection revealed the timber had been purposely hollowed and documents regarding the mission hidden there."

"I never realized that ship was so important," mused Pierce.

"Indeed it was, my friend," added Hotchkiss.

"So, if it is possible to know, sir," continued Pierce. "What were *Perpignan's* mission and destination?"

"North America, it seems, Mr. Pierce," revealed Admiral Tompkins. "The armaments were to equip uprisings amongst French descendants in British North America. Perhaps too, they would arm those in French territories to strike at British outposts. Bonaparte wanted to create enough of a stir in North America to cause us to withdraw forces from Europe to deal with it."

"Surely one ship could not have provided that much?"

"They had plans for further shipments, had this one succeeded. There was an alternative, additional mission as well."

"Sir?"

"The inspectors found a large amount of gold hidden in the ship. Some was in plain sight, painted to resemble ordinary fixtures and utensils. More was hidden in false beams and hollow timbers. The French were to contact the yards where those new American frigates were built and attempt to obtain similar ships of their own. Had that failed, they were to attempt a purchase directly from the United States government. As a final alternative they were to consider purchasing and converting some larger merchantmen."

"Could the French gain enough of a fleet to be a threat?" wondered Pierce.

"No intention to match us," interjected Captain Jackson. "Simply wanted it to be an annoyance, that we would divert some ships away from blockade duties."

"Say what you will about those American frigates." Tompkins took a sip of his wine. "They are big, heavily constructed, and heavily armed. It would be a close thing, against any of ours, assuming comparable levels of seamanship and gunnery. With the number and weight of guns carried, one well-handled could give *Bristol* a run for it. Had the French obtained even a few ships of that nature, we would have had a real problem."

"Enough, Mr. Pierce," continued Jackson, "to cause us to take ships off blockade duty to hunt them! A weakened blockade and a chance for Boney to invade England."

"*Theadora's* capture of *Perpignan*, Nelson's victory at Copenhagen in April, and other events on the mainland have well-skewered his plans. He has finally agreed to a peace. The treaty is not yet fully approved, but two days ago, hostilities between the two nations and their respective allies ceased."

"I see, sir," intoned Pierce.

"I don't see that it will last long. Time, not tranquility is what Boney wants. Yet the fleet is being laid up. Most ships, including the three here now, will be put in ordinary, the crews paid off, and officers set ashore on half pay. Unjust as it is, employment will go to those with friends and influence. Gentlemen, we are, in a word, 'unemployed.'"

Tompkins continued. "Mr. Pierce, were I retiring I would have the opportunity to make promotions: midshipman to lieutenant, lieutenant to commander, and commander to post captain. If I was retiring, you would be promoted to commander."

"I'm grateful of the consideration, sir," Pierce said.

"But I am not retiring. I can recommend a promotion, but with the peace, and the inevitable tightening of the Admiralty's purse, it would not be confirmed. With no vessel to command, it would be a non-promotion at that. You'd still be a lieutenant on half pay."

"I quite understand, sir." Everyone was silent a few moments, and then Pierce continued. "I'll not have problems, sir. I have family and home and should have a tidy amount in prize money to see me through."

"My family is there as well," said Hotchkiss.

"Prize money, Mr. Pierce," began Jackson. "We did earn a fair amount during *Theadora's* commission. But there is some dispute over *Perpignan's* gold. Courts are deciding if it is prize money. Is it French gold or what they obtained illegally? Is it eligible for distribution?"

"Now, Mr. Pierce," added Admiral Tompkins. "I do have an alternative for you, should you be so inclined."

"Sir?"

"There is an organization concerned with exploration that may have need of a most resourceful and daring ship's captain. They may have determined the location of a long-lost, nearly legendary island, and plan to make a voyage to confirm its presence. It would be most advantageous that Great Britain be the first to locate it. Certainly we would not want the French even to be aware of its existence."

"You would recommend me for the position, sir?"

"I would, indeed. But you needn't decide this instant. There is still some time before any expedition can get underway. Enjoy your time ashore. Visit with your family. Get reacquainted with your brothers. But do keep it in mind. Should you choose to investigate further, here is the name and address of the person to contact." Whereupon the admiral handed him a small folded piece of paper. On it was the name Harold Smythe, and an address on the Isle of Wight.

Chapter Seven

Auspicious Meetings

The Solent was agitated, stirred by the strong westerly wind whipping across it. The half gale blew the foam off the whitecaps and sent it flying across the deck of the small coaster ferrying people, animals, produce, and merchandise to the Isle of Wight. Close-hauled on a starboard tack, the huge lugsails double reefed, she hoped to fetch Cowes on this current heading.

Edward Pierce stood easily at the forward weather rail. The wind and spray in his face were exhilarating. He felt refreshed by the sea's onslaught and gave no thought to seeking shelter. Enroute to Newport to call on Mr. Harold Smythe, he had paid for his passage and had boarded the lugger at Gosport.

Pierce had not been afloat for the previous six months. After they met with Admiral Tompkins, he and Captain Jackson had dined aboard the flagship. Both had eaten heartily, as the admiral's stores were much fresher than any aboard *Theadora*. Then they had returned and Jackson had announced the cease-fire to the crew. To make some order out of the fleet's return, *Theadora* had remained at sea another three weeks. The hands had grumbled a little, and even some officers had voiced displeasure at the delay. They did have fresh stores to see them through those last days, thanks to Captain Wyndham of *Bristol*. Jackson declared every third day make and mend and allowed hands not actually on watch to work on items of a personal nature.

The last weeks of a long, arduous commission passed quickly. They anchored off Spithead, and stores and munitions were off-loaded. Canvas, spars, and upper masts were sent down and stowed. Captain

Jackson read the orders that placed the small frigate in ordinary, and at that time, he and all officers were on half pay. The crew was paid off and ferried ashore. For some, it was their first step on English soil in years. Mr. Phelps, three master's mates, and six hands, all volunteers, remained as a caretaker crew.

Pierce went ashore along with Lieutenant Forrest and Midshipman Small, their sea chests wedged against the thwarts of the hired small boat. Ashore he hired a man and his barrow to carry his dunnage. Pierce stayed that night at the *George*, fortunate to find a room, and fortunate to afford it, having received at least a part of the prize money he was due. He waited there for the return of *Bristol* and Isaac Hotchkiss. Then the two half-pay lieutenants returned to their boyhood home together.

At home in the small village outside of Petersfield, the two were welcomed with open arms by both families. There were feasts and festivities, celebrating the return of the seagoing sons. Pierce did not mind talking of life at sea in a general way, even as everyone listened awestruck as he and Hotchkiss described the adventures they had had.

While he was grateful to be home for the holidays, being home wasn't as before. He was at home and yet felt more like a guest. He didn't particularly miss being at sea and in harm's way, but he felt restless and agitated. He had left home nearly a decade earlier, a young lad not sure if the path he had somewhat reluctantly chosen was the right one. Now he was back, in all respects a man, a lieutenant in the King's Navy. He had been places, seen things, and done things that he had never dreamed of. There was much more to the world than the village and the surrounding countryside.

He had no need for employment, due to his share of prize money, and Pierce soon found that he was bored. While he attempted to stay busy, helping his father clean and polish the squire's coach, Pierce found the idea of free time to be foreign to him. As a result, he also groomed and tended the horses. Living what would appear to be an idyllic life, he and Isaac spent many evenings deep in conversation with friends, acquaintances, and strangers at the Crooked Oak Inn. There was always food on the table and drink to be had. The next morning they often awoke with aching heads, churning stomachs, and blurred memories.

Once a month they journeyed to Portsmouth, visited the Dockyard, and drew their half pay from the Clerk of the Cheque. They also checked for possible employment in His Majesty's Ships and Vessels. Neither sought active duty because of the hardships of half pay. Both had done well with prize money, and both had families not in need of their support. Still, Pierce and Hotchkiss felt a need to be back at sea and active in naval service once again. Once they had collected their half pay and made their standard queries for employment, they spent a day or two and a portion of their pay enjoying the sometimes notorious wild life of Portsmouth.

There was a house with rooms to let on Broad Street. The price was reasonable, the rooms comfortable, snug, and clean, and could be had for a day or two. While they could have afforded more luxurious accommodations, they found these convenient and the proprietor hospitable. Each month, they arrived, arranged for lodging, went to the Dockyard, and took in the town. While they had favorite places that they returned to each time, they also endeavored to visit new and different establishments.

During their February 1802 visit, they stopped to eat just up the street from their room. Finished, Pierce and Hotchkiss sat at the table, each nursing a pint, when another Royal Navy lieutenant entered. He was half a head shorter than Pierce, and wore a threadbare greatcoat to fend off the winter's chill. Shrugging out of his outer garments, he tossed them and his hat into a vacant chair. After stamping a bit of warm into his feet, he sat down at a small table.

"An' 'ow are ye t'day, Mr. Rowley?" asked the owner. "What can I get ye?"

"I'm well enough, thank you," replied the lieutenant, rubbing his hands briskly. "A pint of your best and a plate of anything warming would do nicely."

"Mutton stew?"

"Yes, thank you."

Rowley? Isaac had mentioned a Rowley in *Atlas*, where last word placed his brothers amongst the crew. He looked at Hotchkiss. "Do you think?"

"You could ask," his friend answered.

"I could, yes. We'll have another pint and one for him as well. Let him join us if he chooses, and I'll ask him."

Pierce ordered each of them another pint. He quietly ordered one for the lieutenant who sat a couple of tables away. When his beer was served, the lieutenant protested that he hadn't ordered it. The girl nodded toward Pierce, indicating that he had bought it. The stocky lieutenant acknowledged the generosity with a grin and a nod. His mouth was full and he could not politely reply any other way.

Pierce rose and approached the other's table. "I beg pardon, sir, but would you care to join us? I am Edward Pierce and this is Isaac Hotchkiss."

"Unemployed lieutenants, as am I, I'll wager. Misery and company, you know. Delighted at the invitation and naturally I'll accept. By the way," he added, rising from his seat, "my name is Leonard Rowley."

"I couldn't help but hear it when you entered," said Pierce. "I am wondering if you might be the Lieutenant Rowley who was in *Atlas*."

"I was in *Atlas*, yes," answered Rowley. "May I ask as to your interest?"

"I do not mean to be abrupt, but I seek information of my two brothers, believed to have been in *Atlas* during her last commission."

"You needn't apologize, sir. As Nelson suggested, one should not waste time with maneuver, but rather go straight at them. I was fourth for some time and don't recall that a Pierce ever messed in the wardroom or gunroom."

"My pardon, but they were pressed years ago. They would have been amongst the crew, no doubt experienced hands by the time you may have known them."

"That sets a different light on it. As I recollect, there was a gunner's mate, name of Pierce onboard. A topman as well. Good hands, if memory serves. I realized they were brothers, but never guessed a third would be in the service with a commission."

"We gained appointments as midshipmen to find them. Three other friends were pressed as well."

"I am sorry I cannot give you any recent news. I was promoted commander in *Tickler*, a French prize and returned last autumn. As to *Atlas* since my departure, I know very little, except that she has recently returned to Sheerness. If luck is with you, Lieutenant, you may soon be reunited with your brothers."

Rowley momentarily turned his attention to his dinner, but soon he looked up. "I understand a Lieutenant Pierce's actions helped convince the Frogs to sue for peace. Would that be you?"

Hotchkiss added. "My friend was instrumental in capturing of *Perpignan* a year ago. With her taken, the French were quite ready to ask for peace."

"My congratulations, sir," said Rowley. "Now if you will excuse me, my stew grows cold, and I must soon take my leave. A good day to you both!"

"A good day to you, sir!" replied Pierce.

The older Pierce brothers returned home two weeks later. Both had done well in the service, Robert rising to gunner's mate, and John to Captain of the Foretop at the end of *Atlas's* voyage. At first they found it difficult to carry on as brothers and family. The two had been under discipline so long that they could not see past Edward's commission. He was their younger brother, but first in their thoughts, he was a lieutenant. Eventually they lessened their long-held restraint and again regarded him as kin.

Over the course of many conversations, John and Robert told Edward of *Atlas's* voyage to the Mediterranean, her captain's growing detachment, and the exploits of the fourth lieutenant. Having met the man, Pierce wondered if they spoke of the same person.

Pierce thought that with his brothers' return, he would feel complete and content. However, he still felt like a visitor in his boyhood home. He needed to be out and about, at sea, with the wind and rain, the bad food, and the harsh realities of life or death. For two more months he made the journey to Portsmouth, drew his half pay and unsuccessfully sought employment aboard any of His Majesty's Ships still in commission.

As April's trip drew to an end, he took a now well-folded paper from his pocket. "Isaac, my friend, I won't be returning home with you. I'll find this gentleman, the one Admiral Tompkins told me about. Perhaps the offer yet stands, and I will find employment."

"I'm surprised you haven't gone already," said Isaac. "I would join you, but someone needs to tell your family. And Sharon would never forgive me if I miss that dinner next week. But should they need anyone else, keep me in mind."

"I'll do that. But for now, I am merely going to look into the possibility. I'll return within the week."

The coaster's track was not a good as had been hoped, and she was forced to tack again before heading into Cowes. As the small vessel came about, Pierce instinctively observed and rated the crew's performance. He was about to shout an admonishment, but as he was only a passenger, he held his tongue. The small crew did not have the precision and blazing speed of a naval crew, but they were most handy in working their craft.

Under the headlands the wind was less forceful. The waters were still choppy, however, and the coaster pitched and bucked. The motion reminded Pierce of him and Isaac helping his father break young horses years ago. Skillfully the coaster's crew brought her into the small harbor and nestled her alongside the quay with a small jolt. Lines were passed, made fast, and the voyage was over.

Pierce stepped ashore and wondered how he would get to Newport. He could walk, even though it was some distance, if that were the only way. Yet, if transportation were available, he would take advantage.

A wagon loaded with rum kegs rumbled off the quay. Pierce overheard the driver remark that he would be in Newport by nightfall. Pierce asked if company would be welcome, and added that he would pay at least a token amount for a ride.

"It's up to you, sir," the teamster answered. "Sixpence would be good, if you got it. Climb up!"

Pierce dug in his pocket, handed the driver the agreed-upon coinage, and threw his small travel bag behind the seat. After he crawled up, the driver cracked his long whip and they started off. The wagon jolted, lurched, swayed, and bounced. For a moment Pierce thought he would pitch headlong to the cobbled street, but soon he found a secure seat. It was not unlike riding with his father on the squire's coach as they made a mad dash along the rutted byways outside the village. But the wagon proceeded at walking speed. It was the vehicle's design, its load, or the road's condition that made the ride so rough.

The driver was a man of few words, who normally made this journey alone. Pierce was not talkative either, so for a good portion of the journey, they rode in silence. At last the driver's curiosity surfaced and he asked, "You have business in Newport, Lieutenant?"

"I do."

"Might I ask?"

"I am seeing about maritime employment. With the peace, there are far more officers than ships available."

"Aye."

"Perhaps you would know where to find the man I seek. I have an address, but I am unfamiliar with...."

"You know the name?"

"Harold Smythe," answered Pierce.

"Don't know that I'd get involved with that lot, sir," responded the driver. He sipped from a small flask that likely held a sample of the shipment behind them.

"Why would that be?" Pierce had sudden doubts about this employment opportunity. "Are they doing something illegal?"

"No, not that anyone could say. Just odd, he is, sir. Seems to have money. Yet lives in a small place, not much more than what I have, sir. All sorts of visitors, sir. Some right suspicious. Others seem to be all power and influence, sir."

"Sounds intriguing."

"If you want, sir, I'll alter my route some and deliver you there. Won't hardly take me off my usual route."

"I would appreciate it. Perhaps we could arrange a return journey as well?"

"Aye, that could be done, depending upon another sixpence." The driver took another sip from his flask, cracked the whip and returned to his contemplative silence. In spite of the bright sun, the air was cold, and exposed on the wagon, Pierce was chilled by the wind. He wrapped his cloak more tightly about him.

The sun was nearly down, its brightness fading, when the driver stopped the wagon in front of a nondescript cottage. It was sturdily built but showed the ravages of time and benign neglect. The gate in front sagged and the hinges squeaked when Pierce opened it. With some misgiving he approached the door and knocked. He waited, and after sufficient time, he rapped again.

A dog barked, and moments later Pierce heard footsteps approach. The door opened slowly. The old man in the doorway was clad in what had once been fine fashion for a household servant. Now it was worn, threadbare, patched, and darned in many places. Despite the shabbiness of his clothes, the wearer had the bearing of one who had spent a lifetime in respectable service to others. "Yes? May I help you, sir?"

"I am here to see a Mr. Harold Smythe," said Pierce. "I was given his name concerning possible employment while we are at peace."

"Please come in, won't you?" He looked at the dog, black and white, with a touch of tan and gray, one blue eye and one of brown, who watched Pierce guardedly.

"That'll do!" he said. "Junior, that'll do!" The dog relaxed and let Pierce enter the house.

"Whom shall I say is calling?"

"Edward Pierce, Lieutenant, Royal Navy."

"Very well, sir. You may wait here."

The old man led Pierce into a study. It needed a good tidying, looking comfortably used. Books were scattered about, and a tray with the remnants of light refreshment sat on a small table. The table top and other furniture had a slight layer of dust, evidence of days passed since any cleaning. Another table had maps and charts spread out in haphazard fashion.

Curious, Pierce glanced at the top map, which was of the Indian Ocean. It had several positions annotated, and he wondered at their significance. Did they have anything to do with the voyage being planned? He spotted a comfortable-looking chair and, being weary, sat down.

The dog had remained, and now Pierce saw him lying in front of the fire. Was the dog there to guard him? The dog was awake and aware, but paid him no attention.

"Junior?" Pierce said softly. The dog looked. "Junior? How are you, boy?" Hearing the voice and his name once more, the dog relaxed, wagged his tail tentatively, and approached. Junior sniffed at Pierce's proffered hand. With another beat of his tail, he extended a paw as if to shake hands.

"How do you do, Junior?" said Pierce, who gently shook the paw. Junior looked him in the eye and smiled as only a dog can smile, and lay down contentedly under Pierce's feet.

"I see you have made a friend," said a voice from behind Pierce. The accent, or perhaps the lack of one, puzzled Pierce. He did know the speaker was not native to the British Isles. Pierce recognized most local and regional variations of the language, including the influences of other speech used in the United Kingdom. He stood, slowly and easily, careful not to disturb the dog, and turned around.

"If Junior likes you, it is in your favor. I've learned to trust his judgment when dealing with strangers. But since you and he are friends now, you cannot be a stranger. You, I understand, are Lieutenant Edward Pierce?"

"Indeed, I am."

"And I am Harold Smythe." He reached forward and clasped Pierce's hand firmly. Pierce detected warmth, sincerity, and sense of purpose in the handshake.

"Pleased to meet you, sir," said Pierce. "I'm most pleased to meet Junior as well."

"We have hoped to hear from you for quite some time."

"You have?" said Pierce, a slight look of puzzlement coming over his face.

"Indeed yes, ever since *Theadora* paid off and your exploits were published in the *Gazette*. You did read of the adventures of your ship, did you not?"

"Oh yes, I did read them, but my part was quite small."

"As from what was written, yes, but the actual accomplishments were far from small."

"Perhaps," Pierce answered, a bit of a query on his face.

"Ah, my accent!" said Smythe. "It puzzles you?"

"Aye, it does. I can't place it."

"Then let me tell you of myself, and the story behind it. But first, may I offer you a drink? Perhaps you are hungry? We might dine?"

Pierce hadn't eaten since early that morning, before he had boarded the coaster at Gosport. "I would not impose on your hospitality, sir, but indeed I am hungry."

"If you would follow me, then?" suggested Smythe. "While we have a small household staff, we do much for ourselves." He led the way down a short hallway. In a large pantry room, he gestured and said, "We usually eat early, but there should be something left. Please have whatever you would like. Drink? We have several wines, liquors, and other spirits. Beer? Ale? Cider?"

"Cider would be most refreshing," said Pierce, oddly amused and somewhat perplexed by the informality. He had thought that Smythe would ring and have the old man bring something. That he didn't, and that he fetched the crock and poured two tall glasses of cider, told Pierce that this was a man of practicality.

"We have some bread left, and some cold roast beef, sliced fairly thin. You could follow the manner of the Earl of Sandwich."

"And, how is that, sir?" asked Pierce.

"Lay some of the roast beef between two slices of bread. A little mustard or similar condiment so it won't be dry, a slice of cheese and perhaps some fresh lettuce, and you would have a handy meal." Smythe went to work assembling such a meal as he spoke. "I'll do one for you, should you like? I've found it convenient and do so quite often."

"Please, if it isn't any trouble."

With the handy meals ready, Pierce and Smythe returned to the study. Following the example of his host, Pierce sat his small plate haphazardly on the table, picked up the double slices of bread and took a bite. "Delicious, and as you said, 'convenient.'"

Such meals could be made up beforehand, and if kept fresh, might feed a crew in battle or when galley fires were out. Pierce could see other times when such a pre-made meal would be welcome. Boarding and landing parties could both benefit, especially when required duties lasted through regular mess times.

Smythe took a bite, laid the *sandwich* on his plate, and began. "I can tell, Lieutenant Pierce, that you are puzzled. You are puzzled by my appearance, my accent, and even the strangeness of my hospitality."

Smythe's command of English was as good as his own, but his accent caused Pierce to question its origin. He had already decided it was not from the British Isles; nor could he place it in any European region or country. Nor did Smythe appear to be British. He was dark, almost swarthy, and Pierce thought him to be from Eastern Europe, the Mediterranean, or even the Middle East. Perhaps he was Greek, or a Turk? His hair was dark, nearly black, except for what the years had turned white. As to the informality, Pierce found it refreshing.

"Yes, sir, I am puzzled. Your speech, your name, and your appearance confuse me, although I certainly would not disapprove of this hospitality. It almost seems I am home."

"I believe in being comfortable and that guests should be comfortable as well. It's best to make one's guests feel as if they were at home.

"Now, while you eat, I'll tell you a little of myself, and that will lead to the purpose of the expedition." Smythe took another bite and washed it down with cider.

"As you have surmised, I am not British. My birth is a bit of a mystery. Some say I resulted from a dalliance between an East European noble, perhaps even a Royal, and a young peasant girl. I never knew my real parents. I was raised by the Romany -- Gypsies, if you prefer -- although I regard that term with some ill feeling. As I don't know the real truth of my ancestry, I may be Romany myself."

"I can see that in your appearance, sir."

"As can I." He took another sip of cider. "I grew up wandering through Europe. We moved constantly and were often outcasts. Sometimes we were run out of villages, simply because of who we were. Looking back, I cannot always blame the locals. Romany can be rather devious. Our band played it honestly and upright as possible, but others had given us a bad name. Regardless of our conduct, we suffered.

"We spoke our own tongue and the language of the local area. Because we roamed, we learned a new tongue every few months. I still speak many European languages, and have forgotten still more. My English is tempered – accented, if you will -- by many different languages.

"Harold Smythe is of course, not my real or Romany name. When I arrived here, I was befriended by an Englishman named Smythe, worked for him, and since he had no heirs, he left me his estate, such as it was. This place was his, and now it's mine. He was a rare individual who saw that what is inside a person is what matters. He didn't bother much about bloodlines and established heritage. I assumed his last name when he died and picked 'Harold' from the baptistery register of the nearby church."

"Sometimes I think we all should be able to do that," said Pierce. "These days, I suppose every man in England would be Horatio Nelson, even if not blind in one eye and short an arm."

"Quite true!" Smythe clucked his tongue, and Junior sat up. Smythe handed him the last bite of his meal and the dog ate it rapidly. "If you find it is more than enough, Junior will gladly finish it for you."

"I am sure that he would. I'll save him a bite at any rate," said Pierce. He took another bite of bread and beef.

With only one bite left, he held the morsel out to the dog. Junior sniffed at it and then took it, careful to seize only the food and not the fingers that held it. "Very discerning!" said Pierce. "There are dogs at home that will take food and fingers and not think twice of it."

"He is a gentle one," said Smythe, "and yet fearless in the face of danger. He will not back down, whether the threat is to him or one of us."

"A good dog," remarked Pierce. Junior's tail swayed contentedly at the words.

"To continue my tale," said Smythe as he sat back and sipped cider. "We spent many evenings around the fire, telling stories. Some we made up. Others were old, passed on from generation to generation. We often exchanged tales with other Romany or the local populace.

Some legends were old, so old that they had been passed down from father to son, even in the days before Greece, Rome, or Egypt!

"Many concerned Atlantis. Others told of an island or a continent of similar prestige. In some tales, detailed instructions existed that supposedly told how to get there. Since I was a lad, it has been my dream, my quest, to find that island. As I grew older and heard more tales about this island, I wrote them down. And I read any old texts I could lay my hands on.

"I have interpreted and corrected multiple translations, reacquainted myself with archaic forms of measurement, and at last I know its location. Most importantly, I know the way to it!"

"If one knows the location, the way should be obvious. Only geography would create any obstacle in reaching it," Pierce observed.

"But it is not that simple. One must travel a specific route ... pass through certain locations, much like passing through a series of gates. If one approaches the location without going through all these gates, the island simply isn't there."

Pierce shook his head slowly.

"You think I'm not in my right mind?"

"I would hesitate to say that, sir. I sense the hope and the dream. I just can't see it as fact. Can you be certain the island is there? Are your translations correct? Does it exist where you calculate it to be, the path taken to reach it will not matter!"

"Edward, open your mind to other possibilities. I don't know if the island exists, but I believe it does! I don't understand the science or the magic of its presence being dependent upon the course taken to reach it. I don't need to understand for it to be possible. That I have never seen such doesn't mean it isn't true. I simply know that I must try. We must find that island!"

"I quite understand that!" said Pierce, slightly vexed. "But you must be practical as well. What if you make the voyage and find nothing?"

"A second voyage, a third, and a fourth, if need be."

"Why from England? Surely you could start from any of a dozen nations."

"Despite my speech, my appearance, and my history, I consider myself English. At this time in history, England displays a sanity that many nations lack. The English are as free as any, aside perhaps from the Americans. They are still learning to be what they will be, so I would not trouble them with this. With the European affairs as they are, it is best that England find the island, rather than the French."

"They are searching for it?"

"I've heard rumors," confided Smythe. "Should war resume and the French find it, they would have a base from which to launch attacks against John Company and totally disrupt British trade in the region."

"The need to find it first might be why some word circulates about the voyage. Could it be why Admiral Tompkins mentioned such to me?"

"Indeed. We have contacts -- sponsorship, if you will -- financial backing, and official approval. But the whole thing is kept rather quiet. Most who are aware of it know it simply as a voyage of discovery and exploration. Only a handful know of the island, and fewer still know the truth about reaching it."

"It does sound intriguing."

"Yes," continued Smythe. "Do give it some thought. You would do your country a great service. But pray, take time to make the right choice."

"Papa!" The voice came from the doorway, quiet, strong, and melodious, the tones rich and full. "I'm retiring now, and you should let our guest do the same. He is likely fatigued from his journey. Pray, continue in the morning!"

Pierce stood and turned. A young woman stood in the doorway, simply and plainly dressed. She stepped further into the study and he noticed the graceful sensuality of her movements. The everyday dress she wore did not hide a lithe and slightly voluptuous form. Her hair was dark, almost black, but in the candlelight, highlights shone with a rich auburn hue. Her well-formed face was clear and unmarked by scar or blemish, and skin's tone was not unlike Smythe's.

She had called him "Papa." His daughter?

"My goodness!" said Smythe. "I am so driven to complete my quest that I forget my civilities. I've kept you discussing a legendary island and have not introduced my family. Please, forgive me."

Pierce looked at the young woman. She smiled as he said, "I understand the fervor of your quest, sir. It poses no offense to me."

She scowled mockingly at Smythe. "But indeed, it might for me, Papa!"

"Oh, dear child!" said Smythe contritely. "You know as I grow older, my mind doesn't function as it once did. Evangeline, my only child, this is Lieutenant Edward Pierce of His Majesty's Navy."

"Enchanted!" said Pierce, bowing formally.

"As am I," she said and extended her hand.

Pierce had always thought a lady waited for a gentleman to offer his hand, and only then did she reach out so that he might take hers. Nonetheless, he responded and grasped her outstretched hand firmly, yet gently in his. He noticed the strength of the slender fingers; the short-cut nails, and even the slight dryness and roughness of her skin. He did not find the touch at all unpleasant. It was refreshingly normal that a woman used her hands for everyday tasks. He thought to kiss her fingers in the manner of society, but decided against it. He was not of the upper classes, and as far as he knew, neither was she. "I am very pleased to meet you, Evangeline," he murmured, suddenly feeling a little warm.

"I am pleased to meet you, Edward." She squeezed his hand slightly and relaxed her grip. Slowly they relinquished the hand to hand contact. She smiled warmly.

"My dear, you are right." Smythe's voice broke the mood as Pierce stood transfixed. "It is late and he has had a tiring day, I'm sure. We can continue on the morrow."

"I am tired, sir. Would there be a decent inn nearby?"

"An inn? What sort of host does not provide a bed for his guest?"

"I would not want to trouble you, sir," begged Pierce.

"Nonsense! We are always ready for visitors. The nearest inn charges twice what it's worth, and the others are full of vermin. You'll stay here, if I may insist!"

"That being the case, I believe I would sleep very soon and very well."

Later Pierce tossed restlessly. Try as he might, he could not fall asleep. His mind flew from one detail to another and would not stay where he wanted it to. Images of the young lady he had just met continuously crowded in.

She was attractive, if not beautiful in the classic sense. She had a little too much nose and her mouth was a little wider than perfect. But her complexion was clear, her figure beguiling, and her manner self-assured and pleasant. He could easily alter his concept of the perfect woman to fit the reality that was she.

Chapter Eight

A Most Remarkable Lady

As Pierce awoke, he remembered bits of conversation from the night before. A great deal of what Smythe had told him was beyond belief. Still, the man was sincere and had a unique sense of hospitality that intrigued him. And, he had a daughter who had played delightfully on Pierce's mind as he had tried to fall asleep.

A knock sounded against the door. "Yes!" he said, loudly enough to be heard.

"Don't mean to wake you, sir." It was the old man who had answered the door yesterday. "Just me, sir, Hiram. Wondering if you'd like a bath to start the day, sir?"

"A bath?" Pierce struggled to comprehend. He had had a bath at home before he and Isaac had set out for Portsmouth. That had been less than a week earlier. Surely he did not need one so soon.

"Yes, sir. Mister Smythe is right peculiar with baths, sir. Says that it's good to have one every day, he does. And he does, too! May I come in, sir?"

"Certainly, yes."

The door opened and the old man entered the room. He opened the curtains and let some light into the room. "A nice day today, sir. Plenty of sun and only a little bit o' cloud in the sky. If the wind doesn't come up, that is."

"Very likely, I'd say," said Pierce. "What were you saying about a bath?"

"Wondering if you'd like one, sir? Might get you ready for a new day. Mr. Smythe has one nearly every day. Miss Smythe as well. And he's got me and the missus, Gertie, doing so nearly as often. Does feel good, sir!" Hiram paused to allow Pierce a bit of time to think upon the offer. "Never realized sir, until I started, just how dirty a person could get."

Pierce had always thought he was a clean fellow. He bathed when he had to, bathed when facilities were available. Still, the idea of a bath every day startled him. Surely it was unhealthy. Yet, according Hiram, Harold Smythe bathed every day, and he seemed healthy enough. "I suppose I could try it," he said. "Do you need help rigging it?"

"Oh, no, sir, I don't." The old man pointed. "Robe and slippers there, sir. All you need do is to change and follow me. While you're in the bath, I'll lay out some fresh things for you, sir, and we'll have your trappings cleaned and freshened up for you, sir."

By now, Pierce was sitting at the edge of the bed. He stood and struggled out of the night shirt and cap that he had borrowed the evening before. He slipped into the robe and belted it snugly about him.

"This way, sir," said Hiram as he led the way down the hall.

"Mr. Smythe had this room outfitted special, sir, just for baths. He's a bit of a tinkerer, as well, sir, and this is what he's come up with." He pointed out a small chamber, just big enough for one person to stand in. There was a fine metal grate in the floor, and overhead, near the ceiling, a brass pipe that ended with many fine holes. Farther back on the pipe was a pull chain, evidently with which to activate the system. "You can turn it on or off with the chain and toggle valve, there, sir. Water's hot, so check it first. The handle on the wall controls cold water if you need to cool it down some, sir."

"Where does the water come from?" asked Pierce intrigued with the set up

"We pump water into two tanks in the attic. One is the cold water and it just sits there. The other has a small fire under it. We have had lots of practice now in keeping it perfectly warm."

"Looks interesting. I'll have a go."

"Very good, sir, "said Hiram. "There's soap an' a flannel there.

The jar is for your hair, if you want. Mr. Smythe made it, and says it does better than anything that can be found. Towels are right outside, sir. Just come on back to your room, sir, when you're done. I'll have things ready for you."

"Thank you, Hiram," said Pierce. He untied the robe, hung it on a convenient hook, and stepped into the small room within a room. He stood to one side and pulled the chain. A soft spray of water burst forth from the end of the pipe. It was a little too hot and he reached for the knob on the wall. He got some movement out of it and pulled the chain again. That was better. He stepped under the falling spray of water. Within minutes, he felt cold. He nudged the cold water adjustment and slightly lessened its effect. Then he washed himself thoroughly and luxuriously. He tried a little of the substance in the jar and washed his hair as well. Then he turned and allowed the fine falling drops of water to rinse the soap and soil away.

It felt heavenly to stand under the hot water and let it cascade over him. Surely doctors were wrong to insist that a person not bathe often. It was too bad that fresh water was so precious aboard ship, as a bath on a regular basis would be refreshing. Perhaps it could be done with sea water, although no one would stay under such cold water any longer than necessary. But at present he did not want to end the bath. It was warm and comfortable, and for the first time in his life, he felt really, really clean. He liked that.

Pierce stopped the water and stepped out. He shivered as the cooler air of the outer room contacted his skin. Point of reference, he thought, grabbing a large soft towel. The room had seemed warm before, but with his body warmed by the water, it seemed cool. He toweled off, and the exertion and the friction of the cloth warmed him. He put on the robe and the slippers, and returned to his room.

As he stepped into the hallway, Evangeline approached from the opposite end. She too was in robe and slippers and obviously on her way to a bath as well. She smiled. "Good morning, Lieutenant!" she said. "I trust that you slept well? Did you find the bath refreshing?"

"Very much so. Hard to believe they say bathing can be harmful." Pierce realized he was in nothing more that a borrowed robe, and the young lady was also similarly attired. "Excuse me! I'm not properly dressed." His face reddened slightly.

"Neither am I, Lieutenant." She smiled again. "But neither of us is indecent. It's a matter of practicality. We are used to one or another being thusly garbed and pay it no mind. But if it bothers you, please continue and make yourself presentable." She moved past him into the bathing room. "I'll join you for coffee when I finish."

"Yes! Coffee would be fine." Pierce still felt a little flushed.

Back in his room, Pierce found that Hiram had produced a wash basin and a mug of shaving soap. There was also a razor, old and oft-honed, that looked efficient and sharp. He had one in his kit, but used the one provided. He slightly nicked a particular spot, as he always did, but he ended up with a comfortable, close shave.

Hiram knocked perfunctorily and entered with an armful of clothing. "Here you are, sir, somethin' to wear today. Your uniform will be clean tomorrow. If the size isn't good, we'll find other for you. Appears between Mr. Smythe and m' self there's no problem with fit, sir."

"These should do. Thank you, Hiram."

"Very good, sir. If it's not beneath you, sir, join us in the kitchen for coffee. Perhaps a bite o' breakfast if you are in need of it, sir? Mr. Smythe hardly ever has any, an' I've come to see that some do and some don't, sir."

"Most assuredly, I'll join you for coffee. I'm a coachman's son, after all."

"Aye, sir," said Hiram. The old man left.

The clothes were clean and nearly the right size. The coat sleeves were a trifle short, the waistband a wee bit big, and everything was worn and used. But the clothing was comfortable, and when he finished dressing, he caught sight of himself in the mirror. He looked very presentable in the borrowed attire. The dark green of the coat and the palest of yellows in the breeches, shirt, and waistcoat agreed with his countenance and coloration. But he was not used to anything but his blue uniform, and his reflection looked unfamiliar in the mirror.

Pierce adjusted his neckerchief as his mind wandered back to the recent encounter with Evangeline. She was a most attractive young lady. She may not have been a lady by virtue of position or bloodline, but her presence and bearing were enough that she could be. But based on Smythe's origins, could she possess the blood of East European nobility, if not of royalty? Pierce could not fathom any guess as to her mother's station in life.

Try as he might, Edward Pierce could not take his mind off her. He even wondered about the charms hidden under her robe. He scolded himself for having such thoughts about the daughter of his host and prospective employer. He was not a man to work for someone while he planned the seduction of the daughter. Still, he was young and alive, and in some unexplainable, magical way, Evangeline stirred the basic elements in him.

Pierce found his way to the kitchen where sat Hiram and his wife, Gertie. She was an older woman who had worked hard all her life. Surely her life had had times of great joy and times of great sorrow. There was a merry twinkle in her eye and a smile in her voice. "Mornin', Lieutenant!" she said cheerily. "Do with coffee, I suppose? We don't stand on ceremony around here. Cup's on the shelf, and the pot's on the stove. Help yourself, if you don't mind?"

"Not at all. Much like home." He grabbed a sturdy-looking mug and poured it full. Steam rose from the cup.

"Didn't have no chance to meet you last evening, sir. You just call me Gert, or Gertie, whichever you prefer. I'll answer to either, and more, as long as it's not too crude." She smiled warmly. "Now,

Lieutenant, do you like toast, and perhaps eggs with that coffee? Young man like you needs more than that brew to start the day."

"Mama," said Hiram, as he nursed a cup of coffee. "Let the lad wake. If he wants to eat, he knows to ask."

"Perhaps, old man," she said with mock gravity, "you forget we are in my kitchen. Even Mr. Smythe steps carefully here." She turned back to Pierce. "I'll fix eggs, bacon, and toast if you want. If you don't, speak out. Once I've lost the urge, don't ask, 'cause it won't happen."

"That sounds good. Please!" Pierce took a small sip of coffee. It was a little too hot.

Evangeline came into the kitchen. "Good morning, everyone!" she said gaily as she took a mug and poured it full. She added a touch of sugar, and stirred the coffee slowly to dissolve the sweetness.

"Mornin', Miss Vangie," said Gertie. "Your normal?"

"I think so."

Pierce took another sip of his coffee. It was at the right temperature, and its warmth brought him more into the land of the awake. He felt at ease in the warm, cheery, and friendly kitchen. It was almost like being at home. Then he noticed that someone was missing.

"Beg your pardons," he said, "but where is Mr. Smythe?"

"Papa was summoned on urgent business early this morning," responded Evangeline. "He won't be back until late afternoon or evening. He thought you would like to accompany me today. I too have errands to run."

"It would be my pleasure," said Pierce with a smile.

"Excellent! After breakfast, Hiram can harness the team." She smiled.

"I'm done wi' my breakfast, as it is," said Hiram. "I'll get the rig ready. Might need a bit of cleaning since last time."

"No need to rush, Hiram," intoned Evangeline.

"No, ma'am," he said, getting up and stretching. "Time I got busy."

"Him, busy?" Gertie snorted. Then she giggled as he bussed her affectionately and left the room.

A half hour later, Pierce and Miss Smythe were ready. He helped her into the seat, which provided just room enough for the two of them. He walked around to the other side and climbed in. He was about ready to urge the team into motion when she stopped him. "... oh, never mind. I think Junior went with Papa this morning."

"And normally he would go with you?" Pierce asked.

"Much of the time," she replied. "He enjoys riding, right there, behind the seat. I usually take him, if I go alone. He's good protection, but as you are here, I've no need to worry."

"I would hope not!" Pierce said and gave the reins a slight slap across the horses' backs. "More than enough for this light rig, I warrant. One would be sufficient."

"Yes. But they've worked together for so many years that we keep them as a pair, even if a pair isn't needed. Left at the end of the lane."

"Aye aye, ma'am!"

The old horses settled down to a slow trot. Every now and then, Evangeline gave him directions. They stopped at a couple of shops and she purchased items for the household. Most was simply ordered for later delivery. Eventually they found themselves on the road to Cowes.

"Now where are we going?" asked Pierce.

"To Sir Ronald Arthur's shipyard," she said. "Papa thought you should see the vessel we are having built. He thinks if you see we have an actual vessel, you may be more inclined to join us."

"Perhaps." Pierce was noncommittal.

"I've got the next payment to deliver as well," she said. He understood her earlier concern for a protection. Still, a determined rogue would not let a guard dog, no matter how loyal and vigilant, nor a male escort, no matter how brave and alert, stand in his way.

"Ronald Arthur? I have heard of him."

"I would think you have!" she said. "He commanded a frigate near the end of the American War, engaged a squadron of French frigates and nearly beat them all. He was knighted for it, but suffered severe wounds and retired from active service. He's always had an interest in ship design and building. Now he has a shipyard outside of Cowes."

"I do remember hearing about him."

"He most commonly builds small merchant vessels for channel and coastal trade. From what Papa says, he has unusual ideas about ship design and construction. He's willing to work with us and design and build what will fit our needs. He's even willing to overlook our sometimes erratic schedule of payments."

"That is a very generous thing to do."

"Quite!"

Evangeline was silent for a while, and then asked, "What do you think? Can one sail to find an island that exists only in old legends?"

"Quite honestly, I don't think it could exist. In this day the entire world has been explored and all lands have been found. Still, the prospect of finding more is intriguing. I tend to think I would join, if only to be a part of the search."

"You should be in Parliament!" she chided. "You say so much and yet so little."

"Perhaps I am not yet committed. I want the employment, but the ultimate success is not that important to me. But for your sake and your father's sake, I hope the island is found."

"As do I." She went on. "Papa has lived and breathed with this for so long that it would break his heart if it isn't found."

"Surely one could mount a second or even a third expedition if the first doesn't succeed?"

"Yes, but chances for any sponsorship would lessen with each failure."

Evangeline was silent awhile, but at last she spoke again. "Did Papa tell you the real reason he wants to find the island?"

"I gather he wants to prove that the stories he's heard are true."

"Yes, but there is much more to him than that. There is so much more he hopes for once the island is found."

"Indeed?"

"Papa told you a little of his childhood?" she asked. Then she directed, "Bear to the right, here!"

"Aye. Yes, he mentioned it."

"He told you how the Romany were often set upon by locals?"

"Yes."

"Simply because they were Romany?"

"Yes."

"And not because this particular band had ever caused harm in that village or town?"

"Yes."

"Did he say anything about his adult life? How he met and fell in love with my mother, who she was, and what happened to her?"

She shifted on the seat. Pierce was aware of her nearness and the pressure of her thigh. He should shift a bit, ease the numbness in his nether regions, and lessen the contact between them. He reveled in her proximity but he did not want her to know that her contact, no matter how innocent, affected him. If he moved to adjust his position, would she think he moved to ease the touch, and would that make her aware of his awareness? He would sit as he was for a few minutes. She could move if she found the contact improper.

"I don't recall that he said anything about that," he replied.

"By the time Papa was a young man, he had wandered over much of Europe. He had been in the Middle East, Africa, and had served in the Spanish fleet. In Spain, he met and fell in love with the daughter of a nobleman. She was taken by his charm, his bravado, and his exotic foreignness.

"You can surmise that her family did not approve. They would not have their daughter running off with a gypsy rogue. He was forbidden on the hacienda. She was forbidden to leave, unless accompanied an armed escort. They carried on snippets of lovers' communication, aided by a servant.

"They saw their chance, and she was able to slip away. They met, fled, and found a priest to marry them. They lived on the run, hiding from the pursuit her family sent after them. Papa tells me they were happy, in spite of the hardships. He often felt sorry for her enduring that life, and urged her to return home. She would not."

"Undoubtedly a remarkable and devoted wife!"

"Papa says she was very happy. She was without nearly all of what she once had, but never complained. He was always and constantly amazed by her good cheer.

"And they were in love. Because of that love, I was born. Then, Papa says, all was right in their world. They had each other, they had their love, and they had me as a symbol of it. They had help and support from the Romany and the common people. Papa was truly happy and wanted nothing more in life.

"But so very often, the best things are taken from us. The good doesn't always last."

"Sadly, I have learned that that is often true."

"I was three when we were found by those hired by Mama's family. They came to take her home and to a convent. She was disgraced, a sinner, and no longer a part of their family or society. The only solution was to lock her away. To them, Papa was a criminal of the worst kind. A kidnapper! A seducer! He had despoiled a virtuous lady of noble birth and had ruined their honor and reputation. He would be horribly punished, even killed to satisfy their honor.

"We were warned and fled. For a week they chased us through the mountains between Spain and France. Finally we could go no farther. One of them fired a musket at Papa, but his aim was bad. The ball struck Mama and she fell. Papa fired both the pistols he carried, and in a rage attacked with only a sword.

"His sudden ferocity gave him momentary advantage, and he drove them down the trail. "Then he picked Mama up, and he picked me up, and he carried us up into the rough countryside, and he went as far as he could, and then he tended to Mama. He did all he could, but she died in his arms. One of her hands clutched me so tight that it hurt.

"Papa didn't cry, but even I saw his devastation. A farmer helped bring Mama down from the mountain. The local church provided a funeral service and a place for us to stay. It was sanctuary, so those sent by Mama's family could not come for him, or me. The family wanted me, not out of pity or love, but as payment of a debt.

"Papa wrote a letter full of sorrow and expressed his condolences regarding the loss of their daughter. It was also a plea for reconciliation. Their reply was that he must surrender and face charges as the agent of her death."

"How terrible!" said Pierce. He wanted to say something profound and meaningful, but that simple exclamation was all he could trust himself to utter.

"Yes," she replied. "It was terrible. Papa reached out in grief, ours and theirs, and that was all they could do! Charge and try him as her killer! We left that little village in the Pyrenees and went north into France."

"A very sad tale. You and your father truly have my sympathy. But how does it fit with finding the island?

Evangeline was silent for a long moment. She blinked back a tear, leaned against Pierce, and rested her head on his shoulder. Instinctively he put his arm around her and gently stroked her hair. She had shared this sadness from her past, and now there was a warmth between them. Presently she sat up. The spell was broken, and he had to resume the role of a proper gentleman. He started to remove his arm.

"No, that's quite all right, Lieutenant," she said in a quiet voice. "I feel comforted and secure.

"You asked how this ties in with finding the island. It is Papa's dream to find it so that people who are unjustly accused or imprisoned can have a new, free life.

"You see, Papa has realized that in most places, justice is not so blind. The poor, the followers of a different faith, those of another race or nationality are often accused and convicted, not on the evidence, but on their difference. Even in England, it can be said that appearance and money talk. If you or a common seaman were charged with identical crimes under identical circumstances, I think that you would more easily be acquitted. Guilty or not, it doesn't matter. It is your status as an officer. The seaman, being of a lower standing, would more likely be convicted, whether or not he was really guilty."

"I have noticed the same."

"Most people don't. But Papa does. And he knows that sometimes a crime is committed out of necessity. A pauper steals in order to feed his family. A person kills another in self-defense. There are often special circumstances surrounding the facts of guilt.

"Papa has made arrangements to screen convicts sentenced to transportation. Those he can determine to be innocent or victims of circumstance will be offered an opportunity to settle on the island. They will be pardoned and asked to work, both for a wage and to help build the community. When a short contract time is up, they will be free to leave."

"And return to England?" Pierce asked.

"Sadly, no," she stated. "That was a point that Papa lost. They will be allowed to go to the island, and will be considered pardoned, as long as they never return to England. However, in any English colony or territory they would be considered free men."

"In effect, they are still being transported."

"But not to a prison colony. They are being transported to a *freedom colony*."

"I find myself suspect of that idea," he said. "There might be some who would undermine those efforts, or contrive some personal profit. Some may betray what he hopes to accomplish."

"That is precisely why we don't make it common knowledge.

Those chosen won't be told until underway. Until we depart England, they will think they are being transported as sentenced. Should they refuse the offer, they will be liable for later transportation to an actual penal colony."

"That is a little harsh, considering the compassion that seems to guide these efforts."

"Perhaps," she responded. "But we have the whole group to protect. We are not only in England, but throughout Europe and America. Even France! Some of us face different circumstances, and efforts cannot be known by the respective governments."

"There will be more than one expedition?"

"If the first is successful, it will return and enable other voyages."

"For my part, should I command this first expedition," Pierce queried. "I sail, find the island, report the venture's success, and then I am done with it?"

"As you would, or make another voyage."

"Intriguing!" said Pierce, as free of possible commitment as he could be.

"But you mustn't speak about this aspect of it to anyone," she said quietly. "Now, if you'll turn between those posts, we'll be at Sir Ronald's."

Chapter Nine

Her Unique Skill

When Pierce and Miss Smythe arrived, the shipyard's proprietor, ready to eat dinner, invited them to join him. Pierce wasn't terribly hungry, and ate to be polite, rather than to satisfy any physical need.

Arthur was a small man, at the aft end of his middle years. His left hand was missing two fingers, and his left arm moved with a stiffness caused by wounds suffered in an earlier war. He hobbled and favored his right leg. He spoke in a high-pitched, reedy voice, and was prone to a quick temper. Pierce could not picture him on a frigate's quarterdeck in action.

Yet there was no standard mold for a captain. Nelson didn't fit the picture of a naval officer either, not with his small thin frame, his missing arm, his missing eye, nor his famous seasickness and other constant ailments. Yet Nelson was the most successful naval officer of the age. From what he knew of Arthur, Pierce understood that this small, slightly rotund, excitable, and temperamental man had once been a bold and courageous Royal Navy captain.

As the meal ended, Evangeline spoke. "If you will excuse me, I shall call on Lady Arthur. You will not need me for further discussion?"

"Of course, my dear. She always looks forward to your visits. I'll have Dobbs escort you." He and Pierce rose as Evangeline made ready to leave. Inexplicably Pierce felt a small pang at the thought of her leaving, if only for an hour. He had grown used to her presence.

"I sha'n't be long," she said, directing her speech to him. "We'll need to start back soon, unless we return in the dark."

"Quite true," said Pierce.

Sir Ronald bellowed for Dobbs, and when he did not appear immediately, the old captain bellowed again. At last Sir Ronald's personal secretary arrived and escorted Evangeline to visit the shipwright's wife.

"Shall we go to the yard?" Sir Ronald asked. "I could stretch after that dinner."

"I as well, sir."

"Then keep up with me! I hobble, but get where I go in dammed fine time!"

"I am sure of that."

"Don't!" Sir Ronald Arthur was still sensitive to the limitations his injuries imposed.

"I do beg your pardon, sir," said Pierce. After a moment's uncomfortable silence he asked, "How far along is the vessel?"

"Far enough, lad, that you'll see what she'll be like. She'll launch in a couple months, providing that outfit you're getting into keeps up payments. Had they been more regular, could have had the damned thing afloat by now, rigged and fitted out proper."

"I am not sure that I'll take the position. Currently I am merely investigating."

"You can say that, but you'll accept. You are the first of several applicants brought along to see the vessel. And you are the first to escort Miss Smythe on her errands."

"I am flattered on both counts, sir," said Pierce.

"Well, come then!" Sir Ronald stepped out at a faster pace, and Pierce found that it was work to keep up. "We'll stop at the mould loft. I have plans there and a model as well, which will give you an idea of what she'll be like."

In a small office off the huge floor where full sized frames were laid out, Sir Ronald opened a drawer and removed a roll of paper. He spread it across an empty table and weighted the corners. "The building draught of OGS *Island Expedition*," he said. My signature there, and Mr. Smythe's, indicating he approved the design."

"Yes, although if you allow, I wouldn't know that they are genuine or not."

"What the hell?"

"I mean nothing, sir, other than I have never seen either signature before."

"Oh, yes, yes! Quite right! Quite right! Of course it's my signature. His as well."

"I'm sure they are, sir." Pierce looked closely at the plans. He was not well-versed in interpreting such drawings, but was able to get an idea of the shape, size, and overall configuration of the vessel. "From what I can see, sir, it is somewhat an unusual design. I've not seen one quite like it."

"Probably not. English shipwrights are conservative by nature. They change a design very little. Capture a French ship and they might copy the lines. Or someone comes along who's not afraid to explore other options."

From what Pierce could see, the vessel was a little over a hundred feet on deck. She was flush decked, with no fo'c'sle or quarterdeck rising above the main deck. The amidships frame, forward of which everything was bow, and aft of which everything was stern, was farther aft than Pierce would have thought practical. It was equally distant from the bow or the stern.

The shape of the hull was full, flat-bottomed, slab-sided, and allowed only a small sharp curve of bilge as the frames went from horizontal to vertical. Placement of this broadest section so far aft allowed a fine run forward and a sharp entry. This vessel would slice its way through the sea. The after portion of the hull seemed full. It did not exhibit the easy run that Pierce had always understood would provide speed and ease of sailing. It was as broad in proportion to her length as many, and with the fullness of her cross section, she would carry a respectful burden.

"Hmmm!" said Pierce thoughtfully. "I can see you put a great deal of thought into it. It is not at all what I would have imagined or designed myself."

"Of course not! You would have simply copied a vessel of similar size, as nearly anyone would do. They would increase this and decrease that, alter this a little and that a little. But they would not start from the beginning and forget about following traditions."

"Yes, sir. And what may I ask, is 'OGS'?"

"It's 'Our Good Ship,' from what they tell me."

"'Our Good Ship,'" said Pierce. "An interesting expression of optimism, I daresay."

"Hmmph! You could see it that way!"

Pierce studied the draught a while longer. "Brig rigged, sir?"

"Good God no, lad," replied Sir Ronald. "I suppose from the mere stumps shown, you could think that. She'll be a topsail schooner, or a variation thereof."

"Should make for a handy and weatherly vessel."

Sir Ronald rummaged through the drawers and pulled out another drawing. "Her sail plan." He rolled it out across the first. "As you can see, it is different from most schooners. She'll carry the usual fore and aft sails, fore and main. No fore course like most topsail schooners. Fore and main topsails, topgallants, and even royals. Depending on the conditions, she could be handled as a square rigger, or as a fore and aft rig."

"Effective!"

Sir Ronald led the way into a smaller room, one closer in size to a closet. The small room contained a very detailed model of the *Island Expedition*. Pierce was glad to see it represented in three dimensions. Now he could truly realize the shape and proportions of the vessel. He was more impressed with the vessel than ever.

"Now, lad, let's go have a look at it in fact."

"Aye aye, sir! Lead on, if you will."

"But first, I will show you something. Come along and keep up." Sir Ronald was again off at a furious pace.

They stepped through another door and Arthur said, "My test facility. I float a model hull with its bow to the current flowing through the tank. Add enough weight to the mooring system that the hull moves forward against the current, and I can gauge the force required to move the ship. I can alter some characteristic and see if that makes any difference. It took a lot of work, young man, to arrive at the hull of *your* vessel."

"I am very impressed, sir, with your ingenuity."

"No doubt, you should be!" Sir Ronald said pompously. "I believe I've made more advances over the past ten years than others have made in the past hundred, at least concerning hull design. Come now, we have a vessel to look at!"

He led on to the ways, where *Island Expedition* was taking shape. The schooner was far enough along that he could see her final form. As he examined the hull more closely, other things did not appear normal, even when considering the extremely different and even radical hull shape.

"Can't say that I've seen this sort of construction, Sir Ronald," he said. "Another of your innovations, I suppose?"

"Indeed, lad! Brought on by two causes."

"How so?"

"Now lad, when it comes to bigger ships, large merchantmen, ships-of-the-line and the like, there is a tendency to 'hog.' You are familiar with that?"

"Why, yes. The bow and stern, being less buoyant, tend to sink. The keel bows upwards, and the sheer becomes less than originally designed and built."

"Quite right! That was one thing that led to this method. The other is that I can't get suitable framing timbers. I can get all the timber I want, but it's small. Even for a vessel of this size, it's not sufficient for conventional frames."

"Just how do you overcome that?" asked Pierce, who knew the old ship builder would expect him to.

"I use plank in several layers. You can see yourself, here." Sir Ronald pointed with his cane. "The frames are set up as usual, lad, except they are much lighter. There are two layers of planking. One runs diagonally, at an angle to the frames and to the normal fore and aft layer.

"Then, lad, the whole process starts over. There's another layer of horizontal planking, another layer of diagonal planks, running opposite to the first layer, and an inner layer of vertical or 'frame' planking. All these add up to the same thickness as in a traditionally constructed hull."

"And the diagonals tie the whole together, triangulate it, and brace against 'hogging'?"

"Quite right, lad! You're a keen observer." Sir Ronald continued on. "See here? Every so often we double or even triple this inner vertical or 'frame' planking. We set planks on edge against it and continue them into deck beams and the like."

"I am truly impressed. Mind you, if I accept their offer or not, I would like to be on hand when she sails the first time. I'm most curious to see how such a radical design will do."

"I trust that she'll do fine. But I too am anxious to see her underway. Even with research, there are factors that cannot be predicted."

"I suppose such is bound to happen," said Pierce. "Still, I'd give a month's half pay, just to see her underway the first time!"

"I think you would, lad. But why not take the job, accept command, and save that pay!"

It was mid afternoon as Pierce and Miss Smythe drove slowly back to Newport. The old horses were tired in spite of the oats, water, and rest they had had at the shipyard. They plodded along, slower than a man could have comfortably walked. A few white clouds dotted the blue sky. A light breeze blew, putting a slight chill in the air, but the sun, unless hidden behind a cloud, warmed them. Neither they nor the horses were in any hurry to reach their destination. Neither spoke.

There was no anger or irritation, just that nothing needed to be said. So much had been discussed in the morning that each was content in the presence of the other.

It was a lovely spring afternoon, and Pierce was happy, riding in a comfortable although old and worn rig. He was full, the sun was warm on his face, and warm where its rays soaked into the dark green of his coat. Evangeline sat very close because of the narrowness of the seat, and he could feel her presence. He treasured the moment, exalted in the peaceful afternoon and the closeness of an attractive young lady. He thought of other things they could do, but all in all he was simply glad to be with her.

His mind was active. Should he accept command of the vessel he had just seen? Should he say goodbye to England and sail to the other side of the world? Many times the answer was *yes*. He mentally listed the many reasons why he should accept the offer.

But what if war with France resumed? He was an experienced naval officer and certainly would be needed in one of His Majesty's men-of-war to help defend the realm.

Was there any validity to the quest that this lovely girl's father wanted to embark upon? If he undertook this voyage of discovery and exploration, would it come to fruition? Or would it simply be a waste of time, money, and even lives?

Pierce's neck was stiff. He stretched. He moved his head to and fro and looked up, down, and all around. He rolled his head from side to side in an attempt to remove the kinks that had set in. As he looked to his left, he happened to peer along the lane they had just passed over. There behind them was a single rider. He too ambled along at a pace slower than a normal walk. He did not put his horse to a faster gait to pass by them. Did the rider purposely maintain the quarter of a mile that separated them?

Evangeline had all but fallen asleep, and reclined lightly against him. He hated to ruin this perfect afternoon, but another glance at the lone rider told him that he must. "Hate to disturb you, miss!" he said. "But there is a rider aft. Appears he's keeping his distance."

She sat up a little straighter, but did not say anything. Casually she began to look about, as if she had awakened from a nap. She looked at the sky, at the road, and then at a section of stone fence running through a field. At last she craned farther around and saw the rider that followed, matching their pace. "It does seem he has interest in us, Lieutenant. We could stop momentarily, and see that nothing is amiss with the team or the rig."

"And?"

"See how he reacts. If he comes on and rides past, we can assume he is just at the same slow pace. Does he stop, he has interest in us and deliberately maintains the distance."

"A most practical solution," said Pierce. "And if it pleases, call me Edward, or Ed. We've conversed to the point that each of us certainly could consider the other to be a friend."

"And you may address me by name as well. Perhaps, 'Vangie,' as do Hiram and Gert."

Pierce tweaked the reins and guided the team to the side of the road. A gentle tug and the horses stopped, grateful for the respite. He set the brake, slid from the seat, and took two apples from the floorboards with him. He walked to the horses that waited with anticipation for the treats. They nuzzled at him, blew softly, and gently picked the fruit from his open hands. He rubbed the soft velvet of their noses and spoke soothingly.

He bent to the foreleg of one, picked it up and examined the hoof, as if he suspected a problem. He found no defect or indication of any injury. He knew that nothing was wrong, as did the horse, who, indignant at this suspected lameness, stamped and snorted. Pierce spoke calmly and softly and again stroked the horse's muzzle.

While he apparently tended the team, he kept an eye on the rider behind them. The man stopped and dismounted. With his mount standing by, reins dangling in a phantom hitch, the man stood against the hedgerow and relieved himself. Occasionally the stranger turned and looked in their direction. Was it a coincidence that the man needed to answer nature at the same time they stopped to check the team?

He walked slowly around the entire rig, checked everything, made sure that nothing was wrong, and assured himself it would take them to the end of their journey. Satisfied that everything was right, and aware that nothing had been amiss, Pierce climbed up once more. A quick glance aft was rewarded with the sight of the rider mounting his horse.

He sat motionless for a moment and then said, "I can't say he's watching us, but it's too much that he needed to stop at the same time."

"I am suspect as well. And that we've not resumed our journey," said Evangeline, "he holds there." She looked forward again, trying to act unaware of the man.

"It bodes no good, miss -- if I may, Evangeline," Pierce said, and with a cluck of his tongue and a light flick of the lines, started the team moving. "We need keep a weather eye on him and everything around us."

"I'm sure you are right." She looked to the rear again. It was a quick glance, one that would hopefully not arouse suspicion. "He's matching us once more."

A half mile on, the track dropped into a small gully. At the bottom a small stream gurgled under a simple wooden bridge. It was nothing more than timbers and planks laid across the rivulet, which allowed one to cross and not wade in the clear cold water. Beyond the bridge, the lane turned sharply and wound amongst the rocks and trees as it climbed out of the gully.

Wary now, Pierce guided the team across the bridge, their hooves echoing loudly. As they negotiated the sharp turn, three armed and masked men suddenly stepped into the road. Confused and frightened, the horses stopped. One man grabbed the bridles and another pointed a brace of pistols at Pierce and Miss Smythe.

"All right now," said the third, who brandished a cutlass. "We don't mean to be hurtin' nobody. Unless we don't get what we want!"

Pierce set the brake. "And do tell, 'gentlemen,' just what do you want?"

"Why gold and silver! Money, of course! We've seen this rig headed to the shipyard too many times. And each time, work's started on that dammed schooner again. Suspicions are you're carrying payment."

"Aye, we were. But payment was made. We've nothing with us now."

"Don't much believe that. Dandified young gentleman out with a lady. You have a purse on you, and dammed if it doesn't have a tidy sum in it!"

"Perhaps, Edward, we should share with these 'kind men,'" said Evangeline. "I am quite willing to share what little I have."

Pierce whispered at the same time. "My half pay! I need it for my return home!"

"We ain't for no sharing, wench! It's all of it, or, or … and his too! All of it!" said the brigand who held the horses. His coattails were pushed back, revealing a large horse pistol in his belt.

"Pipe down, you!" said the cutlass-wielding robber. Hoof beats echoed near the gully. The rider who had followed them rapidly drew closer.

"Then you shall have all of mine," said Miss Smythe, who fished through her bag. She extracted a small sack of coins and tossed it in the dirt. The third thief warily laid one pistol down and bent cautiously to pick up the sack. He untied the drawstring and poured the coins into his hand.

"Damn!" he exploded. Ain't so much here to be worth it. It's gotta be elsewhere on 'em. Thinks we search and find it!"

"Not yet! See what the gentleman has! Come now, hand it over or I'll run the lady through!" He moved closer to Evangeline's side of the buggy. "You don't want to see the lass hurt, now? Then let's see it. Go easy! Wouldn't want to spoil me payday, spattering your brains all over!"

Reluctantly, Pierce dug his purse out of his coat pocket and tossed it lightly on the ground. The one who had picked up Evangeline's bent over again and examined it. "Damn! Damn! No more in this than the other!"

The rider arrived. "Did we get it?" he asked. "How much?"

The cutlass man responded, "No, damn them! There be nothin' for the trouble. Payment is already to the shipyard! For what these two have, mate, it's scarce pickin's."

"Then take 'em prisoner! Someone will pay for their return!"

"Aye! We'll get our due from them, one way or t'other!" responded the three, nearly in unison.

"Right!" said the man at the horses. "Outta that rig, and lively, now!"

As he spoke, the horses started slightly, and the team jerked forward a couple of feet. The man with the cutlass raised it in threat at Evangeline. She jumped back and bumped into Pierce. The horses moved again. "Damn wench! Get out or I'll do some slicing! The gentleman, too!" he said as he glared at Pierce.

Pierce looked at Evangeline, and she at him. They nodded resignedly and stepped to the ground. The brigand with two pistols stepped close. "Now you, here's one last chance. Where's the rest of it? Tell us an' we won't let no harm come your way!" When neither of them responded, he raised a pistol high in the air, intending to bring it down on Evangeline's head.

His arm dropped. Pierce moved to intercept and deflect the blow. He could not bear to see her so cruelly treated. Even as he moved, and as quick as he was, he was astounded by her sudden transformation. Instantly she was on her toes. Her right arm swung in a vertical arc across her body. As her forearm rose over her head, it collided with the descending pistol. The gun's trajectory was deflected and missed her head completely.

Then her fists set to work in an alternating rhythm. One lashed at her attacker while the other was drawn back, tight against her ribs, ready to strike in its turn. The first blow landed square on the thief's mask. Blood soaked through the cloth. The second caught him in the chest, and the third landed between his legs. He doubled over with a howl of pain and surprise. As he reached the lowest point of his "bow," Evangeline's foot moved in a blurry circle and caught him full on the chin. He grunted and staggered back. She followed and aimed a second kick lower on his anatomy and caught his right knee. He collapsed on the ground. She kicked again, and once more aimed for his head. On his knees, his head was within easy reach of her kicks. Twice, more rapidly than Pierce would have thought possible, her foot struck out. Each time there was a solid crunch and pop. The villain sank closer to the ground and complete incapacitation.

Evangeline's sudden explosion of violence had startled them all, including Pierce. He recovered quickly and reached madly for the cutlass-wielding fiend. He took hold of the man's wrist and immobilized the cutlass. He drove his knee into the man's midsection, and the wind exploded from him. The thief swung his free hand at Pierce, who sidestepped and swung a momentarily free fist himself. His blow connected.

The other two assailants were not idle. The horseman rode down on Evangeline and attempted to strike her with his quirt. Amazingly, she seized it and held on. The sudden pull upset the rider and he tumbled to the ground. "Damn my soul!" he snarled. "Wench fights like a demon. What a time in the hay!"

With a raging scream, he charged at her, his drawn cutlass waving menacingly over his head. She stepped aside at the last moment and stuck out her foot. He tripped and sprawled to the ground. She kicked at the base of his head, but he rolled away. Having missed her kick, Evangeline was off balance. The rogue caught hold of her ankle, and she tumbled to the ground. However, he did not account for her other leg. Before he could take advantage of her position, her free foot lashed out and caught him in the gut. That was enough. He let go of her ankle. That foot followed with a kick aimed slightly lower than the first. Like a ship caught in stays, the man staggered and gave her time to roll away and spring quickly to her feet.

Pierce grabbed his opponent's sword hand in both of his and brought it down across the edge of the buggy. The brigand howled and dropped the cutlass. Pierce stomped mightily on the fellow's foot, then bent and snatched up the cutlass. He brought it down, hilt first, on the man's head, and the villain crumpled to the ground.

He turned to find Evangeline set upon by the remaining two. Amazingly, she appeared to have the upper hand. The dismounted rider had felt the fury of her blows and was extremely wary of any foolhardy attempts to subdue her. The other, who had been holding the horses, also circled warily about her. He was determined not to receive the vicious treatment already meted out to his companions. At a loss over what to do with the young lady who had bested one companion and had nearly beaten a second, the rogue drew his horse pistol. He drew it to full cock and aimed at the girl.

Pierce flung the cutlass with all his strength. The honed edge struck the robber's forearm and sliced through to the bone. Blood exploded from the wound. In pain and surprise, he dropped the pistol. It discharged as it hit the ground, and the ball struck Pierce a glancing blow on his left forehead. Hurting and full of fighting rage, Pierce bounded at the wounded man. He grabbed the fallen pistol by the muzzle, swung it like a hammer, and *nailed* the grip into man's face. He delivered a second blow and the man no longer posed a threat.

"Damn bitch!" growled the one fiend that remained. He made a final lunge at her, and that was his downfall. Again she stepped aside. This time she did not trip him. As he went past, she grabbed his nearer arm and twisted it behind his back. Then she pulled and he spun dizzily around to face her. Her fists moved blurringly in rapid succession, striking repeatedly at his face, his torso, and occasionally, his groin. She interspaced the quick short powerful punches with kicks that seemed to circle around and catch him from all directions.

A kick landed against one knee. Another exploded on the other knee. A third caught him full between the legs. Before he could double over because of the intense pain of his most personal parts, she delivered a blow to his exposed throat. She didn't use her fist for this attack. Her hand was open, the fingers straight and tight together. At the last instant she turned her hand outward and the joint of her thumb struck his larynx with devastating impact. He gasped noisily and painfully for breath and collapsed.

Breathing heavily, Pierce looked about. The four would-be robbers were on the ground. They were unconscious but would not long remain that way.

Evangeline also gasped for air. She was disheveled, her hair partly undone, and dirt and sweat streaked across her face. There was a bruise on one cheek and the beginnings of a black eye. She also looked warily at the unconscious assailants.

Pierce looked at her with awe. What an amazing lady!

"Are you hurt, my dear?" he asked concernedly.

"I think not. Some bruises. Some scrapes. I'll be sore, perhaps black and blue tomorrow." She smiled. "But you, dear sir, are wounded! Your head is bleeding! Here!"

"Yes," he answered and reached a weary hand to his forehead. "I don't think it is of any consequence. We need secure these rascals before they recover, and decide what to do with them."

"Let's be quick, and I'll tend your injury."

Pierce found some line under the seat. They used the cordage to tie each of the brigands' hands together behind their backs. At the same time, eight or so feet connected one individual to the next. He tied the remainder to the horse's saddle and then tied the horse to the buggy.

Evangeline removed any remaining weapons from the assailants and placed them in the buggy. She tightly bound the sliced arm of the one who had tried to shoot her minutes earlier. Was it from the goodness of her heart that she could not stand to see anyone pour out his life's blood? Or was she a bit more practical, bandaging the wound to allow the man to survive and answer for his misdeeds?

Then, with water from the rivulet, she washed the bullet wound on Pierce's head, and wound a bit of cloth about it.

One of the robbers stirred. "Up and at 'em now, lads!" shouted Pierce. "There's a long walk ahead of you!"

Piercc and Miss Smythe resumed their journey homeward. The team hauled the rig out of the gully. Tied to the buggy, the riderless horse followed. Being tied to that horse and each other, the criminals followed as well.

Prior to the attack, Pierce had been in no hurry to reach the Smythe residence. Now he was in a great rush, and he urged the old team to pick up the pace. He did not have any sympathy for those who followed and did not give them the comfort of a slower pace. The quicker pace gave the brigands even less opportunity to free themselves.

Pierce turned to Evangeline. "I must say that since we met, you have intrigued and amazed me. The skills you just displayed are beyond all I could imagine of any lady. Not many men would do as well."

She answered softly. "With the life Papa and I have led at times, skills like that were vital to survival. But it is also because of that life, and meeting people from all over the world, that I have come to possess a little of that skill."

"So it is a particular form of fighting?"

"Some refer to it and other hand-to-hand skills as the martial arts. This particular discipline is known as *Karate*."

"I surely have never heard of it."

"Most in this part of the world haven't. It comes from Japan, and some other nations in the Orient. Now, only the Portuguese have connections there, and those are extremely limited. When Papa and I were in Portugal several years ago, we met a man who had spent time in Japan. He had been able to learn the art and was willing to teach us."

"Such a skill could prove useful to members of His Majesty's Navy."

"Someday I will teach you the little of it I know," she said.

They reached the Smythe cottage. Hiram was there, along with Junior, as they drove into the yard. The dog greeted them enthusiastically, but kept a wary eye on the tired and bedraggled outlaws, growling to remind them of their place. Pierce tied the riderless horse to a hitching ring. Smythe came out and unharnessed the team while Hiram left to fetch the local authorities. After a short interview in which Pierce and Miss Smythe described the transgressions of the four, those individuals were led away.

Supper was over, and Smythe and Pierce sat in the slightly cluttered study. A half bottle of wine sat on the table, and two partially full glasses sat within easy reach. Evangeline helped Gert in the kitchen, and Hiram tended to firewood, water, and other duties.

"Enough adventure for one day, no doubt?" said Smythe, sipping at his Port.

"Indeed, sir!" answered Pierce. "More than enough!"

"What do you think of our vessel?"

"Impressive! Innovative! It is so radically different; I could not predict its behavior."

"But do you want command?" Smythe put his drink down and shifted his seat to more directly face Pierce.

"I do! But I have questions, primarily of myself, that should be answered before I decide."

"I fully understand. But we must have a definite answer by July.

The vessel should be afloat then, and work should begin immediately to sort out her sailing qualities."

"Then, sir, you shall have a final decision no later than the Summer Solstice."

"Excellent!"

"Have there been no other applicants for the position?" asked Pierce.

"Some. Too many were only about the money. That you have not brought it up is a feather in your cap, and more reason that you are our prime candidate."

"I see."

"And even now, Edward, you are not going to ask about pay?"

"I hadn't thought of it. I do quite well on the prize money I received from *Theadora's* last commission. I have my half pay, and family adequately supported by their own means. I am not in any great need at present," replied Pierce.

"But it would not be proper not to pay you for your services, although I understand you are more interested to be active and at sea again."

"True!"

"Still, we should discuss it. Currently you draw half pay as a lieutenant. With your tentative agreement to assume command, the Organization will match that, and you will have pay as if you were an employed lieutenant. By arrangement, when the vessel is placed in service, that you are a naval officer, and that some aspects of the voyage relate to the national interest, the vessel will be commissioned in His Majesty's Navy. At that time you will advance to master and commander. Bur we know that the Admiralty is extremely tight with monies in these times and will not go no further than to pay you a lieutenant's half pay. The Organization will pay you the remainder. There will be certain allowances as well, and you will pocket near to what a captain under three years' seniority would."

"That is most generous, sir," said Pierce. "And should it arise that I be paid or other expenses be met, I would prefer that you meet those other expenses."

"Certainly generous on your part, Edward!" Smythe took a sip from his glass, set it down, and stood. "That we have even a tentative agreement calls for us to seal the arrangement. Here now, a toast."

Pierce had also risen. "To the agreement, tentative as it is, sir!" said Pierce

"The agreement! Any immediate plans, lad?"

"If I'm not imposing on your hospitality, I shall stay tomorrow and perhaps the next day. Then I must return home and make certain arrangements. I have an acquaintance in mind to serve as first lieutenant, if you would have him, sir?"

"With your recommendation, I am sure he would be ideal. Still, bring him when next you visit. Best that I meet him and make a final determination."

Shortly thereafter, Pierce went to bed. He was tired and thought that sleep would come easily. It did not. He tossed about, completely awake, thinking of the day's events. He pondered the strange and daring adventure that he had all but committed himself to, and the radically designed vessel he might soon command. Interspersed with these thoughts were those of the amazing and lovely lady he had met, and whom he had come to know and respect so much in the day gone by. He also contemplated the pleasures of a bath in the morning.

Chapter Ten

Commissioning

When Pierce returned home following his visit to the Isle of Wight, his mother lamented his decision to undertake such a perilous voyage. She could not understand why he did not remain in the small village, drive coach with his father, marry a nice young woman, and settle down. After all those years in the Royal Navy with the countless hours of danger, toil, and bad food, she had thought that he would want nothing more of the sea. It was hard to convince her that this was something he wanted to do. Indeed, from his view, it was something that he had to do. He could not convey his need to be at sea, independent of the land, and away from the stifling confines of home life. Being at home was the same as being a wild animal in a cage. He was fed, cared for, loved -- but nonetheless, caged.

Pierce loved his mother deeply and was ready to reject going to sea again. Had she said, "Don't go, Edward!" one more time, he would have acquiesced to her wishes and stayed. But she didn't, and one day she said, "You know I fear for you when you are gone. But I see that is where you belong. I will miss you terribly, but I will not force you to stay and live a life you find intolerable."

It saddened him to leave her, and yet her willingness to let him go buoyed his spirits, and he left with little regret.

His father, too, wished he would stay, although he understood that should war with France resume, his son could be called away as a King's Officer. He closely recognized the turmoil in his son's heart, and although at home, he was not fully at ease. At their final parting, he too gave his blessing to Pierce's ambition, and turned away so his son would not see the moistness that welled in his eyes.

Pierce tried to enlist his two older brothers into this great adventure. They too had served in the Royal Navy, but not as officers. They had been pressed and had survived the hardships of the lower decks, battles, cruel captains, and incompetent officers. They had had enough of life at sea. One had married, the second was preparing to do so shortly, and they politely but firmly refused his offer.

Isaac Hotchkiss, the squire's son and Pierce's long-time friend, also faced opposition from his family. Finally they gave their blessing, wished him well and a speedy and safe return. Sharon, the apothecary's daughter, was utterly devastated. The two had spent a great deal of time together since Isaac's return. It was her hope that they would soon be married. She could not understand that Isaac, like Edward, needed to be free and at sea. Isaac did solemnly promise that he would return, and reluctantly she had consented to his going.

Pierce and Hotchkiss were active through the spring and summer of 1802. When they went to draw their lieutenant's half pay, they spent little time carousing in Portsmouth. They usually journeyed to the Isle of Wight to see Harold Smythe and to check the progress of *Island Expedition*. Many details needed to be dealt with, and both attacked the problems with a will. Pierce would make suggestions to Sir Ronald Arthur, only to have them firmly rejected. Sir Ronald was a stubborn man, determined to complete the vessel to his own ideas. Still, on Pierce's next visit, changes would have been made that were identical to what Pierce had suggested earlier.

On Hotchkiss' first trip to Newport, Pierce introduced him to Mr. Smythe, who was favorably impressed and approved him as the ship's lieutenant. Pierce contacted the Admiralty to ask that Hotchkiss be appointed by their lordships.

Island Expedition had a captain and a lieutenant, but now she needed a crew. Finding one during the peace was easy. In war, the Royal Navy struggled to man its many ships, but peace found many of those same men unemployed. Pierce and Hotchkiss found they could pick and choose from amongst the best. Often they rejected someone, when before they would have welcomed him, even had he been hauled aboard by the press gang. Former shipmates from *Theadora*, *Ferret*, *Mariner*, and even *Orion* turned up with the hope of signing on. Pierce was afforded the rare opportunity of choosing from men whose abilities, skills, faults, and failures he already knew.

Pierce soon discovered that he served two masters. He was employed by the British Island Expeditionary Organization, under whose leadership the voyage was being planned. It was their vessel he was to command. They had contracted for the design and building of *Island Expedition* and would pay him and the crew a portion of their wages. Yet the King's Government and the Royal Navy had a hand in it. The Navy would promote him to master and commander to command the schooner, even though purse strings were tight and he would continue to draw only a lieutenant's half pay. His requests for warrant officers and midshipmen had to go through the Admiralty. The appointments also had to be approved by Smythe on behalf of the Organization.

Sir Ronald Arthur launched *Island Expedition* on the 4th of July. No one but Pierce recognized it as a date of any significance. As a keen student of the young United States, he knew the day marked the anniversary of their Declaration of Independence.

"Ah, Lieutenant Rowley," said Pierce at the small reception after the vessel was afloat. "I am surprised you are here. I thought you to be at the gaming tables, sir."

"Other requirements have brought me here, sir. A fine vessel it seems. You are to command her?"

"Yes, I shall have that honor," answered Pierce. "With your reputation, you may have had a chance."

"Perhaps, but I have other endeavors occupying me now."

"Nonetheless, it is a most significant date for launching, if I may say so."

"The Americans' so-called Independence Day?" asked Rowley.

"Why, yes," continued Pierce. "It marks the birth of a new nation, the United States, but someday it may mark something more, the beginning of a new era in English history."

"Indeed it may. And may I congratulate you upon your forthcoming promotion!"

"I do thank you, sir," said Pierce. "But I must wait until this newly floated hull is placed in commission before it is in effect."

With the vessel afloat, the work of completing her began. Masts were stepped, rigging rove and set to the proper tension. Sails were made and various stores, materials, tools, and pieces of equipment put aboard.

Pierce continued to feel the tug of two masters. The Navy would not pay the hands until the vessel was in commission. Pierce nearly begged Smythe and the Organization to provide full wages, lest an excellent and experienced crew be lost before sailing.

Determining who was to provide various items of equipage was a constant struggle. Usually the one expected the other to supply or obtain the majority of it. Pierce found that in most instances, that he had better luck with the Organization. The Government's interest in it seemed to extend only to the point where it could reap benefits without spending too much. Nor did the Organization spend carelessly. Yet if a particular item was desperately needed, and Pierce could convince them of its importance, it would be obtained.

The 15th of August saw *Island Expedition* fully outfitted and ready to sail for the first time. The ship's company, dressed in their finest shore-going rig, was assembled on deck, all looking remarkably similar. At a time when no uniforms were specified for the hands, Pierce had pressed both the Admiralty and the Organization to provide sufficient, serviceable, and uniform clothing for the hands. The midshipmen, the warrant officers, and Lieutenant Hotchkiss were in their best or full dress uniforms. The fifteen men of the marine detachment under Sergeant Lincoln added a flash of scarlet to the blue, white, and gold that dominated the assembled ship's company.

Officials of the British Island Expeditionary Organization, including the head of the group, Harold Smythe, and his daughter Evangeline were on deck. She had christened the vessel a month earlier as it slid down the ways. Captain Jackson and Lieutenant Forrest, lately of His Majesty's Frigate *Theadora,* represented the Royal Navy.

Edward Pierce nervously paced the quayside, warm in his full dress uniform. He had grown unaccustomed to wearing a sword, and the weapon swung ponderously at his side. Would he trip over it? Thankfully he did not need to board from a small boat. That would lessen his chances of catching some portion of the schooner's structure. Today he could simply walk aboard.

In the distance, a church bell rang. The forenoon watch was half over, and four bells sounded from *Island Expedition's* belfry. Pierce strode purposefully to the foot of the brow. He stopped momentarily and then placed one foot on the plank. At that instant the pipes started and the drums rolled. With a few measured strides, he gained the deck and stepped aboard. The side boys knuckled their foreheads with white-gloved right hands. The bo'sun's mates saluted with their left, their pipes held in their right. Lieutenant Hotchkiss, the warrant officers, and the midshipmen doffed hats. Pierce raised his in return and was mirrored by Jackson and Forrest. The squeal of pipes and the roar of the drums ceased.

"I will now read my orders," said Pierce in a loud and firm voice.

"Off hats!" shouted Hotchkiss. The assembled crew uncovered, as did other male guests and dignitaries.

Pierce unfolded the paper he had pulled from his breast pocket and began:

"From the Lords of the Admiralty, Whitehall, London, to Master and Commander Edward Pierce, at, in, or near His Majesty's Auxiliary Schooner *Island Expedition*, currently quayside in Cowes, upon the Isle of Wight.

"You are hereby directed, requested, and required to report your person in aforesaid vessel at the earliest instant. Upon reporting aboard you will place yourself in command of said vessel, take charge of said vessel and all persons assigned to or employed in said vessel. You will take it upon yourself to ensure that aforesaid vessel is serviceable, seaworthy, prepared, and equipped for extended periods at sea. Upon determination that these requirements are met, you will soonest, report such fact to Sir Joseph Tompkins, Knight of the Bath, Rear Admiral of the Blue, Commanding His Majesty's Ships and Vessels embarked and deployed upon Special Duties and Assignments.

"You are hereby directed, requested, and required to take into the above named vessel, one Harold Smythe of the British Island Expedition Organization, any other such persons of that Organization that he may require to have in the said vessel, and those persons required by Harold Smythe, or others of the Organization as members their respective staffs. You are further hereby directed, requested, and required to take into said vessel any other person or persons that he or other members of the Organization may elect to bring into the vessel under your command. You are hereby directed, requested, and required to place yourself and the vessel under your command and charge into the services of Harold Smythe and the British Island Expedition Organization, and provide to Harold Smythe and the British Island Expedition Organization such service and perform such duties as they may direct, request, and require.

"You are hereby notified and informed that as a King's Officer commanding a vessel commissioned in service to the Crown, that you and all persons assigned in or employed aboard said vessel are governed by all the rules, regulations, and laws that exist for His Majesty's Ships and Vessels while in said service. You are hereby notified and informed that you and all others serving in the Royal Navy and in the vessel under your command are fully subject to the Articles of War. You are hereby directed, requested, and required to ensure, under pain of the severest penalties, that you and all other persons in aforesaid vessel and in service to the Royal Navy and under your command, do hereby subscribe to, follow, and obey the Articles of War.

"(Signed) Sir John Humphries, Knight Commander, Vice Admiral of the Red, at the direction of Lord St. Vincent, First Lord of the Admiralty. Given under my hand this eighth day of August, in the year of our Lord one thousand eight hundred and two."

He put his orders in his pocket. As he did so, a ball of cloth sailed up the halyards and broke out at the tip of the main gaff. Fluttering in the breeze, the Blue Ensign indicated that the schooner served under an admiral of the Blue Squadron. He turned, faced the ensign, and saluted. The other officers did the same. The little band assembled on the quay struck up a passable rendition of "God Save the King." When it was done, Pierce replaced his hat, the other officers following his lead.

"On hats!" bellowed Hotchkiss.

"Mr. Hotchkiss!" said Pierce. "Dismiss the hands and carry out the routine of the day!"

"Aye aye, sir!" replied Lieutenant Hotchkiss.

"Mr. Hotchkiss!"

"Sir?"

"At your convenience let those deserving go ashore for festivities at the Inn of the Isle."

"Aye aye, sir!" Hotchkiss turned once more toward the assembled ship's company. "Division officers, take charge and dismiss your divisions!"

The ceremony was over. OGS *Island Expedition* was now HMS *Island Expedition*, and Edward Pierce was her captain.

Captain Jackson stepped forward and offered his hand. "Congratulations, Captain Pierce. You do this vessel, this service, and this nation proud. I stay a fortnight in Cowes. Leaving, I will carry any reports to Admiral Tompkins or the Admiralty."

"Most kind of you, sir," responded Pierce. "Thank you, sir! I hope that I will command with the dignity and skill I always saw in you."

"Kind words, lad. You will do fine. Any messages to send sooner may go with Mr. Forrest. He returns in two days."

"Indeed I shall," said Lieutenant Forrest. "And may I too offer my congratulations. No one deserves command more than you, sir. Even," he added, "if it puts you senior to me after all these years."

"I thank you as well, sir. You have been a true shipmate who taught me well during our service together. I trust that you find employment and full pay soon."

Others crowded around, shook Pierce's hand, and offered their congratulations. The crowd of well-wishers thinned, headed ashore to the local inn. Pierce, Smythe, Sir Ronald, and Captain Jackson had each contributed toward a number of bottles of wine, a couple kegs of ale, and several kegs of rum. They had also ordered up the best meal the little inn could provide, with the strict understanding that it was to be provided to whomever happened by that day. They had cause to celebrate.

Soon only Evangeline remained on deck with Pierce. "Is it 'captain' or 'commander'?" she asked.

"'Commander' is the rank I hold, junior to a post captain. But as I command this vessel I am her captain, and have the honor of being addressed as such."

"I see," she said, as she drew a bit closer. "I offer you my congratulations as well."

"But, my dear, it is not I that should receive them. They should go to your father and his organization. They are truly the ones who have achieved something today."

"That is true, Edward," she smiled. "But only with your help has it been possible."

"Then I gratefully accept your congratulations."

At the Inn of the Isle, Pierce found himself in a quiet corner. Captain Jackson was there, a glass of Port in his hand. He sipped it often, but the level of liquid hardly changed.

Pierce noted that that was how Jackson stayed steady. He always had a full glass, which he raised at frequent intervals. Yet for a long time the glass' contents remained at the same level. If one did not notice the tiny sips, it would appear he drank much more. Perhaps this was something Pierce might use in the future.

"Now, Captain," said Jackson quietly. "Even with celebrations going, I must remind you, there may be trouble afoot."

"Indeed, sir?"

"First, I know Smythe's true ambition. I consider myself a humanitarian and support his efforts. Many forward-thinking people do. Others support the expedition for the glory and honor it will bring England. Some in the government see it as a jump on the Frogs."

"Yes, sir? Nothing you've said is unknown to me."

"The French are aware of the expedition. Difficult to keep secret, you know." Jackson sipped his Port.

"It could not be otherwise, I should think." Pierce drank from his mug of ale. "However, peace currently exists with France, so can it be of that much concern?"

"Listen, Captain!" Jackson's voice was soft and confidential. "Will this Peace of Amiens last? The Frogs sought it at any rate. The capture of *Perpignan* hurried it, but they weren't interested in real peace. Rather, they wanted time to regroup and rearm. When they're ready, it'll be war again. Mark my word! It would not be beyond them to disrupt your voyage, especially should they find the expedition's captain directly responsible for taking *Perpignan*. Do consider that Boney would interfere, even during peace."

"There is good sense in what you say, sir. I shall be alert for possible trouble."

"And I would keep an eye out for a former shipmate. There is much speculation about his activities these days."

"And you speak of?"

"Why your cabin mate, lad! Sollars!"

"True, he did his best to make life truly as miserable as he could. Yet I cannot see him in any conspiracy against King and Country, or the aims of this expedition."

"Scarcely believe it myself. Mark you, he is embittered and jealous. He has incurred considerable debt at various gaming establishments. Like many, he hasn't found employment, yet he spends more and more. Now he repays long-standing debts. Plays wildly, loses, and plays again. I understand he no longer collects his half pay.

"He was merely an inconvenience to you in *Theadora*, but he saw you as a real threat and reportedly loathes your success. It would be no real surprise should he take action against you or the expedition."

"Damn the fool!"

"Aye, he'd leap to do you harm, especially if paid. There are French agents about that would pay to stop this voyage."

"But Sollars, a traitor?"

"I can't say he is. I can't say he actively pursues a personal vendetta. But do be aware."

"Aye."

"There's scuttlebutt that he hired those which set upon you and Miss Smythe."

"Hmmm," said Pierce thoughtfully. "It's possible. And if I may be so bold, sir, I've never understood why you didn't have him transferred out of *Theadora*."

"I will admit failure there, Pierce. Thought that I might meet the challenge he posed and mold him to the better. Obviously I did not succeed, and I do hate to own that perhaps some influences from elsewhere helped keep him aboard."

"I never knew you to play those games, sir."

"I've tried not to, but…."

Pierce felt a gentle push at his leg and heard a soft whine. He looked down.

"Why, Junior! What are you doing here?"

Junior whined softly again. Pierce scratched behind the dog's ear and handed him a nearly finished beef bone. The dog wagged his tail for and waited for another pat on the head. Once received, he slipped away.

"Good dog, Pierce," remarked Jackson. "Yours?"

"No, sir. He belongs to Hiram and Gert, Smythe's household staff. Yet he belongs to all that are welcome at Smythe's place. Smythe told me they gain many first impressions of people from how Junior reacts to them."

"I see. And should the dog meet Lieutenant Sollars?"

"It would indeed be interesting to see."

The next day, *Island Expedition* put to sea for the first time. Pierce sailed her with a minimum of sail as he got used to her quirks and peculiarities. Whenever more sail was set or she was set to a different point of sailing, Pierce took the helm, as he wanted to know what the helmsman would experience under any conditions. As they became more familiar with her, they set more sail. The weather that day was cooperative, and by evening they had her gliding over the waves with all plain sail set. Running easily on a broad starboard reach, Pierce remarked, "I'd never 'ave thought it, Isaac, that such an unusually designed vessel could sail so well."

"Nor I," responded Hotchkiss. "There's a lot to be learned here."

"Aye!" Pierce was silent for a moment. "Perhaps, Mr. Hotchkiss, you would be so kind as to cast the log!"

"Aye aye, sir! Mr. Morgan, kindly cast the log! We shall see just what sort of heels this girl has."

"Aye aye, sir!" replied Morgan. He motioned to a young lad, and the two of them went aft to the taffrail. Morgan held the log line firmly in one hand, and with the other dropped the log over the side. "Ready!" he said.

"Turn!" said his partner as he turned over the twenty-eight-second glass. At that exact time, Morgan pulled the peg out of the log and let it stream out behind the schooner, the log line slipping freely through his hands. "Stop!" cried his partner as the last grains of sand fell into the bottom of the glass. Morgan instantly stopped the line.

"What does it show, Mr. Morgan?" asked Pierce.

"I'd scarce believe it, sir. Perhaps I've erred. I'll have another go at it, sir."

"Very well, Mr. Morgan. Make sure you do it properly this time."

"Aye aye, sir!"

But when the second cast of the log was complete, Morgan was still unsure of the reading. "It can't be right sir! It just can't!"

"What does it say, lad?"

"You won't believe it sir, but we're nigh on fourteen knots sir!"

"I do find it difficult. Still, I sense such speed. Tomorrow we'll compare to fixed landmarks."

"Then we'll know for sure!" said Hotchkiss.

"Mr. Morgan, take charge and put us on course to ensure we have sea room for the night!"

"Aye aye, sir!"

The next day the winds blew in gusts from varying points of the compass, allowing them to sample *Island Expedition's* behavior under more adverse conditions. All day the entire crew practiced handling the trim and fast schooner.

That afternoon they exercised the guns. While built for peaceful exploration and transport, *Island Expedition*, like most commercial vessels, was armed. For her type, intended mission, and size, the schooner carried very heavy weaponry. Six twelve-pounder long guns were mounted along each side. In addition, two twelve-pounder carronades were mounted aft, and another pair was mounted forward. These would be enough to deal with most adversaries, unless they chose to show their heels.

For two hours the crew repeated steps of casting loose, running in, loading, running out, and firing. Most were old hands at naval gunnery, and once they were familiar with *Island Expedition's* particularities, practice went smoothly. They tossed empty casks over the side and practiced at them, at first with individual guns and finally with the entire broadside.

At eight bells, the start of the first dog watch, Pierce secured from gun drill. Prudently he shortened sail, much as a merchantman or a foreign man-of-war would do. The daily grog ration had been served out earlier, but satisfied with both schooner and her crew, Pierce ordered that they splice the main brace, serving out an extra tot of grog to all hands. As the hands eagerly queued up for their extra dose of rum and water, Pierce fell in and drew a ration himself.

"All of you, listen! We have done well these past two days. This schooner has done well. You certainly deserve to splice the main brace. To *Island Expedition*, her crew, the Royal Navy, and the British Island Expedition Organization. Here's to His Majesty, George the Third!" He downed his with one swallow. Those who had not already gulped theirs drank in unison with their captain.

From amid the crew came a small voice saying, "Hip, hip!" That was followed by a ragged "Hurrah!" The next "Hip, hip!" was a little stronger, and the following "hurrah" more in unison. The final cheer was loud, enthusiastic, and perfectly in time.

By the time *Island Expedition* rested along the quay again, Pierce and the entire crew were totally familiar with her sailing and sea-keeping qualities.

The day after returning to Cowes, Pierce gave half the crew shore leave. In war, that would have been foolhardy, as many would have run. During the peace, Pierce was confident they would return. They needed to be in a commissioned vessel, if only for food, drink, and a place to sleep. Not many -- if any -- of the hands would fail to show up the following day. He surmised correctly, because next morning, all those that had been ashore were present for morning muster. Pierce gave the other half of the crew the privilege of going ashore.

When all hands had had a run ashore, the work of getting ready to depart began. Much of the supplies and equipment were already aboard, but much more had to be acquired and stowed. Cask after cask of salt pork, salt beef, and ship's biscuit arrived and were struck below. The Organization bought these staples through a commercial ship's chandler, instead of allowing the Navy's victualling yards to provide it, hoping the schooner would have fresher and better quality foodstuffs. Water was obtained through commercial sources, and put in newly made and well- scrubbed casks. The fresh casks might serve to keep the water from turning into the green and growing mass of slime that often sufficed for fresh water in His Majesty's ships. The slop chest was filled with uniforms and general clothing. Items of feminine apparel were also included, as some of the fairer sex would be amongst the passengers.

Pioneering tools -- picks, axes, and shovels -- were procured and stowed. Many woodworking and carpentry tools, necessary once the island was found, were stowed aboard. They also loaded bags of seeds: oats, wheat, barley, and rye; and seeds for various vegetables, herbs, and spices.

During these days before sailing, Pierce was as busy as he had ever been. He could count on Hotchkiss, the warrant officers, and the midshipmen to handle day-to-day tasks and routines. Yet it was ultimately upon his shoulders, and he took active charge of the entire operation.

While he did not directly oversee the stowage of every cask, keg, and bag, he required those who did keep track to report on a regular basis.

Harold Smythe and Evangeline had rooms in the inn, to be closer during the final preparations. Evangeline often took an active role. She acted as messenger between her father, others of the Organization, Pierce, and various merchants and suppliers. Aboard *Island Expedition* she willingly tailed onto lines and helped sway casks and bales of cargo with the crew. She was handy with tools and with a little help, soon mastered many of the knots, hitches, and splices used in the work at hand.

When he had the time, Pierce accompanied her as she made journeys as messenger. He also watched with admiration or amazement as she pulled her weight and helped with the ongoing stowage of equipment and stores.

Unless duties demanded he be aboard in the evening, Pierce generally joined Smythe and his daughter for supper. One evening, following the after-dinner Madeira, Pierce found himself sitting alone with Evangeline.

"You would make a fine seaman, my dear," he observed. "That is, should members of the fairer sex ever be welcomed as fellow crew."

"Not in our lifetime, I would guess. Still, I do what I do to stay busy."

"And you do what you do so well." Pierce paused for a moment, took a sip from his glass, and went on. "Too bad you are not going."

"Yes. Papa has arranged for Henry Dawes to take charge. He trusts him, but...."

"He trusts you more?"

"Yes!" She was silent for a while, perhaps feeling her next words. "I try so hard every day to stay busy! I try not to think! How lonely it will be when Papa sails! I'll miss him! And Edward Pierce, I will miss you!"

"I will miss you. I'm not sure how it would be, not spending a little of each day in your company."

"I must see to the rooms." She rose from her chair, and Pierce did as well.

She stepped closer to him. "I'll miss you. I'll miss you so much!" She moved nearer and he could see the tears flooding her eyes.

Her eyes searched out his and locked upon them. He returned the longing look, as tenderness, desire, affection, and caring all welled up within. Then, without effort by either, she was in his arms, and he in hers. Their lips met.

Pierce luxuriated in the embrace and kiss. He was aware of her closeness, the heat of her body so close to his, and the scent of her hair, her skin, and the lingering taste of Madeira upon her lips. He was aware too, of her eagerness, her hunger, and her desire. He was aware of his own desire, and in the throes of their first embrace, he did not worry that she might notice.

In this white-hot blaze of mutual passion, Pierce's mind functioned as if separate from his fevered and demanding body. She was his, and he could have her, but she was more to him than a simple outlet for his masculine needs. She was not one of the harbor's easy women, one he would forget after a week at sea, or one whose personal happiness did not matter.

While he ached painfully to have her, he wanted her in a higher, even a more spiritual way.

They parted slightly. Still he could feel the rise and fall of her breast. "When you return, my love, I'll be here!"

"My darling Vangie," he said softly, "I shall return to you, as quickly as can be done!"

It was with great joy and nearly unbearable sadness that Pierce returned that evening to HMS *Island Expedition*. Regulation and custom required the captain to sleep aboard. Even had they followed their desires, Pierce would have had to steal away in the night, and to have left Evangeline alone then would not have been at all proper.

Chapter Eleven

The Voyage Begins

Island Expedition sailed a week after Evangeline and Pierce first realized their feelings for each other. Those last days were a nightmare of joy. He forced himself to concentrate upon work during the day. The evenings with her and in her arms were wonderful, yet every evening he reluctantly drove himself from the warmth of her embrace and returned to his plain and bare cabin. In spite of elation in her presence each evening, knowledge of the forthcoming parting dangled like a sword over his head. It was always there, preventing him the unfettered bliss of the moment.

Was he correct to not press his desire and avail himself of her charms? Clearly she had been willing, no doubt desiring and wanting him. Could he have erred in not letting it happen? Had he offended her by not taking advantage of all that was so openly offered? Because he had not seriously tried, did she feel his love was less than it was? Had he been right not to fully enjoy his relationship with her? Would it be better to have sweet memories of what had been, rather than dreams and hopes for what might be? Or was he now hoping for what might never be?

The bright spot of that last week was the squire journeying to see his son Isaac off on the voyage. He brought along Pierce's parents, his unmarried older brother, and Sharon, Isaac's intended bride. The journey was an eye-opener for Pierce's mother and Sharon. Neither had ever ventured far from their own village, and the sights, sounds, smells, and bustle of Portsmouth had been wonderfully strange to them. The trip across the Solent was an adventure, and in that short trip they briefly experienced what Edward and Isaac knew on a daily basis.

It was a proud moment for both when they brought their families aboard *Island Expedition*. Pierce's brother, with sea service experience himself, was well-impressed by the trim and tidy vessel. His mother gasped with wonder and astonishment at the entire structure of the craft and proudly noted that her son was in command. At last she could understand his need to escape the confines of home. His father also radiated pride in his son and the vessel he now commanded.

The squire found satisfaction with the situation and the vessel in which his son would sail. Sharon was proud that her future husband was the first lieutenant aboard such a handsome schooner, although perhaps she wished he were captain instead. She was obviously thankful for a final chance to see him.

Hotchkiss was glad for the visits, both from his father and from Sharon. He too spent many of those last evenings in the company of a young woman. He was not required to be aboard every night, and Pierce often wondered what occurred between them. But he would not, and indeed, could not press his friend for details.

Pierce proudly introduced Evangeline to his family. He had worried that her foreign heritage would cause them not to accept her. However, her grace and easy manner prevailed and they were very much taken with her.

Island Expedition left Cowes and the Isle of Wight, beat along the English coast, and upon reaching Plymouth, anchored in the Hamoaze. She spent two days there as boatload after boatload of heavily guarded convicts and their families were ferried out and put aboard. When each group was aboard, Smythe explained to them the changes concerning their transportation to a penal colony.

"My friends," he said, often to groans of disrespect and derision. "The cases and the charges against you have been reviewed by an organization which I head. We found no evidence that would overturn your convictions or lessen your sentences, but we have found that you are not as guilty, nor as incorrigible as the courts may have thought.

"You have been sentenced to transport to Botany Bay, and transported you shall be. But you will not be going a penal colony. You will be going to a 'freedom colony.' You will not be convicts! You will be colonists! You will be pioneers! Many more will follow and will hopefully find the freedom that has eluded them. Once on the island, you will labor in support of the colony. You will be fairly paid, and after a minimum of time declared free men in a free colony. Once free, you will have the option to leave and go anywhere you choose.

"I warn you, this organization could not persuade His Majesty's Government to recognize your freedom should you ever return to England. Sadly you will not be able to return here as free people.

"As we offer you freedom in exchange for leaving England forever, we offer you the choice of accepting that offer. Any who wish not to go, only say the word to be put ashore. You will return to prison and face transportation at a later time."

Pierce expected the assembled convicts to reject this sudden change in their lives. Yet they sat quietly. They had already resigned themselves to transportation, and where they would go didn't matter. "Mr. Morgan!" Pierce shouted. "Please get these people below and assigned to their berths! The watch below will assist you!"

"Aye aye, sir!"

"See that any chains are struck off immediately!"

"Aye aye, sir!"

That stirred the group and they roared in approval.

"Silence!" said Pierce a little harshly. "Such joyous noise will not do. You must appear hopeless and despairing, if only as a show for those ashore." Smythe nodded his agreement, and the noise settled.

When all the prisoners were aboard and somewhat settled between decks, *Island Expedition* sailed. When they were out of sight of land, Pierce requested the passengers assemble on deck, and ordered all hands to muster aft. He climbed atop a twelve-pounder and grasped the windward main shrouds as he addressed the humanity massed on deck.

"I am Commander Edward Pierce, captain of *Island Expedition*. This is Lieutenant Isaac Hotchkiss. The crew knows what I expect. What I expect of you is quite simple. Follow the rules that will be spelled out shortly. If you do not understand, ask. Ask any of us and it will be clarified.

"This will be a long voyage. Those who wish may sign on as a part of the crew. The Royal Navy will not pay you, but the organization can credit your service aboard toward the time you are declared totally free.

"Should any women so choose, there are tasks and duties aboard that could use a feminine touch."

Pierce explained what life would be like for all aboard. He detailed the arrangements for meals, for water rations, for washing, and for matters of personal necessity. He also told them which areas were off limits to them, those off limits to the crew, and those areas off limits by reason of gender.

"And," he added. "The windward side of the quarterdeck is by tradition reserved for the captain or senior officer on deck. I follow that tradition. My officers follow that tradition. I expect no less from you."

Island Expedition sailed easily through the middle Atlantic. On a starboard reach she cut across the light westerly wind of a pleasant October day. In another day or two, she would point closer into the wind and sail close-hauled to the southwest. Once she neared the bulge of Brazil, she could reach, head south again, and eventually back to the East.

Near the foremast, Jonas Gibbons, schoolmaster, sat with a group of children working their sums on slates or scraps of paper. Two crewmen sat along with them. One, a veteran of decades at sea, had determined it was never too late to learn. The other was not many years beyond those in the class. He understood that his chances for success were better if he could work his sums and read and write on his own.

Harold Smythe had insisted on having a schoolmaster. He wanted the people of this extraordinary expedition to be educated, knowing it was a valuable requirement for anyone attempting to lead a better life. Jonas Gibbons had run a day school near London, but had been unable to support himself doing so. Now he was at sea, teaching a ragtag group of urchins and a varying band of seamen.

Amidships, seamen caulked deck seams. It had been done during construction, but this section had rejected that initial attempt. Or did the quality of the original work not meet the first lieutenant's approval? With the voyage going smoothly so far, Hotchkiss needed to keep the hands occupied. Opposite the caulking party, the bo'sun instructed several landsmen in the art of long splicing. Some of the attentive students were younger, less-experienced crewmembers. Others were passengers, eager to learn and assist in the daily operation of the ship.

Near the wheel, Commander Edward Pierce strode the deck easily. The windward side was deserted, allowing him the captain's hallowed sanctuary. He glanced about, seemingly without interest, comprehension, or notice. But he did notice. He saw the various activities and work on deck. He noticed the work aloft, as topmen made routine repairs and upgraded the rigging. He noted the direction and force of the wind and, without a glance at the binnacle, calculated the ship's course by instinct. Pierce crossed to the helm, looked at the compass, and was gratified to see he had guessed correctly.

"Keep her at that, Mr. Spencer!" he said to the young master's mate serving as officer of the watch.

"Aye aye, sir!" he replied.

Spencer repeated to the helmsman, "Keep her at that!"

"Aye aye, sir!"

Pierce moved to the taffrail and looked at the wake left by the vessel's passage through the water. It was straight as an arrow, the way it should be. A steady light wind and an experienced crew would do that. A good hand at the wheel and *Island Expedition* would sail just as he wanted her to, just as he willed her to. Pierce watched the ripple of the wake as it receded astern. He observed it to gauge the helmsman's skill, but now he was in his own world, his thoughts many miles and many days away.

In all his years at sea, he had never felt such loneliness. Even during those first days aboard *Ferret* he had not been so lonely. He had been homesick, perhaps seasick, and indeed frightened. He had been constantly apprehensive for what the next moment, the next hour, or the next day might bring. And as well he had wondered about the far-distant future.

But now, Evangeline was always on his mind. He would not see her for years perhaps, and he wondered how empty a man could be.

Slowly Pierce returned from his mind's journey home. Once again he checked the straightness of the wake. He turned and brought his gaze and his thoughts back aboard. He headed forward.

Traditionally, a Sunday morning would find a King's ship ready for inspection, decks holystoned, gear stowed neatly, and hands at quarters in their best outfits. With the confusion and the effort of getting passengers and crew organized, Pierce found that formal Sunday inspections did not yet fit into the ship's routine. Nearing the foremast, he decided to make an informal and unplanned tour. He would gain a truer indication of conditions than from any planned and orchestrated affair

The head was clean and fresh. As he watched, a hand thoroughly cleaned the starboard seats of ease. He had been brought before Pierce two days ago for a minor violation. With passengers aboard, and with his own aversion to flogging, he had assigned the culprit to clean the head. "Very good, Jones! Shipshape!" he remarked.

"Aye, sir! Thankee, sir!" Jones started at the voice, and again when he saw Pierce.

The manger was in the triangular forwardmost part of the lower deck. *Island Expedition* had aboard three cows -- two with calves -- four hogs, three goats, two sheep, and a coop of chickens. They provided milk and eggs, even if in a limited supply. The fresh foodstuffs rotated through the ship, rather than being reserved for any particular group. When the animals' feed ran out, they would be slaughtered and provide fresh meat to all on board.

The crew's berthing was aft of the manger. It was unusual because bunks were built into the very structure of the ship. Each crewman had his own, complete with storage drawers under it. The drawers could be secured, and Pierce noticed that many crewmen had obtained locks. They could be assured that no one else had access to any of their prized possessions.

He had been relieved to find the hands taking so readily to the new berthing arrangements. It was novel, convenient, and most reveled in having even that small amount of space as their own. The bunks, stacked three high, enabled more men to occupy a smaller area.

The galley stove, or camboose, was just aft of the crew's berthing. Its smoke pipe, known as "Charlie Noble," rose through the upper deck and higher than a tall man into the air. The space to either side of the stove was fitted with benches, work tables, and equipment. The camboose was large, more suited for a small frigate, rather than a vessel like this. Wisely, Smythe's group had insisted on a large unit. With the large numbers embarked, the coppers were filled to capacity whenever a meal was in the making.

The coppers were full now, boiling up the day's dinner. Pierce lifted a cover and sniffed at the steam and vapor billowing out of the pot. "A quite savory aroma, Mr. Eubanks," he said.

"Thankee, sir! Lobscouse today!"

"I thought as much!" It would be welcomed by nearly all. No matter how well a meal was prepared, some always complained. *Island Expedition* was fortunate to have Thomas Eubanks as ship's cook. He was a culinary artist, and in spite of the questionable stores he had to work with, and the large number he had to provide for, he always provided the best meal possible.

Continuing aft, Pierce came to the passengers' quarters. Passengers were also provided with bunks, rather than with hammocks. The forward section was for single former convicts and was nearly the same as the crew's berthing. Families occupied the next section, and women traveling alone, the aftermost section of passenger berthing.

As he passed farther aft, he met, greeted, and spoke with many of the onetime convicts. He promised to look into complaints, answered their questions, or engaged in a moment's conversation.

Pierce left the areas set aside for the passengers and found himself in the stern cabin. A long table extended along the centerline. At its aft end, the three stern windows let in light, and with one slightly opened, a little breeze as well. There were sleeping cabins along each side where ship's officers and Organization officials berthed.

The aftermost cabins were slightly larger. Pierce's was to port and Smythe's to starboard. If this had been a true man-of-war, Smythe's may have been assigned to a flag officer. Flag and captain would then share the center cabin for dining and as a day cabin. But with the size of *Island Expedition* and the number aboard, the dining area was shared by all officers, including the captain and the leader of the expedition. Pierce had a small writing desk in his cabin, and when he felt inclined to eat alone, he could do so there.

He very rarely ate dinner alone. As he grew older, he found that he rarely ate all three meals every day. He wanted his coffee in the morning and often drank cup after cup as he dealt with the details of command. One good meal a day was generally sufficient for him. He did enjoy eating, and when he ate, he ate enough to last. If he ate three times a day on a regular basis, he would continuously need larger uniforms.

When he did eat, it was usually with the other officers and Organization staff at the long central table. This served as the captain's dining cabin, the wardroom, and the gunroom, its identity rotating amongst the three. If it were not considered as the captain's table, then he had a standing invitation to join the others for dinner. When it was the captain's table, they all had a standing invitation to join him.

There was enough room that two or three more could join them, and the appropriate hosts generally invited someone. Pierce normally invited one or two of the hands. Some felt ill-at- ease and out of place, and Pierce never insisted that anyone attend. The wardroom usually asked passengers from amongst the single men and women. Those who would mess in the gunroom, if they had a gunroom, often entertained a transported family.

Many guests were surprised by the fare set on the table. The food was the same as was served in their normal mess location. Pierce, Smythe, Hotchkiss, and the warrant officers ate the same meals as did everyone on board. Their meals were not prepared in any special location or fashion. Occasionally the day's hosts would have something prepared as a treat, or in honor of a special guest. However, specialties such as plum duff, suet pudding, or spotted dog were usually provided to all.

Pierce debated a return to the open deck above or a descent farther below. He chose the latter. Aboard most vessels of this size, this level would be partial sections of deck that overlapped the hold. Because the vessel had been designed for a most unusual mission by a most unusual shipwright, the orlop was a complete deck. To fit it in to the schooner's structure, certain compromises had been made. Pierce, who was not quite six feet in height, had to stoop to clear the deck above, and had to consciously duck under the even lower deck beams. He found it easier to move in a crouch.

There were tiny cabins, berthing for warrant officers and senior midshipmen along each side of the after part of this deck. Outside the cabins, casks, kegs, bales, and bags of provisions occupied every available space. Pierce checked that they were all securely wedged against their neighbors, and that lashings were tight.

Moving forward, Pierce came to the sick bay. The location was contrary to normal, but it was here because of the schooner's peculiar mission. It was low enough in the vessel that during any combat, it could serve as an operating theater for the amputations and other gross medical treatments the surgeon might be forced to provide. Here too, and all along the deck, casks and bales of provisions and equipment were piled and stowed in every available space.

The magazine was aft of the mainmast and guarded by a marine. Through the locked hatch and wet fear-naught curtains there was enough powder to blow *Island Expedition* to splinters. Light was provided by lanterns hung behind double-glazed windows. Only specifically authorized personnel were permitted to enter, and when they did, they wore felt slippers to lessen the chances of a stray spark igniting the powder.

"Any problems?" asked Pierce as the marine came to attention. "I trust you are staying awake!"

"Aye, sir. No problems, sir!" Pierce saw the red-coated marine swallow hard as he suppressed a yawn.

"Carry on! Should Sergeant Lincoln find you asleep, I would have no recourse but to order appropriate punishment!"

"Aye aye, sir!" The marine suppressed another yawn.

Between the mainmast and the foremast, the deck was broken by an enormous open hatchway. Narrow gangways continued along either side, but were piled nearly solid with stores and equipment. Pierce opted to use the catwalk along the hatchway's centerline. At midpoint, he scrambled down a ladder and into the hold, where the majority of provisions and equipment were stowed. His practiced eye noticed that everything was wedged and stowed correctly, and that lashings were properly done.

He checked under the deck and around the exterior of the magazine. Then he looked under the forward most part of the lower deck, again paying particular attention to the proper and secure stowage of all items.

He inspected the actual construction of the schooner, and with satisfaction noted no signs of structural failure. Six or seven inches of water sloshed about in the bilges. Sir Ronald Arthur had built a tight hull. At this point they pumped out every other day, and the amount of water removed was minimal. Pumps had been manned that morning and there would be no need to do so for some time. He climbed back up.

The forward most part of the orlop was the domain of skilled seamen and artisans. The Bos'un's Locker was here, where Cartney and his mates stowed supplies and tools, and where they did much of their work, unless it was required to be done on site. The carpenter, Mr. Cook, the sail maker, Mr. Neilson, and even the gunner, Mr. Harris, had space for work and stowage in this area. The purser, Mr. Gray, also worked from here, as it was quite handy to the stores and provisions he issued and accounted for. These spaces were neat and squared away, just as would be expected of experienced hands and warrant officers. However, now they were not at their tidiest, work being in progress at the time.

Pierce was pleased with the overall condition of the schooner, and properly credited his first lieutenant. Hotchkiss kept hands the busy and ensured that everything was properly squared away.

Below and out of the sunlight, Pierce squinted and blinked upon emerging onto the weather deck. He walked aft, past the children at their lesson, and the bo'sun teaching long splicing. He moved along the ship's boats nested atop the hatch gratings.

Flush decked, *Island Expedition* did not have an actual quarterdeck, but as he neared the helm, Pierce entered the area that was treated as such. Upon his approach, the officer of the watch and others moved and left him the desired windward side. He paced slowly at first, the fixtures on deck allowing him twelve steps forward and twelve steps aft.

Pierce did not normally pace the deck as some did. Many captains strode several miles a day and did not venture more than a few yards from the same spot. After his self-guided tour below, it felt good to be in the open again. They were far enough north that there was a slight chill, and he walked to warm himself. As his exertions took effect, he lessened his stride.

Seven bells! His watch showed eleven twenty-nine. In a good mood, he did not berate the midshipman of the watch for the minute error. He seriously doubted that it could have been much closer. Time for the noon sightings approached, and in a moment or two, he would go below for his sextant. Because they were making to the west, actual noon would be later than his watch indicated, so he had plenty of time.

When actual noon or the sun's highest point was determined, he would set his watch to it. In fact, the entire vessel would adjust its time to match the sun.

He stood for another minute and went below to his cabin. He momentarily reveled in the privacy afforded the captain. It was not a large cabin and some might have described it as minuscule, but it was his. He did not have to share it with anyone, especially not a loud obnoxious senior lieutenant, as he had done aboard *Theadora*.

Pierce had seen Sollars just prior to the voyage, nearly colliding with him, as each pursued his own business at Portsmouth Dockyard. They had briefly and formally exchanged greetings, Sollars directly and openly respectful of the epaulette on Pierce's left shoulder. However, Pierce had distinguished an aura of contempt beneath the veneer of good manners.

Pierce took his sextant from its case, gathered up some scraps of paper and a pencil, wound his watch, and returned to the quarterdeck.

As he waited, other officers appeared, each with his own sextant.

They stayed to leeward and gave him sole occupancy of the windward side. Pierce had insisted from the beginning that all officers calculate the ship's position daily. It was good training for them, and served to validate his plot. One day he might be incapacitated and unable to establish the position. Then, one of them would have to do so. Usually the majority placed the schooner within sight of his calculated position, and it was possible that one or more fixes were more accurate than his.

It was nearly noon. "Gentlemen," he suggested. "I think we can look for opportune spots. It's close to the time." Purposefully, but without haste, the officers moved forward. Because of the schooner's current heading, the best view of the sun would be from the port bow. "Mr. Spencer, you may put her two points into the wind!"

"Aye aye, sir!" Spencer gave the order to the helmsman and had the sails trimmed for the best efficiency on the new course. This slight change put the sun more on the port beam and allowed easier sightings as noon approached.

Pierce moved to port, and forward of the main shrouds, he found a spot not shadowed by the foresail. He made sure the sextant's dark lenses were correctly positioned, and pointed it at the sun. He deftly adjusted the mirrors so the sun appeared to touch the horizon. He noted the reading on the scale and a moment later repeated the process. The sun was a little higher on the second try. Still not noon.

Pierce repeated the process every few moments. Now, each time he took a sighting of the sun, he noted the time and the elevation. When two readings showed no increase in elevation, and the third showed the slightest of decreases, he paused. It was noon, but in the tradition of the sea, he waited for his officers to report the fact to him.

He watched as Midshipmen Morgan, Andrews, and Steadman nodded their heads in apparent agreement. Morgan approached Spencer, and that individual then came to Pierce. "We show it as noon, sir," he said ceremoniously.

"Very well, Mr. Spencer, make it noon!"

"Aye aye, sir!" he replied, and nodded to the attendant midshipman of the watch. Mr. Hadley turned the half-hour glass and started the sand running again. At the same time, he signaled a hand stationed by the belfry.

"Ding ding! Ding ding! Ding ding! Ding ding!" The bell echoed throughout *Island Expedition* as official noon was again established. Immediately the bell was followed by the bo'sun's mate's pipes as they called the watch below. Hands were piped to dinner, and those who assumed actual duties expectantly awaited a momentary relief so they too could eat.

As eight bells struck, Pierce went below. He noted the time on the ship's chronometer as well as upon his watch. With some basic calculations, he determined the time that had been on the larger, more precise timepiece when official noon had been declared. That particular instrument, a wonder of precision workmanship and accuracy set to Greenwich Mean Time, indicated the time difference from that noon and their local noon. With that information, Pierce calculated their longitude -- or distance east or west of Greenwich.

Today, the chronometer showed nearly two o'clock when the sun reached its zenith. They were well to the west of Greenwich and London. The sun's elevation at noon was translated into their latitude, and that placed them somewhat south of the Azores.

Pierce already knew this. He had pricked the chart yesterday, and in twenty-four hours and some minutes, the schooner could not have traveled that far. Still, definite progress had been made.

Four bells in the afternoon watch. Pierce had gone to his cabin, updated his log and personal journal, and was again on deck. As the bell chimed out the time, eager faces looked aft expectantly. "Sir?" asked Hotchkiss, now the officer of the watch.

"By all means, Mr. Hotchkiss!"

"Up spirits!"

That call was the one most anticipated by the hands. Pierce had decreed that passengers too could partake in the grog issue, and many of them also looked forward to this moment.

Pierce had been at sea long enough to know that the daily ration could cause problems. He had served aboard, or had heard of ships that had no real control over the process. Aboard his ship there would be none of that sort of chicanery, nor would he abide anyone drinking to excess. As a result, anyone issued a grog ration had to drink it on the spot. It could not be carried below, saved for later, or passed to another for a twist of tobacco or other luxury. Pierce intended that the process prevent anyone from getting drunk.

He did have a good crew, one of the best, but he knew and understood the British seaman. Many would risk anything for an additional tot of rum, but he would not give them the opportunity as long as he commanded *Island Expedition*.

Smythe exercised control over the passengers' spirit consumption, as many of them had the same desires as the crew. Should either group obtain an excess of grog, what goods or services might be exchanged for additional issues of the seaman's ambrosia?

A fortnight later, after they had finished their evening meal of boiled beef, potatoes, and peas, Lieutenant Hotchkiss proposed a toast. "A glass be raised by all. Today is the ninth of October, and it marks the birth of our esteemed captain, and my long-time friend, Edward Pierce!" Glasses were raised, and Hotchkiss continued. "To your health and happiness, sir," he said. He drank, as did the others.

"The captain's health and happiness," various voices intoned.

Pierce sat slightly embarrassed. He had noted earlier the date's significance and had hoped it would pass without any notice. Only his old and dear childhood friend knew or would have brought it to the other's attention. Hotchkiss was of a sentimental nature and took sharp notice of birthdays and other anniversaries. Even as he wished nothing had been said about his birthday, had his friend not brought it up, he would have felt slighted.

In turn, Pierce raised his glass and said, "The health and happiness of all at this table! To *Island Expedition* and all who sail in her! Their health and happiness!"

"To us and this schooner!" the assembled group said as all took another sip from their cups.

At a discreet nod from Hotchkiss, Mr. Midshipman Hadley intoned, "Gentlemen, the King! God bless our Sovereign, King George the Third!"

"The King! God bless him!" they replied, toasting the Royal Health.

Later, sleep did not come for Pierce. He had enjoyed the fuss made over his birthday and the cabin's friendly warmth that evening. But something was missing, and he searched for what it was. He lay dead tired, and yet he was wide awake. It would have been a most complete evening, had she been present!

With his thoughts again of Evangeline, Pierce was reminded of his loneliness. That loneliness kept him awake all night.

Chapter Twelve

A Royal Visit

As the voyage progressed, life became an unchanging set of routines. "All Hands" was piped every day at four bells in the morning watch. "Up Spirits" sounded at four bells in the afternoon watch. Hands were piped to meals at the same unvarying times. The captain's inspection, Divine Services, and reading the Articles of War occurred on Sundays. Particular days of the week meant gun drill was held, or all hands were exercised in setting and taking in sail.

One day of each week was established for competitions. One watch or other group was pitted against another for the best time at tasks of seamanship or sport. Perhaps it was to see which battery could load and fire its guns the fastest. Competitions were not limited to the crew, and many involved passengers against passengers or against the crew.

Even the meals served became a part of the weekly routine. Sundays meant lobscouse and a plum duff for all. Boiled peas with salt pork were served on Thursday.

The weather had been fair and cooperative since the start. Yet on occasion, squalls came up, soaking all on deck. The wind's sudden increase often required that sail be shortened quickly. These sudden storms broke up what by now had become a very monotonous routine. As they progressed farther south, the occasional storm was welcome, as the rain and wind cooled the air, the schooner, and its people.

Several passengers took Pierce's advice and volunteered as crew. A few were experienced seamen, and with others that were quickly trained, Pierce found himself in a unique situation. *Island Expedition* was nearly over-manned! Even in the beginning of the voyage, she had been very fully manned by her assigned crew.

A week after his birthday, Pierce and Hotchkiss revised the Watch, Quarter, and Station Bill, the document that listed each man's duties for each action and situation that might arise. The overall solution, although not unheard-of, was very rare in the Royal Navy. They became a *three watch ship*.

Rather than having all hands, other than officers and idlers, assigned to the port or starboard watch and on duty every four hours, the crew was divided into port, starboard, and amidships watches. Besides the watch on deck and the watch below, there was now the *off* watch. When watches were changed, those just relieved went from watch on deck to off watch status. Four hours later they became the watch below. This off watch was indeed off. They were not called for anything but the most urgent situations, those that required the presence of every man jack aboard. Regardless of the time, the off watch could take to their bunks and enjoy four or more hours of uninterrupted rest. While there were exceptions to the rule, they were extremely limited. To seamen who spent their entire lives on duty every four hours and who were often called out as the watch below, this was a Godsend.

The three-watch system was not simply for the crew's benefit. It made better use of the large numbers of crewmen and volunteers, and long ago Pierce had noted that many mishaps aboard ship were due to the hands' constant fatigue. He hoped that with at least four hours' rest, and more probably eight, all crewmen would be better rested and more alert.

Amongst himself, Hotchkiss, and O'Brien, Pierce established the duty command watch. The individual on duty was simply the one contacted should unusual circumstances warrant it. Pierce usually assumed that role during forenoon and afternoon watches. Hotchkiss covered the dog watches and the evening watch, and O'Brien the mid and morning watches. But as captain, Pierce expected to be called at any time should his presence be required.

Pierce knew Hotchkiss as well as he knew himself. Childhood friends, they had served together long enough in the past that there was never any real disagreement between them. However, O'Brien was a bit of a mystery. He had been a master's mate in *Mariner* when Pierce had served aboard, and they had indeed sailed together. But the fit between them was not yet established. Pierce had hoped for the services of Phelps, master of *Theadora*, but he was still assigned to that ship as it lay in ordinary.

Officer of the watch duties rotated amongst the two senior midshipmen and two master's mates. Morgan and Andrews had served with Pierce aboard *Theadora*, and he considered them to be lieutenants in every sense, other than to have passed an examination board. Should they perform well during this voyage, and should he give them proper recommendations, he was confident they would gain commissions upon returning. Pierce knew the master's mates as well. Spencer and Dial had both been midshipmen in *Orion* during his time aboard. After his departure to *Theadora*, both passed their examination, but had not been commissioned. Instead they had chosen to serve as master's mates.

Townsend, Hadley, and Steadman served as midshipman of the watch. Townsend and Hadley had served with Pierce aboard *Theadora*. They were both excellent in this capacity but were not yet ready to act as officer of the watch. Pierce hadn't known Steadman until he had reported aboard, being recommended for this appointment by a friend of Lieutenant Forrest. At this point in the voyage, Pierce had a most favorable impression of the dark and swarthy lad. His appearance was what Pierce imagined Smythe's might have been many years ago. Upon occasion, Steadman admitted to, or even insisted he was of Gypsy or Romany ancestry.

As *Island Expedition* sailed further south, the days got warmer. Yesterday they had passed south of the Tropic of Cancer. Now Pierce sat in his cabin, making entries in the ship's log as a rivulet of sweat ran down his back. He dried his hands on a trouser leg so the moisture on his fingers would not wrinkle the page.

A cooling and refreshing squall would be welcome. Perhaps a bath would fit the bill? He remembered baths at Smythe's house in Newport. With a little cooler water, one of those would be wonderful. He longed to feel cool, clean, and refreshed, rather than like the salt beef boiling away in the coppers. With a sigh he resigned himself to suffering as did everyone on board, and as predecessors voyaging in tropical waters had done in the past.

He did resolve to be as comfortable as possible. He stood, crouching slightly under the beams, and took off his uniform. That was better. He opened the stern window a bit farther and got a breeze through the cabin.

"Wyatt!" he called to the marine outside. "Pass the word for Mr. Hotchkiss!"

"Aye aye, sir!"

He heard the call passed forward and throughout the schooner. Hotchkiss appeared moments later, his uniform soaked through. The first lieutenant looked rather disheveled and melted in the heat.

"Isaac, old friend, pray, climb out of that coat! You look nearly boiled in it."

"Quite a good idea!" Hotchkiss said as he gratefully removed the heavy uniform. "But I cannot remain here. I'll need to be about my duties, and I shall be right back into that boiler."

"That is not what I imply. It is warm enough that we need not wear the coat."

"Regulations? Decorum, sir?"

"It's my belief, sir, that any regulations are for the colder climes of England. They are also meant to establish an officer's authority and position, which we have done. No, I say those regulations be damned as of now. Please inform all that uniform coats are no longer required.

Much warmer, and we will abandon neckerchiefs and waistcoats as well."

"Aye aye, sir! Seems a sensible thing. I do worry about the apparent disregard of regulations." He paused. "You are not vexed for this insistence?"

"No, sir, not at all. It is your duty to caution me. And the hands too may rig according to temperature. But are there any complaints of impropriety, heads or other parts will roll!"

"Aye aye, sir!" Hotchkiss turned to go.

"Wait just one moment, if you would." Pierce quickly rearranged the items on his desk. He spread the chart in front of them both. "By my plot, we should cross the line, the equator, in a week, maybe two. I understand that it is customary for some sort of ceremony to mark the occasion."

"I believe it is the custom. But as neither of us has crossed, I am not sure what it entails."

"Nor I, Isaac. Perhaps some on board have, and can be of service in this matter."

"I shall seek out any that have crossed, sir."

"Thank you. What we do should not be some wretched debacle of gross and totally obscene behavior."

"Aye, sir!"

Hotchkiss left and Pierce finished his log entries. The cabin was too hot, and he went on deck. Those on the quarterdeck vacated the windward side for him. He did not take advantage, but proceeded aft to the taffrail.

Smythe was there, staring at the schooner's wake, much as Pierce had done on numerous occasions. A brisk breeze blew from the port quarter, and with the top hamper between them and the sun, the spot was rather refreshing. *Island Expedition's* course was nearly to the south, only one point still to the west, and at this time of day they sailed nearly into the sun.

"It seems that it is going well," remarked Smythe after some moments.

"It would seem so," said Pierce in reply. "We make good daily runs. The schooner is a joy to command. With the crew we now have, and without passengers, she'd put up a strong fight if called upon."

"We requested heavy armament, as the war was still in progress. There was always a chance to encounter a privateer, or a French or Spanish man-of-war. It was imperative we be able to defend ourselves." He paused and moved to follow the main topgallant's shade as it traced its way across the deck.

Then he continued. "It would be most unfortunate, should we need to fight with the passengers aboard. Far better that we sail now, during the peace."

"They are holding up well," commented Pierce. "At sea just shy of eight weeks now. Not long for a seaman, but…."

"Most were resigned to transport. That we've altered the destination hasn't affected their state regarding the voyage itself. Yet, I sense boredom and unrest."

"In a week or two they will have a chance to recoup some sensibilities."

"How so?"

"We cross the line soon, and there will be a celebration to mark the occasion."

"Well, that we should. I've crossed before, so if you need help, please!"

"Most assuredly, sir," said Pierce. "Might I point you in Mr. Hotchkiss' direction? I fear I have pushed the task of arranging any ceremony at him. And with your permission, I may send him your way."

"By all means, sir."

The conversation drifted on to other things. At length Smythe asked, "You received secret orders in Plymouth. Would I be amiss to inquire into them?"

"No. As we are beyond thirty degrees west and thirty degrees north, secrecy is no longer required."

"I see."

"Quite simply," said Pierce, who offered the information without being asked, "We are to call at Cape Town. While there, we are to let our search for the island be known. Bonaparte surely has agents there, and one will no doubt quickly depart for Paris. Our agents would note this and send word or gain passage to England at the first instant."

"I see," said Smythe again. "And?"

"I suppose His Majesty's Government is most interested in what French, or even Dutch reaction is to our voyage."

"A bit of intrigue then, is it?"

"Nor do we hide the island's search when we call at St. Helena."

"But it is British."

"It is indeed, but while we are at peace, there may be French agents there as well. And should they tip their hand regarding any resumption of hostilities. . . ." Pierce and Smythe both moved again as they endeavored to stay in the shade.

A week later Pierce awoke in the gray pre-dawn to a stifling hot cabin. He was soaked with sweat and wondered momentarily why he had been called to consciousness. Four bells had sounded, and he could hear the commotion of all hands being roused out of their hammocks. Morning muster was the one time the off watch was required to violate their four uninterrupted hours of rest. How tired and groggy they must be with only a couple hours of sleep!

He had slept most of the night, once he had reconciled himself to the stickiness of the warm evening. Yet as he lay in his cot, he felt as if he had slept hardly at all. It took real effort to remain awake, and even more of an effort to get up.

He washed his face, wondering if the water in the basin cleaned or further dirtied it. The wetness refreshed him slightly. He quickly dressed, went on deck, and indicated that he was not ready to occupy the windward quarterdeck. Forward, he went below to the galley. He had a mug and the coffee pot on the stove was partially full. Eubanks knew that coffee best be ready when the captain came after a cup. Most ship's captains would have a steward make this trek and bring the coffee to the cabin. He had never appointed anyone to those duties, and this far into the voyage, could not see that he would. It was no trouble to fetch his own. He simply insisted that freshly brewed coffee be ready.

In spite of the heat that oozed from the very structure of the schooner, even at this early hour, Pierce relished that first cup of strong, steaming, hot coffee.

He edged back to the quarterdeck, dodging clusters of seamen mustering by divisions. He caught Dial's eye and nodded slightly. The master's mate uttered a few words and the windward side cleared. Pierce enjoyed the solitude and slowly sipped his coffee. He still had an unfinished dream running through his mind and he allowed it to linger. He was awake, on deck, but not ready to begin the day.

"Ahoy the ship!" The hail came on the heels of a loud splash. "Come aboard?"

Pierce noticed with an inward grin that Dial and Townsend, presently on duty as officer and midshipman of the watch, had both jumped with a startled suddenness.

"Who's hailing?" asked Dial rather loudly.

"Davy Jones!" the voice answered. "Come aboard?"

Dial was totally bewildered and looked about helplessly. He looked at Pierce, his countenance begging for a solution.

"Perhaps you should let him aboard, Mr. Dial!" said Pierce. "If I am correct, Davy Jones is a person of privilege. Were I you, side boys and bo'sun's mates!"

"Davy Jones? Privileged? Side boys?" Dial was perplexed. He quickly recovered. "Aye aye, sir! Mr. Townsend, prepare to render honors!"

Moments later the side boys, some wiping sleep from their eyes, formed up along the starboard entry port. "The Most Honorable Davy Jones, please come aboard at your convenience!" said Townsend, reciting the words Pierce had given him an instant earlier.

A head of wild tangled hair under a soaked and dripping cocked hat appeared even with the deck. The pipes twittered, and the side boys saluted. The wet and bedraggled figure heaved itself on to the deck and stood dripping. It lifted the soggy misshapen hat in salute to the quarterdeck, a salute that was returned with due ceremony by the ship's captain.

The strange visitor made his way to the captain, dripping seawater on the recently holystoned deck, and no doubt irritating the first lieutenant. Moving aft, the stranger busily unwrapped a parcel of tarred canvas, and as he reached the spot where Pierce stood, took out its contents.

He unrolled the scroll, and in a loud voice read: "I, Davy Jones, Royal Scribe and Emissary of His Most Royal Majesty, Neptunus Rex, Ruler of the Raging Main, present greetings to you and your vessel, sir, from his most Royal and Salt Encrusted Majesty!"

"Master and Commander Edward Pierce, captain of His Britannic Majesty's Schooner *Island Expedition* at your service, sir. How may we be of assistance?"

"From sources unknown, we have learned that you mean to proceed on a generally southerly course, cross the boundary of our realm, that latitude you define as zero degrees or the equator. As Ruler of the Raging Main, His Majesty King Neptune can not permit passage of any vessel into his realm without it and its occupants being found worthy to continue."

"And you are here to pass such judgment?" asked Pierce.

"No, sir, not I," responded Davy Jones. "I have brought a list of requirements that you must fulfill before His Majesty comes aboard and determines your worthiness." He handed a list, written on yellowed and stained paper, to Pierce. "You have until eight bells in the forenoon watch to prepare for His Majesty's visit. He will, of course, have the Royal Entourage with him."

Pierce looked at the list. "There is a lot to be done, and in a very short time. We turn to at once. May we offer you our hospitality, sir?"

"Thank you, Captain," said Davy Jones with polite air. "I must return and report that this vessel will be ready for the Royal Visit." He proceeded to the entry port. Once again the side boys saluted and the pipes twittered as Davy Jones went over the side. There was a splash and the Royal Scribe was gone.

"Mr. Dial!" roared Pierce.

"Aye, sir?"

"We've work to do, and a lot of it. Call all hands, including the off watch!"

"Aye aye, sir!"

"I'll meet with all officers in five minutes, here on the quarterdeck!"

"Aye aye, sir!" Dial turned to fulfill his duties.

Soon the officers and were assembled around the captain. "It appears everyone is here, except... No, here comes Mr. Cartney now." The bo'sun hurried to join them, his hair wet and his clothes damp and twisted, much as if he had dressed quickly while still wet.

"Gentlemen," began Pierce. "Today we are to receive a Royal Visit from King Neptune, Ruler of the Raging Main. He has requested certain preparations be made for his Visit, and we shall have them completed when he arrives."

He continued, detailing to each just what was to be done. Shortly, they each had groups of seamen engaged in various tasks, all of which were deemed necessary to prepare for the Royal Visit.

Boats were hoisted out and towed astern. Two timber frames were built and set even with the foremast, one to either side. These were lined with spare canvas, which was then tarred and greased, making them impervious to water. Once these basins were complete, they were filled with water, hoisted by bucket from the sea, or from the discharge hoses of the pumps.

Into that water went a variety of vile and nasty ingredients. The cask of salt pork declared unfit two weeks ago went in, as did rotten cabbages and moldy potatoes. The cook personally added a great portion of slush and uneaten burgoo from breakfasts of the past week.

Six chairs were brought from the stern cabin and set on deck, just forward of the mainmast. One was elevated above the rest, placed upon short timbers laid on the deck planks. Two mess stools were set aft of the vats of foul and disgusting water. Beside each was an opened cask of slush, tar, and soap, mixed thoroughly with the worst of the schooner's fresh water to form a revolting lather. Two swabs and two mock wooden razors of enormous size stood nearby.

The pumps were checked and rigged with hoses leading forward over the knightheads and into the head itself.

With these nefarious arrangements were made, an air of excitement and expectation manifested itself in everyone on board. There was anxiety, to be sure, but hands and passengers both relished the change in routine. They worked willingly and good-naturedly, despite the fire of the sun in the sky. Most of the passengers were on deck, lending a hand where they could. Others tried to stay out of the way, but with the hustle and haste, they too were swept up in the action.

Mr. Andrews' working party set about testing the hose to the starboard head. Four stout tars put their weight onto the pump handles and the water flowed. However, when they built up a high rate of flow, a connection separated. The broken hose flailed about, soaking those nearby.

In mock revenge, those so unceremoniously doused grabbed buckets and filled them from the sea. Before anyone could prevent it, these daring avengers saturated the hands at the pump. One of those took up the hose, bid his mates pump for dear life, and took after the bucket brigade.

On any other occasion, Pierce would expect petty officers to instantly put a stop to such horseplay. If others did not, he certainly would do so. Today however, he let the joyous riot continue. More passengers and crewmen became involved, soaking and drenching others. Laughter and high spirits echoed over the deck, and in his best estimation, none was caused by unauthorized consumption of spirits.

Soon someone caught an inadvertent elbow and thought it a bit more than called for. Tempers flared and fists swung. Blows landed, instantly ending the merriment.

As quickly as the scuffle started, Cartney's mates broke it up. The flare-up was extinguished as it began, and the antagonists brought to the quarterdeck. The impromptu excitement faded.

Pierce eyed the two before him. They were soaked, crestfallen, and out of breath. They glared at each other when they thought he wasn't looking. He could see the uncertainty and fear in their faces. They had been fighting; a direct violation of regulations, and could be swiftly and severely punished.

Most captains would not account for what led to the altercation, nor the lingering results of punishments awarded. But Pierce recognized what had led to blows being struck. He acknowledged that he had let the excitement continue longer than he should have. With the coming visit of King Neptune, discipline should take a different turn. He would not excuse their behavior or let their actions go unpunished. He simply would not make more of it than it was.

He glared at them for another moment. "You both know the regulations about fighting?" he said, his voice flat and emotionless.

"Aye, sir, I do," said the first quietly.

"Me as well, sir," nodded the second.

"Is there still any anger between you?" Pierce asked. "Is it over?"

"Think so, sir!"

"Aye, sir," came the second's answer.

"Very well, then. I'll see a true heartfelt handshake. When this visit from Neptunus Rex is over, you will clean the heads. And you will clean them until St. Helena. Now, aloft to the mastheads with you!"

"Aye aye, sir!" both said with barely detectable sighs of relief.

"You are on my short list! Any trouble from either of you, and I shall not be as lenient as now. Mark my word on that!"

"Aye aye, sir!"The two shook hands, and with a nod from Pierce, left the quarterdeck. One ascended to the main topmast head, and the other to the fore topmast head, there to stay until King Neptune arrived.

O'Brien approached and touched the brim of his hat. "Beg pardon, sir, but you've said what we feel something ain't right, that we should call it to your attention."

Pierce nodded in reply to the master's salute and said, "I have made it clear that within bounds of reason and discipline, you bring your concerns to me."

"Aye, sir. And what it is that bothers me, sir, is that those two are getting off light for fighting. Most captains would've had 'em flogged or would've stopped their grog for a week!"

"You disapprove of my disciplinary measures?"

"Don't know I'd say that, sir, beg pardon."

Pierce sighed briefly. "Mr. O'Brien, I do not worry should you disapprove. If you do, then you do."

"Aye, sir, I suppose then, I do."

"When the Articles of War and other regulations give a captain leeway into how infractions are punished, we must use it to the fullest extent. We must look at all the circumstances of the infraction. Then we must assign a punishment that fits. Flogging is not always the punishment called for.

"But do not think that I am easy. I can and will order the severest punishments, should they be required. Flogging those two would ruin their spirits, as well as their backs, and put a damper on the day's celebration. Good order and discipline isn't about having subordinates fear us. It's also about having them follow and support us."

"Aye, sir. But next time? The next fight? Them knowing they'll only clean heads and be mastheaded?"

"All factors will be weighed, and punishment will reflect that incident alone."

"Aye aye, sir!"

"You realize, Mr. O'Brien, most captains would not stand for any questioning of their methods."

"Indeed, sir! For that I am grateful. Beg pardon, sir." He touched the brim of his hat again and moved off.

By six bells in the forenoon watch, *Island Expedition* was ready for King Neptune's visit. "Mr. Hotchkiss, you may pipe to dinner. We'll ensure full bellies for what may await us."

"Aye aye, sir!"

An hour later Pierce and the others took the noon sightings. Notified by the officer of the watch that it was noon, Pierce called, "Make it noon! Sound eight bells!"

As the bell chimed, Pierce faintly heard splashes and voices aft.

A much louder splash was followed instantly by a hail. "Ahoy, the ship! Make ready and make way for His Majesty, Neptunus Rex, Ruler of the Raging Main. I, Davy Jones, Royal Scribe and Royal Emissary, have spoken!"

"We are most pleased to have His Royal Majesty visit this unworthy vessel," said Pierce loudly. In a quieter voice he turned to Hotchkiss. "Call away side boys and marine honor guard, if you will, sir!"

Hotchkiss acknowledged and bellowed for the side boys, the marines, and the bo'sun's mates. They all had been awaiting this call and immediately formed up abreast the port entryway. The Royal Party had acquired the gig and now waited alongside.

"Come aboard?"

"Aye, come aboard, Your Majesty!"

A battered and tarnished crown appeared even with the deck.

The pipes started caterwauling and the crown was followed by King Neptune himself. His hair was long, matted, and the color and texture of oakum. His beard, much the same in appearance, covered the Royal face and fell in dripping masses to his waist. His garments clung damply about him, and whereas they were purported to be of the finest cloth available, they appeared to be old sailcloth draped haphazardly about him. Neptune clutched a makeshift trident in his right hand. It had once been a boarding pike, but had two extra tines riveted to it.

He struck the trident's haft sharply against the deck. "Avast there, mate! Belay that damned screeching! Hoist my flag!"

At the Royal command the pipes fell silent. Hopkins hoisted a black balled bit of cloth to the peak. A sharp tug on the halyard broke the flag out into the wind and the Jolly Roger flew alongside the Blue Ensign.

Others of the Royal Party began to climb the side of the *Island Expedition*. First was Davy Jones, the Royal Scribe and Emissary. After him came the Royal Princesses. Surely no king had ever sired such ugly and undesirable females as had Neptunus Rex. Their long unkempt hair was the same color and texture as his. They were dressed in old linens wrapped about their persons and secured about their ample waists with lengths of cord. They giggled bashfully, and hid their countenances behind their hands or their fans. At least two of the princesses could have shaved better that morning.

The last on deck was the Royal Baby, an *infant* fully the size of a grown man. His diapers were of stout sail cloth, stained, dirty, and reeking. For a child of such tender years he had an extensive growth of hair over his upper body, matted and curly on his chest, back, and upper arms. Like his sisters, the youngster had forgotten to shave, and a dark shadow manifested itself on his face. His bald baby head showed signs of stiff and bristly stubble. A mixture of slush, tar, paint, and varnish adhered to his ample midsection.

"Welcome aboard, Your Majesty!" Pierce said and bowed low and elaborately. "We have seats for you and the Royal Party." He indicated the chairs placed on deck, one of which was raised slightly higher than the others.

"Very well, Captain Pierce!" Neptune replied with a slight impatience. We shall be seated, and then to business."

"As you desire, Your Majesty."

Neptune and his party sat. "Is everyone on board topside?" he queried.

"Yes, Your Majesty," answered Pierce.

"Now see here, Captain! Ye seek passage into my realm with this scumbucket garbage scow and these scurvy dogs of crew and passengers?"

"Yes, Your Majesty! But I would hesitate to describe this vessel or her company in such terms," Pierce responded.

"Silence thy tongue, ye lubberly polliwog! Ye are as I say! Until inspected and found worthy, ye shall not enter my realm." The Ruler of the Raging Main stood and rapped solidly on deck with the haft of his trident. "Let all that have previously been tried and found acceptable come forward!"

Four hands, two warrant officers, and three passengers stepped forward. Neptune called each by name and heaped praise and good wishes on them. Still, he was offended that they were aboard a vessel infested with so many detestable, slimy polliwogs. He was particularly insulted that they had dared sail with a captain never before found worthy. Neptune offered that they could redeem themselves by assisting in the Royal Court's inspection and examination.

Those individuals took up their stations, and Neptune ordered everyone else to kneel and crawl about on all fours. Pierce refused, but when a Royal Princess and a Loyal Shellback approached menacingly, he humbled himself and dropped to the deck.

"Captain Pierce, ye shall be the first examined. A true and loyal crusty Shellback must know the art of kissing. He must know how to joyfully terrorize the young with his stubbly chin to their bellies. Kiss the Royal Baby's Royal Belly!" Neptune roared.

Pierce sought to protest, but with the approach of the enforcing Princess and Shellback, he acquiesced and crawled to the foot of the Baby's chair. "Oh good!" squealed the giant toddler in a deep and booming voice. He suddenly clasped his hands behind Pierce's head and pulled the captain's face into his greased and tarred midsection. He rolled Pierce's face about in the grease and fat for a moment and let go.

Pierce straightened, spat out a chunk of pork grizzle, and waited.

Neptune spoke again. "Members of the Ancient Order of the Deep are well-groomed and clean-shaven. Proceed!"

The two enforcers escorted him to a stool aft of the foremast. When he sat, the first of two stationed there quickly lathered his face and head with the ill-smelling concoction. The second Shellback honed his mock wooden razor and with a few quick and deft movements scraped away most of the vile mess.

"My loyal subjects are clean! You, captain, need a bath!" With that, the two escorts, the Royal Barber, and the assistant bodily lifted Pierce from the deck and deposited him in the port side vat.

He climbed out the forward end, covered from head to toe in the most awful and obnoxious substances. Was he permitted to remain standing?

Soon he heard the pumps being put in operation. A trickle of water, and then a steady stream blasted against him. The coolness of the seawater refreshed him and removed most of the odious materials. He rotated under the jet of water and delighted in the cleansing spray.

"Captain, ye may join the Royal Party. Ye have passed thy examination. Now bear witness to the testing of these scurvy, slimy polliwogs. Come and sit!"

"I am most grateful, Your Majesty!" said Pierce.

He took the chair vacated by the Royal Princess. He watched as the crew and passengers were inspected and found worthy to venture into King Neptune's realm.

Rather than escorting each individual through to the bath before starting with another, the Crusty Shellbacks and Royal Party members drove one after another forward and through the examination. As soon as one had kissed the Royal Baby's belly, another was having his face and head rolled about in the grease and fat covering the infant's ample gut. The Royal Barbers worked unceasingly and without pause, lathering and quickly shaving each individual that passed into their hands.

As fast as one individual stepped out of one of the large vats, another was placed in it. The pumps worked unceasingly now, and two constant streams of water played over the ever- changing party of new Shellbacks on the foredeck.

It should not be said that Neptunus Rex did not respect the delicacy and dignity of the fairer sex. For those who objected to being so rudely treated, he allowed they need only kiss his hand as a sign of fealty, and plunge one arm up to the elbow in the bath's dubious mixture.

He extended the same leniency to smaller children, and those that were particularly frightened, he passed on the word of parents or other adults.

When everyone on board had been examined, found worthy, and stood soggy and unkempt about the deck, Neptune stood. He rapped his trident against the deck and said, "Captain Pierce! In Our Royal pleasure we have examined this vessel and company. All are deigned worthy, and ye have our leave to continue thy voyage. In honor of all now being Loyal Shellbacks, we insist ye splice the main brace!"

Chapter Thirteen

Port Visits

It was December, but south of the Equator it was summer and quite hot. Pierce and the officers of His Majesty's Schooner *Island Expedition* stood their duties in shirt sleeves, uniform coats being stowed in their respective cabins. Their desired course was east by southeast as they sought the tiny island of St. Helena. Unfortunately, the winds came out of the very point to which they were heading, and they were forced to tack across their intended track. For every mile gained in the desired direction, they sailed three, four, or even five miles on port or starboard tacks.

It was now that the schooner's sail plan made its benefits known. With her square sails furled tight about their yards and nothing but fore and aft sails, *Island Expedition* could lie closer to the wind and make better progress to windward than any square-rigged vessel. Because of the nature of the fore and aft rig, tacking or wearing ship was simpler. More of the work involved could be done from deck, rather than aloft, and fewer hands were needed to accomplish each evolution.

As the days progressed, Pierce tacked after the forenoon watch was called, after the first dog watch had begun, and finally once the midwatch had been set. As it worked out, the ship was on a starboard tack twice and a port tack once on any particular day. The next day it would be on a port tack twice and on a starboard tack once.

Island Expedition drew ever nearer St. Helena as it described a great jagged path, a hundred miles or more to each side of the line leading directly to that island. Pierce and the other officers sighted and measured the sun every day at noon. The position was plotted and slight corrections made to place them on the correct course. On the ninth day of the month, they determined they had reached St. Helena's latitude. Now their desired track was directly east. They came about and set up close-hauled on a starboard tack. That would suffice until they fetched the East India Company's outpost. Practical considerations demanded an occasional short run on a port tack to counteract any leeward drift to the north and keep them to their desired course.

The wind was fresher, and stirred the sea into choppier larger waves. Some staysails were gotten in, and at times the officer of the watch was forced to order reefs in the large mainsail and foresail. Still, *Island Expedition* thundered on, her port side deep in the water as the wind pressed her over. She drove her sharp bows into the sea and sent up clouds of spray and foam. Once in a while she met a particularly large sea, and her bows would crash into it, sending masses of water, spray, and foam washing along the deck to soak those there.

Pierce found it exhilarating. He stood on the windward quarterdeck, the wind in his face as the spray whipped about him. It was refreshing and cool, even while they were in the tropics and the temperature quite warm. The schooner had settled into a predictable motion, pitching and rolling with the passing of each sea. He balanced easily, instinctively, as he casually glanced about him. Yet in that casual glance he perceived many things and knew all he needed to know about the schooner.

Then his mood darkened. Even though he was reveling in the brisk excitement of this day at sea, something in his life was missing. He had never been to sea with anyone special waiting for him. True, his parents had waited when he had first sailed as a midshipman. But never had he left a young lady behind. For the past weeks he had tried to keep Evangeline out of his thoughts, because if he didn't, his loneliness would drive him mad. It took a great effort not to think of her. He wasn't always successful, and once his thoughts were of her, they would prey upon him for hours. He would be unable to sleep, despite the relaxing motion of the ship and the wind that made below decks much more comfortable.

Today Pierce could not prevent his mind from wandering back to England and the waiting Evangeline. He pictured her in the dress she had worn while standing on the pier when *Island Expedition* had cast off to head into the Solent. He pictured her in the bonnet that she wore that day, and how she had smiled bravely and waved.

He recalled their first meeting, how something had stirred deep within him, and how he had decided that if she did not fit his ideal of the perfect woman, he would change that ideal to fit her. He thought of her direct honesty and practicality, as when they had met attired in their robes, enroute to or from the bath. He remembered her skill and mastery of an Oriental fighting technique when they had been waylaid by brigands.

She had offered to teach him, but in the hectic days before sailing there had never been time.

It had been wonderful, just to be with her. He recalled the longing and want he had felt when they were together, and the conflict within, as he balanced animal desire for her with respect, decency, and true affection. His mind turned to the last days they had spent together and how their passions had come forth. With sweet pain and sadness, he remembered their first professions for each other, and the sweet deliciousness of their first embrace. Those next few days until *Island Expedition* sailed had been pure bliss, and now were a wonderful but tortured memory.

As he thought more, his mood darkened. He had known her only a few months. Their expressions of love had occurred in the last weeks of their time together. She had promised to wait until he returned. He in turn had promised to return to her, and he would do just that. But could a young woman of such grace, beauty, desires, needs, and wants, forsake those urges for the next few years? Could she stay intent on their beginning relationship and not be swayed by anyone she would chance to meet?

Pierce began to think he was a fool. Were her feelings as intense as he imagined, or as strong as his? Should he have pressed the physical issue to its conclusion, and at least be able to claim memories of that pleasure, regardless of the future? Perhaps that was what she had wanted as well. Gone three months now, was he a dim memory, a fool who failed to avail himself of her charms, a fool out of sight and out of mind, perhaps for years?

He wondered darkly. What was she doing now? Was she on the Isle of Wight waiting for and missing him? Was she enjoying the company of other young men, another naval officer perhaps? Was she being courted and more by a merchant of Newport? Was she with a general, an admiral, or a captain? Could she even be in the company of a common laborer, a private soldier, or an ordinary seaman?

Pierce checked himself momentarily. For his entire life he had fought to not make distinctions of rank in such matters. But he wasn't classifying them one against another. He was classifying them against himself. No matter who it might be, he tortured himself unmercifully to think she could be with someone else.

His anger at these unknown and imagined competitors faded. Now his sadness, his loneliness, caused his wrath to turn upon her. His fevered mind again saw himself as her foolish toy. He heard her careless taunting laugh as she paraded her latest companion before him, failing to see his hurt and anger. Mentally he composed impassioned tirades to spout violently should he return and find she had not respected his love. His blood boiled as he thought of the confrontations, and the duels he would fight in her honor. No, not her honor, but his misguided sense of honor and his feelings of betrayal when he found that she had all but forgotten him.

The unfounded rage churned within and he wondered if he would strike her, hurt her, defile her, even slay her, should he return and find that she had passed on their life together. Yet he was a gentle, forgiving person, and no matter what would be found upon his return, any sign of her affection would wash the hurt, imagined or real, from him.

The starboard bow dug into a larger-than-usual sea. Spray drifted along the deck and soaked Pierce, his miserable spirit many miles away. As the saltwater dripped from him, his despairing thoughts ebbed, and again he was aware of his surroundings. The wind had come up a bit. Much more and he would need to order another reef. Now, however, things were fine.

St. Helena should be very near now. His calculations earlier in the day had shown that they should sight the tiny island any day. That depended upon the accuracy of the noon sightings, the accuracy of the chronometer, and his mathematical prowess. They were at the correct latitude, but determination of longitude was more of a chance.

Pierce urgently hoped for landfall. He needed a change in the constancy of being at sea. As captain, he was concerned for supplies and the well-being of both passengers and crew. They still had plenty of fresh water, but it was long enough in the casks to be foul and unappealing. He and the crew could drink it for a long time yet, but passengers were already complaining about its quality. Perhaps they could also obtain fresh meat and vegetables to liven up the fare set before everybody. Fruit -- especially lemons, limes, oranges, and apples -- would be welcome.

"Deck there!" the fore topmast lookout bellowed. "Deck there! Land! Land! Three points to starboard!"

Morgan, the officer of the watch, acknowledged the lookout's hail. "Very well, Jones!"

Then he turned to Pierce. "Land's been sighted, sir! Three points to starboard!" He knew Pierce had heard, as Pierce had been on the quarterdeck all along. Still, duty and tradition led him to report with some formality to the captain.

Pierce, in the last vestiges of dark despair, thought to tell Morgan that yes, damn it, he knew, as he had ears and was aware of what happened on his ship. He checked himself and simply replied, "Thank you, Mr. Morgan. Be so kind to put us on a port tack!"

"Aye aye, sir." Morgan shouted orders. The bo'sun's mates piped, and hands appeared. They let go the headsail sheets, the helm was put down, and her way carried her into the wind and beyond. Headsails were sheeted home, and the mainsail boom swung across, inches above their heads. The loose-footed foresail was sheeted to the other side as well. The *Island Expedition* righted from the port heel she had maintained for the past several days, sat perfectly level for a few seconds, and then dipped her starboard rail toward the seas.

Pierce desired they head to the southwest portion of the island. When most opportune, they would come about, head northeast on a starboard reach, and fetch Jamestown on the island's northwest corner.

At noon the next day, *Island Expedition* anchored in James Bay. Immediately, a party of East India Company officials came out in a plain but sturdy long boat. Arrangements were made for watering and restocking fresh provisions. Pierce made it clear that he would allow the crew ashore, one watch at a time, except for those restricted to the ship. Due to the passengers' official status as convicts, they could not be set ashore unguarded. Pierce and Smythe knew they needed to be away from the schooner more than members of the crew did. The Company finally let them ashore to stay in a secure and guarded camp. Pierce used that time to clean and disinfect the schooner.

Watering and stores were completed by Christmas, but contrary winds kept them harbor- bound until the first days of 1803. While there, Pierce oversaw re-supplying of *Island Expedition*, the cleaning of her 'tween decks, and routine but necessary repairs. In the evenings Smythe, a varying selection of officers, and Pierce dined aboard any of a number of East Indiamen in port at the time. Occasionally they dined ashore with the governor or other respected company officials.

On the second day of the year, Pierce awoke with a headache and a nauseated stomach. Although he had tried to exercise careful control, he had drunk more than he should have. He freshened himself at the basin in his cabin and went forward to the galley. He needed coffee, and today it seemed that he would require a gallon or more. Pierce reached for the pot atop the galley stove. He hoisted it easily, an indication that it was nearly empty. If it were not full, it was old. Today, especially today, here and now, he wanted fresh coffee. Strong, yes, but brewed recently, not strong because it had cooked since Nelson was a midshipman.

Eubanks was ashore and the last liberty party had not yet returned. His mate was to the side, pounding biscuits with a marline spike, making crumbs for the next offering of lobscouse. Evidently the cook's mate had forgotten the standing order that coffee always be ready for the captain. Absorbed in his work, he did not see the captain.

Pierce poured a shot of the remaining contents. The aroma reached his nose: oily, bitter, strong and old. It was exactly what he did not want. His stomach churned, and the deck rose and fell alarmingly. He shuddered slightly and flung his mug across the deck.

Franklin jumped when the crockery shattered against the bulwark. He dropped the marline spike on his foot, howled in pain and surprise, hobbled, and tried to make the proper honors. "Good morning, Captain! Sorry, sir, but didn't know you was here, sir!"

"I don't much bloody care whether you knew I was here or not!" growled Pierce. "You are amiss in your duties, damn your eyes!"

Franklin's countenance took on a terrified and questioning look. "S-sir?"

"Coffee! Damned hot fresh coffee!"

"There's still some in the pot, sir," suggested the cook's mate.

"The hell, you say, Franklin! I drink that, and all aboard will know exactly what my dinner was this past evening. I wouldn't drink that whale piss were I at sea a year!"

Franklin did have his wits with him. "Beg pardon, Captain, but I'll see to it at once!"

Pierce's stomach rolled again and in his mind the ship rolled as well. "No, not for my sake! But others will want some. We've not had a death aboard yet this voyage, but...."

He turned and headed for the upper deck where the fresh breeze might clear his head and reduce the rebellion in his midsection. "Damned incompetence! Just a damned cup of coffee. A bloody damned cup of coffee!" He said it primarily to himself, but with the aim that the cook's mate might also hear it.

Pierce shuddered again as a wave of nausea washed over him.

The morning breeze helped clear his head. With his head clearer, the protestations of his middle eased. A shore boat came alongside to return the last of the crew allowed ashore. Apparently many of them felt worse than he did. Too bad for them that he had not had his coffee. Normally he would commiserate with them and their lingering drunkenness. He would go easy on them as *Island Expedition* got underway. He would let the worst beg off duty, go below, and pass out before they returned to work.

But today he would show no mercy or concern for their condition. He would drive them, and he would drive himself. In spite of his generally kind nature, and general abhorrence of physical punishment, he gave great consideration to having Franklin flogged. Perhaps he would pull Eubanks' warrant and have him flogged as well.

After hands had been piped to breakfast, the tasks of getting the schooner underway began. Pierce no longer had time to think of revenge for his missed coffee.

The convicts, as the East India Company officials thought the passengers to be, had been returned aboard the day before. The last crewmen allowed ashore were back aboard. Fresh water and fresh provisions were stowed. *Island Expedition* was ready for sea again.

Pierce left the actual task of getting underway to his first lieutenant. Hotchkiss had also imbibed too much the evening before, and in his present ill temper, Pierce was simply mean to his friend, who suffered the effects even more. A fleeting bit of guilty conscience crossed his brow, but he successfully dismissed it. Later, when effects of the previous night had worn off, he would apologize. They had been friends for many years, and Hotchkiss would shrug it off and say nothing was adrift between them.

At sea, when the schooner was on the course ordered, he went to the galley carrying another mug. He had brought a set of six with him. Four were left, as he had broken one earlier as well. Now he had this one, and the coffee was fresh and he could drink it. He poured himself a full steamy cup and retired to the privacy of his cabin.

Island Expedition's course was nearly south, bound for Cape Town and the Cape Colony. Captured from the Dutch during the war, it had been returned to them by the Peace of Amiens. As peace existed, Pierce, Smythe, and the British Island Expedition Organization would not find any difficulties there. Hopefully they could once again obtain fresh water and fresh provisions, and be on their way into the Indian Ocean.

Smythe wanted to start the final search for the undiscovered island as well-stocked as possible. They did not know how long it would be before they found it, if indeed they did find it. If the island were not found, they would have to deliver their passengers to Botany Bay.

To do so would be to admit failure, which Smythe was not at all prepared to do. His one driving ambition was to find a place where the passengers, erstwhile convicts, could re-establish themselves as free men. He would sooner die, sooner they all died at sea, rather than see them turned over to the notorious prison colony. He had promised them their freedom, and he would see they got it, even if they died at sea as free men.

Pierce agreed that the search for the island should be carried out to the utmost, but he stopped short of letting all perish, should their search prove fruitless. They talked of this often. One would sometimes concede a minor point, but for the most part they were separated by a gulf of devotion to the cause. Pierce had long admired Smythe's dedication to his special mission, but he could not agree with the finality that Smythe was evidently prepared for. He fervently hoped it would not come to that.

The journey to the Cape Colony was arduous. Their course lay into the wind, and they were forced to tack and sail many miles to gain a few. They changed course, tacked or wore once a day, unless Pierce ordered ship-handling drills. He did that every second or third day, but when the drills ended, *Island Expedition* would be on the tack assumed at the start of the forenoon watch.

They held gun drill as well, to keep the crew sharp in defending the schooner. Pierce preferred they use powder and shot, but the noise alarmed the younger passengers. Thus drills were usually conducted *dry* and the guns were not actually fired.

Contests between watches, divisions, and individuals continued. They kept both the ship's company and the embarked passengers occupied. In the evening there was music, as many had talents in that area. They would sing, loud, boisterous and off-key, or soft and gentle, the entire group quiet and misty-eyed. Occasionally they convinced Gibbons to bring a book and read while everyone listened with rapt attention to the story.

Early in February they were on the same parallel as Cape Town. Out of the consistently southerly winds, they were now able to run before the westerlies as they headed toward the tip of Africa.

They anchored at Cape Town on the 12th of February.

Their reception was cordial and correct, if not warm. Arrangements were quickly made for watering and taking on additional fresh stores. Pierce noted in his log that while water and provisions were readily available, they paid premium prices. They did not tarry long there, anxious to be on to the final stretch of the voyage, but also not to ruffle the feathers of their one- time enemy.

Smythe, Pierce, and several other officers dined with the governor one evening. Also partaking in the meal were the captain and senior officers of a twenty-four-gun French corvette that also happened to be in port. When introduced, Pierce noted a gleam of unresolved recognition in the other captain's eye. There was something familiar about the Frenchman, as well.

Later the two captains found themselves able to converse somewhat privately. Pierce spoke no French, but the other's English, although not perfect, was suitable for their needs.

"M'sieur Capitaine Pierce, I believe you are somebody I have met before."

"I sense the same, Captain Cartier. Perhaps in battle? I was at the Nile as fifth lieutenant in *Orion*. Earlier I was midshipman in *Ferret* and then *Mariner*. When the Peace was signed, I was third aboard *Theadora*."

Mon Dieu! M'sieur!" exclaimed the Frenchman. "*Theadora*! We set a trap to capture her and she tabled, how you say, turned it around for us."

"Turned the tables?" offered Pierce.

"Oui, 'turn the tables.' And now I know you, m'sieur. The English lieutenant sent to board our poor *Rose Marie*."

"The barkentine?" asked Pierce.

"Oui, m'sieur, the barkentine." Cartier's face clouded momentarily. Then it brightened. "I am glad I did not kill you."

"As am I! You may have, had not Jackson brought *Theadora* alongside at that instant. You do your fencing master proud, sir," said Pierce. "As it is, I have a scar, an annoying ache when the glass falls, and at that time a uniform ruined, suitable for only routine duties aboard ship."

"For you, m'sieur, it is with luck I am distracted. You also are skilled with the blade. But you do not kill me. Why?"

"To render you unconscious served the same purpose. It eliminated you as a threat to my life and our capture of *Rose Marie*. And no man, even one's enemy, should die if it can be avoided."

"A man of compassion, I think you are, Capitaine. How strange you serve an occupation devoted to death and destruction?"

"I've never thought of naval service that way. I was brought up to hold life -- all life -- dear. As to the service, we fight only in defense of our kingdom. Should we exist and were never called to perform that deadly duty, it would be for the better."

"Oui, Capitaine, you are as I say, a man of compassion. I see fierce loyalty to your king and country as well. I also see a loyalty to friends and all people. It suits you to be involved in this expedition. I sense M'sieur Smythe is also a man of compassion."

Pierce should have been shocked that this French officer knew of their search for the mythical island. Yet, earlier he had casually let it be known to all at the table. He was sure that others from *Island Expedition* were mentioning it. Indeed, he had secret orders to let slip the purpose of their voyage while in Cape Town.

The Government feared the French might also try to find the island. Its supposed location would make it ideal for raids on British shipping in the East Indies and Indian Ocean. Should the French learn the English were searching for it, that knowledge might spur them to action, and perhaps that would indicate just when the current uneasy peace would end.

"Perhaps I have said too much. It is strictly a British affair. I would not want you thinking we seek the island in any strategic sense. We simply want a place for those convicts and debtors who otherwise are fine and outstanding subjects. A place where, in Smythe's mind, they are no longer considered prisoners, but free men."

"I understand perfectly, M'sieur Capitaine. Whether I report your voyage to Paris or not, word will reach there. M'sieur Bonaparte is suspicious and surely will read more into it."

"That would not surprise me, sir."

"As we know of your search, you should know we have investigated a possible expedition. Perhaps for many of the same reasons you profess."

"Nor does that surprise me."

"But whether or not it is underway, I will not, nor cannot say." Cartier took another sip at his glass. "Perhaps we have each said more than we should?"

"Quite possibly," returned Pierce. "Let us leave the intrigue to others. Another glass, sir?"

"Indeed, sir, that would be ideal." Cartier refilled both glasses from the decanter. "I think, Capitaine Pierce, that were we not opponents because of nationality, we would be friends."

"Perhaps."

"I am French. I will fight for France, whether we are a monarchy, a republic, or are governed by such as Napoleon Bonaparte. Yet I admire the English. You have so much of what we do not."

"How so, Captain?"

"Freedom, m'sieur! Freedom! And you balance that freedom with responsibility and national loyalty. You have age-old traditions and a continuous history. We cut loose from our past, and without it we struggle to regain what should have been kept."

"The 'baby and the bathwater'?"

"I do not understand?"

"An expression, sir," said Pierce. "Meaning you destroyed more than required."

"Oui, m'sieur. But as I have said, I will fight for France, despite what she lacks. And Capitaine Pierce, should we meet again, I hope it is in similar circumstances. Should we be at war, I would do my utmost to defeat you."

"And I you, Captain."

"But now peace exists, and I wish you a successful voyage." Cartier reached out his hand.

Pierce shook the proffered hand firmly. "I too wish you fine sailing as you complete your own journey."

Island Expedition got underway the next day, and when well out to sea, and after supper had been eaten, Smythe asked that Pierce and the other officers stay for a few minutes.

"Friends," he said. "We are now into the real heart, the real reason for our journey. To successfully accomplish it, navigation and piloting must be perfect."

"And why, sir?" asked Morgan, who as senior midshipman acted much as a second lieutenant. "Have not our skills been satisfactory?"

"Oh they have been quite satisfactory, sir," answered Smythe. "But from today, they will need to be that much finer. There are locations we must reach precisely. These points are at sea, out of sight of known landmarks, and we will have no means of verifying our position."

"Sir?" O'Brien looked to Pierce for clarification.

"Gentlemen, this may be hard to fathom. You may not believe it. I am not sure I believe it. As I understand it, we must cross specific points on the map, in a specific order, and in a specific direction, in order to reach the island. To sail directly to the position of the island would avail us nothing, or so I'm told."

"No!" emphasized Andrews. "Such could never happen! We can approach any island or continent from any direction! If our plot is good, we would fetch it!"

"Quite, so, I should think," stated Townsend.

"I would agree," replied Pierce. "But there are many mysteries in the world yet to be explained."

"You are correct, Captain," said Smythe. "I don't fully understand the mechanics of it either. What I do know comes from many sources. Each mentions that a specific course must be sailed, or the island will not be found. Extensive research has enabled me to pinpoint key locations that must be crossed in order to reach the island."

"Sounds like five-water grog to me, sir!" said O'Brien. "Beg pardon, sir!"

"I understand, Mr. O'Brien. I cannot explain it satisfactorily, even to myself. I feel, as opposed to knowing, that reaching each point exactly and in proper succession is what we must do."

"Thus, gentlemen," said Pierce. "It matters not to me, nor to Mr. Smythe, that you believe. I merely ask that we follow along with it. I shall endeavor to navigate more precisely than ever, and I expect that you will all do the same."

Chapter Fourteen

Destination Found

From Cape Town, *Island Expedition* sailed south. After two days with the prevailing wind against her starboard side, she altered course and headed east before the wind, the great main and fore sails out to each side, wing and wing. When they reached sixty degrees east, they changed course again and sailed northwest on a port tack. Seas were choppier and the wind stronger than Pierce would have liked. Due to the wind, he could not shake the last reef out of the topsails and was forced to keep a reef or two in the huge fore and aft sails.

Luck was with them and the skies were always clear when they took their noon sightings. The results were compared to their intended track, and corrections made to bring them to the ideal. They were headed to a spot on the chart labeled only as *one*. Smythe had handed Pierce the longitude and latitude of this location a day after leaving Cape Town. Furthermore, he had said, "We must be on a westerly course as we pass through this location. Otherwise once we clear Africa, we could reach directly for it."

Because they had to pass through the site while heading in a westerly direction, they sailed past and tacked back to the spot.

The sightings taken on the 28th of February indicated they had reached the proper parallel, and were a day or two east of the mysterious location. Because their destination lay directly into the wind, Pierce was forced to sail in tight zigzag fashion. They stayed on each tack a scant few miles to each side of the intended course, which meant plenty of work for the hands. To lessen that and to keep the handiness of *Island Expedition* at the utmost, all square sails were gotten in, and she ran close-hauled under fore and aft sails only.

Pierce, Hotchkiss, Morgan, and Andrews all took noon observations on the 2nd of March. Their individual calculations placed *Island Expedition* within a mile or two of a common location, a mere five leagues from the hypothetical number *one*. Immediately Pierce had the crew 'bout ship onto a starboard tack.

To increase the precision of their pilotage, they shortened sail, and only enough to ensure something more than steerageway remained exposed to the gusty winds. Every time the glass was turned, they came about, keeping within a couple of miles of the intended track. Smythe did not know how accurate their navigation had to be as they crossed that particular spot, but Pierce was determined to be as precise as possible, and as they drew nearer, the time spent on each board became shorter.

They sailed on, through the dog watches, through supper, and into the evening. Pierce remained on deck and relieved those individuals scheduled as officer of the watch. The delicacy and precision required was such that he would trust it to no one else. He had not lost confidence in the others, but felt the final approach to *one* was best left in his hands. Twilight came, and with it, the slightest chill. Pierce sent Steadman to see if coffee were available. As it was, he fetched two mugs from his cabin. At the galley stove he poured them full and returned to the quarterdeck, where he offered the second to Hotchkiss.

"Mr. Steadman, you and the others may go for coffee if you care to. One at a time, and be quick about it."

Darkness was nearly complete. The wind slackened; the sky was clear and filled with stars. A quarter moon hung low and reflected enough light that it was not difficult to see. *Island Expedition* buried her bow in a large sea, and spray flew aft. Pierce checked his watch in the binnacle's light. Nearly time to come about again. He was altering course every fifteen minutes, so fine was he determined to be as they crossed that particular location.

As he dropped his watch into his pocket, Pierce had the oddest feeling. He had been on deck since the forenoon watch with only a few short breaks. He had done that many times, and never had he felt as if he had been there forever. He seemed as old as Creation, and yet with every heartbeat he was a newborn. He discovered things, ordinary things, for the first time, and marveled at them. Often near the end of a long day, he would feel as if it had lasted a very long time, but that sensation always passed. This time it was more pronounced and would not depart. It grew stronger.

Below, a baby cried. That Hennessey lad, he thought, calling to mind the one birth that had occurred on the voyage. No one, not even Maggie Hennessey, had known she was with child, although Pierce found it hard to believe that a woman would not know. But she was, in his mind -- and he hated to think that way -- an ignorant, stupid woman, married to an equally ignorant and inconsequential little man. The child had been born between St. Helena and the Cape Colony.

Little Isaac bawled again. He was named after Pierce's friend, the first lieutenant, who had been the duty command officer when the baby had arrived.

The remaining calf bellowed as if panicked, and the helmsman muttered a low profanity.

"Beg pardon, sir!" Hopkins said. "Ne'er seen nothin' like it, sir!"

"How's that?" Pierce asked. His own voice sounded distant to his ear.

"Compass spun completely, like we was boxin' it, sir. But she's been steady as can be on course."

"Now?"

"Right as rain! Beg pardon again. Them kinda words on the quarterdeck, sir."

"Perhaps you had cause."

"Aye, sir."

"My God!" Hotchkiss exclaimed. His eyes were wide and a hint of terror flicked about in them. "What in God's Name was that?"

"A momentarily confusion of the compass, or perhaps the helmsman," replied Pierce. "I hope it isn't a sign...."

"No, sir! Not that, sir!" Hotchkiss was nearly beside himself in his fright, and it fast approached a full panic. Odd, that such a slight distraction could affect Pierce's friend that way. Isaac had always been the cooler of them.

Hotchkiss continued on. "Ed! You didn't see it?" The use of his captain's first name on deck attested to the first lieutenant's growing apprehension and maddening confusion.

"See what, Isaac, my old friend?" Pierce recognized his shipmate's state of mind and did not correct his lapse of quarterdeck etiquette. Clearly, a more personal and comfortable approach was needed.

"The stars! The stars, Ed! We weren't just looking up at 'em. We were amongst them. There was the sea, and then there wasn't. An' the stars were below us as well! And we were there, right among them, like we were the stars themselves, or the moon, or...."

"I'm sure you saw what you've described. Unfortunately, I chanced not to see it, although I have had a strange feeling of timelessness."

"And I, sir, which we were in a full gale and becalmed at the same time." Steadman volunteered his observations of the past few minutes.

"Strange," Pierce said. "Each experienced something unusual at the same time. Yet for each, it was different. Could the baby and the calf have experienced something similar?"

"Stars! Stars all around us! Close as could be, sir!" Hotchkiss still seemed confused, although he was less terrified and less prone to an all-out panic.

Smythe came on deck. In the darkness he stumbled against the ringbolt of a starboard twelve-pounder train tackle. He caught himself and remained upright. "'One,' I believe, gentlemen!" he shouted in triumph. "We have passed through number 'one'!"

This simple explanation was enough for Pierce's friend.

Immediately the remaining look of terror and panic left Hotchkiss's face. "Tell me, sir," he said to Smythe. "What did you see?"

"The island we journey to find, Mr. Hotchkiss. Only for a moment, and perhaps as it was thousands of years ago. I was nearly asleep in my chair. Perhaps I was asleep. Suddenly I had a view of the island, as if I were a bird, looking down from the highest point of the sky. My eyes, moments before so heavily closed, were open, and indeed, I was fully awake."

"And you realized that we had crossed 'one'?" Pierce asked.

"Merely my supposition," Smythe replied. "I don't see that it could be anything but."

"No doubt you are correct," Pierce continued. "I hear confusion and perhaps near panic. I shall try to explain what has happened. Of those not actually on watch, I would expect your assistance."

Later, Pierce took Hotchkiss by the elbow and guided him away from the quarterdeck. When they were comfortably away from the others, Pierce asked quietly, "I was worried for you, dear friend. Are you shipshape now?"

"I believe it has been put to rights, sir, by Mr. Smythe's explanation."

"Another thing we don't understand. Perhaps we are not meant to. Like you, I find strange comfort in a straightforward and reasonable explanation. Yet how strange that each experienced or saw something different."

"Strange indeed, sir. Tomorrow, I will gather more impressions from crew and passengers."

"Capital idea! Perhaps now Mr. Smythe might have the coordinates of 'two' ready. Mr. Andrews can have the deck." Pierce yawned and drank his now-cold coffee.

Island Expedition remained on the same course for the rest of the night. As Smythe still had not presented him with the coordinates for *two*, Pierce allowed the schooner to sail easily to the west-southwest as the day wore on. As the forenoon watch drew to a close, Pierce and the other officers prepared to take the noon sightings. But when he instinctively gauged the sun's position, Pierce thought it lower in the sky than it should have been.

A little before noon as indicated by the glass, Midshipman Steadman began measuring the sun's height above the horizon. Even with steady westward progress since yesterday's observation, the sun should reach its zenith not much later than it had the day before. They could not have sailed far in twenty-four hours. Others joined in shooting the sun. The glaring ball rose higher in the sky, and *Island Expedition* seemed poised at that last minute before noon was declared. The hands on Pierce's watch continued their progress around the dial, indicating noon, and then some minutes after.

"Damn my soul!" said Hotchkiss quietly. "Something is truly amiss."

The helmsman yawned.

"We've made more of a westing than imagined," said Pierce as he focused his sextant on the sun once again. "If our latitude is correct, we still have a while to noon. Perhaps, Mr. Hotchkiss, some relief for the helm and other duties. Those lads have had their time on watch, regardless of what the sun indicates."

"Aye, sir! A current, do you suppose? We surely could not get so far any other way." Hotchkiss fell in with O'Brien and passed along Pierce's desire that the helm and other duties be relieved.

Four bells in the apparent afternoon watch drew near before the sun reached its highest point in the sky. Immediately upon being told that noon had been established and declaring it to be so, Pierce and the other officers set about determining their position. While all were well-versed in comparing local time as established by the sun at its zenith and Prime Meridian time as kept on the chronometer, this day found all of them at it for a much longer period of time. Finally Pierce sighed in disgust, grabbed a scrap of paper with his results scribbled on it, and went on deck. When he found no one there, he summoned the midshipman of the watch. "Mr. Townsend, do you find the others and bid them join me."

"Aye aye, sir!"

Moments later, the schooner's officers appeared. None looked directly at anyone else, nor attempted to meet Pierce's gaze. "Gentlemen," he said. "I trust your delay in determining today's plot is due the same situation I experience."

"Indeed, sir, if repeated working of the figures places us where we should not, could not be?"

"Well ashore on Madagascar, Mr. Hadley?"

"Why, yes, sir!" replied the midshipman in amazement. Relieved, the others spoke out, their captain revealing that his computations resulted in the same impossible plot as theirs. A quick comparison of solutions revealed that all had placed *Island Expedition* within a couple of miles of each other. Yet that determined location was not where logic would allow it to be.

"We seem to be in agreement," nodded Hotchkiss. "But can this solution be accurate? Do we navigate based on this, or do we *dead-reckon* from yesterday's fix?"

"If I may intercede, gentlemen," said Smythe, arriving on deck with a piece of paper and handing it to Pierce. "I would use the fix most recently determined, despite its implausibility."

"I would be loath to enter such into the ship's log, Mr. Smythe." O'Brien glowered. "Whatever would be said upon returning to England?"

"An unpleasant prospect, to be sure, gentlemen," said Pierce. "Yet Mr. Smythe must offer his advice with some amount of wisdom behind it."

"In truth, I do. Within the legends it is mentioned that one might seem to sail across dry land or find that he has journeyed the equivalent of several weeks in the course of a single day."

"Impossible, sir!"

"Yet do we not have proof? To have sailed the distance from yesterday's plot to today's should take a week, perhaps two. Yet your calculations prove we did so in a single day. I delayed in presenting the coordinates for 'two' for that very reason. If you check that location upon your chart, you will find it well inland on the continent of Africa. However, as we are supposedly well ashore on this rather large island, I have no difficulty in desiring you to sail to this location."

Pierce took the paper and glanced at the latitude and longitude written thereupon. "It seems we are now embarked upon a most unique voyage. If you will, Mr. Hotchkiss, call all hands, set all plain sail, and shape a course to the northwest."

"Aye aye, sir!"

Noon occurred the next day as it should have, a scant few minutes later than it had been established the day before. Pierce felt relieved when their plot showed them to be in the Mozambique Channel between Madagascar and the African mainland. As the schooner continued to the northwest, Pierce and all aboard expected land to be sighted at the next instant. None was.

Ten days went by from the time *Island Expedition* passed through *one* until she passed through *two*, and souls on board experienced much the same as they had during the earlier transit. Once again, Pierce had that strange feeling of timelessness. Hotchkiss once more saw the schooner sailing in the heavens, buoyed not by the sea, but by the universe itself. While they passed through *two* at midday, he still saw stars. Because he had an idea of what caused the vision, he did not panic. Smythe saw the island that was their destination, allowing that on this second occasion, details were more intense and clear. "A sure sign," he remarked, "that we are drawing nearer."

With some effort, Pierce got used to the idea of being upon the open sea while the plots calculated placed them well ashore on established land masses. He had seen navigational errors in his younger days, and if truth be told, had made several himself. It was not unheard-of for a novice pilot to theoretically place his ship upon a large island or continent. But when several people computed the position daily, it was more than simple error that placed them in such unlikely spots.

Sometime after crossing *three*, Smythe passed the location of *four* to Pierce. "Two more to go, Captain," he said. "Here is number 'four'."

"Deck there!" the foremast lookout hailed. "Land to starboard!"

"About time you noticed, Williams," replied Dial, the officer of the watch. "It's visible from deck. And you sleeping aloft!"

"No sir! I swear, sir!"

The mainmast lookout chimed in. "Beg pardon, Mr. Dial, sir, but it did just appear. Wasn't nothing at all, sir, and then, there it was!"

"Damn!" muttered the master's mate. "Both asleep." He turned to Hadley, the duty midshipman. "Take their names! Respects to the captain and that land is sighted!"

"Aye aye, sir!"

"Belay that, Mr. Hadley!" said Pierce. "I heard!" He mounted to the deck from the after companionway. "But do take their names as requested. We'll deal with that later."

People began to crowd on deck and line the starboard rail. This was their first sight of land in nearly two months, and what was now in sight would be home for many of them. "On the deck, there!" shouted Pierce. "Remember we are still at sea. Leave room that hands can do their duties! And see that you mind your duties!" He did not want the excitement of landfall to detract from the jobs at hand.

Smythe arrived on the quarterdeck excitedly happy, and from his broad grin obviously relieved that the island had been found. "Well, Captain, I believe that you've done it! Based on today's plot, this must be it, although I thought it would be another day."

"A day after two months, a position from legends and old stories, sir -- I'd say we have it dead to rights," replied Pierce. "The only trouble is one of shipboard discipline and duty. Both lookouts failed to see it until visible from deck. I've had no problems with the hands' performance, but this means measures need be taken. I fear cleaning heads or polishing brass will not suffice."

"You need not worry about that, Captain."

"How so?"

"In some stories the island appears suddenly and is close enough to be seen from deck. Perhaps it is related to the special course needed to arrive here."

"I'll keep that in mind, sir," said Pierce. Then he turned to the first lieutenant. "If you would, Mr. Hotchkiss, shorten sail as you think prudent! Alter course toward the land in sight!"

"Aye aye, sir!"

"I thank God that we found it," said Smythe quietly. "It eases my mind considerably. I truly did not want to take them to Botany Bay."

"Weren't you prepared to remain at sea until all perished?" asked Pierce. "We argued frequently over that conviction."

"I'm afraid you have me, sir. Perhaps I exhibited such conviction to hide my doubts and fears. I'd not have let these good people perish for my pride. In the interests of their safety and very lives, we would have steered for that damnable penal colony."

"Indeed I am relieved to hear it, sir. Your dedication to that fatal point over the last few weeks gave me cause regarding your mental state. No doubt you took that position in the way a captain will pose as being of sterner stuff, that he will not be seen as soft."

"Quite probably," said Smythe. "If you will excuse me, sir?"

"Aye. We'll heave to prior to darkness setting in. That, or risk an unseen shoal."

"A sensible thought."

There was lightness in the older man's step. Smythe had been under more strain than anyone had known. The success of the voyage had been fully upon his shoulders, and should it have proved a false dream, Smythe's failure would have been his ruin.

Pierce was relieved to know his navigation had been up to the task, although he vowed not to take sole credit, as the other officers had all contributed. More than once they had found errors in his daily fix. As well, he had sometimes found mistakes in their solutions. That was why he had them all plot the position each day. Now he could sail with any of them and be assured the navigation and pilotage would be of the very highest quality. They had brought *Island Expedition* through a terribly complex journey. With land in sight, proof of their skill was at hand.

Dusk fell as they drew closer to the island. They were close enough that a few details could be discerned. Pierce noticed several high peaks, some of which were covered with snow. Not wishing to approach a strange coast too closely at night, he gave the order to heave to.

"Mr. Hotchkiss, ensure the watch on deck is alert, and the watch below is ready if called. There may be hostile forces ashore. We need good lookouts to watch for shoals should we drift, or for any sign of attack."

"Aye aye, sir!"

"Mr. Harris!"

"Aye, sir?"

"You will see all guns are ready!"

"Aye aye, sir!" the gunner replied. He had not neglected his duties during the course of the voyage, but a final check of the weapons' serviceability would not be unwise. With the schooner hove to off an unfamiliar island, no one could be sure that those twelve-pounders would not be needed before morning.

"Mr. Morgan, as officer of the watch, please note that we are off an unknown shore. You will, and you will pass to your relief, the need for all hands to be alert and focused! We do not wish to drift upon a reef, nor do we wish a surprise attack."

"Aye aye, sir!"

Pierce went below. He was tired, but still he could not bring himself to dress down and crawl into his cot. Too many thoughts raced through his mind. Much of what they had seen or experienced could not be explained by any sort of logic. They had sailed on the open sea even when navigational solutions had showed them well inland, not only on Madagascar, but also in Africa and the Indian subcontinent. Now they had sighted land where none was shown on his charts, and where it surely would have been discovered in the past.

During the last few weeks, Pierce had begun to wonder if they had passed over to a world of sea and sky only. Had they gone beyond the ocean's edge? They had not sighted land since Cape Town, even though they had sailed close to many known islands, and directly over locations where land should be. Perhaps, he had thought, they would remain in this *all sea, no land* world forever, eat their slowly spoiling stores, drink their stale water, and sail on and on until all perished.

Would he ever see Evangeline again? Would he ever see his parents or brothers? Perhaps he would never again set foot on English soil. No more would he sit in some alehouse with fellow officers and tell of voyages, commissions, and desperate actions against the enemy. Never again would he be honored to discuss the service with his mentor and friend, Captain Granville Jackson. He would not even have a chance to continue the ongoing animosity with Lieutenant John Sollars.

Finding the island they had set out to locate meant a finality to the outward voyage, a point from which they could return. With the convoluted course and the time required to reach it, the island would be worthless to England or France in a strategic sense, should war resume again.

But how would he report this to the Admiralty? If he turned in reports and logbooks showing them sailing across known land masses, he would be a laughingstock. His skills would be questioned, and most certainly he would be court-martialed for incompetence. He could not explain what had transpired during the last part of the voyage, and he could not adequately defend the charges that would be brought against him.

Awake and angry that his mind would not stop working, Pierce put his uniform back on and went on deck. Midshipman Andrews now had the duty.

"How is the coffee?" asked Pierce, who noticed the steaming mug in Andrew's hands.

"Passable, sir. Hot and not too bitter. Shall I fetch some?"

"Thank you, but I'll go myself."

Pierce went down the forward companionway. He moved quietly through the crew berthing area. At the camboose he found a fairly clean mug and poured it full. The aroma that met his nose was not unpleasant. It was better than expected, based on Andrews' description. Coffee had been remarkably fresh since they had left St. Helena, and he hoped that it was not because of his ill temper that morning. He insisted that it be ready and fresh in the morning. Otherwise he would take what was available, or if it were too old, he would do without.

He was grateful for its relative freshness now. He knew he should sleep, but at the same time knew he wouldn't. He would remain awake and on deck, and hopefully not get in the way of the watch. As he tiptoed to the forward companionway, he wondered how many others aboard had trouble sleeping this night.

Pierce awoke at four bells in the morning watch. Slightly confused, he found himself seated in a folding canvas chair, with his head pillowed on a boat cloak and a gun breech. He remembered hearing eight bells as the midwatch ended, and Spencer relieving Andrews who had suggested his captain go below as he looked God-awful tired.

"Out on his feet," were the words Andrews had used. Pierce had declined, and Andrews brought the chair up from the cabin he shared with Morgan. Pierce had fallen asleep standing. Andrews had guided him to the chair, and with his boat cloak as a cushion, had let him rest his head on the gun carriage.

Sheepishly Pierce got to his feet. He hobbled because of a loss of circulation in his right leg. It burned momentarily as blood flowed back in to it. He saw Spencer, officer of the watch, nod knowingly at Townsend, midshipman of the watch. Townsend scurried forward and returned with a steaming mug of fresh coffee. "Coffee, sir? Fresh brewed, sir!"

"I thank you, Mr. Townsend. Fetch some for you and Mr. Spencer, should you want it!"

"Thank you, sir, but beg pardon, sir, we have ours."

Pierce stood by Townsend. "I hope my presence did not distract from the morning watch."

"Not at all, sir. Hardly knew you were on deck."

"I recall a time aboard *Theadora* when you slept through the watch."

"I thought we were done for, what when I awoke and saw the captain on deck, sir."

"Had it been other than Jackson, I'm sure consequences would have been most distressing."

"Painful as well, sir," said Townsend with a slight grin.

"No doubt. Let's move to starboard so these fellows do a proper job on the deck."

Together with Spencer, they moved to the starboard quarterdeck. Pierce limped slightly, as circulation had not yet fully returned. Several hands worked their way aft along the port side. The pumps had been rigged and two hands hosed the deck with seawater. The next individuals strewed sand, trying their best to spread it evenly. Five seamen came next, and on hands and knees worked their way aft, scouring the deck with holystones. The heavy stones and sand ground away the dirt and grime. Another pair of hose men rinsed the sand and dirt overboard through the scuppers.

When they reached the taffrail, the detail reformed and started forward along the starboard side. In fairness to the labor-intensive task of using the holystones, those previously so occupied now manned the hoses and the sand buckets. The former hose men and sand sprinklers manned the holystones and scrubbed the starboard deck.

The three officers moved back to port. It was growing lighter and the world, what they could see of it, was slowly colored in by the rising sun. Where the sun did not yet shine, all things were in shades of gray. A light fog lay over the water, and dimmed their view of the island. But it could be seen, although fog and clouds, gray and dismal at dawn, floated in the trees, nestled in valleys and canyons, and obscured the higher peaks.

Smythe was on deck now. "I somehow pictured this as more tropical," he said. "More as the West Indies, or St. Helena."

"What you saw when we passed each site wasn't this island?" questioned Pierce.

"Oh, I believe it was. I just did not pay attention to indications of climate. In spite of the fog and clouds, the place may be warmer than it appears."

"True, sir, and in the Southern Hemisphere, we approach winter, rather than summer."

"A rugged-looking coast line, from what I can see," said Hotchkiss as he joined them. He studied the island intensely with the glass he carried. "A hand who sailed with Vancouver said it reminds him of the more northern regions of the Pacific Coast."

"Remembering stories heard as a child," Smythe continued, "the island might be more temperate than tropical."

A commotion erupted at the forward companionway. Several passengers hauled their possessions on deck, packed and ready to go ashore.

"Avast there!" roared Pierce. "Take that dunnage below! We'll not land nor set foot ashore until we've found a suitable place! We'll explore from the sea and find a location best suited to our needs. We will make sure the place is not occupied, and if it is, make proper arrangements for our arrival."

"Well said, Captain!"

"Aye, sir. To land on this stretch of coast would be disaster. I see boats stove in, do we try. Injuries and deaths as well, sir," interjected Lieutenant Hotchkiss.

"My thoughts, exactly," said Pierce. He roared again. "Mr. Cartney! See that those belongings are sent below and stowed properly! No one on deck with dunnage!"

"Aye aye, sir!" The bo'sun and his mates shepherded the anxious passengers and their bundles below.

"Now, gentlemen," said Pierce, addressing the small congregation that had formed on the quarterdeck. "Once all have a good breakfast, we'll follow the coast south. Whenever on deck, work to chart the coast line in detail. Upon our return to this place, we will have some idea of the island's geography."

"Aye, aye, sir!" the several of them replied.

Pierce was suddenly very hungry. In the excitement of discovering the island, he had forgotten to eat. His stomach growled menacingly.

He joined the others for breakfast in the combination dining cabin, wardroom, and gunroom. He had oatmeal, white sausage, ship's biscuit, heated to soften it slightly, butter that was only slightly rancid, a final crock of raspberry jam, and as always, coffee. With all the coffee drank lately he could, no doubt, remain awake for the next three days. But as he ate, he grew sleepy, and yearned to lie down for a few minutes.

Chapter Fifteen

The First Visitor

A week and a half after landfall, *Island Expedition* eased northward along the island's east coast. She carried enough sail to give her a bit more than steerageway. With the island blocking the westerly wind, the sea was calm, stirred only by the mild breezes that survived in the island's lee. Everyone crowded the port rail to stare at what would soon be their new home.

The day after sighting the island, they had set sail, following the coast line south. The why of that direction was known only to Pierce, and if pressed, he would have admitted to a mental coin toss. Circling the island in an anti-clockwise direction had won. Many on board had thought they would go ashore at the first landfall and be done with it. They would off-load the colonists, their dunnage and supplies, give the hands a run ashore, find a stream of cold fresh water and refill the water casks. Smythe would have none of that, nor would Pierce.

The shore sighted the morning after initial discovery was not suitable for landing. There was considerable surf, evidence of reefs, sandbars, underwater rock, and other obstacles. What little beach existed was steep and rocky. The hills and cliffs started their climb to the heavens at the water's edge. Had a boat made it successfully ashore, there would virtually be no place for anyone to go. Many had grumbled when Smythe and Pierce made it clear that they would not immediately land, but reason had eventually triumphed. Sailing completely around the island would let them develop an outline of the coast and gain an idea of its size and shape. They had a chance to find a better landing site, and perhaps the ideal place to establish the colony.

Safety of both passengers and crew was also a concern. According to the old legends, the island had not been occupied for hundreds of years, although that did not mean it was uninhabited now. Voyaging around it would allow them to see smoke or other signs of human presence. Should any current residents prove hostile, it was better to discover that before landing.

Ten days later, they had not seen any evidence of recent habitation, but they had spotted remnants of those who had lived on the island long ago. On several of the headlands and sheer high cliffs, ruins of ancient stone fortifications stood. Imposing even in decay, and nearly covered with fir, spruce, cedar, and other vegetation growing rampant over them, they must have been splendidly impressive when a long-forgotten people had lived there.

The quarterdeck was more crowded than normal. Because of the island's position relative to the schooner and the wind's direction relative to both, the captain's portion of the deck was not reserved to him. The ship's officers were there, trying their best to draw a chart of the coast line. For the midshipmen and the master's mates it was a very thorough and ongoing lesson.

As per Pierce's instructions that first morning, they spent the majority of their free time on deck. When one spotted a notable feature along the coast, he sighted in on it with the ship's compass, or his own pocket compass, and obtained the relative bearing of that feature. He denoted the time that the reading was made. Later he took another bearing and again noted the exact time.

Those on watch kept a very accurate track of the schooner's movements, noting the exact time any course correction was made, and the heading upon which they settled. The vessel's position was updated and corrected each day when the noon sightings were taken. When the truest possible ship's track was added to the chart, and the hourly updates penciled in, it was fairly easy to establish where the schooner had been at the time any bearing was taken on any landmark. By taking a second sighting, they could triangulate and exactly locate the feature.

Pierce did not expect any one individual to come up with a complete map of the island. He would combine the data collected, and would use an average if the location of a particular object varied extensively. Several people were involved in this, and he was sure that they could soon have a fairly accurate map of the island.

Because of this activity, Pierce had forsaken the privileged windward side of the quarterdeck. Now, he stood patiently on the lee side and watched the activities with a calm air of indifference, although as always, he was attuned to the schooner's very being.

"It appears a rather large island, at that," said Smythe, joining him away from the bustle and activities.

"Quite large, it would appear, indeed."

"In some of the stories, it is described more as a continent."

"Then we may be a sea six months yet before returning to our start."

"Terms are relative, Captain. I presume we have already passed a good portion of the western side, the southern edge, and now have made great progress along the eastern coast. Unless it is an odd-shaped peninsula, we should be well on our way toward circumnavigating it."

"It is large enough that I cannot imagine it being uninhabited. It appears to offer much of what a people would desire in a homeland."

"The reasons for its desertion are in the stories. Even though it is referred to as a continent in some tales, what I have seen shows the size to be about what I would expect."

"We've seen several inlets. Do you fancy any of them as a place of landing?" asked Pierce.

"I daresay the one we sighted the first day along the western coast."

"With the chain of small islands along its southern edge, or a large bay or a passage between two separate isles?"

"Quite!" answered Smythe. "If this is the island for which we have searched, that bay corresponds with the legends, and would indeed make the best site upon which to go ashore."

"When we reach our starting point, we'll head there under as much sail as she'll carry."

At that instant the main topmast lookout hailed. "Deck there! Shoreline's fading to windward, sir!"

"Fading away or changing in nature, there?" shouted Hotchkiss.

"Fading away, sir. No sign northward, sir!"

Hotchkiss glanced at Pierce who nodded almost imperceptibly. The first lieutenant turned to the helmsman. "Starboard your helm! Easy, now!" Then he roared, "Hands to the sheets!"

As the wheel turned, each spoke's shadow emerged as a unique piece of light-deprived wood that crawled across the deck. Then it merged into the larger constant shadow before being replaced by another making the same journey. *Island Expedition* swung her graceful bow to the northwest, and the wind shifted from her port beam to her port bow. Under jib and mainsail only, it was simple for the well-trained and practiced crew to sheet home and properly trim the sails. Now she was only a point off of her best effort against the wind, close-hauled on the port tack.

Still, the land faded away. When it was nearly invisible, even from the masthead, Pierce ordered, "'Bout ship!" They headed southwest on a starboard tack until the shore was again in sight. Here, as the coastline ran west across the presumed northern edge of the island, they could not constantly parallel it as they had before. Their desired path was nearly into the wind, and as superb as the schooner was, even she could not sail directly into it. They tacked along this portion of the coast, making short boards to keep the land in sight. Each time they neared the shore, Pierce ordered leadsmen into the chains to take soundings.

The sun sank lower into the sky. As the fiery glowing orb touched the horizon, Pierce ordered them back on a port tack, and they stood well out to sea. When the shore was a smudge on the southern horizon, *Island Expedition* hove to.

On April 23rd they anchored in a well-protected harbor, the upper portions of the bay seen the day after sighting the island. While they had found several smaller bays that could prove serviceable, they had set course for this one, the consensus being that it offered the most of what they sought.

The bay was a large, its opening to the sea miles wide. Then it turned south, almost as an inland sea. The peninsula along the bay's western shore had high rugged hills that blocked the constant west winds. The eastern shore was a large expanse of lowlands, heavily forested but suitable for habitation. Several streams entered the bay, bringing icy waters from the far-off mountains.

Entering the confined waters, Pierce ordered leadsmen into the chains. But even with the tide at its lowest, the entire bay seemed deep enough for the largest known vessels. In the near future they would take soundings throughout and fully determine the bottom.

Ruins of old fortifications perched on the headlands they had passed. However remote the possibility of an attack, Pierce allowed that those sites would stand the establishment of shore batteries. Stowed deep in the schooner's hold were four brass nine-pounder long guns, each with a knocked-down field carriage. They would be ferried out to those headlands, hoisted, and manhandled into position in the ruins.

Farther south along that western sliver of land, and nearly opposite of where they were now anchored, the ruins of another fortress rose above the timber. That would provide an excellent lookout site. With an improvised spar and a set of signal flags, it would provide them with a nearly instantaneous warning of any approaching vessel.

Anchored securely, sails furled tightly, *Island Expedition* rolled imperceptibly in the calm waters of the bay while a gentle rain fell. Cold gray clouds hid the higher peaks and ridges, and put a chill in the air. In spite of the damp, everyone was on deck and anxious to be going ashore. Pierce knew that a more methodical approach was called for.

"Mr. Andrews! You will take the longboat, Sergeant Lincoln and ten marines! Put in there, where it looks like an old stone quay! Send the marines one way. You and the boat's crew go the other! See what's in the immediate vicinity! Mr. Smythe will go with you, should he choose. If he desires, allow him to be the first to step ashore."

"Aye aye, sir!" responded the second senior midshipman, who for the entire voyage had fulfilled duties more suited for a lieutenant.

Smythe joined in. "It is quite all right that Mr. Andrews or someone else in the landing party has the honor of first stepping ashore. I have other tasks now and daresay that I shall not go ashore for some time."

"Thank you, sir!" said Andrews. "Perhaps one of the passengers? One who will make this their home? We are only providing transportation."

"Most admirable, Mr. Andrews," said Pierce. "You do realize you pass a chance to go down in history, do you not?"

"Indeed, sir. But as I've said, such an honor should go to one who will be living here."

"Perhaps, sir, we should consider this a reconnoiter, and not record it as the official first landing. That could occur later when all are truly prepared for it," suggested Midshipman Steadman.

"I would abide that," replied Smythe.

"As would I," seconded Pierce.

"And I as well," said Andrews.

"Excellent suggestion, Mr. Steadman," offered Hotchkiss.

"Mr. Hotchkiss." Pierce spoke again. "Kindly take the cutter and go across to the southern headland! See what can be done to get the nine-pounders into the ruins! We must have some defense established as soon as possible."

"Aye aye, sir!"

"Mr. Townsend! You will take the gig and go directly across the bay! See what can be done to establish a lookout post in that tower just visible from here! We may need to rig a spar upon which to hoist signals."

"Aye aye, sir!"

"Now, everyone! All of you understand this! We believe the island to be deserted. Yet it is evident people were here at one time. Neither you nor your men are to destroy, deface, or in any other way defile any of what they may have left. Nor do you offer harm to any creature, unless it is a threat to you! Understood?"

"Aye, sir!" came the collective reply.

Pierce had mentioned the last after many conversations with Smythe during the course of the voyage. According to Smythe's recollections, the original inhabitants had been forced to leave because they had squandered away the island's rich resources. They had taken and used with abandon, and had not renewed, preserved, or conserved. Smythe was most anxious not to destroy any artifacts or ruins left behind, as these would offer invaluable information about the earlier residents. He did not wish that this present group do anything that might be seen as heresy toward or defilement of the original inhabitants' faith or beliefs.

Smythe then climbed into the lower port main shrouds. "My friends!" he shouted. "My friends!" The general uproar died away and they turned to face him.

"My friends! We have done it! We have arrived at our destination, and for that we should be thankful and most appreciative. A moment please, to thank God and Providence, or whomever you should believe responsible for our good fortune!"

He continued after an appropriate pause. "I know that we are anxious to be ashore and about our new lives. But first we must thoroughly investigate and establish our presence here. We must determine where and what will provide shelter for us. We must remember that in the Southern Hemisphere, April signifies the approach of winter, rather than summer.

"Have patience and all will soon be ashore and settled in our new homes. I will ask the captain that tomorrow we all go ashore, and being Sunday, perhaps have some manner of feast in honor of our arrival."

Indeed the next day, everyone went ashore. The weather was clear, although a bit of a chill clung to the air. A huge roaring fire was built on the beach, and as much of a special meal as could be provided from the ship's stores was prepared. Pierce allowed all but a handful of ship's company ashore as well, and then recalled some ashore to relieve and allow the remainder to also set foot in the new land.

The next day, work to establish the colony began in earnest. Having sounded the waters up to the ancient quay and finding them sufficient to float the schooner, *Island Expedition* was warped alongside and gangways rigged. They had brought with them immense quantities of canvas and sail cloth, rolled, folded, and stored in the hammock nettings which were not used for such. Should nothing else be available, this material would provide tents for shelter until more permanent structures could be erected. Three large tents were indeed set up, one for families, one for single men, and one for unaccompanied women. Two slightly smaller tents provided a headquarters and a communal kitchen.

Smythe's thought, he had once told Pierce, had been to construct houses of wood, similar to the cabins on the American frontier, built of logs stacked one atop the other. But as they explored the area, he realized that many of the ruins were dwellings for individual families. Many were in a remarkable state of repair and needed only a good cleaning to be habitable again. All evidenced features of construction designed to provide warmth in winter and coolness in the summer. Smythe suggested that it would be more expeditious to use structures already in place. That was agreed to, but he cautioned them all not to claim any particular structure until he had a chance to look it over. He did not want anyone cleaning out a new home without first determining that nothing of historical significance remained.

On Wednesday the 18th of May, Pierce awoke at four bells in the morning watch. He had slept in the headquarters tent in spite of the custom, tradition, and the rule that a ship's captain sleep aboard every night. But here, thousands of miles from any naval authority, and only yards from his ship, Pierce relaxed that rule to allow himself a night ashore.

It was cold and he momentarily wished to dive back into the warmness of his cot. Pierce dressed quickly and peered out the flaps of the tent, both at the shoreline and the hills behind him. Frost lay heavy on the ground and clung to the trees and bushes. Puddles from yesterday's rain were iced over.

A week after their arrival and first landing, Pierce had revised the ship's routine. While the crew was still divided into port, starboard, and amidships watches, they did not rotate every four hours as at sea. Instead, each watch was on duty for a twenty-four-hour period. The *on deck watch* remained aboard and tended to normal work and routine upkeep. They rotated the few actual duties amongst themselves, and if not actually required to be awake, slept on board. The *watch below* helped out aboard *Island Expedition*, or went ashore to help with various projects in the colony. When they knocked off following the day's work, they were off duty. The *off watch* was duty-free throughout the day and the next morning would be on board as the *on deck watch*.

Pierce included himself and his officers in this arrangement. He took charge of the starboard watch, gave charge of the port watch to Hotchkiss, and direction of the amidships watch to O'Brien. Morgan, Andrews, and Spencer acted as second in charge of each watch. Today the starboards were off duty, and Pierce planned take full advantage. He knew Hotchkiss and O'Brien would keep both the watch on deck and the watch below busy for the day.

Perhaps he would take a newly constructed punt, row across, and explore around the lookout and signal tower. He would get a loaf of bread, some sliced salt beef, some cheese, and a bottle of wine. He would traipse through the woods and scramble over rocks like a lad half his age. He could leave the cares, worries, and responsibilities of command behind for a part of the day. Although the morning was cold, complete with frost on the ground, the sky was clear. The day promised to be bright and warm like many they had already experienced.

He particularly relished the thought of a meal alone, where he could eat his fill of the newly made soft bread. An oven had been built ashore, and with what remained of the flour, several loaves had been baked, and more were being made daily. It was delicious and easy to chew, heaven on the palate, compared to the tough stale ship's biscuit, the hard tack that they had eaten for so long. The hardtack did keep for months aboard ship, spoiled only by the usual bargemen or weevils.

But first he needed a cup of coffee. His nose told him that coffee was making, and at the cook's tent on the quay, he found it ready. Halfway into his second cup, Pierce chatted idly with Smythe and watched the sun's rays break through the gray mists and burn away last night's frost. He had plans for the day, a rare chance to get away from his duties and responsibilities, and yet there was no hurry to set about it. As he was about to take another sip of coffee, Mr. Steadman, the day's duty midshipman, appeared at the tent flap. "Beg pardon, sir. Mr. Hotchkiss sent me."

Pierce felt the comfort of a rare and much-needed day off fade away. His first thought was to tell Steadman to report that the captain could not be found. His second was to jump on the midshipman for the quality of his shave and send him back aboard, suitably chastened and mentally beaten. He fought down the growing temptation to act on either of the ideas. The mood of the day, the expectation of a day of leisure was gone, and he struggled within not to betray his sudden gloom as he asked, "Well, sir, what is it?"

"Mr. Hotchkiss, sir. He says to tell you the lookout is signaling, sir. A small boat or canoe is approaching the bay, sir."

"Very well. Tell Mr. Hotchkiss that I will be there shortly!"

"Aye aye, sir!" Steadman moved quickly enough that Pierce could not hasten him further with a derogatory comment. At that moment, he wanted very much to do that.

"Visitors?" questioned Smythe. His coffee cup was nearly empty, but the slices of bacon between two of bread were nearly untouched. The food sat on a plate on his improvised desk.

"It would appear so."

"Any danger or threat?"

"I doubt it. If it is a small craft or canoe they cannot be any real danger to us, should they in fact be hostile."

"I have wondered how long before we had contact with any people in the area. And now it appears that my wonderment is being answered."

"Aye. While I do not see any danger, I'll see that proper steps are taken to fight the ship." Pierce finished the coffee left in his cup and threw the dregs outside. "Now, I'll go see what this is about." He headed for the schooner.

Pierce bounded up the gangway and stepped aboard. There was no ceremonial piping or other time-honored tradition to welcome him aboard. That was as he would have it with the vessel made fast to the quay and everyone coming and going with regularity. He saluted the quarterdeck and the Blue Ensign flying from the staff. Hotchkiss returned the salutes.

"Welcome aboard, sir," he said.

"I imagine it is good to be back after one night," commented Pierce a little testily. "Now, what is going on? I did have plans for the day, and...."

"So sorry that you've been unaccommodated, sir. The lookout has signaled. A small craft, evidently a canoe, is paralleling the outer coast, northbound."

"Have they an idea of the number of men onboard?"

"No exact number, but no more than two or three dozen, if that."

The lieutenant continued on after his captain did not immediately respond to that information. "I daresay, sir, with that small a force, if it is a force, they pose us absolutely no threat."

"You are quite right, I'm sure. All the same, we will make preparations. See that the duty marines are in full kit, ready to repel an attack, or to act as honor guard if we welcome them as visitors."

"Aye aye, sir."

"And the second-best bower out a half cable length! Springs to the capstan should we need to fire anywhere other than our immediate broadside!"

"Beat to quarters? Recall the off watch?"

"We'll not need to do that. It will take the canoe the better part of the morning to round the point and come down the inlet. You may choose to see the seaward guns loaded and ready to run out!"

"Aye, sir! The watch below on board or close at hand? Mr. O'Brien said he would have them ashore later in the day."

"I had such thoughts myself, but the situation does not warrant. Except for what we've discussed, today, at least the morning should be as any other."

"Quite so, sir. Will you remain on board?"

"I think not, Mr. Hotchkiss. We have time yet, and I will take some slight advantage as a member of the off watch. I'll return by eight bells in the forenoon watch, earlier if necessary. If I wander off, I'll leave word ashore as to where I can be found."

"Aye, sir."

Pierce saluted the quarterdeck and the Blue Ensign again, and stepped ashore. His salutes again were returned by Lieutenant Hotchkiss.

Pierce looked at the cutter nearly halfway across the bay, ferrying over those that would man the lookout for the next twenty-four hours. The men presently at the station would be back in an hour or two, and he could speak with those who had actually seen the mysterious craft.

He would get honest, direct answers to his questions, as most considered lookout duty to be a privilege. Manning the remote site allowed them to get away from the schooner and the officers, and was almost an overnight picnic. Normally three or four hands and a petty officer were detailed for the day. They took their own food, plenty of water, and a limited supply of spirits. Pierce knew the British tar's propensity to overindulge should the opportunity be available, and thus he strictly limited how much was allowed. He required they remain alert and signal the approach of any vessel to *Island Expedition*. However, the men made arrangements to divide up duties and rest periods amongst themselves.

Six bells in the forenoon watch. Pierce had finished speaking with the off-going lookouts. Steadman again found him to say that the canoe had altered course to round the northern tip of the peninsula. Apparently the craft intended to enter the bay. In another hour they would be able to see it from *Island Expedition*.

"Thank you, Mr. Steadman. Tell Mr. Hotchkiss that I shall return aboard at eight bells."

"Aye aye, sir!"

As eight bells sounded, Pierce again went aboard His Britannic Majesty's Schooner. He exchanged formalities and a few pleasantries with Andrews, who now had the watch, and went below to his cabin. He fetched his best glass, returned to the deck, and immediately climbed the main shrouds.

He reached the main topmast crosstrees and made himself comfortable. He hadn't been aloft in some time, but the instinct and habits learned in years at sea were not forgotten. Soon he felt he as if had been aloft daily for the past several months. What bothered him was pressure on parts of his body not used to such a perch. He trained his glass at the point where the strange craft should soon appear. Pierce did not have to wait long. He had lowered the glass momentarily to wipe away the tears caused by the cool stiff breeze. When he resumed scanning the headland, the canoe was visible.

As he watched, the canoe altered course gradually, and it now headed almost directly at him. It drew closer, and with his glass he was able to distinguish many details. It was a large craft, forty or so feet long, as estimated against the figures on board. Closer examination showed that the craft was not one canoe, but two. The two hulls, each carved from a single giant log, were connected by a sturdy platform that ran slightly above the gunnels for nearly the entire length. A single sail was set on a stay leading from the bows to a bipod mast that stepped well aft. It was in effect a single gigantic jib or staysail. To Pierce it may not have been the ideal rig, but it obviously aided the men along each side, who paddled strongly in unison.

Sore from his unaccustomed time aloft, Pierce returned to the deck. He came sedately down the shrouds rather than hand over hand down the backstays. He no longer trusted the strength and sureness of his grip to do as he had done when a midshipman.

On deck he spoke with both Hotchkiss and Andrews. He cautioned them to ensure the hands acted properly, that they showed proper respect for the approaching visitors, and that they did not allow the strangers' appearance or attire to affect their decorum. Then he went ashore and passed the same request to Mr. O'Brien for the watch below, busy within the colony.

Back on board he went forward and again trained his glass on the canoe. It was closer now and he could make out more detail. While it was hard to get an exact count, he estimated that eight or nine were along each side, digging their paddles forcefully into the water. Another dozen or so stood on deck between the hulls. At times he could see an individual seated upon an elaborate chair forward of the mast. Most were dressed in what looked like buckskin. The strangers resembled North American Indians as pictured in the book that Hotchkiss' father had. The bows were carved into stylized representations of various animals and were painted in bright and nearly garish colors.

By four bells in the afternoon watch, the canoe was close enough that Pierce could hear the rhythmic chant as the paddlers drove it rapidly through the water. As the paddles lifted in unison, their wetness caught the sunlight and flashed brilliantly.

Off *Island Expedition's* port bow, a word was shouted in an unknown language. The paddling stopped instantly. Swiftly the huge single sail was gotten in, the mast unstepped and stowed, and at another word, the paddles resumed their work. A drum set the tempo for the paddlers' stroke. A new and different chant accompanied it.

The strange craft passed smartly along the schooner's port side.

One of the hands detailed to grease the forward carronade's elevating screw observed, "No doubt, Jack! Gotta be them noble savages we been hearin' about."

"Aye, Tom. But noble?" answered his mate.

As the comment was made, the individual on the chair turned slightly and looked directly at the schooner. His face remained blank and he resumed his forward gaze.

Pierce glared. "Belay that, I say! You will keep your opinions to yourselves. Report for duty with tomorrow's watch on deck!"

"Aye aye, sir!" They were embarrassed at being overheard by their captain, and most assuredly dismayed that they would have another day's duty before any liberty was granted.

The canoe continued on. The strong rhythmic paddling drove it forward at speed. It was astern of the schooner now, and Pierce wondered what they were about. Soon they passed the end of the quay and were off a gently sloping gravelly beach.

At another word in that unknown tongue, the portside paddlers held their blades in the water. Twin steering paddles were put over, and the starboard paddlers exploded with a flurry of strokes. The canoe spun to point her bows at the beach. All the paddlers gave four powerful strokes and the bows slid onto the gravel. The paddlers jumped over the side and with a mighty unified grunt hauled the craft farther up the beach. One on the forward portion of the deck leapt ashore and made a line fast around a tree stump. He returned aboard and helped the others extend a portion of the deck forward and down to provide a ramp to shore. The old man on the chair moved. He stood and twisted slightly, stiff from sitting for a long time. With great deliberateness he proceeded forward and down the ramp.

Pierce hurriedly left the schooner and was joined by Smythe, Townsend, Dial, and O'Brien. They met the old man and four of his companions abreast the starboard quarter. The other strangers remained with the canoe. Their postures were guarded, but they showed no sign of hostility.

Both groups stopped when they were two paces apart. Pierce wondered how they would communicate. The old man stepped forward, cleared his throat deliberately, and said. "Not savage! Not noble! Me Shostolamie! Dream chief, Kalish People!" He grinned slightly and looked at the schooner, at those who had made the disparaging remark. The old man's eye twinkled.

Smythe stepped forward. "Harold Smythe, leading this expedition to find and settle the island. Captain Pierce, commanding His Majesty's schooner, *Island Expedition*."

Pierce took a small step forward. "And the ship's officers." He gestured, indicating those he spoke of.

Shostolamie extended his hand. "You do when meet," he said, and solemnly shook everyone's hand. He named the four with him, and after each introduction, that individual solemnly and rigidly shook hands with the English contingent.

The ceremonies of the initial meeting over with, the old man said, "Me chief! You chief! We talk!"

Chapter Sixteen

A Different World

"You have had a long journey," said Smythe. "Would you rest or have something to eat and drink? The others at your boat?"

"Shostolamie not hungry now. We drink and talk. Other Kalish have food, have water. Stay at canoe. Guard canoe. Watch far away you not kill dream chief. You not kill Kalish!"

"We would not consider such a thing!" Pierce addressed the old man directly. "You would believe such of us?"

"Happen sometimes," stated Shostolamie. "Strangers think Kalish People not smart. Say this, mean that. Make promise, not keep. Say protect. Kill! Destroy!"

"I hope that is in the past," said Smythe. "Such things are known to us as well. It is an extreme belief in one's own superiority, or extreme contempt for those felt inferior."

"Many words, Stranger Chief Smythe! Me un'stand. All people different. All people same. Different people not bad people."

"Well put," volunteered Hotchkiss, who joined them.

"I would hope we each see the people we are," continued Smythe, "and not the outward differences. Then we may make progress."

"Many words, Stranger Chief. What do, what not do, that say more."

Pierce understood Shostolamie's wariness. Contact between different cultures was always a perilous undertaking. One usually believed itself superior and felt the other to be of lesser worth. He recalled several historical instances that fit. From the beginning of the European conquest of the Americas, native peoples had been subjugated, conquered, enslaved, and betrayed. Obviously the Kalish had

had other contacts, perhaps with Europeans, and had experienced the bitter and vile taste of broken promises. For reasons unknown, these Kalish now sought contact with a new group, but the pain of past contacts, conflicts, and betrayals put them in a defensive mode.

"You and your friends are most welcome, Dream Chief Shostolamie," responded Smythe. "We will eat soon, and you may join us. Now, we will hear what you have to say. This way, please!"

"Well, very good!" said the old man with a slightly pompous air. Pierce wondered if the pomposity was ego or a disguise for the relief felt at the relatively warm reception. Perhaps the dream chief's initial refusal to eat had also been one of wariness.

There was a brief scramble at the headquarters tent as they improvised a conference table. Various crates, kegs, chests, and barrels were finally arranged so all could sit comfortably. Should anyone have a drink at hand, there was a place for it as well. Out of habit and for self- protection, Shostolamie and the four Kalish sat where they could see the entrance. Still wary, they did not wish anyone to approach unseen.

When everyone was finally seated, Smythe said, "You have something to say to us, Chief Shostolamie. Say what you will!"

"Thank you, Stranger Chief Smythe." He stood and cleared his throat again. Was this a way to overcome nervousness? "Say before, me Shostolamie! Me Dream Chief, Kalish People!"

"Dream chief?" asked Hotchkiss.

"Me tell what dreams mean. What dreams say. Somebody have dream. Troubled. Tell me dream. I tell what it say. Sometimes me dream. Dream tell about Kalish People. Dream tell about whole world."

"A clairvoyant, perhaps?" suggested Townsend.

"Not clairvoyant! Dream Chief!" The tiniest bit annoyed, the old man scowled ferociously but with no real menace at Townsend and continued. "One time have dream. Have big dream. Three times moon eat good, get fat. Three times moon no eat. Moon get small. All bone. Go away. Me come here."

"You had a dream and three months later you have come here?"

"Me say that. Tell you dream?"

"Certainly."

"Tell what dream say, not what dream was. Different. Dream chief know what dream say from what dream is."

"Fine, sir," said Smythe. "If you would tell us?"

"Dream say, 'Shostolamie, take big canoe. Go Island of Ancient Ones. Go Island of Stone Lodges. Go Stone Island. Strangers there from another world. Different world. Look like strangers, talk like strangers in Kalish People's Land. Not same. New strangers help Kalish People. Help all people. All People make strong nation. Someday land of Kalish People be great nation."

"I am sorry to say, Shostolamie, that we are not here to help anyone with battles or conquests. We are simply attempting to find...."

"Me know. Your people leave home. Chiefs say bad. You say they not. Come here. Bring here. Not in cage. Not beaten. Here they free."

"Well, yes," said Smythe, amazed at the old man's accurate and brief assessment of his mission. "How do you know all this?"

"Me Shostolamie, Dream Chief, Kalish People."

"I daresay, Mr. Smythe, he has you at that," said O'Brien. "We were nearly to St. Helena before I figured out our purpose. He's here half an hour and understands as well as we do."

"I'm afraid you are both right. I am astounded that you know so much about us. But we are not prepared, nor do we desire any part in local warfare or power struggles."

"Aye," said Townsend, broaching a thought that had also occurred to Pierce. "What if this is a French trick?"

"French? What French?" asked the chief, who appeared to be genuinely confused.

"A people much like us," said Pierce, "They speak a different tongue and have a different chief. For many years they have been our enemy. Currently there is peace between us, but...."

"French? Never hear those people. You talk Kentish like strangers in Kalish Lands, but you not Kentish."

"We are English. Some might be from Kent, but there are other places in England. There are other British kingdoms, all with the same king or chief. Some amongst us are originally from France, some from America, and elsewhere. The tongue we speak is English."

"Shostolamie no hear these peoples, no hear these nations, no hear those tribes. Different peoples! Different world! In Kalish Lands strangers from Kentland. Speak Kentish. Some strangers Picts. Some strangers Galwaians. All Tritonish. Kentish people, Tritonish people all time fight Gallicians. Big war now."

"Gallicians?" asked Pierce. "Do you know any of their words? Any of their tongue?"

"Me know good, like me know Kentish."

"What sort of things would a Gallician say?"

"Call man 'M'sieur.' Say 'Oui.' Words like water over rocks in river. Speak fast fast. Hard listen. Hard un'stand. Hard hear what say. Hard know what mean. Kentish speak slow. Words clear like water in lake."

"Thank you, Chief Shostolamie," said Pierce as the reality of the situation sank in. "I think I understand now."

He was silent for a moment. After collecting his thoughts he turned to the others. "When the chief said he came here to meet strangers from a different world, that is exactly what he meant. We are from a *different world*! It is not Old World versus New as the Americas relate to Europe. It is a *new* and *different world*."

"I don't see that it could be possible!" exclaimed O'Brien. "We know exactly where we are on the charts. We did not fly through the heavens to any planets that are said to be worlds as well!"

"Consider, Mr. O'Brien, that we speak of charts that show no island this size after there have been many, many voyages through this very area? Remember as well, our track on that chart has us voyaging over solid ground, miles inland from well-known and established coast lines."

"A bit puzzling, I must admit," said the sailing master. "I still would suggest, sir, that perhaps there is an error in the charts? Perhaps an error in our navigation?"

"An error in the charts? Certainly that cannot account for the distance inland we show our passage to be in places. Navigation? It is unlikely that all could have erred so much and in the same way. Surely, sir, one would have detected such an error. I do not hold your protestations against you. I appreciate your role as devil's advocate, but do consider the possibility of what I propose.

"And remember," continued Pierce, "each time we crossed the specified points along our path, everyone on board reacted differently. Further, do you recall that our next fix often placed us hundreds of miles from where we should have or could have been? Perhaps those points were the steps of a ladder, one taking us out of our world and into a new one."

"Quite a stretch, I admit," said Smythe. "Yet it fits with what has transpired. We followed the exact and precise route so the island would be here when we reached it. I understood there to be some mystery in achieving our goal, but I never thought we would, in fact, journey to a completely different world."

Pierce went on. "In this world there are apparently parallels with the world we know. We speak English, but here, the same tongue is Kentish. Things are the same and yet they are different. The Gallicians must be the equivalent of the French."

"It would seem to be so, Captain Pierce," remarked Smythe. "Chief Shostolamie, do you follow the reasoning?"

Shostolamie huffed a bit. "One man, that man," he pointed at Pierce with his chin. "Un'stand what Shostolamie say. Different world! Me say that."

"I can't say it's the Gospel truth," said Townsend. "As a working theory, I'll go along with it. As the captain says, it may be related to our experiences when we crossed those points."

"No doubt, Mr. Townsend," agreed Hotchkiss. "Those were indeed some remarkable experiences. Crossing those points may have had a greater effect than we realize."

"It is difficult to comprehend, and yet it appears the best explanation of our presence here," said Smythe. "But we must remain true to our original purpose. We must not become involved in any conflicts in this world. We must remain loyal to our world, and not be diverted by events in any parallel nations we find here."

"You say, Harold Smythe, Chief of Stranger People. You believe. One day, someday, things different maybe. Someday soon. Then help Kalish People. Help all people in Kalish Lands. Someday soon. That me say." Shostolamie abruptly folded his arms across his chest, grunted, and nodded his head for emphasis.

"I seriously doubt that we'll change his mind, sir," said Townsend to Smythe.

"Mind no change. Mind like jaws of bear. Not let go. No can change. Dreams tell me! No can change what will be!"

Smythe took a different tack and said, "Perhaps we are too hasty to reject your predictions and expectations. We shall need to see what happens, and then perhaps we can act upon them. At this point, we will not promise any help, but we will not deny it outright."

"Good for now. But you see! Someday you help all people in Kalish Lands!"

Eight bells sounded, marking the end of the afternoon watch and time for supper. Many settlers were already preparing meals in their new homes. Others ate at the communal kitchen along the quay. Ship's company ashore ate there as well, while the watch on deck had their meals delivered. A small fire in the galley stove reheated food prepared ashore and provided hot coffee, tea, or cocoa for those on board.

Pierce was hungry. He had had coffee early that morning, and had sampled a bite of freshly baked bread, but that was all. "Gentlemen," he said. "I believe it is time for supper. Shall we?"

"Of course, Captain," said Smythe. "Chief Shostolamie and his party would join us?"

"What eat?"

"I would imagine there will be salt beef, boiled until tender. Perhaps some vegetables, seasoned for flavor. We'll have freshly baked soft bread. Much better and easier to chew than ship's biscuit."

"Jones caught several salmon in the stream to the south," added Hotchkiss. "Eubanks said they would be ready for this evening's supper as well."

"A welcome change from the ship's stores."

The chief sniffed, for the smell of cooking wafted through the flaps of the tent. "Think me not hungry. Smell food. Smell it cook. Now hungry, we eat!"

He spoke to the four who accompanied him. They smiled and spoke amongst themselves. One left quite hurriedly. "Bring others at canoe."

Together the English and the Kalish stepped to the cook's tent. Soon, everyone had a plate or platter of food and a glass or mug of drink. The Kalish refused to drink any spirits, and settled for water. The old chief's eyes brightened when he saw that coffee was available, and he returned to the headquarters tent with his platter piled high and his mug full to the rim with coffee. The Kalish who had been with Shostolamie remained and ate in the tent, but the others returned to the beach and their canoe.

As the meal drew to a close, Smythe suggested, "Perhaps, Chief, you would tell us of your land, and the troubles that beset it?"

"Indeed, sir!" interjected Pierce. "It would help us to know where it is." He took a sip of coffee.

"This smart man," said Shostolamie. "Drink coffee. Me drink coffee.

Me Dream Chief!" He chuckled, amused that he and Pierce both had an affinity for the hot brew. "Coffee good drink, but water better. Tell Kalish people not drink rum. Make crazy. No remember. Not good drink rum. Not good drink wine."

"Sage advice. But of your lands?"

"Where Kalish people live since time of Ancient Ones. Kalish People. Touroc People. Yaida People. Many People. All people like Kalish People live there. Life good. Hunt, fish, grow corn, grow pumpkin. Eat good, make babies. Fight other people, take corn, take pumpkins! Stop fight, have feast. Make babies. Life good!

"When Grandfather's Grandfather's Grandfather little boy. When voice still like woman voice, strangers come. Strangers look yellow rock, shine like sun. Strangers look rock, shine like water in sun. Strangers bring gifts to Kalish People. Bring gifts all people. Strangers say, 'This not your land. Go away! We give these, you give us land.'

"We say, 'No, land not to give. Land for all. We not go.' Still we say, 'Thank you what give us.' Strangers say, 'Give you iron pot, you give us land. Go!' We say, 'No! Kalish People not go!'

"Strangers mad. Bring sickness. Make Kalish People sick. Make other people sick. Many die! Kalish fight strangers. Many die. Soon only little bit Kalish People in Kalish land. Only little bit Touroc People in Touroc Land. Little bit Yaida People in Yaida Land! Little bit people in any land!

"More strangers come every day. Strangers like stars. Strangers fight other strangers! Kentish fight Gallicians, fight Cordobians. Cordobians fight Gallicians. Everybody fight everybody. Strangers make Kalish People, make Touroc People fight. Tell People to fight other People. Tell fight other strangers. More die!

"When Shostolamie young man, not Dream Chief, Kentish strangers in Kalish Lands have big anger with Kentish in Kentish Lands. Big fight. Say, 'No treat like Kentish people. Maybe we not Kentish. Maybe we Vespicans. Listen no more, big chief beyond big water.'"

"A revolt?"

"Sounds like the American War," commented O'Brien.

"Indeed," answered Pierce. He turned to the old man and asked, "Were they successful?"

"Land called, 'Vespican In' pendant Lands.' Tell Kentish strangers go away. Kentish go."

"Quite similar to the United States," remarked Pierce.

"And now?" urged Smythe.

"Now big trouble! This many lands." Shostolamie held up all ten fingers. "This many great chiefs." The ten fingers remained. "Each land have council. Great council for all lands. Great council say, 'Do this,' council in one land say, 'We not do.' Nobody do. Fight all time what do. No fight with weapons. Fight with words. Nothing happen."

"It would appear," said Hotchkiss, "their independence is not without faults."

"Aye, sir!" put in Townsend. "An ineffectual government, it would appear."

"The Americans went through much the same," offered Pierce. "But they adopted their written constitution and seem destined for a great prosperity."

"We know, sir, you have an admiration for the Yanks!" said O'Brien. "Mind you, sir, I'm not to be seen complaining of it."

"I did not notice you were," continued Pierce. "I allow that I hold a certain admiration for our former countrymen. They are engaged in a noble experiment, and lately it appears they may well succeed."

"Aye!"

"But what of this world?" asked Townsend. "What of the Vespicans? How does that affect us?"

"That is a question that I must evaluate further, Mr. Townsend. Now would you kindly pass the decanter this way, good sir?" Smythe poured a little Port into his long-empty glass. He took a sip but did not swallow for a long moment.

After he did finally swallow, he looked at the Kalish dream chief. "Chief Shostolamie, are we in any danger here?"

"Danger, Harold Smythe?"

"Yes. Is there any threat to us here? From the Kentish, the Gallicians, the Cordobians, or anyone else? We are few in number. Will we need to defend ourselves?"

"Island sacred for Kalish and other Peoples. Strangers afraid to come here."

"Is there any threat on the island?"

"Not worry. Ancient Ones say you belong here. Ancient Ones know you here. Dreams say you here. Dreams say island for you."

"Quite reassuring, Chief, but why are strangers afraid to come here?"

"Long time past, strangers come. Make houses. Dig yellow rock that shine like sun. One day somebody die. One day yellow rock all gone. Bad things happen. Strangers afraid, go away. Other strangers come, make houses, look for yellow rock. Plant food, like Kalish plant corn, plant squash, plant pumpkins. Soon everything die. Strangers leave, no come here again."

"And the same will not happen to us, Chief?"

"Say before, not worry. You belong island!"

"I hope you are right, Chief," said Pierce. "But where are the Kalish Lands?"

"There!" He looked toward the east.

"Far?"

"Paddle, sail twelve suns find island. Paddle two suns, find you."

"I see. Would it be unwise to sail and look at your lands?"

"Want to see? Go see."

"Would there be any danger?"

Shostolamie thought for a moment and said, "No can say no danger. Always danger on big water. Storm break ship, sink ship. Maybe pirates take ship. Maybe Gallicians see, think you Kentish ship. Maybe Kentish see, think you Gallician ship. Always danger, go big water."

"Are many Kentish and Gallician ships hereabouts?"

"Few. Most far away, close to own lands." He looked to the west and thrust his jaw in that direction. "Far away. Far away."

"You are thinking to go to sea?" asked Smythe.

"I am. We should have some knowledge of the surrounding area. Nor is it good for the hands to be ashore more than need be. They need to be at sea, refreshed in the duties and skills that erode while here."

"I see."

"You prefer we remain?"

"No, I do not hold you. You will need to leave, as it is. You must return and make your reports to the Admiralty and the Organization. My reports must be delivered as well."

"True enough," yawned Pierce. "Excuse me."

"Good sign," said Shostolamie. "Talk long time. Eat good. Bellies full. Everybody sleep now. Talk when sun come back."

"It is late," said Hotchkiss. "I must return aboard to give Mr. Andrews his relief."

"May we offer you a place, Chief?"

"Stay with Kalish People, come with me."

"Why to be sure, I did mean the whole of your group."

"Me know. Stay Kalish People. Sleeping robes in canoe. We go now." The dream chief spoke briefly to his companions. Abruptly they got to their feet and left.

All day Pierce had debated whether to stay ashore, or return aboard and spend the night in his cabin. As their guests departed he made up his mind. "Mr. Hotchkiss, I shall return aboard with you. I fear that I would not sleep well anywhere but in my own cabin."

"Aye, sir."

A hint of frost hung in the air, and with the stars clear and countless, the prospect of a truly cold night faced them. Aboard *Island Expedition*, Pierce filled a brazier with coals from the small fire in the galley stove. It would ward off the chill in his cabin.

He carelessly tossed his hat on the writing desk, and hung his uniform coat over the chair. Although the cabin was cold, he dressed down and slipped on his night shirt. This was his one indulgence toward personal comfort for the night. It felt good to get out of the clothes he had worn all day, and some he had worn since the day before. A good, really hot bath would feel wonderful now. But it was too cold, and he was tired enough to not let such strange desires have much of a hold on him. He slipped into his cot, recoiled from the cold linens, and thrashed about vigorously as he attempted to generate a little warmth. He wondered if Mr. Gray had followed his orders and had issued additional blankets. An arm appeared and lay across the blankets. Not so overbearingly cold, Pierce again relaxed and sank deeper into blessed unconsciousness.

Then thoughts of the day's events and conversations wormed their way to the forefront of his remaining consciousness. The overpowering desire to sleep lessened and he was awake. There were so many things to think of. The thoughts ran through his mind and played in his head like great fleets of ships in the confusion of battle.

Try as he might, he could not accept being in a world different from where he had grown up and served King and Country. Yet proof was there, as much as could be found, and it all indicated the impossible. Were he to rise and look at their track on the charts, it would show them sailing across both land and sea. This island was right where the old legends said it was, but it was not on any modern chart. Being a landmass of relatively large size, why had it not been previously charted? That it wasn't offered proof that the island was in a different world.

From his name, appearance, and indeed his language, Shostolamie and his companions were comparable to North American Indians. How did the chief know they were here? Pierce put no stock in the supposed abilities of others to divine the future, although he acknowledged and even believed a little in luck. He felt it sometimes played pivotal roles in battles at sea, but he allowed that skill, knowledge, and training played a bigger part. Alongside an enemy ship, he would be more confident that his gun crews' skills would carry the day, rather than hope for a lucky shot to strike a fatal blow.

How strange that they had left England and sailed halfway around the world, only to find themselves in a situation nearly the same as what they had left. His England and this Kentland were apparently much the same. How closely parallel, he didn't know. He was aware that the same language was spoken, and that both had lost colonies across the sea. But was Kentland the same as England in other matters? Did the average Kentishman enjoy the same freedoms and liberties as did the average Englishman? Was there a King George the Third on Kentland's throne?

The Vespicans must be equivalent to the Americans, their name apparently derived from the last, rather than the first name of the continent's namesake. Pierce could admire them as he did the former British colonists of America, especially since the Vespicans were not former British subjects who had rebelled against his king. These people had fought and won their independence from a sovereign not his, a monarch to whom he would never owe any allegiance.

Smythe preferred the colony avoid outside contact, either here or in the world whence they came. He wanted them self-supporting and self-sufficient. But they would not be able to obtain all they needed on the island. To send to England or to acquire needed items by force or deceit would be highly impractical and dangerous. It would make more sense to establish contact with some nation or group in this world. Their presence would eventually become known, and it would be best to be allied with someone -- if not for defense, at least for trade and commerce.

But with whom? Kentland was too far away, and even its equivalency with England might pose a problem. They might be expected to swear fealty to the Kentish Crown and become a Kentish colony.

Gallicia and Cordoba were apparently close enough to France and Spain that they would not want anything to do with them. A forced allegiance would be swiftly obtained and brutally kept. With the many years of war had fought against both France and Spain, he could not see any relationship with this world's variants.

Pierce reasoned that the little colony of former British convicts would do best to establish contact with the Vespicans. Even that would require a great deal of caution, should Smythe see that as an option. Would the Vespicans see commonality with them and not be threatened by their Englishness -- or indeed their Kentishness?

In the near future, Pierce would take *Island Expedition* to sea and learn what he could about this new world. Now he would sleep. He heard the quiet muffled sound of eight bells as it sounded the end of the evening watch. He heard the quiet voice of the ship's sentry announcing that all was well. Midnight, and indeed time to sleep. His eyes closed again; this time they stayed closed, and his awareness faded into the dark.

Chapter Seventeen

Exploring a New World

The clang of the ship's bell jarred Pierce awake. He hadn't slept enough and wanted to roll over and return to the comfortable world of his dreams. In the instant of wakefulness, he thought it was oddly bright for that time of day. The footsteps and voices of crewmen on deck were muffled and quiet, more so than if they were taking extra care not to disturb him.

He could not fall back asleep. Awake now, memories of yesterday's events flooded his consciousness. From their visitors, they had learned the supposed truth about the island. Today they would meet again with the visitors and hopefully have any unresolved questions answered. Beyond that, he had plans for the future employment of His Majesty's Schooner *Island Expedition*.

He threw back the blankets, swung his legs over, and sat up. Damn, it was cold! He thought again about remaining in the warmth of his cot. Rejecting that option, he found his slippers, wrapped a blanket about him, and went forward.

With the passengers gone, he could proceed along the lower deck to the galley. He toted one of his mugs, although he wasn't sure if coffee would be ready. Lately he had allowed that requirement to ease, as coffee was nearly always available in the cook's tent. Should none be available this morning, he vowed not to begrudge the cook. Still, he fervently hoped that someone had the foresight to provide fresh coffee.

As expected, several hands were gathered around the warmth of the stove. As Pierce approached, they stiffened to attention and made way. "Stand easy, lads," he said. "I am still in the off watch and not yet ready for the day. I only seek coffee, should any be had, and perhaps some hot water that I might shave."

"Aye, sir."

"Mornin', sir."

"And morning to you as well," Pierce said.

"You're in luck, Captain," said Franklin, the cook's mate. "Coffee's made not more than half hour ago, sir. Here, let me fill that for you."

"Thank you, Franklin. And might there be hot water available?"

"Certainly, sir. On the forward side, sir. Some help?"

"Thank you, but I shall manage."

Perhaps Pierce should have accepted the offer. With the kettle in one hand and his mug in the other, he had a devilish time keeping the blanket about him. Finally the blanket slipped away; he shivered in the cold morning air, and hurried the remaining way to his cabin. He set the hot water and coffee down and retrieved the blanket.

Minutes later, Pierce had sparingly washed, shaved, and had put on clean clothes. Because of the cold, he wore heavier wool stockings, and seaman's duck trousers and boots, rather than silk stockings, breeches, and shoes. He wore a knit fisherman's jersey, a gift from his mother, under his shirt. Because of its bulk, he tied his neckerchief loosely around his neck, in the manner of the lower deck.

When he arrived topside, the cause of the extraordinary brightness was apparent. The night before, the skies had been clear, and an endless number of stars had twinkled in the heavens. During the early morning hours, clouds had come, borne on a steady, gentle wind. They had dropped their contents, not as rain, but as snow. A layer of powdery white coated the deck, rigging, and spars. Stepping on deck, he nearly slipped in the snow.

Hotchkiss was aft, his neckerchief tied over his ears to keep them warm. "Good morning, sir!" he said. "Thought holystoning would not serve. A layer of ice would never do."

"Quite true, Mr. Hotchkiss. But if we aren't at it, we will have just that, even from our steps. You might see that the hands sweep off what they can. Sand the decks for better footing."

"Aye, sir!" Hotchkiss turned to Midshipman Andrews, who understood immediately what was required and went forward to form a working party.

"I believe, sir," said Pierce, "that come eight bells, or sooner, you and I may be needed in further consultations with our visitors. I suggest that you find something for Mr. Andrews to put the hands to, aboard or ashore. Come midday, the port watch will be released from duty requirements. All hands to be aboard before the forenoon watch tomorrow."

"Aye, sir! Shall we be putting out then?"

"Indeed, or as soon as can be. As I remarked last evening, we need to learn of our surroundings. Shostolamie's revelations have created a new set of priorities. Despite Smythe's insistence that we remain apart, we may find ourselves involved after all."

"Do we manage to stay unentangled, better to know what occurs around us."

"My feelings, exactly," said Pierce. "Now, my dear friend, you look half frozen. I'll take the deck. Go below, shift some dry clothes, and have a warm drink."

"Capital idea, sir!"

Alone, other than hands sweeping snow and sprinkling sand, Pierce slowly paced the portside quarterdeck. Oddly, they were tied up with the starboard, rather than the port side to the quay. The terms had originated when ships were steered by an oar mounted on the right, or *steering board* side, and moored with it away from shore to prevent damage. Moored as they were, bows north, and the prevailing winds from the west, the port side was often the weather side as well.

Before they put to sea, he would go along the schooner's seaward side and check her trim. Lighter with the colonists and supplies offloaded, she would be more out of the water. It might be required to add ballast, or at least shift what there was to put her in the best trim. A good look from fore and aft would be warranted as well, to make sure she was on an even keel.

At Pierce's insistence, *Island Expedition* had been kept as ready for sea as possible. They would need to send up topmasts, topgallant masts, and cross upper yards. Those were common evolutions, although labor-intensive and back-breaking work. It would sweat the remnants of rum and other spirits from those who would overindulge the last evening ashore.

"Captain! Captain Pierce!" a voice hailed. Pierce stepped to the starboard rail. Smythe, Chief Shostolamie, and Jonas Gibbons, who also served as secretary and aide-de-camp to Smythe, were there.

"Here!" shouted Pierce.

"Can you come ashore, sir?" said Smythe.

"Of course, sir! And Mr. Hotchkiss? He's below for the moment!"

"Should he wish to, Captain. The chief and his party are preparing to leave!"

"I shall be along presently, and perhaps with Mr. Hotchkiss, should he so wish!"

"Join us in the headquarters tent, if you would, Captain!"

"Aye!"

Pierce found the morning's gathering even less formal than the meeting the evening before. A great fire roared in the tent's central fire pit. Smoke rose to the center and escaped through vents at either end of the canvas structure. A coffee pot from the cook's tent hung suspended over the fire's edge. Pierce had brought his mug with him, and now poured another cup before he sat down.

Shostolamie, who also had an affinity for the hot drink, rose and poured himself a second cup. "Me say, 'thank you.' Not meet strangers before, make Shostolamie feel like home. You treat good, like person. Treat same as you."

"I know of no reason why we shouldn't," said Smythe.

"All same, much thanks. Soon go to land of Kalish People. Maybe come again. Maybe others come. Maybe canoe? Maybe ship? If ship have this flag, no worry, friends." He drew a rectangle in the ground. "This color of night sky when no clouds, no moon. In middle, sign like this, color like snow. See ship this flag, know it friend." He drew a four-pointed star, or the most basic of compass roses, one that indicated only the four cardinal directions.

"I do hope that any further visitors do not try to have us to aid your people, or those referred to as Vespicans. We are grateful for the hand of friendship, but I reaffirm our desire not to engage in others' affairs."

"What you say, what you want, not matter. One day, you help Vespicans. Help Kalish. Ship come one day, bring what need. Big cold come soon. Ship bring warm blankets, bring furs, bring skins. Ship bring cows so babies can drink milk. Bring cattle so can eat fresh meat."

"That would be most welcome, and we thank you. But we have nothing to trade or offer as payment."

"Pay later!"

Before anyone could respond, Shostolamie refilled his cup. After he had blown to cool it and had taken one mighty gulp of the steaming brew, he stood and said earnestly, "Friends from another world. One thing you swear, you stay Island of Ancient Ones, Island of Stone Lodges?"

"Please don't ask us for help, Chief," said Smythe. "I have been most clear on that."

"Not ask that. On island have many trees, many deer, many fish in rivers. Not chop all trees, kill all deer, catch all fish. Chop tree, plant tree. Two deer? Shoot one, eat one. Let other have baby! Let one fish live. Let young fish grow, be big fish. See two, catch one, eat one."

"We shall endeavor to do that, Chief!" said Smythe.

"Indeed, sir, we will," said Hotchkiss. "Mr. Smythe has already insisted on it."

"Know why?"

"I have an idea," remarked Pierce, "based upon what Mr. Smythe has told us, but I would hear it from you."

"When Ancient Ones here, long time gone by, island like now. Many trees, many animals. Plenty eat. Ancient ones kill all deer, catch all fish, chop all trees! One day have no trees to build lodges. No deer, no fish to eat. One day water no good. No water for drink, no water for corn, for pumpkins. Ancient Ones leave, go away. Ancient Ones no live on island no more. No can live here no more. Go away. Where, no one know."

"We will do our utmost, Chief!"

"Good! Shostolamie go home soon, but come back maybe. If others come, make welcome!"

Aboard the schooner a half hour later, Pierce found Morgan on the quarterdeck. "If you would oblige me, Mr. Morgan, please that all hands, the watch on deck and the watch below, man the port rail. We must give them a proper send-off!"

"Aye aye, sir. A gun salute?"

"I think not. They may not know our customs, and interpret it as a hostile act."

"Indeed, sir. And are the customs of those supposedly like us the same as ours?"

"Perceptive, Mr. Morgan. You have heard some details of yesterday's meeting?"

"Yes, sir. The only thing discussed this morning."

"And by now half of what you have heard is wrong."

"Aye, sir! Scuttlebutt. But I'm certain the honest truth will appear when it's needed."

"You can be assured of that, Mr. Morgan," said Pierce. "Now if you will see to manning the rail!"

"Aye aye, sir!"

Pierce watched intently as the Kalish loaded the large twin-hulled canoe. Shostolamie walked up the ramp and took his seat on the elaborate chair forward of the mast. The ramp was retracted. It fit snugly under the deck that connected the two dugout hulls. Others in the group pushed the craft into the water and leapt aboard.

At a guttural shout, paddles dug into the water, and backed the canoe away from the shore. Another command caused those to starboard to paddle forward, and those to port to paddle in reverse. Swiftly the native craft turned to point its twin prows toward the open sea.

When the canoe neared *Island Expedition's* stern, Pierce nodded at Morgan, who called the hands to attention. When the Kalish delegation drew abreast the stern, Pierce nodded again, and the midshipman signaled the bo'sun's mate of the watch. The pipe's shrill tones screeched in the cold quiet air as the canoe passed alongside. Pierce and Morgan stood at attention and lifted their hats in salute.

Aboard the canoe, Shostolamie rose. He turned to face the schooner, as did other Kalish not tasked to paddle. He raised his right hand, palm outward, and held it at shoulder level as they passed alongside. Near the bow, and as the bos'un's mate ceased piping, the old man slowly waved three times. Pierce and Morgan relaxed their salutes, and the hands along the rail stood easy. Morgan dismissed and sent them about their normal duties.

Pierce watched the canoe proceed toward the harbor mouth. When the light snow that had begun to fall again hid them from sight, he turned and went below.

Pierce tried to think of how to write this latest episode in the log so that it would be believable. The visit of local indigenous people was quite unremarkable, but the information they conveyed was beyond belief. How would he ever record it and not have the entire Admiralty wonder if he had lost his mind? And for that matter, how would his other entries be received? For the time being, perhaps, the best option was to record and detail the events as truthfully as possible, and let the reaction, good or bad, happen as it would. Everyone in the colony and crew had experienced the same events and apparent contradictions, and should his accounts ever be questioned, he would have their verification.

Two days later they warped *Island Expedition* away from the quay and toward the anchor that had been set out from shore. Originally placed as an aid to maneuver the schooner should it be necessary to fight, it now provided some sea room on what was effectively a lee shore. When they were *up and down*, they set a minimum of sail and established a port reach. The anchor came free and was soon at the cathead.

Pierce brought her closer to the wind so that they could clear the land that jutted out just north of the quay. They passed the point with good margin and maintained the same course to stand well out in the harbor. Then he eased her a bit, set the course at north, and ordered a trifle more canvas shown to the wind.

He momentarily left the deck to Hotchkiss and went below. He wanted to look at the newly made charts that showed the entrance to the bay, and determine what route they would use to get to the open sea. He had several options, and weighed the need for adequate sea room against the ease of maneuvering. Pierce debated a few minutes, and elected the simplest option. He had a vessel and crew that he normally would expect to successfully navigate the most difficult route, but they had not been to sea in nearly a month. Many had been ashore the night before and were not clear-headed enough for intense and complicated sail-handling.

Later, when they cleared the two larger islands to either side of the entrance, Pierce set course directly south and remained as close to shore as possible. "Mr. Hadley, be so kind as to fetch my glass, would you?"

"Aye aye, sir!"

Pierce scanned the peninsula that hid the colony from view.

Somewhere along its top, he should see the ancient structure left by the island's original inhabitants. That bit of stonework served as a lookout tower for the British Island Expedition Organization's settlement. They had erected a spar so they could hoist signal flags and pass information across the bay to the settlement and the schooner as it lay along the quay.

Recently the spar had been extended so it could be seen more easily from the sea. Pierce had said nothing directly to Townsend a day earlier when he detailed him to remain and take charge of the lookout station and shore batteries. He hoped the young midshipman would have the presence of mind to acknowledge the schooner's passage and not cause her captain to think the shore detail was already neglecting its duties.

Something caught Pierce's eye as he glanced at the ridgeline. He put the glass to his eye and looked. He didn't see signal flags, but rather the Union Jack, which had been hoisted on the tower's new signal mast. As he watched, a hoist rose up, little dots of dark bundles that immediately broke out into multicolored signal flags.

As he waited for a lookout or a junior officer to report it, Pierce's anger began to rise. It was surely time to get the hands to sea and remind them of what it meant to do one's duty. Someone should have seen it by now.

"Deck there!" cried the foremast lookout. "Signal from the lookout station, sir!"

"Very well. Mr. Hadley, take my glass. See if you can make it out!"

"Aye aye, sir!" Hadley took the proffered glass and studied the hill top intently. He made a few quick notes on a scrap of paper pulled from his uniform pocket, and then consulted the signals book. Pierce preferred the signal midshipman translate or interpret signals without the book, but Hadley was still relatively new at it. Pierce said nothing.

"Our number, sir," said the midshipman, his head in the book for only a moment. They say, 'Good luck,' sir."

"Thank you, Mr. Hadley. You may acknowledge. And ask the combined age of all hands now at the lookout tower!"

"Aye aye, sir! Combined ages, sir?"

"Yes, Mr. Hadley. We will ensure they are there and alert, that they didn't hoist a pre-made signal."

"Aye aye, sir!"

Moments later, the requested signal broke out in *Island Expedition's* rigging. In response the signal flags ashore were hauled down, indicating receipt of the schooner's inquiry. Soon, "In progress" was seen, and moment's later the flags flew that indicated the answer to the question.

"Not a bad showing, Mr. Hotchkiss, for those ashore. Can't say we were all that sharp aboard, however. Their signal should have been seen and reported much earlier. Make it known to all hands that I will not stand for such delays!"

"Aye aye, sir, but I might count myself at fault as well, sir."

"How would you be considered at fault?"

"I saw the signal hoisted as well and waited to see how long until reported. I could have reported it at the time you first saw it."

"In that case, good sir, I own a portion of blame myself. We both saw the signal and did nothing about it."

"Other than to check reaction times."

"Let us not worry about our individual failings. We saw it, but apparently, no one else did. We will see that such never occurs again."

"Aye aye, sir!" replied Hotchkiss.

"Now, be so kind as to wear ship and set us upon a port tack, northwest by north!"

"Aye, sir!"

"Crack on what you think prudent. We shall maintain this heading for some time!"

"Aye, sir!"

The schooner came about quite handily, but in his present irritation, Pierce wasn't happy with the evolution. They quickly set more sail and bore away to the northwest. In the late afternoon, they let her fall off and headed north. As evening came and darkness crept upon them, Pierce and O'Brien dead reckoned the day's run. They agreed that they were well north of the island. As the dog watches ended, they let her fall off even more, and for the next four hours carried on to the northeast. When the mid watch was called, they put her directly before the wind and headed directly east. The wind was light, and they set even more sail. The schooner fairly flew over the water.

With the mid watch underway, Pierce went forward to get a needed cup of coffee. He wanted it known to the cook and his mates that coffee should be available throughout the night. It was cold and would get colder before morning. Pierce passed through the berthing area and saw that all hands had one or even two new blankets issued and on their bunks. If the men could not be warm and dry on deck, they should at least have the opportunity to be as warm and dry as possible when below.

As the forenoon watch began the next morning, Pierce ordered all hands aft. "Men!" he said loudly. "Men! We are at sea again, finally without passengers or cargo. We need to be at sea! Yesterday's performance points that out. We've been ashore, tied up at that old stone quay, and it shows. We're rusty!

"Today, we will drill! We will drill and practice all that there is to practice! Gun drill! Sail drill! We will practice coming about, wearing ship, shortening sail! We will practice repelling boarders! We will practice boarding a hostile vessel! We will drill tomorrow as well! And we will drill the next day, and the next! When we return, there will not be a better-handled, better-fought ship in this world, or any world!"

Despite the watchfulness of the bo'sun and his mates, and the sharp glances of the officers and warrant officers, a low rumble of moans passed through the assembled crew. Pierce heard it too, just as he heard the efforts to strangle it, but he did not worry about it. It was as much a sound of relief, for with the promised drills, the hands would be busy and not subject to the boredom that often infects ships underway.

He continued. "Listen, all of you. If you do not know, we have found ourselves in a new and different world. We sail east, seeking land where our charts tell us there is none. We will gain a better idea of this strange world and its unknown lands. Not knowing how we may be received by any residents of these shores, we will close only until land is sighted from the masthead. We will not detail the coast as when we circled the island. We seek only a general idea of where land lies.

"When we are sufficiently drilled in all tasks and duties and have a general idea of the lands to the east, we will return to the colony. When we see that Mr. Smythe and the colonists can function on their own, we shall return to England!"

That brought a murmur of approval, along with, "Three cheers for the captain!" There were also requests of "Three cheers for England!" and "Three cheers for *Island Expedition*!" Then the cheers came. "Hip hip, hoorah! Hip hip, hoorah!"

"Now lads, let us be sharp! Everyone properly and warmly dressed and with a full belly, and we'll be about our work! Mr. Hotchkiss, you may dismiss and carry on!"

"Aye aye, sir!"

As promised, they drilled. They drilled at the guns, again and again, until they could fire as rapidly as possible. Pierce walked amongst them, designating this man wounded or that boy killed, forcing them to work the guns with partial crews. He suddenly announced the enemy was on the opposite side, so that gun crews had to man the opposite battery. Then he detailed more hands as out of action and unavailable to help man the weapons.

When all hands were exhausted from the effort and looked forward to a secure resumption of the daily routine, Pierce indicated another imaginary enemy along side. The drill did not end. He called for a renewed effort at the guns, and exhorted those hands remaining to increase the rate of fire.

While they fought this imaginary battle, they maneuvered. They steered to take advantage of the foe or to escape the most destructive of his broadsides. Men were called away from the guns to handle the schooner, even while Pierce insisted a furious rate of fire be maintained.

At four bells in the afternoon watch, Pierce decided the opponent had had enough and had attempted to flee. *Island Expedition* set out in pursuit and crowded on all sail she could carry in the now-blustery winter conditions. Dinner had not been served due to the battle drill, but a meal was made available. As the drill was conducted as realistically as could be, the galley fires were out, and all hands ate cold rations.

On the quarterdeck, Pierce gnawed on ship's biscuit. He held a joint of cold salt pork in his other hand, and alternated between mouthfuls. He washed it down with swallows of cold coffee. Because the hands ate their cold meals at action stations, it was only right that he do the same. When he finished, he allowed time for all to eat their fill before continuing the scenario for this particular drill.

"Mr. Hotchkiss!" he bellowed, a last crumb of biscuit falling from his chin. "Our opponent is dismasted and we are nearly up to him. Get the men back to the guns and prepare to open fire!"

"Aye aye, sir!" The guns rang out and sent shot screaming into the invisible imagined enemy.

"Refuses surrender!" said Pierce, narrating and guiding the action. "You there! You're killed. Stand away from the gun! You are wounded! Splinter to the thigh. To the orlop with you now! Hard to starboard, there! Get those staysails in! Cross her stern! Now! Fire!"

When it seemed *Island Expedition* would be victorious, the unseen opponent was reinforced by several larger and more powerful warships. Pierce ordered a final broadside as a show of defiance, and cracked on all sail the schooner could carry to escape a truly hopeless situation.

It was well into the second dog watch when Pierce announced the drill was over. The galley fire was lighted, the guns secured, and the schooner returned to a more normal routine. Even though *Island Expedition* berthed her crew in bunks rather than hammocks, the call "pipe down hammocks" signified that hands could turn in. They did so willingly, and nearly all were asleep as they became prone.

The next day provided much of the same. There was constant, grueling exercise at the guns, at making sail, and at maneuvering the ship. They drilled and exercised until it could be done as quickly as Pierce could ever hope for, and until all hands were dead tired again.

The third day repeated the strenuous efforts of the first two. That night, Pierce called all hands for a simulated night action. He normally wanted all hands to have proper sleep, but knew that any enemy would not be as kind. Thus, tired and sleepy men were roused out of sound and deep slumber to once again stand to their guns and fire them hot, smoking, and reeking into the hull of an unseen and imagined enemy.

During the days of practice and drill, the schooner made her way east. Progress was not always great because of the variety of courses sailed in the execution of drills. Five days after Pierce had addressed the crew, the call came from aloft. "Land in sight! Four points to port, sir!"

"Very well! Mr. Dial, make a note of the time, will you?"

"Aye aye, sir!"

"Call all hands to 'bout ship! A starboard tack will do nicely!"

"Aye aye, sir!"

With land sighted, *Island Expedition* turned away and headed to the southwest. The location of the sighting was marked on the charts. After a few days, they altered course and again sailed to the east along a more southerly parallel. Several runs at different latitudes against this unknown shore would give them a basic understanding of where the lands of the Kalish and the Vespicans lay.

Chapter Eighteen

An Unfortunate Encounter

Monday, the 13th of June, was cold and blustery as *Island Expedition* once again progressed eastward. She was under minimal sail and eased through the foam-flecked, spray- spewing, cold gray water. Pierce thought to exercise the guns, to fight another imaginary enemy, and to urge the hands to even better efforts with the twelve-pounder long guns and carronades. He needed a scenario, a script from which he could direct the actions of his ship and the actions of the unseen foe. Today he could not concentrate in order to devise any scene in which *Island Expedition* would need to fight.

The drills and exercises over the past weeks had sharpened the crew to a razor's edge. More drill would likely dull rather than further sharpen the perfection that had been obtained. It was time to slack off and let the hands be about normal ship's work.

When Pierce decided to explore the world around the island, he had hoped to converse with any of the ships that they might meet. He hoped that these at-sea meetings might help him to better understand the world where they now found themselves.

They had spotted several ships over the past several days. Perhaps they were merchantmen, carrying cargoes to and from this land to the east, this new nation called or referred to as Vespica. It puzzled him that none wanted to close and exchange greetings. Many, upon sighting *Island Expedition*, set more sail and steered away from her. Pierce did not pursue, as he did not wish to appear hostile or belligerent. But one day, one of those unknown ships would desire news or contact, and he would have the meeting he hoped for.

"Never, my friend," he remarked to Lieutenant Hotchkiss as they stood, bundled against the cold biting wind, "have I seen so many, so afraid to communicate with another." He rubbed his hands and tried to warm his numbed fingers.

"Shostolamie mentioned war. We haven't determined the flag of most we've seen, nor do we know the whole of it. They may think us privateers or pirates," responded Hotchkiss. "Perchance we resemble a ship of a hostile navy?"

"You are no doubt correct. Still, what I wouldn't give for a short conversation with someone of this world!"

"It does feel that we are here but not a part of it." Hotchkiss was silent for a few moments. Then he asked, "Do we exercise the guns today?"

Pierce was surprised that his friend asked. They had been friends since childhood, had shared many adventures and escapades, but in his duties as *Island Expedition's* first lieutenant, Hotchkiss rarely inquired into Pierce's immediate plans. He imagined that Hotchkiss felt in his bones just what his captain thought and planned.

For that reason, and the surprise of the inquiry, Pierce did not answer right away. Two or three replies came to mind, but he decided against them. He could reply as he wished, and his friend would take no offense. Even if Hotchkiss received any cutting remarks personally, felt insulted or belittled by the manner in which he was spoken to, words could not be any stronger than their friendship.

Before Hotchkiss repeated his question, Pierce simply said, "No. We've done enough lately."

"Aye aye," Hotchkiss replied. He would have agreed, regardless of the decision.

"Now, sir, might you go below? You've been on deck a great while, and appear chilled to the bone. Perhaps Eubanks has a fresh pot."

It was amazing how their relationship changed almost instantly. Moments ago, Hotchkiss had been the respectful subordinate who dared ask his captain about plans for the immediate future. Now he was the old friend that tried to see to his comrade's comfort, and who now treated him like a small child without the sense to come in from the cold.

"Coffee does sound good, and Lord knows it's cold. Andrews can have the deck to himself, I suppose." As he turned and headed for the companionway, he made enough of a commotion that Andrews saw it from the lee quarterdeck and moved in unspoken acknowledgement. "Keep her as she is, Mr. Andrews!"

"Aye aye, sir!" he responded.

Pierce and Hotchkiss retired to the relative warm of the great cabin.

Eubanks had recently brewed a fresh pot, and when he learned that the captain had gone below, he sent Franklin aft with it.

Pierce was grateful for the timely arrival of the scalding brew. He poured a great steaming mug of it for each of them. He sipped at it and took in as much as he could. The warmth spread slowly to his inner core and then to his nearly numb extremities. He had been on deck for a long time. He finished the first cup and poured another.

It was fortunate that Eubanks had brewed a fresh pot. Pierce was on the verge of being in a temper, and had the coffee not been ready, that slight inconvenience might have put him in one of his rare foul and black moods. Earlier he had thought to demean his friend and first lieutenant's intelligence when replying to a question that he had posed. Surely that was a sign that his mind was agitated.

"Strange, isn't it?" asked Hotchkiss.

"Isn't what?"

"To be this cold in June."

"But we are in the Southern Hemisphere."

"Understood. Yet it's odd to think of these present months as winter. To my mind it is summer, the long warm days of summer that we should feel now."

"I would welcome just one day as it was when we crossed the line. To go on deck in shirtsleeves."

"And even then be too warm," added Hotchkiss.

"Then we would wish it a little cooler. We are never satisfied with the climate. But temperature doesn't matter as long as we have the wind."

Conversation faded and each sat alone with his thoughts. Pierce drifted into a realm where he wasn't awake, and yet he wasn't asleep. He was aware of being on board, in the cabin, at sea, and of the ship's routine going on overhead.

Yet his mind wandered. He was aboard *Theadora*, as the trim frigate sailed in the West Indies. It was wonderfully warm, and tomorrow they would anchor at Kingston. There was a young lady he longed to see, if Captain Jackson would permit him time ashore. But wait! He was captain of the frigate. Jackson now commanded a seventy-four.

What was the young lady's name? It started with an "E," as did his. Evangeline! That was it! But she wasn't in the West Indies! She was on the Isle of Wight, waiting for his return. She would surely warm his chilled bones! Her embrace would not merely warm him; it would set his very soul afire. A smile played upon his face as he thought of her. So warm, so lovely, the perfect wife of a frigate captain.

His head nodded twice and then fell forward. He heard the lookout hail from the masthead. A sail in sight to windward! Bellowing inquiries aloft. A friend? An enemy? What action should he take?

He was about to order *Theadora* to beat to quarters, when he became aware of a gentle rapping, soft and muted in the background. As he gave orders for battle, the rapping, the knocking, became more insistent.

Pierce was asleep. He had been dreaming, but there really was a repeated knock at the door. "What is it?" he barked, not sure if he was aboard the frigate or the schooner.

"Mr. Morgan's compliments, sir, and to tell you that a sail has been sighted," replied Midshipman Steadman.

"To windward?"

"Why yes, sir. To windward, sir."

"Thank you, Mr. Steadman. You may tell Mr. Morgan that I'll be along shortly."

"Aye aye, sir."

Pierce checked his watch. In the hour and a half since he had come below, he had fallen asleep in spite of two large cups of coffee. Isaac had left him to his rest in the somewhat private solitude of the great cabin. He yawned mightily and wished a return to his dream and the warmth of the West Indies. Then with images of himself as a post captain in command of *Theadora* lingering in his mind, he put on his greatcoat and went on deck.

The southwest wind was still cold, and *Island Expedition* ran across it on a starboard broad reach, headed just south of east. With minimal sail she coasted along easily, even though she could have tolerated more canvas in the moderate breeze. Somewhere, the wind had been much stronger. The remnants of large seas left over from a powerful storm swept under her as she pitched and rolled gracefully. Now and then these swells and the occasional cross sea met and exploded into clouds of spray that sent a chilly mist across the deck.

Pierce shivered after being in the warmth below.

"Now, Mr. Morgan, tell me about this sail that's been sighted!"

"Aye, sir. Not more than a few minutes gone by, sir. Maybe ten? Sorry, but Mr. Steadman says it was devilishly hard to get your attention."

"I doubt that has anything to do with the vessel sighted. It is not Mr. Steadman's duty to report on my responsiveness. Nor is it your duty to relay the same back to me."

"My error, sir, and, my apologies!"

"Accepted! Now, about the ship?"

"Yes, sir. Mainmast lookout saw her, just off the starboard quarter. Sent Mr. Steadman to tell you, and Mr. Dial aloft to have a look, sir."

"Very well. Mr. Dial, anything?"

"Aye, sir. Ship rigged. Topsails an' t'gallants. Looked to be on the opposite course."

"Looked?"

"Yes, sir. She's seen us, sir. Altered course just as I got to the cross-trees, sir"

"And her heading now?"

"Before I came down, sir, looked to be making for us. Hard to tell at that distance."

If the master's mate had seen three masts blend into one, that ship must be heading directly for them. To sail away would be into the wind, or closer into the wind than any vessel known was capable of.

"I'd venture to say she is attempting to close us!"

"Aye, sir. It would seem she is."

"Perhaps we'll have a chance at a meeting, sir," said Hotchkiss. Pierce hadn't been aware of the first lieutenant's presence, but as a good second-in-command, he had been there all along. That, or his childhood friend and comrade had arrived quietly and without notice. He was fast becoming the ideal first lieutenant.

"It would seem," answered Pierce. Perhaps today was better than he thought.

"Deck there!" the lookout hailed. "Royals, sir. She's set royals. Studding sails too!"

"Still closing?" Pierce roared back.

"Aye, sir."

"Must really desire speaking with us," remarked Morgan.

"It would so appear," said Pierce with a sudden twinge of apprehension. Why should this vessel seek to close them? Every other sail sighted had maintained or increased the distance. His suspicion grew as he imagined what the captains of those other ships would have felt, had he attempted to run down to them.

"More sail, sir? Alter course?" asked Hotchkiss.

"I think not," answered Pierce. "But do ensure all hands are alert.

Clear the ship for action at your convenience. Do not beat to quarters or strive for any record time. But we will be ready if yonder ship is belligerent!"

"Aye aye, sir! The guns?"

"Load! Do not run out! When we are ready, the men to be in normal activities about the deck. We must not appear alerted or defensive."

Pierce did not keep the ship's guns loaded and ready for action. He preferred the extra time to properly charge them at the start of a drill or bonafide action. The powder in an always loaded gun could dampen and be useless when needed most. The gun would need to be drawn, and the advantages of being pre-loaded would be lost. In the event of fire, loaded guns could cook off and discharge. A fire at sea was enough of a problem without the added danger of uncontrolled detonations.

"Aye aye, sir!" Hotchkiss moved off and delegated different tasks to the midshipmen, warrant officers, and senior petty officers.

After the days of incessant drill that Pierce had insisted on, the crew quickly transformed *Island Expedition* into a fighting machine. The canvas screens and light wooden bulkheads that provided privacy for the senior officers were removed and stowed below. Chairs, tables, stools, and other furniture disappeared from their normal locations. The decks were sanded. The guns were cast loose, checked, loaded, and temporarily secured again. Harris retired to the magazine to fill cartridges.

Pierce hailed the lookout. "What now, Thomas?"

"Still closing. Still studding sails and royals, sir. Hull up now!"

"Mr. O'Brien, your best men at the wheel! Rig relieving tackles as well!"

"Aye aye, sir!"

"I can see her from here, sir!" said Morgan. He raised his glass for a better look.

Pierce went below and fetched his best glass. He scanned the southeast horizon and saw it immediately: a small square of white, steady against the ever-changing patterns of grays. A quick focus and he could make out the royals, topgallants, topsails, and the studding sails that rose along either side of them. She was headed directly for them.

Pierce's anxiety increased as he watched the strange ship close the distance. He had urgently wanted to meet and converse with a ship of this world, and now with the opportunity at hand, he was worried. No ship that simply wished contact with a stranger would come on so aggressively. An alteration of course was understandable, but to set more sail than prudent with current weather conditions, and to sail directly at the other vessel, did not suggest peaceful intent. Pierce would have closed the distance in an easier and less hostile manner. Why did this ship seek contact when every previous one had actively avoided it?

The knot in his gut grew larger. He felt the old urge to visit the head. It was fear, and at once he was ashamed, and yet he welcomed it. He still reacted as before to the prospect of battle. He just hoped no one else could detect it.

"Ship's cleared for action, sir!" said Hotchkiss, touching the brim of his hat. "Might I allow the hands a bite to eat? Eubanks says that it was ready and still warm. I could send a few at a time?"

In his present state, eating was the last thing Pierce wanted to do. Yet a good captain always made sure his men were recently fed when facing danger.

"Very well, pipe to dinner. One watch at a time, and no one lingers!"

"Aye, sir."

"See that Mr. Gray issues a tot to all hands. It'll take away a bit of this chill."

"Aye aye, sir!"

The stranger was hull up from deck now. Through his glass, Pierce could see white foam and spray leap around her bows. She came on strong and purposefully, driving over, through, and sometimes it seemed, under the sea. A strong ship, she was well-handled, and well able to carry that amount of canvas in the gusting winds. The wind had picked up from earlier in the day.

Pierce saw the dark hull and the single yellow stripe that marked the gun ports along either side. Most certainly she was a man-of-war or a privateer. A merchantman with dummy- painted gun ports would never approach in such a manner.

"Mr. Hotchkiss!"

"Sir?"

"Pray have the reefs out of the main and fore sails! We'll go topgallants as well. Ease her a bit, another point or two before the wind!" A modest increase in sail and a slight change of course should give the approaching ship the impression that she had been sighted. Pierce still hoped that a peaceful meeting and ship-to-ship communication could take place. Perhaps his apprehension was misplaced, and his suspicions about the rapidly closing stranger were wrong.

He did not like that *Island Expedition* was to leeward. Here in uncharted and unknown waters, the schooner was, in effect, on a lee shore. Eastward there was land, and he hated the thought of running up on it during the heat of battle. Far better if he were to windward.

The schooner's motion changed as her speed increased. Pierce glanced at the approaching ship. She altered course as well, so as to keep *Island Expedition* dead ahead. Then the stranger changed course and headed a point south of east, as opposed to the schooner's east-northeast heading.

All aboard had a good broadside look at the stranger. She was a neat, trim, and deadly ship rigged sloop-of-war. "Reminds me of *Ferret*," remarked Hotchkiss.

"Perhaps," responded Pierce. "But there are more guns here, and quarter galleries as well."

"Truth sir, this one isn't sparred as heavy. Eighteen guns, I'd say."

"Nine-pounders, I'd wager, unless she's got carronades. If they have carronades here," offered O'Brien.

"She's signaling, sir!" hallooed Spencer. They watched a string of black balls rise into her rigging and break out as colored signal flags.

"Are you able to comprehend them, Mr. Spencer?" queried Pierce.

"Look the same as our signal flags, sir," he answered. Then after a few minutes with his face buried in the signal book, he piped up. "They don't decode to anything intelligible."

"Neither code nor plain spelling?"

"No, sir! Here, sir, see for yourself!"

"I will do just that, Mr. Spencer." Pierce looked at the master's mate's scribbled notes. "While the flags are the same, do they represent the same letters and numerals?"

His question went unanswered as smoke mushroomed from the stranger's port bow. They heard the sound of the shot seconds later and saw a splash fifty yards ahead.

"Clew up, Mr. Hotchkiss! Mr. O'Brien, ever so gently to starboard! Mr. Spencer, hoist the interrogative!"

While his premonition of the stranger's hostility was reinforced by her shot across the bows, he did not want to justify her aggressiveness. With square sails clewed up, *Island Expedition* would lose way and appear to comply with the sloop's "heave to" command, the shot across her bows. Easing the schooner to starboard would better present her guns to the sloop. Depending upon how the unknown ship reacted, *Island Expedition* would be across the other's bows, if only for a brief moment.

The interrogative soared up the halyards as the schooner lost momentum. The last vestiges of steerage way acted on the starboard set rudder and her bows swung gently south. The flags broke out, and an instant later the sloop backed her topsails, checked her way, and pivoted to starboard. Her port broadside erupted in smoke and flame.

Aboard *Island Expedition* splinters flew, gouges appeared in the deck, lines parted, and holes appeared in the sails. A shot came through a gun port, careened off the muzzle, and struck two men at the next gun. One dropped straight to the deck, his right arm gone. The other spun around violently. Blood flowed and even flew from his severely mangled hand. The second victim came to a rest, and bit his tongue nearly in two, attempting to stifle a scream. Others suffered less-damaging or non-life-threatening wounds. Most injuries were from splinters caused by the crash of iron shot against the schooner's wooden structure. Some were caused by pieces of top hamper falling from the damaged rigging.

A block landed where Pierce had stood a second before. He glanced at it with a strange nonchalance. He still had a charmed ability to avoid serious injury. The fear that had earlier threatened to overwhelm him was gone. Now that the first shots had been fired, he was angry that the stranger had ignored a clearly peaceful and submissive move.

"Damn!" said Midshipman Andrews. "She's English! Look at her ensign!"

All within hearing glanced at the sloop. There, snapping in the brisk breeze was apparently the White Ensign of the Royal Navy. "Mr. Andrews!" roared Pierce. "Call attention to our colors. Be so kind as to dip and raise twice!"

"Aye aye, sir!" The Blue Ensign was lowered slowly several feet and hoisted again to the peak. Once again it was slowly lowered before being raised to its normal location.

In reply to this reminder, the sloop braced her yards around and commenced a port turn. She had not lost as much headway as had the schooner, and was now directly ahead. Her turn placed her across *Island Expedition's* bows. Pierce had the jib, foresail, and mainsail sheeted home. They caught in the wind. As *Island Expedition* gained steerage way, Pierce ordered the helm alee in an attempt to turn inside the sloop. That would hopefully lessen the time that the schooner's vulnerable bows would be exposed to the sloop's guns.

"Mr. Hotchkiss! If that son of a bitch fires again, you may return the compliment in kind! And does he fire, and you return it, fire as your guns are served! Pour it on!"

"Aye aye, sir!" answered the first lieutenant. "Mr. Morgan! Mr. Andrews! If we fire, all guns target her mainmast! Pass the word!"

The sloop's port broadside flowered into deadly blooms of smoke, flame, and hurtling iron shot. The schooner's port bow took the brunt of it, and a few shots struck the small boats nestled on the main hatch. In a normal prelude to battle, they would have been put in the water and towed behind. With the odd circumstances of this encounter, doing so would have indicated hostile intent.

Much handier, *Island Expedition* turned inside the curve negotiated by the sloop. They were port side to port side. The six port side twelve-pound long guns and the pair of twelve- pound carronades were ready, double-shotted. The sloop's nine-pounders and eighteen-pound carronades had just fired, and her gun crews worked feverishly to reload.

Hotchkiss would not give them the chance. Previously authorized by his captain, he roared, "Mind your aim point! Fire as your guns bear!"

Singly, but in rapid succession, the guns spoke in real anger for the first time since commissioning a year ago. The recent drill and overall experience of the crew paid off. Shot after shot struck the sloop. Pierce saw a veritable cloud of wood, splinters, cordage, iron, brass, and body parts fly high into the air. The debris settled back to deck or into the sea. Amidships the sloop was a battered mass of ragged holes, smashed bulwarks, and fallen top hamper.

"Keep her hard over, Mr. O'Brien! Head sail sheets!" The momentum of her turn carried *Island Expedition* through the wind. She headed west for a moment, and then west- northwest. North and beyond she went, while the port gun crews labored feverishly to reload and run out their guns.

After the exchange of broadsides, the sloop had continued her port turn. Then she put her helm over and commenced a starboard turn to reverse course and present her loaded and ready starboard battery to the schooner's stern. The sloop's captain had not accounted for *Island Expedition's* maneuverability. Before his ship was halfway through the planned turn, the schooner had described more than a half-circle. As the sloop pointed directly east, the schooner faced north-northeast.

"Starboard battery! Fire!" yelled Pierce. Again, double-shotted twelve-pounders bucked, cracked, and roared. Smoke and flame rushed from the muzzles. Like wild beasts fighting the nooses of their captors, the guns lurched inboard with a vengeance, and were violently subdued by the heavy breeching ropes.

The stern and quarter gallery windows aboard the sloop shattered. Shot tore through the stern and sent up clouds of splinters. Sails shivered as gaping tears appeared, and a rain of blocks and cordage, along with bits of mast and yard, crashed onto the deck. A mizzen backstay parted.

"Keep to the turn, Mr. O'Brien!"

"Aye aye, sir!" The master reinforced the directive to the men at the wheel. "That'll show them bastards, sir!"

"Mr. Hotchkiss! Port battery!"

"Aye aye, sir!"

The schooner continued her rapid turn to starboard. Now she bore east and rapidly continued in the arc of her turn. The sloop seemed to hesitate, apparently undecided as to continuing her starboard turn or reverting back to a port turn. For an instant she steadied and settled on course to the east-southeast. Then slowly her bows swung to the north as she elected to turn to port.

Island Expedition's course was south and beyond, close-hauled now, as her fore and aft rig allowed her to lie closer to the wind than the sloop could ever hope. Her port battery once again bore on the other vessel.

"Port battery! Target the main mast! Fire!" Hotchkiss ordered. "Send those false English straight to hell!"

Guns roared and spat forth flame, smoke, and destruction. More holes! More clouds of splinters! More agony aboard the sloop! The mizzen mast swayed perilously.

"Damn!" said Pierce. "We don't know main from mizzen! But it'll do, should it come down."

As the guns fired, Pierce ordered, "Helm aweather! Get those port side guns reloaded! Follow her around!"

Like children playing follow-the-leader, *Island Expedition* followed the sloop in the turn. Positioned off the larger ship's port quarter, her guns bore on the foe while she remained out of the line of fire. Hotchkiss passed the word for independent fire, and as quick as each crew could load, they fired. The port battery kept up a continuous rolling broadside of cannon fire. After every shot from the schooner's twelve-pounders, great clouds of splinters rose from the enemy vessel.

The sloop continued to turn and headed closer into the wind. Pierce wondered about her next action. Would she pass through the wind and settle on a southerly course? Would she halt the turn, assume a port tack, and head east? Was there another reason for her going this close to the wind?

The schooner described a gentle arc as she easily followed along in the port turn. She ran before the wind for the briefest of moments. Then she headed more and more to the north, first on a port broad reach and then a port reach. All the while, the port battery kept up a steady, accurate fire.

The sloop was close hauled on the port tack and lay as close to the wind as she dared, headed a point north of west. She steadied and then her bows swung north. Pierce saw the change. On a port tack herself, *Island Expedition* was like a bulldog that refused to let go. The sloop had tried to snap its tormenter off. The change allowed the English to bring their under-used starboard battery into action. "Ease your helm!" said Pierce quietly. "Hold her there! Starboard battery, Mr. Hotchkiss!"

"Aye aye, sir!" The starboard bow dipped into a larger sea and spray, wet and chilling, flew over the deck. Nearly westbound, the schooner passed astern of the sloop as it headed north and continued to turn east.

A helmsman muttered a variation of the old intonation as the enemy came under the starboard guns. "For which they are about to receive, may we all be truly thankful!"

"Silence there!" spat Pierce. "Take his name! I'll not have such remarks from any and every man jack aboard!" He smiled inwardly, as this twist on the saying was appropriate at the time. It was far better that the other ship be on the receiving end of the pending broadside than he and his crew. For that, he was indeed, truly thankful.

"Now, Mr. Hotchkiss!"

"Fire!" yelled the first lieutenant, his voice raw and coarse with continuous shouting and the irritation of gun smoke. The guns boomed, banged, and cracked. Splinters flew from the sloop.

As shot swept along the man-of-war's deck, she suddenly reverted to a port turn. Hotchkiss saw the impending danger. "Starboard battery, reload! Reload and quickly, lads!"The schooner's momentum had carried her to where the sloop needed only a small turn to bring her portside guns to bear.

Now, about to receive the full force of a broadside, Hotchkiss invoked the more traditional saying. Quietly, under his breath he began. "For what we are about to receive."

"May we truly be thankful!" concluded Pierce. "Starboard battery, fire as you are ready! Independent fire! Fire as your guns bear!" He watched smoke and flame burst from the sides of the ship rigged sloop. "All hands, 'bout ship! Helm alee! Lively, lads, lively now!"

Enemy shot struck home just as the schooner's starboard battery fired. Masses of splinters and chunks of wood, pieces of sail and metal fittings roared through the air, even as the gun crews went about reloading again.

As broadsides were exchanged, *Island Expedition* began her next maneuver. She tacked, passing through the wind and presenting her unprotected stern when the enemy could not take advantage. Having just fired, it would be some minutes before the sloop's port battery could again pose a threat.

Much quicker in the turn, *Island Expedition* passed through the wind and found herself on a starboard tack and then a starboard reach.

"Port battery! Fire as your guns bear!"

The turn continued. Nearly before the wind, the port side guns roared again. The sloop's portside guns boomed as well, just as her bows faced directly into the wind.

Perhaps it was a lucky shot from *Island Expedition*. Perhaps it was the concussion of the sloop's own guns. Perhaps it was a mistake in seamanship, but the sloop missed stays as she attempted to follow the schooner through the eye of the wind. "By God! We have her now!" hollered Pierce with grim satisfaction.

Chapter Nineteen

From the Jaws of Victory

"Back the topsails!" yelled Pierce. "Ease foresail and mainsail sheets! Hold her! Mr. Hotchkiss! Port battery! Independent fire! Quickly now, while we have her!"

Hotchkiss passed the word to the gun crews. The drill of recent weeks paid off. Quicker than anyone thought possible, each gun fired, was loaded, and fired again. In spite of the cold raw wind, many crewmen stripped to the waist as their exertions wrung great rivulets of sweat from them. Each gun crew loaded and fired as fast as they could. Soon the schooner's port side blazed fire and smoke, spitting out a deadly hail of iron shot on a regular and continuous basis.

The guns fired, rearing back against the breechings. When reloaded, they were run out, and when all clear, the gun captains pulled the lanyards. The locks atop the guns snapped, and the shower of sparks produced ignited the powder charges. The detonations again flung death and destruction at the enemy, while hurling the guns inboard.

As the cannonade continued, the low gray clouds parted. The sun, low on the northwest horizon, bathed both vessels in diffused light and feeble warmth. The sun's rays bounced off the water, illuminating the cloud remnants and billows of powder smoke in shades of red, yellow, and orange. Light reflected onto the shattered stern of the sloop, allowing those aboard *Island Expedition* to see her name painted across the stern. *Hawke,* it read. Pierce noted the name of their foe for the first time. They had often been astern of her, and should have made out the name much earlier, but had been too busy fighting to notice and too angry to care.

Taken aback, *Hawke* gathered sternway and rapidly narrowed the distance between them. She sailed stern-first into the continuous fire from the schooner. At any moment she would put her helm over, get her bows out of the wind, and trim sails to resume normal forward progress.

Pierce watched the shattered stern draw nearer. Which way would her captain turn? He instinctively prepared two sets of orders, dependent upon whether the sloop's stern swung to port or starboard.

He felt justified to have suspected the stranger's direct and strong approach, and to have taken all possible precautions. But at what cost?

Five crewmen were dead, their frail bodies no match for cascading iron shot. Others had met their end impaled by jagged splinters or crushed under debris from aloft. More were wounded, some quite grievously.

Morgan, senior midshipman and acting second lieutenant, lay below, his knee shattered by a rampaging round shot. He would likely lose his leg, if Matheson the surgeon hadn't yet taken it off. Simmons, gunner's mate, had a sharp and jagged splinter embedded deep in his gut.

Pierce grimly wondered about the butcher's bill aboard *Hawke*. She had suffered far worse, having received innumerable broadsides, and had sent very few in return.

Island Expedition had been bruised, battered, cut, and pummeled, but she had not been pounded into a wooden, bloody pulp. If she were a living, breathing being, she was not so injured as to prevent full use of all faculties. She was not bleeding to death. No bones were broken.

Hawke's mortality, were she a living entity, was more in doubt. Her stern was shattered. Shot holes and gouges pockmarked her sides. Rigging was torn, missing, and incomplete. Although still standing, her weakened masts threatened to go by the board. She was a gravely wounded creature and as such, very dangerous.

"Rudder's over, sir!" shouted Hotchkiss over the guns.

Pierce snapped out of his momentary reflections.

"It's to port!"

Hotchkiss had wrapped a rag about his head, and red showed forward of his left ear. Pierce was shocked to see his friend wounded, although it was a relatively minor injury. Hotchkiss was still on deck, the damage done to his countenance not affecting his performance of duty.

If *Island Expedition* remained as-is, she would soon be broadside to broadside with *Hawke*. He issued the orders he had formulated earlier. "Lee braces! Bring those yards around! Helm aweather! Mainsail and foresail sheets!"

With the wind once again behind the sails, the schooner leapt forward and gathered speed and steerage way. With the helm hard over to port, she turned and headed north, then northeast, then east. Before the wind she flew from the sloop-of-war.

Caught in irons, *Hawke* had sat briefly, bows into the wind, and then had slid stern-first through the water. All the while she underwent a terrific and terrible pounding from the schooner's guns and took longer than expected to get her helm over. If her wheel had been shot away, she would have needed the time to rig relieving tackles.

With noticeable sternway and her rudder to port, she would turn her bows north. Her starboard guns would soon bear on the schooner.

Handy and nimble, *Island Expedition* leapt into motion, surged forward, and turned away. With each second, she gained more distance from the sloop. She was not out of range, but each yard gained lessened the chances of a hit or severe damage. Having guessed correctly at *Hawke's* most probable course of action, Pierce could describe nearly a full circle and again pass astern of the sloop. On a port tack, the starboard battery could further pummel her.

Hawke's stern swung south. Wind came over her port bow, and then her port beam. Yards were braced around and sails filled. Pierce watched intensely and gauged the angle of her guns and the position of his own vessel. Any second now and she would open fire. That point reached, her tattered sails began to draw. As the wind checked her sternward movement and began to thrust her forward, *Hawke's* mizzen topmast, weakened by repeated broadsides from the schooner, and with backstays shot away, collapsed. It folded in upon itself and fell in segments straight onto the deck. The quarterdeck was buried in spars, canvas, and cordage. The main topgallant mast came down as well.

The sloop's starboard battery got off a ragged ineffective broadside. Most of the shot missed, and those that did strike caused only cosmetic damage, wounding no crew nor any vital parts of the schooner.

Island Expedition circled, came into the wind, and passed through it. On a port tack, she came up on the battered and partially dismasted sloop-of-war. The schooner's starboard guns were run out and menacingly pointed at the battered *Hawke.*

"Ease your helm! Starboard battery, fire aft of her! Any gun crew whose shot strikes home will be at the gratings tomorrow!" He did not want to cause any more death, injury, or destruction on board the devastated warship. The hands recognized his motives. They also knew that despite his known distaste for the cat, he would indeed flog every man of the gun crew whose shot might hit the sloop.

The broadside roared out, flames from the muzzles bright in the darkening gloom of evening. Seven splashes were seen slightly astern of *Hawke.* The eighth was near the sloop's mizzen chains, where the water raised wetted the shambles of her afterdeck. Would his last broadside convince the enemy captain to surrender?

Pierce saw her portside guns being angled aft to better bear on his schooner. They spat fire and smoke, but not one shot struck home.

Hawke drifted helplessly, the mass of spars and canvas trailing overboard acted like a rudder and a sea anchor. The foremast still stood, and its presence in the wind caused her bows to swing to starboard. Pierce reduced sail, and *Island Expedition* maintained her position off the sloop's stern.

"One more as before, lads!" he ordered. The starboard guns were now reloaded and run out.

"I'll stop every man's grog, should any shot strike her!" The guns boomed and bellowed as they had only moments before. Eight splashes appeared, two closer than he liked.

There was frantic activity on the sloop-of-war as her crew desperately chopped away the wreckage of the fallen mizzen topmast. Red blood-tinged water flowed from the scuppers. She had been holed below the waterline and as they pumped her out, the discharge washed away the gore.

The sloop had fought a most courageous engagement, but could do no more. Pierce silently wished for his counterpart to give up and end the bloodshed.

"Edge in closer, Mr. O'Brien!"

"Aye aye, sir." The master's face was dark, streaked with powder smoke and congealed blood. He had been splattered when a nine-pound shot had smashed a man in two at the wheel.

"Closer! Closer still!"

"Aye aye, sir!"

The rack of speaking trumpets had been smashed and none were at hand. "Mr. O'Brien," Pierce said. "I'll need your mouthpiece, sir, if you will part with it!"

"Of course, sir!" O'Brien handed his speaking trumpet, his badge of office and duty insignia, to his captain. Normally he would not to part with it for dear life, but these were not normal times.

Pierce scrambled onto the starboard rail, held on to the fore shrouds with one hand, and raised the trumpet with the other.

"Ahoy the *Hawke*! Do you strike, sir?"

No reply came. It appeared as if he had not even been heard.

"I beg you, sir! Strike and end the carnage!"

A figure detached itself from a group working frantically to clear the sloop's deck. He stepped to the port rail, used his hands as a megaphone, and bellowed. "Damned I am that I yield to a damned pirate and rebel! I'll sail this deck under before I surrender to any ship flying that accursed flag of disloyalty and rebellion!"

Pierce was stunned and puzzled. The same flag that danced in the breeze at the mainsail gaff also flew over the *Hawke*, nailed to the spare pole serving as a flag staff.

"Her flag, sir! It's different!" said Jack Haight, one of the younger boys aboard, the powder monkey at the gun nearest Pierce's location. "Look at the colors, sir!"

In the gathering twilight Pierce saw what he expected, a large white rectangle with a red cross, and in the upper quadrant, at the hoist, the Union Jack. The Union Jack repeated the Cross of St. George, symbolizing England. Behind it was the white on blue Scottish Cross of St. Andrew, and the red Cross of St. Patrick.

Then Pierce spied the difference. The colors were reversed! White portions were still white, but what should have been red was blue, and what should have been blue was red. While *Island Expedition* flew the blue, rather than the white ensign, sharp eyes aboard *Hawke* had noticed the reversal of colors in the Union Jack itself.

What would Pierce have thought or done, had he spotted a ship flying colors with the reds and the blues reversed? If a group hostile to King and Country used a reverse-colored flag as their insignia, perhaps he too might close and fire on their ship.

It had taken the better part of the afternoon for them to realize the differences in the flags, and then it was a young, poorly educated boy who first noticed it. Pierce supposed they had not noticed because the shapes and patterns fit, and seeing those familiar shapes, the question of color had never arisen.

"Very sharp there, lad!" Pierce said. "I'll note your contribution in the log."

"Why, thankee, sir! Thankee!" Haight beamed at this recognition from his captain, and turned back to his duties an inch taller.

"That clarifies a great deal," remarked Hotchkiss.

"Aye, it does," agreed Pierce. "But they must at least agree to a cease-fire. We have no quarrel with them. I don't wish to sink, capture, or destroy that ship. Nor do I wish to kill or wound any more of her crew."

"But to convince them?"

"A tough nut, to be sure."

Pierce put the speaking trumpet to his mouth once again. "You need not surrender, sir! A cease-fire? Clear your wreckage? See to your wounded?"

Hawke's captain had returned to helping clear his ship of wreckage. He straightened up wearily but did not reply.

Pierce hailed again. "Your choice, sir! We will stand off or come alongside and assist! Your choice, sir!"

The other replied. "And once these things are done? Will we resume the fight?"

"By then, sir, we may find it need not continue! I shall not fire unless fired upon! That will hold true even when your decks are cleared and your wounded attended to!"

"Very well! Come alongside if you wish!"

"I assume this also pertains to boarding parties and hand to hand as well, sir?"

"You would think so ill of me, sir?"

"No, sir, I do not question your honor. It is simply a point upon which I must be sure as to the safety of my ship and crew!"

"Understood! At your convenience, sir!"

Pierce tucked the trumpet under his arm and raised his hat in salute to the sloop's captain. That individual, hatless, touched thumb and forefinger to his brow. Then he turned back to the work of clearing away wreckage.

Pierce stepped down to the deck. "Mr. Hotchkiss!"

"Sir?"

"All guns to be loaded, grape and round shot! Do not run out, and let one man remain at each gun!"

"Aye aye, sir!" Hotchkiss turned and passed the orders to Midshipman Andrews and Master's Mates Spencer and Dial, who in turn would see to their implementation.

"Mr. O'Brien, lay us along their port side! Gently! Gently! We go to aid distressed seamen, not to carry an enemy by boarding!"

"Aye aye, sir!"

Pierce clambered into the lower main shrouds. "Lads, we've fought a good fight, but it's over! We are angry for what seems an unwarranted attack! But we set that anger aside to assist fellow seamen regain their ship and tend their wounded.

"By God, I'll have any man jack at the gratings who abuses, steals, or plunders in that ship. Should any disregard that, this will be a dry ship for the remainder of the voyage! I will pour all spirits into the sea!"

Pierce paused and then he hollered for the bo'sun. "Mr. Cartney, take a party aboard to aid their bo'sun. Campbell can carry on with our own work!"

"Aye aye, sir!"

"Where's Chips?"

"Sounding the well, I believe, sir," answered Hadley.

"Have him report as is convenient!"

"Aye aye, sir."

Mr. Cook, the carpenter, appeared shortly thereafter. "One shot hole below the waterline, sir. Forward. Plugged and holding. Fifteen inches, but pumps are gaining, sir"

"No danger then, Chips?"

"Oh no, sir! None whatsoever! She's still a tight little thing, just not as pure and untouched as before!" He grinned. Hopkins, who was at the helm, snickered slightly.

Pierce caught the implication and the helmsman's reaction, but gave no sign that he had. "In that case, repair aboard *Hawke* when we are alongside. Take what men you need; aid in plugging shot holes and pumping out!"

"Aye aye, sir."

"Mr. Steadman, kindly ascertain Dr. Matheson's capacity to aid *Hawke's* surgeon!"

"Aye aye, sir."

As repair and assistance parties were being organized, Pierce watched O'Brien bring *Island Expedition* gently along side the battered *Hawke*.

Should he request the sloop's captain to join him on the schooner? Or should Pierce allow him to remain at his tasks and meet him aboard the sloop? Practicality won and he decided to board the other vessel and meet his counterpart there.

Pierce took the pistols from his belt and laid them on the binnacle. He thought to leave his sword as well, but it would not be a hostile act to board while it was sheathed. It was part of the uniform.

The two vessels lay aside one another and rested like two prize fighters pummeled so severely that each held on to the other for support and rest. Fenders had been hung and lines passed to secure them together. O'Brien had brought *Island Expedition* alongside *Hawke* so that their entry ports were aligned. Planks had been laid across the narrow gap to facilitate movement between the schooner and the sloop.

Pierce halted at the plank and eyed the movements of the vessels and the motions of the joining planks. He didn't want to misjudge his step and fall. He could swim, but the water was cold, and prolonged immersion would be hazardous to his well-being. Pride also played a part, as he did not wish either crew see him go for an unplanned swim.

Within seconds, he saw enough of the motions. He stepped across briskly and onto the deck of *Hawke*, and headed aft in search of her captain.

Around him, men were busy, both those of the sloop and those from *Island Expedition*. They all worked together to repair the most obvious damage. They pursued a common goal even though an hour ago they had done their utmost to sink the other's ship. But that was the way of combat at sea. Ships fought ships, but once the fighting was over, all were men of the sea, and all men of the sea were brothers.

Pierce had been in action many times. He had been aboard ships seriously damaged by a powerful enemy, and he had boarded ships after they had been pounded by his own. He had seen worse, but this sloop-of-war had taken a severe beating.

He felt no thrill at the victory. He would not gloat over the defeat of a nominally larger ship. He took no delight to step aboard the vanquished foe. This ship posed no threat to Great Britain. They probably did not even realize the existence of the British Empire. Pierce had not fought in defense of King and Country as he would have if *Hawke* had flown French, Spanish, Dutch, or even American colors. He had fought only because he had been fired upon. He had been forced to return fire and beat down and smother all aggression and belligerency in his opponent.

Pierce found the captain at the after end of the quarterdeck, engaged in efforts to clear away the wreckage of the mizzen topmast. Two bodies lay under the fallen cross trees, broken and grotesquely bent by the shower of debris. The sloop's captain wearily directed the work, and at times stepped in and lent a hand.

"Captain?" said Pierce quietly, almost afraid to intrude upon the man's endeavors and thoughts. "Captain?" he said, just a little louder.

The sloop's captain stood slowly and turned around. He was taller than Pierce, somewhat over six feet, and thinner as well. He appeared to be not much older than Pierce, and if not for the strain of combat, the resulting dishevelment and soil, might have been considered a handsome gentleman

"Most noble of you, sir," he said. "I didn't think Galway Rebels had such a degree of breeding and sophistication. More as if you were a King's Officer, or an old-line Gallician sea officer. Since their Revolt, those we meet are, for the most part, unrefined and dastardly brutes."

"Captain, you are low at this moment, so I will not take offense at being called a Galway Rebel. I am not aware of that aspect of Irish troubles. I do assure you that I am a King's Officer, commissioned in His Majesty's Navy as Master and Commander, and captain of His

Majesty's Schooner *Island Expedition*. Edward Pierce, at your service, sir!"

The struggle to believe was evident on the other's face. He composed himself and simply said, "Horatio Newbury, Commanding Master, His Regal Majesty's Sloop-of-War *Hawke*."

"You do not believe me," said Pierce. "In your face I see you would know the truth. But we are each as claimed, unless there is more to you than evident. However, the real truth of my existence may be difficult to understand."

"Very perceptive, Captain. At the instant, I am ashamed of defeat and yet grateful for the assistance you lend. This shall put an end to any hope I may have had for a post captaincy in the near future." Newbury's head sank. "We agreed only to a cease fire, but should you wish my sword and my ship, I am powerless to prevent it."

"I proposed a cease-fire, and that is all we need between us, sir. You are not my enemy. I do not need your ship as a prize, nor your sword as a trophy."

"Most gallant of you, sir. While I still feel that you are of the Galway Rebellion, I will not accuse you of the same."

"Very honest and forthright, I must say. Now, join me aboard *Island Expedition*. Surely I have a bottle left un-shattered. Galley fires are going and Eubanks is boiling up double rations of peas and salt pork. Enough, I believe, that we can offer your men a portion. I will have the same, as I have no stock of cabin stores at hand. You, sir, are most welcome to sup with me, such as the fare may be."

"But I must remain to direct and assist in clearing and repair efforts."

"Nonsense, man! One can only do so much. All do better with full stomachs, including you and I, sir. If there is no one to take over in your stead, I will send Midshipman Andrews. He is second amongst the young gentlemen, and for some time has performed duties more as those of a lieutenant."

"Very well, captain," replied Newbury. "Perhaps it is best we continue our discussion below. The hands will be grateful for a hot meal. But first I must visit my wounded. I'm afraid, sir, that your accurate and heavy fire played havoc amongst us."

"Most distressing! Dr. Matheson should be aboard and aiding to that end, sir, providing he has fulfilled duties to his own shipmates."

In *Island Expedition's* cabin, where Pierce's sleeping cabin would be when bulkheads were replaced, and having split a bottle of Madeira, the two captains were silent and deep in individual thought. The visitor, Newbury, spoke. "Amazing that ship's biscuit and only warm salt pork and peas would touch one's palate so well! A most talented cook, sir."

"He does a fair deal at that! And this far along, he has the coffee hot and fresh in the morning."

"Never developed a taste for it. Hot tea or cocoa suits me more," responded Newbury. They lapsed into another silence, which was ended by the appearance of Hotchkiss and an officer from the *Hawke*. "Jarvis, my first lieutenant," stated the sloop's captain.

"And Hotchkiss, my first lieutenant," said Pierce. "Yes?"

Hotchkiss replied. "We are working at something for a mizzen topmast. They have spares that will serve for the main topgallant and the yards."

"But nothing for the mizzen topmast, I take it?"

"Aye, sir. Not even close, sir," added Jarvis. "Unless we rig just to see us to port?"

"And?" queried Newbury.

"We've got a spare fore topmast aboard that looks near the same, sir," answered Hotchkiss. "If we might offer it to them?" The last remark was directed at Pierce.

"If it can be transferred across expeditiously, and that we don't overextend the hands doing it."

"It shouldn't pose any problem in either area, sir."

"Very well, Mr. Hotchkiss, you and Mr. Jarvis may see to it. I would advise that as you can, give the hands some moments of rest and some supper."

"Aye aye, sir."

"Good advice, Mr. Jarvis. You will undertake the same advisement regarding our people. Ensure that you also have a meal and a little rest!"

"Aye aye, sir!"

After the lieutenants left, Newbury appeared to be deep in thought. Then he spoke. "Captain Pierce, I am very grateful for your assistance. That we are in such a state is my fault. Nevertheless I felt I had you to rights. It did not occur to me that a vessel presumed to be a Galway Rebel pirate would be so well-armed or fight so uncommon ferociously.

"And, captain, I hesitate to say this, and I pray my words do not offend you. I still harbor suspicion as to your real purpose. You claim to be a King's Officer, and a member of His Majesty's Navy. Yet, I do not recollect your name on the Commanding Master list. I recall no ship with the name that is painted across your stern. Your flag is that which of late has been adopted by those seeking Galway independence. Further, your uniform, and those of your officers, do not meet with current regulations for such.

"My signal for you to heave to was met with a coded profanity that the Galway Rabble uses in great insult to the King."

"I did not comprehend your signal, sir, and hoisted the interrogative," Pierce replied, unaffected by Newbury's sudden prying and suspicions. "A coincidence that it meant different to you. No insult was intended."

"Quite understandable. I do not fault your conduct, sir, either during the engagement, or now with your provision of assistance. Yet I wonder how you are what you claim to be, when everything tells me it isn't so."

"Perhaps, sir, I speak of different worlds," said Pierce. "I and this schooner are indeed as I say. But you do see we do not serve the same Navy, nor the same King."

"Perhaps it is as I suspect?"

"Not as you suspect, sir. Allow your mind free rein over your knowledge of the world."

"How so?"

"I don't fully understand it either, but picture it thusly. We can define our exact location on this deck in relation to the centerline and the stem or stern of the vessel."

"It requires no effort on my part to see that, sir!" Newbury was agitated at the beginning of the explanation

"Please follow me, sir, and it will all be made clearer." Pierce took a last sip from his glass. "Now, Captain Newbury, if we have those measurements that define our location here, we could go on deck and position ourselves in the same exact spot that we are in now. We would be in the exact place we are now, and yet we would not be."

"I don't follow, sir?"

"You sir, your world, your King, the Navy in which you serve are on this very deck. My world, my King, the Navy in which I serve are on another deck. By luck or design we have found the 'ladder' that connects the two worlds or decks."

"Am I to believe that on that world, on that deck, there is a Kentland, a Grand Triton, a Galway, a King Geoffrey the Fifth?"

"No, sir! But there is an England, a Great Britain, an Ireland, and a King George the Third! There are many similarities, although from what we have seen, the worlds are not exact parallels. Even the geography doesn't correspond."

"A very interesting story, I'm sure," mused Newbury, raising one eyebrow. "I do find it hard to fathom. You appear a generous and honest man, sir, so forgive me to not readily accept this explanation."

"It is a stretch," Pierce nodded.

"You will understand I still harbor those suspicions I had when we first encountered each other."

"Were I in your place, sir, I would also," commented Pierce.

Mr. Steadman clattered hurriedly down the aft companionway. Had bulkheads and doors been in place, he would have knocked, but he was suddenly face to face with the two captains. "Beg pardon, sir," he said.

"Yes, Mr. Steadman?" asked Pierce.

"Mr. Hotchkiss's complements, sir, and that four sail are sighted, bearing southwest, sir."

"Thank you, Mr. Steadman. My compliments to Mr. Hotchkiss, and I'll be on deck presently."

"The weather has cleared since we've been below," offered Captain Newbury. He looked out the stern windows, two of which had been shattered by the guns of his own ship. "It is bright enough that a sail can be seen a good distance way."

"Quite so," Pierce agreed, looking in the same direction. "I must go on deck and see to the safety of my ship. After our encounter, sir, I distrust the sight of other vessels. And four at once is risky."

"I must add, sir, that now, perhaps we have you!"

"How so?"

"Unless I am mistaken, what approaches is the main body of the Flying Squadron. *Hawke* was scouting ahead when we spotted you. At the same time several sail were sighted to the northwest. The Flying Squadron set off in chase of those, and I came to investigate you. Now that you have won our encounter, it seems that you will yet end up defeated. You have my sincerest apologies, sir, for your misfortune, but I will see duty done, and justice will prevail."

"I've not yet surrendered, sir. This, as you have experienced, is a most handy ship. Fast as well."

"Aye! But it is a considerable force that approaches. More, I daresay, than your young gentleman reported. A force under whose broadsides you would not long survive."

"I had not particularly thought to fight, sir. I know the odds, even if all of them were as *Hawke* or even this. Instead, I shall flee."

"All very well, sir. They are to windward, and would have you, should you choose to run between them. Leeward? You realize we are near on a lee shore?" Newbury remarked smugly.

"I suspect such, but of its exact location I am not be certain."

"If you are very good, if this ship is as you say she is, and as I have seen, you may indeed have a chance. Slim, but still, a chance."

"Now, Captain Newbury, I must ask you to return to your ship! I and my men will bid you and *Hawke* adieu! I hope that the repairs are satisfactory and sufficiently complete, for they must cease as they are. Now!"

"I quite understand. I do wish you luck, sir, although I feel that you will not succeed."

That small knot of fear and anxiety gnawed at his gut once more. Pierce silently cursed himself for this latest turn of events. Not knowing of the Flying Squadron was no excuse. It irritated him that Newbury had been a part of it, and had not told him. Yet *Hawke's* captain was not obliged to do so. More, in his duty, Newbury was required not to tell him.

It was Pierce's fault that they were in this new predicament. If he had not been so generous and concerned for the safety and survival of a ship that had earlier tried to destroy him, he would have left her there, wallowing semi-dismasted and threatening to sink in the cold choppy sea.

It was not time for self-incrimination. It was time to act! He hastily escorted Captain Newbury to the weather deck and the gangway. "You will excuse me, sir, for seeing you off with haste!"

"Understandable, sir," said Newbury, stepping across to his own ship. "Mr. Jarvis! Clear *Hawke* of all men from the schooner. She is leaving!"

On board *Island Expedition*, Pierce also began shouting orders. "Mr. Hotchkiss! Every man jack aboard, immediately! Mainsail and headsails in five minutes! Guns manned, loaded, and run out -- quickly, now!"

Chapter Twenty

Captive

Pierce was determined not to surrender without attempting to escape. He recalled *Island Expedition's* hands from *Hawke* and cordially but without ceremony sent Newbury back aboard. Then he hoisted the schooner's huge main and fore sails, topsails and topgallants, and sped away from the sloop, racing wing and wing before the wind.

He watched through his night glass as the newly arrived ships convened at the *Hawke's* location, hove to briefly, and set out in pursuit. One remained alongside the battered sloop to aid in repair, much as *Island Expedition* had recently done.

The schooner flew over the water and by dawn the pursuing ships were hull down. The five sail, spread like a giant net, were sure to snare *Island Expedition,* if only they could gain more speed. But if something drove their prey back to them, their speed deficit would not matter.

Eight bells sounded aboard *Island Expedition* and the forenoon watch was set. The foremast lookout hailed the deck, reporting breakers dead ahead. Pierce swung north to parallel the reef, and on the schooner's best point of sailing, hoped to forereach on the ships approaching from windward. Barring success at that, he thought that he might close to long cannon shot, feint one way, sail another, and hopefully pass through the enemy ranks close-hauled. Once to windward, the sailing qualities of *Island Expedition* would allow him to beat to windward more easily and efficiently than those strange, ominous warships.

The British schooner had maintained a port broad reach for nearly an hour when white water was again sighted ahead. Pierce judged the positions of the closing ships, their speed, and the wind against his own position, and reluctantly determined that he could not break through to windward.

With the Flying Squadron even closer, he would not have had any chance to reverse course and pass along the entire line and around the other end. *Island Expedition* was no match for any one of the vessels bearing down upon her. The schooner had a dozen twelve-pound long guns and four twelve-pound carronades. The smallest approaching ship was a sixth-rate, larger than *Hawke*, and mounting twenty-two guns. He could take her, if he handled the schooner adroitly, if his crew handled the guns efficiently, and if the opposing captain was ever so hesitant. Pierce thought to take on the small post ship, engage in a twisting battle of course changes and broadsides, and worm his way to windward.

That would work if they were the only two ships on the sea. The small post ship was accompanied by a small frigate, two larger frigates, and a seventy-four. The sloop was at the far end of the enemy's front, making it impractical to attempt an escape past her.

The rapidly nearing foe did not run blindly at him, content on fixed courses and luck. They continuously altered course slightly, sometimes one at a time, sometimes in unison, as they closed in, narrowing the gaps between them, and not allowing any avenue of escape. An attempt to fight and run through them would have been futile and suicidal, and he had no intention of destroying his ship and killing his crew, or himself.

As seven bells rang in the cold air, the forenoon watch nearly ended, Pierce came to the conclusion that there was no escape. He used his hands as a speaking trumpet to address the crew.

"Men of *Island Expedition*! We have journeyed far. We have endured all the sea and wind could bring against us. We have had strange encounters that no one before has ever experienced. We have fought, at her insistence, a ship larger and more powerful, and fought her to the point of surrender. You have shown the fullness of spirit and abilities as fighting British tars!

"You have also shown great kindness, for I saw the effort you put forth to help our former adversary. You have the hearts of warriors and the compassion and generosity of true men!

"But now, the force approaching is large, powerful, and determined. It would be madness to fight them. I will not throw your lives away in any insane attempt.

"As it is, our only option is to heave to, lower our colors, and hope for true justice."

The somber silence that fell upon the schooner roared like a thousand-gun broadside, and Pierce nearly wished he had ordered a hopeless and desperate attack on the two-decker.

Bitterness and despair rose in his throat, threatening to choke him, as he finally ordered, "All hands, 'bout ship! Mr. O'Brien, the starboard tack, if you please!"

"Aye aye, sir!" the master quietly and solemnly answered.

When *Island Expedition* settled on that course, Pierce ordered sail reduced little by little, and as the other ships closed to long cannon shot, ordered the main topsail aback. A gun was fired to leeward, and the Blue Ensign hauled down.

The strange ships approached cautiously, their guns run out and crews at the ready. They surrounded the schooner; the sloop and a large frigate passed by and hove to so as to prohibit any flight before the wind. The other frigates blocked any attempt to flee on either a port or starboard tack. The two-decker positioned itself to windward of the defeated schooner.

Small boats put off from the ship-of-the-line and the larger frigates. They brought boarding parties to seize *Island Expedition* and ensure she did not mount any last-minute acts of desperation. Knowing the odds were against him, Pierce did not contemplate such action, and instructed the crew that none should be undertaken.

Pierce offered his sword to the young lieutenant who approached him warily but openly on the schooner's deck. "You may keep it, sir," he said. "Captain Newbury passed to us his gratitude for your kindness following your recent engagement and his opinion that you, sir, are a gentleman."

Pierce and Hotchkiss, the schooner's only commissioned officers, were taken aboard the seventy-four, which they learned was rated as a *seventy-six* in the Kentish Navy. The *Duchess Irene* was the center of the Flying Squadron, flying the pennant of Commodore Sir James Hargrove. Her captain was Thomas McKenzie.

The two English officers were pleasantly surprised when asked to join the commodore and the other captains for dinner that evening. Pierce thought that if truly considered pirates and rebels, they would have been locked away in some secure location.

They were treated more as guests aboard the flagship. As the meal progressed, they became party to an informal inquiry regarding Captain Newbury's conduct. Their own actions made favorable impressions upon the assembled captains.

As the last bottle of wine made its way around the table, Sir James finally said, "Lest we forget in the midst of mutual admiration, these two are suspected pirates and rebels. Yet, certain things in their actions and their records and logs point to something else. I have not the training, nor the time to reason it. We have our duties, gentlemen, so let us pass this matter along, and let those qualified, determine the disposition.

"Captain Jackson, as *Furious* is longest without stores, you will provide passage for them to Brunswick, New Guernsey. Deliver them to our consulate, replenish stores and water, and return with the prize crew and guards sent aboard the schooner. Lieutenant Jarvis of *Hawke* will command the schooner to Brunswick."

Pierce was in no position to object. It did not matter who commanded what once had been his ship. Having dealt with Jarvis the evening before, Pierce knew *Island Expedition* would not be in the hands of a complete stranger. The selection also told him, that as the junior captain in the squadron, Commander Newbury was highly thought of by the commodore.

Despite defeat at Pierce's hand, Newbury's silence had allowed the squadron to capture supposed Galway Rebels. Having his first lieutenant assigned to command the captured vessel was a vote of confidence for Newbury. As the announcement was made, Pierce detected a release of tension and a beam of pride on Newbury's face. Nor did he detect any signs of disagreement upon the faces of the other captains. They stood behind Newbury, or were relieved not to lose an officer of their own to command the prize.

Sir James continued. "Written orders will be sent shortly. Bear in mind, Captain Jackson, that they will be treated as guests. Proper measures may be taken that they do not escape or damage your ship, but...."

"I understand completely, Sir James." From the look on his face, it was plain that Jackson would have preferred no restrictions be placed on his handling of the prisoners.

Pierce thought it odd to be a prisoner of one with the same name as his former captain and mentor. Vaguely there was a resemblance between the two. Granville Jackson of HMS *Theadora* was younger, more slender, and of a kinder, more pleasant demeanor. By the time dinner aboard HRMS *Duchess Irene* ended, Pierce had determined that Lowell Jackson was a man of a different and perhaps darker nature.

They accompanied Jackson back to *Furious*. True to Pierce's earlier impression, Jackson remarked, once they were out of earshot of the flagship, that he "would just as soon the two of you be chained and locked in the bread room. But I have orders, and they will be obeyed."

"We are most grateful for that, sir," Pierce had said.

He was dead tired and wanted only to sleep. At the same time, he subtly tested the character and mood of his jailer, probing, looking for any sign of weakness that he and Hotchkiss could employ to their advantage.

"Orders are orders, and obedience is the key to victory," Jackson replied, as if by rote. "Obedience is the key!"

Aboard *Furious*, Jackson barked orders. He turned the junior lieutenants out of their cabin, moving one in with the master and the other in with the surgeon. Pierce and Hotchkiss were given the vacated cabin, which would be locked nightly. During the day they would have full run of the ship, accompanied discreetly by a marine guard. They were granted access to the wardroom for meals, provided the wardroom members agreed to their captain's suggestion. From what Pierce came to understand of Jackson, that suggestion could be taken only as a request or a direct order.

Their sea chests and belongings were brought from *Island Expedition*, and after having been searched for weapons, contraband, or seditious materials, were placed in the minute cabin. Prior to being locked in for the night, they were allowed a few minutes' relaxation and a chance to become acquainted with members of the wardroom.

The only light came from a fire that burned low on the grate. The flames danced, and hypnotized Pierce into a feeling of peaceful contentment. He lay on the floor, several blankets and pillows under him for comfort and more over him for warmth. Evangeline was nestled snug, warm, and contented against him, asleep. They had sat together for hours under the blankets, watching the flames leap and warm the small room. They had talked, loved, and relished the togetherness after so many years apart. Pierce did not have the urge to be aboard ship and at sea, so perfect and grand was the moment.

The fire died down, and a sudden draft snuffed out the remaining flame. Darkness closed in, and for a moment he could not see. He eased his position slightly and tried not to disturb her, hoping to find a placement comfortable for them both. In the enveloping gloom he could not feel her presence, nor hear the soft sounds of her breathing. Darkness, more intense than any caused by the lack of light, cascaded over him, and washed away his joy.

Pierce heard four bells, and thought the motion of *Island Expedition* strange. Was something wrong? The shouts and cries of the crew beginning a new day reached his ears, but the voices that stood out from the general din were not familiar. The shouts of "Out or down!" and "Lash and stow!" were recognizable, but he could not place the voices that produced them. It was not Campbell and Davis, the schooner's bo'sun's mates, whom he heard.

He opened his eyes. The cabin was sufficiently bright that he could make out larger details. He swung his legs over and sat up. There was another suspended cot close by, and as his eyes accommodated the dimness, he saw that it was occupied by Isaac Hotchkiss.

There was a sharp rap at the door, and a voice, loud but not demanding, that simply said, "If you two is up, you can get yourselves about at your pleasure!" A key clicked in a lock, and chains fell away.

Hotchkiss stirred uneasily in his cot. Pierce still sat upon his, not yet fully awake, tired, aching, full of despair and self-loathing. He had surrendered his ship, sent his men into captivity, and due to their captors' suspicions, perhaps to their deaths. Had he not been so anxious to speak with a ship from this world, he would never have allowed that strange sail to approach so closely. *Island Expedition* could easily have outdistanced her, sailed over the horizon in a matter of hours, and could even now have been sailing as Pierce desired.

He could have reduced the sloop to a complete shambles. He had purposely sent the last two broadsides wide, but they could have easily thundered and smashed into and through the battered craft. More could have followed. Then with his foe completely destroyed, Pierce could have sailed away, left her to the mercy of the wind and wave, and the questionable abilities of her decimated crew to keep her afloat.

His damned compassion for fellow seamen had prevented him from taking such action. Had he not remained far into the night along side his former foe, the Kentish Navy's Flying Squadron would never have caught him. He would not be locked in this stuffy cabin, bound for who knows where.

"You awake, Ed?" asked Hotchkiss in the gloom.

"I'm awake, indeed, Isaac," he replied and automatically shifted to their boyhood friendship in place of the quarterdeck formalities they had observed for so long. "Although under these circumstances I would much rather be asleep."

"As would I," said Hotchkiss, who sat upright and swung his feet over to the deck. "Rather strange, if you ask me. Prisoners on one hand and guests and even fêted for our accomplishments on the other."

"Men of the sea recognize one's abilities and skills, regardless of nationality. There is that bond between all. These of the Kentish Navy are no different in that from any British officer."

"Well put! But did you notice the atmosphere of gloom and suspicion in the wardroom? They seemed most reluctant to be themselves."

"As if they are afraid of something or someone."

"Exactly, Edward!"

"But now, Isaac, we have been uncaged. Let's be about some coffee and perhaps a chance at breakfast. We'll have enough time on board to fathom their fears."

Later, during the forenoon watch, Pierce walked the quarterdeck, feeling strange and out of place on the lee side. He was not the captain or the senior officer on deck, and so was not entitled to that preferred spot. He was with young Mr. Roberson, detailed to keep him company, and perhaps to ensure that no escape was attempted. It was also possible that the midshipman would try to discover something that would prove him a pirate and a Galway Rebel.

The young man was pleasant, knowledgeable, and agreeable. He was quite open in his admiration of Pierce's handling of *Island Expedition* against his own service's *Hawke*.

"I gave Mr. Hotchkiss my copy of *Johnston's Geographic World Atlas*," he said. "He asked if I had any literature on board, especially from which he could learn more of the world. Beg pardon, but how could one gain a commission, and not know world geography?"

"He does know it, and well. But neither he nor I know the geography of this world."

"Still the tale of different worlds, sir? I'd give it up were I in your shoes. Just don't think it would wash at a trial or court-martial, sir."

"I would not believe it possible, had I not experienced it myself. By now the senior officers of this squadron have looked at the charts we had aboard. Those would surely prove that we are from a world different from this one."

"They might, sir. But in my short experience I've learned that those in charge can see what they want, if it suits their or the King's interest."

Pierce did not reply, but continued to pace slowly up and down the quarterdeck. "Perhaps I am intruding, sir, by keeping up with the conversation. I'll step aside and allow you the privacy of your thoughts."

Mr. Roberson was most intuitive, thought Pierce, who nodded in the affirmative and continued his walk.

The pace and step became second nature and Pierce was deep in thought, his mind on many things and in many places at once. He had nearly reached the point of being totally oblivious to all around him when orders were shouted and pipes started to squeal.

"All hands aft! All hands aft to witness punishment! All hands!"

Jackson was on deck in full dress uniform. He carried a sheaf of papers in one hand, and wore a look of haughty superiority upon his face. He caught sight of Pierce. "Ah, Commander Pierce. You are in time. You shall see what I meant, that obedience is the key! Most importantly, Pierce, it is punishment that ensures obedience!"

"I had thought, sir, that as I am not ship's company, I would go below and not intrude upon ship's routine."

"Nonsense," said Jackson. "I think you should see the discipline of the Navy and learn why your rebellion will not succeed. Obedience will win, and you will see the consequences of a lack of it."

Pierce was all but ordered to witness the upcoming punishment.

"Mr. Roberson!" said Jackson. "Commander Pierce will join us for this session of discipline. Run below and desire his compatriot, Mr. Hotchkiss, do the same!"

"Ay-ye, aye, sir!" Roberson stuttered and was visibly flustered at being addressed by his captain. He touched the brim of his hat and took off at a run to fetch Hotchkiss. Pierce wondered that the young man could be so flustered by his captain. Ten minutes earlier he had been relaxed, respectful, and in control of himself, conversing with Pierce in an intelligent and easy manner.

Hotchkiss arrived, somewhat out of breath, and twitched the last portions of his rig into proper trim. He glanced inquiringly at Pierce, whose return look answered to the uncertainty of the situation. Jackson indicated a place for them.

"Johann Schmidt, foretopman, step forward!" roared Jackson. From amongst the assembled crew, the named man stepped forward hesitantly. "Come! Come! Let's not dawdle! You are reported as the last man on deck when the watch below was called! Have you anything to say?"

"No, sir!" said Schmidt weakly. The ashen pall of fear showed through the darkness of his sun- and wind-burned countenance.

Jackson nodded and two hands seized the unfortunate Schmidt. His shirt was removed. The man's back was unscarred.

"Damn, he's made it this far in the commission without a touch of the cat," said Jackson. "But he will learn obedience, and he will earn the wages of disobedience! Seize him up!"

Schmidt was tied to the grating that stood lashed to the bulwark.

"Four dozen, Mr. Bo'sun!"

Pierce was shocked by the severity of the ordered punishment, just as he was appalled at the circumstances of the punishment itself. There always was a *last man* in any evolution, and it was contrary to his nature that one should be punished simply for being that man. He had served with captains that had sometimes resorted to such measures to speed up a lackadaisical crew, but never had he heard so many lashes ordered.

He forced himself to watch as the bo'sun's mate made ready. Pierce was dismayed to see punishment would not be administered with a standard cat-of-nine tails, but rather with a larger, heavier, and more destructive *thief's cat*. The first blow had not landed and in the cold air, not much above freezing, Pierce felt himself break into a sweat.

The drum rolled. When it ended, the bo'sun's mate flung his arm back and brought the vicious cat down with all his might upon Schmidt's back. The crack of its impact against skin, flesh, and bone resounded over the deck like thunder. "One!" The drum rolled again. "Two!" And again the drum rolled. "Three!"

Each blow knocked the wind out of him. Before he could fully recover and draw a full breath, the cat landed again. Against the pain, and in an effort to not cry out, Schmidt bit his tongue. Blood streamed from his mouth as well as from his back. "Four!"

Pierce felt light-headed. He wanted to sit and put his head between his knees. He had felt this way the first time he had seen a flogging, years ago aboard *Ferret*. His response had been the same every time he had been required to witness it. Now it was time to gaze elsewhere, to look at the horizon or an object aloft, and turn his mind to other thoughts. He had learned long ago that he could effectively leave the scene of the brutality and transcend to a state where such was not taking place. "Five!"

Pierce was in a trance. He heard the drum rolls. He heard the crack and splat of the cat against the man's back. He heard the number of the blow.

"Sixteen!"

But he did not see the blows land and knock the wind from the victim. He did not see the skin of his back disappear under a smear of blood and torn flesh. He did not see the bo'sun's mate run the tails through his fingers to remove bits of flesh, or shake them out on the deck.

Pierce was only conscious of the roll and pitch of the frigate, the effort to maintain his balance, and that block abaft the foremast. It was newer than the rest, weathered to a lesser degree. He stared at it so intently that he could make out the wood's grain, even as far away as it was.

"Twenty-seven!"

The drum rolled. The tails landed once more with a crack. Schmidt was unconscious and did not respond to the latest blow.

"Forty-eight!"

"Very well, cut him down!" said Jackson as he consulted the papers in his hand. "Tom Williams, able seaman, step forward!"

Again it was a minor offense, if it could be considered an offense at all. Once more the severity of the sentence, three dozen lashes, shocked Pierce. He tried very hard to maintain his composure and to appear nonplussed and unaffected by the excessive brutality. He wanted to run headlong to the rail and empty his stomach into the cold churning sea. He wanted to sit for a moment and let this dizziness and weakness leave him.

He also felt a blind rage toward Captain Lowell Jackson, and wanted to rush him, strike him to the deck, and halt the senseless cruelty and brutal punishments. But discipline instilled over his years of service prevented his acting upon his instincts. He remained as he was and noted the offenses and the number of lashes specified, and the names and count of offenders. God, there were a lot of them; it evidently had been some time since punishment had been meted out aboard *Furious*.

"Ralph Whitcomb, landsman, step forward!" snarled Jackson.

Momentarily coming out of his self-induced fog, Pierce saw that this individual had to be helped from the ranks. So afraid was he that he could barely walk.

"Cut down in your hammock three days running. Anything to say?"

"I… I…" was as far as the man got.

"Five dozen, if you please! Lay on with a will! A little light for the last man. Any more like that and you'll dance with the cat as well!" Jackson stared malevolently at the bo'sun's mates. The three had rotated, either after a dozen blows, or after every victim, but they had done so much, that short rests did not allow their arms to regain full strength and effectiveness of the blows desired by their captain.

The next victim was seized to the grating and his shirt ripped from his back. Pierce felt an inaudible gasp pass through the crew. He shifted his gaze from the rigging and saw that even before the first blow, that this man's back was a bloody, beaten pulp. It oozed and festered, little rivulets of blood flowed here and there and seeped out amongst the dried and blackened scabs left by a very recent flogging. Whitcomb slumped against the ropes binding him to the grating.

"Captain! Captain! I say, sir! You can not flog this man, sir! He has not recovered from his last! He needs time sir, for the medications I've prescribed to do their work!"

The speaker was an older man, dressed in a uniform of a bygone age, if indeed uniform at all.

"Can't! Can't? You say, Doctor! The man is a malingerer. He's playing this to keep from work and duty! Can't?"

Jackson was red with anger. "By God, Doctor Lycoming, you will never tell me what I can and cannot do aboard my ship! This man will be punished for his offense, unless you would volunteer to take his place?"

"I am of a standing not susceptible to the cat, sir!"

"As I thought, Doctor! Anyone to take this man's place?"

Pierce watched the assembled crew for a volunteer to take

Whitcomb's place. He was not surprised when no one stepped forward. Aboard this ship, every man had a very good chance to dance at the gratings and did not need to submit to that agony for a shipmate.

The thought that he should volunteer passed briefly through his mind and left just as quickly. It was a noble thought, but not one that made sense. Jackson would be mad to allow an officer, even an apparent enemy, to be flogged. Should he actually volunteer, Pierce would be just as mad. With his aversion to merely witnessing the ghastly spectacle, how could he in his right mind ever consider submitting himself to it?

"Well, then Mr. Bo'sun. The duty is yours!"

The drum rolled and the cat fell with a crack and crash. The previous victims had been silent, and had stifled their cries and expressions of pain. Some had bitten their tongues, and others, small pieces of leather or cloth provided by mess mates and friends. When the first blow landed upon Whitcomb's already tender back, he screamed in agony.

"One!"

He screamed at every blow until the seventeenth, when he passed out. The eighteenth through the sixtieth lash fell on the back of a man so completely unconscious that his body did not even instinctively respond to the savage blows.

"Sixty! Five dozen, sir!"

"Cut him down! Division officers, dismiss your divisions!"

Pierce wanted desperately to get below and away from the scene of such gross brutality before his weak dizziness would be noticed. His stomach threatened to forcefully empty itself. He hoped to disappear down the companionway before Jackson could corner him and expound on the merits of the severe beatings that had just been administered.

Nearly at the ladder, Pierce thought that perhaps he would make good his escape. But Jackson headed straight for him, with an obvious wish to engage in conversation. Pierce looked at Hotchkiss and communicated his desperation, even with that quick glance. The unspoken message was received and Hotchkiss moved to intercept the frigate's captain.

Quickly Hotchkiss asked Jackson a question about quarterdeck armament and diverted him away from a conversation with Pierce, who quickly thanked God.

Pierce made his way down the ladder to the gun deck. One more and he reached the berth deck. He headed aft to the wardroom and hoped against hope that no one was there.

Earlier he had noticed that in the very aft end of the ship, under the massive tiller and tiller ropes, in areas partitioned off as the wardroom privy, that there were two small ports that opened to the sea. He needed such a place now, where he could hang his head over the water, and if his stomach lost the battle within, spill its contents and not allow any sign of his weakness to linger and betray him. There too, he could cling to the port sill and recover his strength.

The starboard door was shut, that privy quite possibly in use. He stepped quickly into the port cubicle, shut the door and wrenched open the port lid. The cold spray kicked up by the ship's rudder, and the cold wintery air washed over him. He breathed of the cold refreshing dampness, and thought that he might recover. He didn't. He shuddered as waves of nausea overcame him, and the scant contents of his stomach were forcibly ejected into the sea. That over, he felt better and sat down, bent nearly double from the waist. After some minutes he felt better. Pierce set the place to rights and stepped out.

As he entered the wardroom, the starboard door opened and one of *Furious's* lieutenants stepped out, pale and ashen. Remnants of a cold sweat soaked his neckerchief. He looked at Pierce with sympathy. "My God, sir! I thought I was the only one!"

"Evidently not, Lieutenant ... Lieutenant?"

"Lieutenant Nelson, sir. Oliver Nelson."

"Strange I do not remember when your name is the same as one of my Navy's greatest leaders," said Pierce. "But I doubt that you and I are the only ones affected. Of a crew this size there are bound to be more. In these matters I'm sure one would strive to hide it from mess mates and friends."

"I will not speak of it, sir, past this moment and trust you return the faith as well?"

"Indeed, it shall be so. I hope you are not too inconvenienced, being put out of your cabin."

"In honesty, sir, it is awkward. But in a week or two, you'll be sent ashore at Brunswick, and Barry and I will have our place again."

Dinner was piped soon thereafter, and Pierce and Hotchkiss joined *Furious's* wardroom for the meal. Hotchkiss ate heartily, but Pierce's stomach was still uneasy. He ate a bite of stale biscuit and sipped at an unknown white wine that was passed around the table. Finished with their meal, the others returned to duties and the daily routine of shipboard life. Pierce and his friend remained.

"I think we see what the rot is amongst this crew, sir," offered Hotchkiss.

"Aye! That was the most brutal session of punishment I've ever seen. I hope to God I never do so again!"

"As do I!" avowed Hotchkiss. "And did you hear? One lieutenant on watch and watch because not enough of his division were on report. Another on continuous watch because too many of his division were."

"Not at all the way I was taught," Pierce said in a low confidential voice. "To watch this crew work is not a pretty picture! They are fast and precise, but they are driven to it, and fear any failure or deviation. There is no spirit, no initiative in this crew."

"They perform as machines at their officers' bidding. And the officers are marionettes under Jackson's control. You would not have fared well with this Jackson, my friend," said Hotchkiss.

"I have already seen them press on despite danger to shipmates, or self, only so that they do not upset routine, and are not the last off the yard or last on deck."

"I am not a praying man, Edward," whispered Hotchkiss quietly. "But I will say a prayer for the men of His Regal Majesty's Ship *Furious*. Daily!"

"As will I, Isaac! As will I!" Pierce leaned back.

Chapter Twenty-One

Mental Doldrums

Whitcomb died on Friday, the 17th of June. Pierce connected that day and the original Good Friday nearly two thousand years earlier. He did not believe Whitcomb could compare directly to the Redeemer, other than having been a human being, and as such, he certainly had deserved better. Pierce had not even known of Whitcomb until two days earlier, when he had been flogged nearly to death at the order of Captain Lowell Jackson.

Pierce had never been a friend of the cat and shied away from flogging at every turn. Should he ever be required flog a man, he would never have ordered the number of lashes that Jackson had. He would heed the ship's surgeon and never flog a man still recovering from a previous beating.

Whitcomb's death saddened and angered Pierce. That confused him, because he had not known the man. But his death by his captain's order, despite the surgeon's protests, for what seemed minor offenses, got to Pierce, and he did not sleep well for several days. It was all he could do to be civil to Jackson.

At times Pierce thought that for a shilling or two at most, he would lay into Jackson with whatever he might find lying about. With great effort, Pierce kept those urges contained. In spite of his white-hot ire, he saw the entire situation and strove to not make it worse. He was by all accounts a prisoner aboard *Furious*, but had the freedom of the ship during the day, thanks to Commodore Hargrove's orders detailing how he and his first lieutenant were to be treated. Without those express directives, the situation might have been grim, as Jackson had remarked very early on that he would as soon put them in irons. While

Jackson had observed that obedience was the key, how obedient would he be if provoked? Would he cast aside the literal intent of his orders and place Pierce in irons? Despite their brutal treatment, how would *Furious's* crew react to an assault upon their captain?

Maintenance of personal comfort was not why Pierce labored to restrain his anger. Accused of being Galway Rebels and pirates, Pierce had planted a seed of doubt in Commodore Hargrove's mind. He would not do anything to prevent the gestation and growth of that seed. More importantly, he had the well-being of Lieutenant Hotchkiss and the crew of *Island Expedition* to worry about. His men were prisoners aboard their own vessel, sailing in formation with *Furious.* Presently commanded by Lieutenant Jarvis, it was manned by a prize crew from ships around the squadron. Pierce was reasonably assured of their safety under Jarvis, but worried about Jackson's or his superiors' reactions, should he be angered excessively. Additionally Pierce had to consider the settlement on the island. Were he to anger the Kentish Government, it might prove disastrous to Smythe and the others. It was far better to endure the pain of a strangely personal loss, the rage of intense personal hatred, and strive to gain an ally.

Smythe opposed alliances with organizations or nations in this world where they now found themselves, preferring they reside in isolation. When he had first charted the island's location, that certainly seemed possible. But in the world where the island actually existed, that solitude did not exist. Practicality seemed to demand they seek harmonious relationships with neighboring peoples.

Staunchly loyal to Great Britain, Pierce first thought to seek ties with the nearly parallel Grand Triton, but present circumstances soured him on the idea. Having long admired the infant United States, he wondered if good relations with the Vespicans might be beneficial. They were, as he understood it, the nation nearest the tiny settlement.

These thoughts calmed him, and Pierce vowed to work with Jackson and other Grand Triton officials to disprove himself a Galway Rebel and a pirate.

In spite of reasonable and logical choices, the next weeks aboard *Furious* seemed never- ending. One long day blended into the next.

After the excessive and extreme punishments meted out that first day, Pierce hoped that long intervals existed between visits from the cat, but the lash called regularly. Thrice a week, or even daily, hands were called aft to witness punishment. Man after man was seized up and flogged brutally for minor and often contrived offenses. Such was the numbing dread of the cat that hands pressed too hard and trampled or pushed shipmates to avoid being yet another victim. Their haste and recklessness caused serious injury and even death with such regularity as to seem a normal part of the ship's daily routine.

Pierce brooded over losing his ship, surrendering, and being a prisoner. It irritated him that, with alternate decisions, he could have prevented the current situation. Regardless, two days later he might have sailed *Island Expedition* into the midst of the Flying Squadron and been in the same predicament. But it had happened, and he could not and would not forgive himself.

Despite his self-loathing, and his intense hatred for Lowell Jackson, Pierce seized the opportunity to learn all he could about the world where he found himself. The wardroom, where he and Hotchkiss were at first tolerated and then welcomed as guests, was friendly, helpful, and even sympathetic. Through general conversation, direct questions, and keen observation, Pierce and Hotchkiss learned of the world as their new-found acquaintances knew it.

Pierce had been essentially correct when he had suggested to Newbury that while the two worlds were similar, they were not exact parallels. The geography was different. Much of what equated to Europe and the northern hemisphere was in this world's southern hemisphere. North seemed to be exchanged for south, and east and west were reversed as well. The shape and position of land masses differed and could not be approximated by rearranging the map of one world to end up with a map of the other. Pierce and Hotchkiss learned most of this from *Johnston's Geographic World Atlas*. They spent hours studying maps and charts that portrayed the current world. What they learned of the world of men, they gained from conversations and the remarks of others. Many situations were similar to the world they knew, but again, things were not exactly the same.

The current troubles in Baltica, Europe's equivalent, could be traced to the Vespican Revolution. Like the American Revolution, the Vespican rebels had first objected to not being treated or considered in the same way as people of their parent nation. As the war had progressed, the Vespicans had ultimately obtained Gallician and Cordoban aid. The help was not in support of Vespican independence, but rather an attempt to subdue their hated enemy, Grand Triton.

The war to free the Kentish Colonies had bankrupted Gallicia. The higher taxes imposed on the populace, along with rumors and tales of the personal freedoms gained in Vespica, had caused revolution to sweep the countryside. As in France, the Gallician Revolution had ended up as an instrument of revenge and had created terror and fear far beyond what had existed previously. With some sort of order established, the revolution had begun to avenge the wrongs perpetrated over the years.

The revolutionary armed forces, purged of all leaders of noble or aristocratic influence, had begun a campaign of conquest and consolidation. The foremost aim of the Gallician Revolution was subjugation of their old antagonist. After more than ten years of war, the two nations had agreed to, and had signed, the Peace of Rouen. That treaty had not lasted and war had resumed. If peace here were over, Pierce wondered whether the Peace of Amiens had ended as well.

The Tritonish had ongoing problems with the Galway Rebels. The Galwayians chaffed under Tritonish rule, and occasionally rose in revolt.

They were now aided and incited by Gallicia in an attempt to create diversions and dissension within the Tritonish Islands.

Pierce was dismayed to find Vespica not paralleling America as closely as it could have. Their independence gained, the ten former Tritonish Colonies became the Vespican Independent Lands, and true to that name remained as independent as possible, even of one another. A Joint Council existed, but it was ineffective, and each Land did as it chose and disregarded the wishes, aims, and well-being of the others. Dissent, mistrust, and antagonism between the former colonies grew to where they were often nearly at war with one another.

With no cooperation, it was impossible for the Joint Council to present a united front against any real or perceived threats. Although no one nation openly attempted to assert sovereignty over the Lands, Grand Triton, Gallica, and Cordoba operated freely and at times unscrupulously within the new state. Each maintained an embassy in Bostwick, New Sussex, the current capital of the untried nation. They also established consulates in the capitals and trade centers of the individual Lands. In the various Lands, one power or another was more or less favorably received, and the influence of particular Baltican nations could be seen in certain Lands and not in others.

Despite the war between Grand Triton and Gallicia, a truce existed in Vespica. All parties grudgingly recognized it as a sovereign nation and neutral territory. Neutrality was strictly observed, often with ships of the warring nations lying close at anchor in Vespican harbors. Embassies and consulates were often located next to each other, and staff members of one were often guests and visitors at the other. While the great powers observed the sovereign neutrality of Vespica, they carried on a quieter, more hidden prosecution of the war. Larger Vespican cities were rife with political intrigue, espionage, forbidden dalliances, and illicit affairs.

Brunswick, *Furious's* destination, was the largest city in New Guernsey. Both the Tritonish and the Gallicians had consulates there.

The waterfront boasted many fine shipyards, warehouses, and supply depots that for a price would repair, rebuild, or resupply any ship, regardless of origin. It was common to see a Tritonish ship alongside a victualling pier with her Gallician counterpart astern, both receiving stores from a common warehouse. Ships of the Tritonish Navy's Flying Squadron put in at Brunswick in regular rotation to replenish. It was easier to put in there and pay a little more, while being assured of the quality and quantity of the supplies. Otherwise, they would have needed to sail a great distance to those Vespican territories still under Tritonish rule. *Furious* would have made this voyage anyway, as she was the longest at sea and due for such a visit.

Pierce and Hotchkiss were aboard as a matter of coincidence. Sir James Hargrove would have bundled them off on the first of his ships headed to any port. As fate would have it, the ship was *Furious,* and the port was Brunswick, New Guernsey. Not convening a court-martial, or shipping them to Kentland for trial, indicated doubts about their being Galway Rebels. Unsure of their innocence, he had them sent to New Guernsey to allow the residing Tritonish Consul to determine their fate.

Sir James had remarked that with the Gallician privateers and warships on the prowl, he could ill afford the loss of even one vessel to ferry suspected Galway Rebels to Kentland. But it was routine to send one vessel at a time into Brunswick for supplies. A prize crew gathered from around the squadron would not seriously deplete any ship's manning. The hands would return aboard *Furious*, and be back before they were ever missed.

Pierce appreciated the Commodore's predicament, and as the days enroute to Brunswick passed slowly, he was grateful for the man's consideration. The doubt in Sir James' mind gave Pierce a glimmer of hope, while memories of the cordial reception by the squadron's captains and the crew of *Furious* buoyed his sagging spirits.

A week after their capture, Pierce and Hotchkiss noted, along with

Mr. Belknap, *Furious's* sailing master, that they had reached the shortest day of the year. The long hours of darkness suited Pierce's dismal and gloomy mood. With the thought that the days would gradually grow longer, and that he would soon be away from Jackson's savage cruelty, Pierce felt a little better from time to time.

Pierce awoke early on the 3rd of July. It was Sunday, and he looked forward to the day. Jackson, in spite of his heavy-handed punishments, observed the Sabbath in his own way, and that way was reflected in the ship's routine. It was the one day when hands would not be called to witness punishment. They would muster, be inspected, hold a short prayer service, and be read the Articles of War. Although worded differently from those of the British Navy, the Articles of War carried the same strict demands for all in His Regal Majesty's Service.

Following Sunday quarterdeck formalities, hands were dismissed and Jackson took a surprisingly casual tour of the ship. But woe to the man whose gear or assigned area did not meet the standards of Jackson's discerning eye. He did not mete out punishment on Sunday, but names were taken, and later in the week, those deficient would be called forward. Sunday afternoons were generally turned over to make and mend or declared rope yarn Sunday, allowing hands to relax and keep busy. After dinner, unless one had had his stopped, all hands received a double ration of spirits. It was just enough to placate the beasts Jackson thought the men were, but not so much that they lost their fear of him.

On that particular Sunday afternoon, as the weak ineffectual sun sank lower in the gloomy sky, the lookout hailed and reported land off the starboard bow. In rare good spirits, Pierce did not object, even privately, when Jackson approached.

"Ah, Commander Pierce, if indeed you are such," he said.

Being in a good mood for once, Pierce did not let the remark get to him. "It appears that your visit with us will soon be over."

"It does, sir," Pierce mused.

"We stand in under topsails until nightfall and heave to through the night. Should we go blundering in during dark, the Vespies are likely to think it's an attack. Shouldn't think they could cause any real harm, but it would upset the nature of the place."

"Very prudent, Captain."

"It is according to standing orders, as well as being included in my orders regarding your transport."

"My impression of the commodore is of a man who thinks of everything," said Pierce. "He appears to be one who tries to see all aspects of the situation."

"Aye, he is. For his and Kentland's sake, I hope that he does not allow opposing views to cloud his adherence to duty."

"I do follow you, sir."

"As I have said, obedience to one's orders is the key to success. You can swear I faithfully carried out my orders regarding your transportation. I make no secret that my preferences for your treatment would be very different, had I not those orders."

"You have made that known from the beginning. We are most grateful that you elected to follow those orders rather than your personal convictions."

"Obedience is indeed the key, Commander, and in order to fulfill that sacred obligation, one must sometimes set aside one's personal convictions. I would suggest, sir, that you and your friend get a good sleep tonight. You will be much in demand come the morrow."

The next morning when Pierce went on deck, he found *Furious* dressed out as if for the King's Birthday. Midshipman Roberson caught up with him as he pulled his greatcoat more tightly about him in the chilly dawn air. "Here, sir, some coffee. Mr. Hotchkiss has told us of your affinity for it."

"He has, has he?" said Pierce, for once in his normal, short-tempered, but quite harmless, before-coffee mood. He grasped the mug eagerly.

"He says, sir, that you can be a real bear, before your coffee."

"He says that as well, does he! Well, damn him to hell, Mr. Roberson. And damn me as well. He's right, you know. I'm not fit to be around until I've drained that second or third cup."

But today Pierce was right with the world after only the smallest of sips from the first cup. Roberson's direct honesty and open friendliness, coupled with respect and deference, substituted for the coffee. There was also the knowledge that shortly he would bid adieu to HRMS *Furious* and her cruel and overbearing captain.

He took a sip and looked about. "Tell me, Mr. Roberson. Why do you dress the ship out so fine today? Is this done each time you enter port here?"

"Oh no, sir. Usually we just add their flag to the halyards and sail right in. Today's the Vespican Celebration of Independence, sir. We do it to acknowledge their sovereignty. Some say it humors them and we get a better price on the salt horse and rum."

"Independence Day? Fourth of July? Same as the Americans, it would seem?"

"Sir, I don't follow...?"

"No, I don't suppose you would. America, or the United States of America are former British Colonies that gained their independence from England, just at Vespica did from Kentland. They celebrate their independence today as well."

"Quite the coincidence, if I might say so, sir."

"And do you know, lad," asked Pierce, now in a positively jovial mood, "that our schooner, the *Island Expedition* there, was launched a year ago today?"

"Of course I wouldn't have known that, sir."

Furious remained hove to until after the hands were piped to breakfast. Sail was set and trimmed and she headed in to shore. The harbor at Brunswick was large and it was well into the afternoon watch when the best bower was let go.

The captain's barge and the long boat were hoisted out. Jackson embarked in the barge, and Pierce and Hotchkiss were escorted ashore in the long boat by the affable Mr. Roberson. Captain Jackson assigned a detail of armed marines to the long boat to ensure his prisoners did not make a break for freedom.

At the hard, disagreement arose with the Vespican militiamen guarding the harbor in regards to the armed Tritonish marines. It was eventually decided that the marines would remain in the long boat and that only unarmed seamen would step ashore, if only to hold it fast and allow passengers to disembark. Warned of the desperate character of the two, the militia sergeant agreed that his men would serve as escort and guard to the Tritonish Consulate.

Jackson, who had already landed, bade Mr. Roberson remain with the boats, and to keep a watchful eye upon the seamen and marines. This place was, he remarked, "too much a temptation for common seaman, and large enough for one to be lost without trying." Because many an average tar would diligently seek to be lost, it would be best that Mr. Roberson kept a close watch on those in his charge.

Two apparently trustworthy seamen from the barge's crew were detailed to carry their sea chests. That task was made easier as two old men with barrows appeared, and for the coins Roberson offered, agreed to transport the chests.

Pierce and Hotchkiss shook Roberson's hand, said "Goodbye," and realized that they were seeing a new friend for perhaps the last time. Then accompanied by Jackson, the two men wheeling their sea chests, and escorted by Vespican militia, they set off for the Tritonish Consulate.

Life in Brunswick was rather comfortable. Pierce and Hotchkiss were given rooms in the large house behind the consulate, where many staff members resided. Midshipman Morgan was given a room so he could more comfortably recover from the loss of his leg. The other midshipmen and warrant officers were billeted amongst the junior naval, marine, and army officers attached to the consulate. The hands were moved ashore and assigned living quarters amongst the soldiers and marines who guarded the consulate and provided ceremonial details as needed.

Pierce and Hotchkiss each gave their parole, and were permitted to move about the consulate building and grounds as they chose. When Morgan recovered sufficiently from his wounds, he too would have the same freedom. The other midshipmen and warrant officers had the same privileges, but had to report nightly to the guard detail's officer of the day. The consulate staff wanted Pierce to vouch for the hands, but he would not do it. While not opposed to their chance at liberty, he felt it should not be at his word. A compromise was reached and Pierce vouched for the trustworthiness of the hands in general. Each man of *Island Expedition* then gave his parole. They too were free to come and go about the grounds, but were restricted from areas where only higher-level staff personnel were permitted. They had to muster daily with the guard detail's duty sergeant.

A week after their arrival, Brunswick's mayor granted the officers and warrant officers free access to the city and countryside. A week later he allowed the same to the rest of the crew.

Pierce was grateful for the kind conditions imposed during this internment. They were more guests, rather than prisoners, although guests not allowed to depart at their own choosing. He worried about endless days with nothing for the hands to do. As good a crew as they were, idleness and a bit of freedom would soon spoil them. Like so many seamen, they enjoyed their drink, and when they had had too much, trouble followed closely behind. For their own safety, and to maintain a favorable impression, both upon the consulate staff and the local populace, some arrangement was needed to keep the hands busy.

He chaffed at the thought of *Island Expedition* lying nearly abandoned, tied up and guarded only by Vespican militia or Kentish marines. The schooner was a potential prize of war, and his access to it was most strenuously guarded. He argued successfully that it would deteriorate if virtually abandoned, and if eventually declared a prize, its value would be much less. He eventually won permission to send small groups aboard during daylight hours to repair and maintain the vessel. He was grudgingly allowed to have a midshipman or warrant officer and two hands to remain aboard at night as a security detail. Finally, he was allowed to let those seamen that chose to do so work on a regular basis in the dockyards that lined the harbor.

Once again Pierce established *Island Expedition* as a three-watch ship. The first day, hands were sent to deal with upkeep and maintenance of the schooner. The next day that group worked in various shipyards, and on the third day, they had liberty.

To help prevent even a partial crew from overpowering the marines guarding *Island Expedition*, Pierce and Hotchkiss were not allowed aboard together. Following the same reasoning, neither was permitted to spend the night on board. Yet, had everyone ever managed to be aboard at the same time, could they have left? The schooner was moored in the inner harbor, and they would have to pass many docked or anchored merchantmen to gain the outer harbor. A word from the consulate to any Kentish ships in port would be all that was needed to halt their progress.

Until the situation changed, they would not leave of their own accord.

Almost immediately, Pierce and Hotchkiss were in demand as honored guests at dinners and other evening affairs. It was strange that although virtual prisoners, suspected of rebellion and piracy, they were the most popular social commodity in the city. The first night ashore, they had been treated to a late supper as guests of Lord Sutherland, the Tritonish Consul. The next evening there was an official dinner of welcome, which was attended by all of great importance in Brunswick. Guests included a sizable delegation from the Gallician consulate located across the square.

The next day, the Gallician assistant military attaché sent a tailor to measure and make new uniforms and appropriate civilian wear for them. Pierce and Hotchkiss both objected to being provided clothing by the enemy of their current host. Lord Sutherland, however, allowed that what the Gallicians would spend for the garments would not be available to supply their ships calling at Brunswick. They relented and the new garments were made and presented to them.

During those first days, Pierce often met for lengthy discussions with Lord Sutherland. He was a man of easy, polished manner, and accomplished most of what he did by delegation. After he read Commodore Hargrove's report concerning *Island Expedition*, he concurred with that opinion, and assigned Major Howard of the consulate marines to investigate further.

Pierce expressed his confusion over the celebrity status accorded them, even while suspected of piracy and rebellion. Sutherland noted that they were a novelty in a place where things remained the same day after day and year after year.

Regardless of suspected political and national leanings, they had fought a superb battle against one of the best in the region. Captain Newbury and *Hawke,* he was told, had once defeated a thirty-two-gun Gallician frigate. Pierce had come along with a smaller ship and fewer guns, and had reduced the sloop-of-war to a shambles. All appreciated a well-fought battle, regardless of the victor's alliance.

Pierce, Hotchkiss, and the hands of *Island Expedition* settled down to life as well-treated and celebrated prisoners at the Tritonish consulate in Brunswick, New Guernsey. A routine as regular as clockwork evolved, and it was followed as rigidly as if they were at sea.

Pierce spent every third day aboard, caught up on logs and journals, and ensured all was ready for their departure, should it ever be allowed. When Hotchkiss was aboard, Pierce was generally deep in conversation with Lord Sutherland, Major Howard, or other officials at the consulate office. Every morning he visited Morgan, and checked on the young gentleman's rehabilitation while he had that all-important first cup of coffee.

On the day that neither went aboard, they often explored the town. They found many interesting shops and visited many local merchants, shopkeepers, and artisans. Invariably, they came upon a welcoming public house when hunger and thirst asserted their presence. After a few times, they had found one that quickly became their favorite.

The proprietor came to expect the two supposed naval officers every third day. They spent cautiously but well, ate, drank, minded their manners, and were respectful of the establishment, the other guests, and the staff.

Word spread to the rest of the crew that the captain and first lieutenant favored this place. For several days, Pierce did not see any of *Island Expedition's* crew in the Frosty Anchor. Perhaps they felt the place to be off limits because the officers frequented it. He let them know that if they had liberty, they had the right to be there.

Often, as Pierce, Hotchkiss, perhaps Andrews, and even the rapidly recuperating Morgan sat, groups of crewmen came in. Normally they edged to the other side of the room and left the officers their *sea* room. If they should have to, they sat closer but did not intrude onto the present *quarterdeck*. When he felt generous or in good spirits, Pierce might buy a round for the hands. Occasionally they dug deep into their pockets and collectively bought a round for their officers.

Evenings usually meant a formal dinner or other event. Pierce soon tired of that, and once a week or so, begged off from the night's engagement. He tried not to pass up a second event hosted by the same party. Most, he knew, would abide one absence, but not two.

It was a fair and easy existence, but Pierce fretted. His life, career, and present commission were at a standstill. He was becalmed, even if in a region of cool temperatures and pleasant surroundings. He did not feel the heavy oppression, as he had aboard *Furious*, where Captain Jackson's brutality made him seem stranded in the stifling unbearable heat of the tropics.

Chapter Twenty-Two

Dangerous Diversions

"I'm damned tired of this, my friend," moaned Pierce. "Sitting in a colonial port, watching our vessel rot at the pier, and not able to put to sea. We can't return and let Smythe know what we've found. Damn, we can't leave this Godforsaken world where we don't belong!"

Nursing his fifth mug of beer, Pierce was quite full of it by now, and drank slowly. He belched. In his own estimation, he wasn't drunk, but did feel the effects. Humphrey, the proprietor of the Frosty Anchor, noticed the effect and smiled. The coins that had paid for it weighed noticeably in his pocket. Pierce had been there enough for Humphrey not to worry about any rude behavior as the brew worked its magic. He appreciated the business brought to his place by the strange naval officer from a far-off land, and if the story could be believed, from a different world as well.

"To be sure, we aren't rotting in jail, or slopping about in a prison hulk," said Hotchkiss, with two empty mugs before him. After last night, he had only recently desired to imbibe again.

"We may as well be. Still, not a damned thing to do, except drink beer, or those interminable damned dinners, damned concerts, damned poetry readings, and damned recitals. Hurry along and play ship's captain a few hours every third day! May as well be in jail."

"Dinner? At the Mercers' this evening, I believe. Going?"

"I'm of a mind not to," mumbled Pierce.

"But you have excused yourself from their company twice. They will think you find them unfit to visit."

"If they do, I could not care less, Isaac!" Pierce took another slow pull at his beer.

"I'm sick to death of these damned dinners and evenings with the elite of this damned place! Miss 'aren't I perfect,' pock marks, pimples and all to my right! Mrs. 'fifty years ago I was a beauty,' to my left! Put with the one across the table, they provide enough intellect to carry on a conversation. And the husbands, and sons, and brothers as well ... damn, you'd think those living in a seaport would know a little of the sea!"

"Yes, many are no sharper than the breech end of a carronade. But the major from the Gallician consulate?"

"A few exceptions, yes," announced Pierce.

"And, we do eat well."

"Aye and I've already let the piggin' string out in my new breeches. Good, yes, but not every damned day! Better on ship's stores and a meal like these once a month."

"In which case we would be done with this place and at sea."

"Aye," Pierce said, raising his mug again.

"I do think you should come tonight, Edward. Captain of the packet from Malden should be there. Conversation with him may further acquaint us with this world."

"True enough, and you tire of passing my regrets and apologies. For your sake, friend, I'll go. Also, we may learn more of this world."

He tipped the mug one final time and drained it dry. Pierce set the mug down a little loudly and Humphrey offered a refill. Pierce shook his head and laid a coin on the table. Standing, he needed a moment to find his balance. With Hotchkiss's support, he set course for the door. Perhaps he had drunk more than he thought. And he was hungry.

At the Tritonish consulate, they made their way through the offices and chambers and into the house behind it. In his room Pierce decided he needed a bath and a shave. He rang for the valet and requested a tub, hot water, and a good razor.

The man informed him that at this time of the day, that much hot water was not available. There was enough for a shave or for a quick wash, but not at all enough for a bath.

"Best get a fire lit, man!" said Pierce. "I'll have my bath, as I'm expected for dinner tonight, and I'll not go smelling like the gutter!"

"But, but, sir! It won't be possible."

"And check with Mr. Hotchkiss that he might want one as well!"

"It just won't be possible, sir! And two of you? I just can't, sir!"

"You had best jump to it, man! You'll bring as much as you can! Now!"

"Yessir!" gulped the departing valet, desperately hoping to escape the presence of one who had strange ideas about a bath in midweek.

"Damn you! It's 'Aye aye, sir!'" The man cringed slightly and finished his exit. Pierce smiled, perversely pleased with causing discomfort to one of the domestic staff. He pulled off his coat and waistcoat and tossed them haphazardly on the bed. He sat in the chair and his eyes closed, only to open once more. They closed again and stayed shut.

The arrival of the tub awakened him.

The valet and his assistant put the tub in the room and filled it from the buckets that others carried in. They left and returned with kettles of steaming hot water and added that to the tub. They left one full kettle, a small basin, and its stand, to be used by the irascible master and commander for his shave.

"There is enough for Mr. Hotchkiss, lad?" Pierce asked the young man as he laid out the mirror, razor, and shaving soap.

"Enough for what he requested, sir."

Pierce strained to keep his eyes open and focus on the fellow. Despite the haze of his condition, he saw that the lad was sharp, and had made the only sensible reply. When they had checked with Hotchkiss, he had no doubt requested only enough for a shave, and had indicated he could do with only warm or even cold water.

Pierce stripped off his clothes and got in the tub. It was warm, but not scalding hot as he would have liked. Should he summon the valet, complain, and punctuate his displeasure with choice remarks about the man's parentage? Luckily it was warm enough and of sufficient depth that he could submerge as much of his carcass as he chose.

He grabbed the flannel to lather and wash. It was such a miserable way of doing it, he thought, remembering the little room in Smythe's house. There he could set the temperature nearer his liking, and as long as it flowed, have the advantage of clean water to rinse away the grime and the dirty soapy water.

With legs, arms, and upper torso washed, he stood to wash his mid-section, and noticed his expanding waist. Should that keep up, he would again need to let out the lacing in his breeches. Should he continue to enlarge, he would need to obtain larger garments.

Pierce stepped out, splashing water on the towels protecting the floor and beyond. He toweled briskly and rubbed some warmth into his limbs. Shaving, he cut himself only once, and not under his chin where he usually did.

Because of what in his meager wardrobe was clean, and because his Tritonish hosts preferred it, he was soon dressed in civilian attire. He felt odd not to be in service blue and without gold buttons and lace. His left shoulder missed the weight of his one epaulette.

Still, when he checked his image in the mirror, he was not displeased with the picture he presented. The stark plainness of the black coat, waistcoat and neckerchief contrasted with the white shirt, breeches and stockings. The coat fit well, although he considered it dated when compared to what he had last seen in England. A gentleman's evening sword and a small brimmed hat rounded out his rig.

Ready to depart, Pierce and Hotchkiss arrived at the consulate's front door as Lord and Lady Sutherland drove off in the carriage. "They will send it back for you gentlemen," announced the marine sergeant having charge of the door.

Samuel Mercer was a merchant with interests in shipping and shipbuilding, who traded in various commodities from around the world.

It was said he engaged in the sale and transportation of slaves, but he downplayed that part of his business, as New Guernsey officially disallowed traffic in human beings. As a prominent member of local society, he hosted lavish dinners and often invited the Tritonish and Gallician consuls, their wives, and selected staff members as guests.

Despite the chill of the season, the dining room was warm. The many candles, the great number of guests, and the fires at each end of the room added to the heat.

Mrs. Mercer was a large, buxom, obnoxious woman. Born poor, she had married up to be the proud wife of a successful man, a true pillar of the community. She bustled about. "Would the gentleman prefer another glass? Would Lady Smith care to sit here? And here finally, Commander Pierce! Along with Lieutenant Hotchkiss! Let me show you to your seats."

Finally all were seated. Mercer asked a long convoluted blessing, basically requesting his continued good fortune and acknowledging his leading role in the community's prosperity. The *amen* brought an audible sigh of relief, and the dinner began. By now, Pierce had been to many dinners in Brunswick. Often, the dishes served, and the protocols observed, were familiar to him. He well could have been in England or North America. In other instances, the dishes and deportment seemed completely foreign, emphasizing his presence in a different world. His appetite sharpened by the hour and the effects of his earlier beer, Pierce could have eaten while completely neglecting the other guests.

Seated opposite him was the assistant military attaché from the Gallician consulate, who had provided much of his current wardrobe. To either side of the Gallician major sat wives of Tritonish consulate staff. They were boring, plain women who fit his image of three equaling one in any intelligent discourse. Next to one of these ladies sat Captain Robards, lately arrived from Malden and captain of the packet ship *Emerald*.

Malden was the capital of Kentland and hence of Grand Triton. The arrival of a ship from Kentland was to be celebrated, for it would have brought news, the latest in fashion, and even passengers.

One of those passengers sat to Pierce's right, and was by local convention his partner for dinner. It surprised him to learn that she was Mrs. Lowell Jackson, wife of the captain who had brought him to Brunswick. As he politely forked small portions of sea pie, he stole a sidelong glance and decided she could have had better than Jackson.

The lady's fair skin was wind burned and tanned, a usual result if she had spent time on deck during the passage from Kentland. The sun had bleached her light brown locks to a pale yellow, and amongst them there was minor evidence of gray. She was an attractive woman, although evidence indicated her years to be beyond his. Pierce guessed that she might be some ways into her thirties.

She had moved with a fluid grace and obvious awareness of her yet-considerable charm. He noticed that her gown covered little beyond what was required for decency's sake.

"I understand, Commander Pierce," she said between bites of roasted lamb, "that my husband had the honor of conveying you to Brunswick."

"Indeed, he did, ma'am," he answered politely.

"And how did you find him, sir?" she asked.

Pierce found the wording amusing and replied, "I was not aware he was missing. He was always aboard ship, the best I knew. Had I been asked, I would have aided in any search for him." For once he was able to maintain a totally solemn expression.

She and the others sat dumbfounded, thinking he had mistaken the intent of her question. He grinned slightly and at once the Gallician picked up on it.

"He has us all, I daresay!" laughed the Gallician.

"Yes, quite!" interjected one of the ladies seated beside him.

"How amusing, Commander," said Mrs. Jackson. "I was meaning what you thought of him? How the two of you got along?"

Should he answer truthfully and tell her that he had been totally disgusted by Jackson's treatment of his crew? Should he explain that the conditions that Hotchkiss and he had traveled under were due to explicit orders from Commodore Hargrove, and not the result of Jackson's own desires?

"Being strangers, ma'am, and that Mr. Hotchkiss and I were, and are, under suspicion, our relationship with the captain was correct and civil."

"Silly me," she laughed. "I needn't have asked. It's what I would have expected. But what else would one say in company and to his wife?"

"Mrs. Jackson hoped to arrive and surprise her husband when he arrived to take on stores," announced Lady Sutherland.

"And I have caused that to go awry," murmured Pierce. "For him to deliver us, he sailed earlier than scheduled. Please accept my apology, Mrs. Jackson."

"My dear Commander, think nothing of it." She smiled and a reached out to reassuringly squeeze his hand. "We all know that wind and tide play havoc with the best plans of men and ships. I may well have arrived after his visit, regardless of any unscheduled intervention."

"I am relieved you do not hold it against me, ma'am."

"But what will you do, Mrs. Jackson," asked the lady directly across from her, "while you are here and he is out to sea? It may be some time before he is back."

"Still, he will be back, and much sooner than to Kentland. Here I can see him every few weeks, or wait at home and not see him for months. Perhaps years." She took a sip of wine and a bite of lamb. "I shall find enough to busy myself while waiting. Perhaps I will eat like this every day, get fat as a pig, and see if he recognizes me, ha ha!"

Pierce had cooled from the fluster of his moment of decision, but now the warmth returned. Mrs. Jackson had shifted slightly in her chair, and had slipped her left foot behind his right. She gently flexed her foot and allowed her shin to gently nudge his calf. He caught her scent, floral and sweet, but not overpowering. It was enough that he noticed and realized her nearness. He grew warmer still, and hoped desperately that it did not show. He should not accept what were obvious advances, but the means of refusing escaped him.

"I've had to adjust my breeches twice," he announced in response to her last remark. Hastily he added: "They do serve a hearty meal in these parts of this world."

"I've been to great dinners in Malden, and oft times, I believe, those people cannot have done better than what's before us tonight. Most excellent!" she said.

"Yes indeed," remarked Lord Sutherland. "We should say very well done, and thank you to Mr. and Mrs. Mercer. Theirs is always a most delicious and bountiful table."

"With such a variety as well. I've learned to eat sparingly at their table, lest I be ready to burst before the first remove," added Lady Sutherland. "In three days, I believe, dinner shall be at the consulate, and I hope that Mrs. Jackson finds our table as well-laden."

"Oh, I shall! I know I shall!" She shifted again and changed the position of her lower limb against Pierce's. "It is so good to have a real dinner for once. I apologize, Captain Robards, but even at the captain's table, sea-going meals are not all they could be."

"There were storms and squalls, ma'am, such that the galley fires were out much of the time," said the packet captain, who had been silent for much of the meal. He looked strangely at Mrs. Jackson. "I too rejoice in the fare now set before us."

Pierce caught the glance Robards turned in the lady's direction, and wondered of any connection during the voyage. "I have seen times," he said, "when salt pork, dried peas, and biscuit without a frigate's complement of bargemen seemed a feast!"

"As have all who journey upon the sea," responded the packet captain.

"I meant no disrespect as to the quality of your table, Captain," said Mrs. Jackson. With coolness toward the packet captain, she continued. "I thought to clarify that earlier."

"Oh, it was most clear, dear lady. Just two seafarers with memories of victuals unfit to eat, or starve."

"Of course, sir."

The dinner continued. Pierce ate well but found it hard to concentrate on his plate or the conversation. His dinner partner constantly sought discreet and unseen contact with him. Should he act as if he didn't notice, make some covert move to acknowledge her subtle signals, or somehow reject her advances? He grew warmer and warmer. But with the warmth of the room and with all that everyone had consumed, everyone was flushed. No one could tell that his heated condition was from a different source.

Conversation evolved into other matters, and the principal participants shifted as well. Smaller, two- and three-person chats broke out amongst the diners. At the far end of the table, Hotchkiss engaged in lively and animated talk with an attractive but slightly plump young lady. She was the daughter of another merchant, Mercer's business rival, and yet his close friend. Mrs. Jackson chatted amiably with the Gallician major, the women to either side of him, and with the gentleman to her right. All the while she kept up her signals of interest to Pierce. She moved in her chair, breathed deeply, and her bosom lifted and swelled. Had she timed it so he could not help but notice? She slipped her shoe off, and with her stocking-footed toes, gently massaged his lower leg.

Another remove. Another wine. More conversation. More laughter. The evening wore on and Pierce was in a quandary. He enjoyed the meal -- and frankly, the illicit attention of his dinner partner. Should he follow his base instincts and let develop what she seemed to hope would come about?

As he grew more sated with the food and drink and more intoxicated by her nearness, he lost track of time, of others present, and heard or understood little of the conversation around him. He was filled with wanton desire for what he knew was forbidden fruit. She was married, and whether his attraction to her were genuine or a result of atmosphere and wine, he should not aid in the deception of her husband, even if he utterly detested the man.

He thought of Evangeline. Did he not owe her his fidelity, loyalty, and honesty? They had made no promises, other than that he would return and that she would be waiting. It had been a struggle for both of them, but they had refrained from final completeness of their passion. He knew he wanted more than a moment of enjoyment with her. He had always felt that with someone special, it would not do to rush.

It had been nearly a year since he last held Evangeline in his arms. But she was thousands of miles away, on the other side of the world. He was a man with needs, wants, and desires, all of which were dangerously stirred and fanned by this woman seated beside him. He recalled that someone once said that no man was married once past Gibraltar. He now understood what that meant.

"Commander! Commander!"

"Oh, yes?" he responded.

"Fill your glass, there, Commander Pierce. We are about to drink the health of all sovereigns and heads of state represented. You will honor us and offer to the health of your king?"

"Of course, milord," he said and filled his glass. "Ladies and gentlemen, I give you His Majesty, King George the Third, Sovereign of the United Kingdom of Great Britain and Ireland!" He raised his glass.

"George the Third!" the others echoed, as they lifted their glasses to take a quick sip from them. Pierce was pleased that everyone drank to his king, even though some no doubt thought him mad. Obviously, George the Third, England, France, America, and his entire world resulted from delusions and a strange imagination.

"Major du Champlain, if you would, sir."

"Oui. Of course, m'sieur. Even though we are at war, here we can gather at the same table and enjoy a meal, a little wine, and a little conversation. We can honestly drink to the health of another's king, ruler or leader. I give you to the health of Nicholas Bartholomieu, Prime Director of the Gallician Republic!"

"Hear! Hear!"

Faintly Pierce heard someone say, "I'll drink his health, does the lack of it put the bastard in his grave!"

"Major Howard?"

"Yes, quite, milord. To His Regal Majesty, Geoffrey the Fifth of the Unified Kingdom of Grand Triton and Galway. His health and success, ladies and gentlemen!"

"His health! Hear! Hear!"

Pierce noticed that many Vespicans drank the health of the Tritonish king with a little more enthusiasm than that of the Gallician first director. He also thought he saw many Gallicians raise their glasses but not drink anything from them.

Mercer stood. "My good friends and honored guests. In Vespica, we do not have kings or prime directors. Please join me in drinking the health of the Honorable Richard Randolph, Governor of the Land of New Guernsey!"

"The Governor! His health! Hear! Hear!" Once again glasses were raised, and Pierce noticed that many took more than a sip.

"And," continued Mercer, "the health of the Vespican Joint Council and the health of all Vespicans, the true rulers of these Lands!"

"Hear! Hear!" Was there a slight mocking tone on the part of some Tritonish and Gallicians?

Glasses were raised once again, and finally all the official toasts were done. Continuing, they drank to the health of Commodore Sir James Hargrove, commander of the Regal Navy's Flying Squadron. They drank to the health of Rear Admiral Rochambeau, Hargrove's Gallician counterpart.

Eventually, as the wine, the brandy, and other spirits flowed, they drank to the health of those present. Lord and Lady Sutherland were toasted. General Benardette, the Gallician consul, was wished a long, healthy, and happy life. The various aides, attachés, and special guests were all mentioned and their health, well-being, and prosperity wished for and drank to.

Pierce had drunk too much. The room and everyone in it were in a fog. A string quintet played in the corner and furnished a background of pleasant and pleasing sound. He heard it, but noticed more the absence of music between selections.

He found it odd, despite his inebriated state, to witness representatives of two hostile nations toast the health and well-being of the other. From half-heard comments and barely noticed behaviors, he sensed the hostility, mistrust, and subterfuge lying below the surface conviviality. The major Baltican powers regarded the Vespicans mere caretakers of a land that one or the other would someday rule. The Independent Lands of Vespica were a stage for the grand play of world domination that Grand Triton and Gallicia continued to act out.

Pierce once again found himself in conversation with Mrs. Jackson. Dinner had ended, and dessert had been served. Remnants of dishes and foods sat on the table, and individuals helped themselves to what they desired. Several bottles of brandy, rum, whiskey, and decanters of wine were available and the diners poured their own choices. The table-wide conversations had ceased, and small groups or pairs carried on individual, independent, and unrelated talks. "Lady Sutherland has told me your incredible story. Tell me, Commander," pressed Mrs. Jackson. "Is this England you are from the same as Kentland?"

"I couldn't say, ma'am, having never been to Kentland. I believe there are similarities, but…."

"You think I humor you, Edward? May I call you Edward?"

"If you so wish, ma'am."

"And you must call me Leona!"

"Of course, Leona."

"But you do think I humor you? That I do not believe your tales of another world?"

"What you believe is of little matter. I know it exists. We journeyed along a complicated course to get to this world. Continued inaction and indecision by Grand Triton's local officials now prevent my return to others from my world, or to my world itself."

"But as a man of the sea, surely you know such things take time. And there is so much one can do while waiting."

She shifted her chair abruptly and sat nearly facing him. Her knees pressed against his. She leaned forward slightly, either to emphasize her remarks or to afford Pierce a closer view of her cleavage. Whatever her motive, he noticed, and again felt overly heated in a very warm room.

"We are both waiting. You wait to leave here, and I wait to see my husband. But must we wait alone?"

She reached for his hand, grasped it, and squeezed.

"A very tempting thought, Leona. How near I am to acting upon it."

"And what stops you, sir?" she smiled.

"You are a married woman, and I've someone waiting. Despite the temptation, I strive to maintain myself as a true gentleman."

"My dear Edward, you have such noble and fine ideals." She leaned a little closer. "But we are here, and they are both far, far away. I do not know your lady and can not speak of her patience. I can speak of him, and tell you that once at sea, he is no more married than a tomcat."

"I'm sorry that is so."

"You needn't be. From what I've seen, that is more often the case, is it not?"

"In many instances, I am afraid it is."

"But why fight it? We should take advantage of what comes our way." She adroitly moved her chair even closer and pressed more of her knee and lower thigh against him. She took his hand again and pressured it affectionately, warmly, wantonly.

Pierce was positively on fire! The pounding of his heart and the throbbing in his head were both magnified by her closeness. Her aroma, both of her perfume and the underlying scent of her being, intoxicated him. He could not help but focus his gaze upon her barely covered, rising and falling bosom. The pressure of her knee, along with the touch and squeeze of her hand, were nearly more than he could bear. It was such delicious and wonderful torment! His wits all but escaped him and he could not coherently reply to her latest remarks. He could develop no further argument against what she apparently proposed. A vestige of doubt and reluctance remained -- and strangely, he did not want it to fully disappear. He did not want to succumb to the fire that burned deep within him.

"Perhaps more wine?" he asked, struggling to regain his composure and self-control. "Shall we try this one?"

"Please, pour me a sip, Edward."

The overall revelry carried on into the late evening. Several gentlemen were asleep now; the wine and other spirits, combined with the large meal weighed heavily upon their eyelids. Two or three still sat at the table, their heads cushioned on their forearms or their blank unseeing faces turned to the ceiling. Others sat in larger, more comfortable chairs about the edge of the room, their unfinished drinks on small tables near by.

A small number of women dozed, snoring and sputtering unconsciously and unfashionably. Small groups or pairs of people still talked, some in a highly animated fashion, others in a more desultory manner. Discussions grew heated, and voices rose in pitch and volume as opinions were offered, rejected, and vehemently insisted upon.

The Mercers' household staff slipped through the room, clearing away the plates, dishes, and flatware where they could. They also swept and wiped up spilled food and drink. Guests began to leave, bundling into greatcoats, shawls, capes, muffs, mufflers, gloves, and mittens to combat the cold night air. Lord and Lady Sutherland appeared behind Pierce's chair.

"Commander, we shall take our leave now. You of course may stay as you desire. We shall send the carriage back, should you wish it?"

"Mr. Hotchkiss?"

"I believe he is seeing his dinner partner home."

"Perhaps I should offer safe conduct to Mrs. Jackson?"

"By all means, Commander Pierce," said Lady Sutherland. "It is most gallant of you."

"Yes, milady. It is one's duty, is it not? If Mrs. Jackson would allow me to see her safely home?"

"I would be most grateful, Commander. It may not be safe this time of evening."

"Indeed not, ma'am. And may I inquire whither we journey?"

"Of course, you do not know, Commander!" exclaimed Lady Sutherland. "Mrs. Jackson has rooms at the consulate. You were out when she arrived. When you returned, she had already departed!"

"Then shall we send the carriage back for you, sir? Or would you prefer to go first and send it in return for us?"

"We can remain a while longer, milord," replied Mrs. Jackson. "It may take me time to find my things."

While they waited, Pierce remembered his manners and thanked Mr. and Mrs. Mercer for inviting him, for the delicious dinner, and for an interesting and entertaining evening. Very properly he helped Mrs. Jackson find her wraps, and helped her bundle against the icy outside air. When the carriage returned, he helped her aboard, and tucked the blankets and furs snugly about her. He climbed in, pulled the remaining covers over his chilled legs, and signaled that they were ready. The horses took off at a slow walk, their hoof beats muffled in the slight snow that had fallen earlier in the evening. The iron tires crunched in the whiteness, and once he felt them slip sideways.

It was not far to the Tritonish consulate. Pierce had often walked the distance as he explored and journeyed around Brunswick. But at this late hour and with a lady in his care, it was best they ride. It was cold in the enclosed coach, but with the blankets and the warming pans, surely not as bitter as a walk would have been. They pulled up at the consulate. He helped Mrs. Jackson out, tossed a coin to the driver and one to the footman, and then hurried his charge inside out of the cold.

Through the darkened consulate proper they went, with her arm in his. The walkway to the residence house was unheated and both shivered from the chill. Once inside she said: "My room is second to the right. Here!" Pierce opened the door and they stepped through. She closed the door.

Chapter Twenty-Three

The Healing Man

Despite pursuing various pleasures to the point of hardly having slept at all, Pierce awoke at his regular time. His head ached and his stomach churned, and while he would have preferred to go back to sleep, duties required him to be up and about.

She snored softly and he thought it strange, as such sounds were not usually associated with women. He carefully slipped from under the covers, took care not to wake her, put on enough to be decent, and tiptoed out of the room. He shivered in the unheated passageway and quickly entered his own room. He fought the temptation to fall into the unused bed, rang for the servant, and waited.

"Good mornin' sir! Trust you slept well, sir!"

"Coffee, a basin, and some hot water! Now!"

"Of course, sir! Rough night, sir?" The man was too damned cheerful.

Pierce growled.

"Shall I fetch you some breakfast, sir?"

Pierce stomach churned.

"No! No damn breakfast! God, no damn breakfast! I said 'coffee' and 'a basin and some hot water'! That's all I said, damn you, and that's all I want! Now get at it afore you get your back striped!"

"Perhaps the commander would like a splash of brandy in his coffee?" The fellow was cool, obviously used to guests and residents waking up in disgruntled states.

"No!" Pierce yelled. The noise of his own voice echoed painfully in his ears. "Coffee, that's all! And the basin and hot water!" He moaned agonizingly; the servant comprehended, and left.

While he waited for his coffee, Pierce brushed his teeth and rinsed his mouth. He felt better having gotten the taste and feel of old wadding out of his mouth. He dashed a little cool water onto his face, and that revived him a bit more.

The coffee and basin finally arrived, along with a kettle of hot water. Pierce washed and refreshed himself, and paused often to take long sips of coffee. The man had brought a full pot, so with one cup quickly down his throat, Pierce poured a second and kept the hot soothing beverage flowing to his tortured insides.

He dressed in one of the uniforms made upon their arrival in Brunswick. Today it was his turn to be aboard *Island Expedition*. He'd work on his logs and diary, and direct the watch aboard in preserving and preparing the schooner for sea. He knew that most of what he could have them do would be make work. Other than stores and a full crew, the schooner was ready to leave. She had been ready for the past several weeks, and lacked only permission of the Tritonish consul or higher authority to be underway. Half aloud he muttered several obscenities referencing the situation, and left the room.

First he stopped to see Midshipman Morgan. During the battle with HRMS *Hawke*, Thomas Morgan had been severely wounded, and Dr. Matheson had been forced to remove his lower right leg. Healing had progressed nicely during the voyage to and during the first weeks in Brunswick. Morgan had been well enough to have joined them for a couple of dinners, and had gone to the Frosty Anchor more than once.

Pierce had optimistically hoped that by the end of August, the stump would be sufficiently healed for work to start on a substitute leg, but now there were complications. The stump had grown sore and inflamed. For a while, the young man had bravely insisted upon accompanying his shipmates to various functions. Now the limb was so tender that Morgan could not think of going along.

Dr. Matheson was as competent a ship's surgeon as there was, but was at a loss as to how to proceed. He knew the stump had become infected, but with his limited medical knowledge, the poor doctor was unsure as to how to treat it.

Lord Sutherland had responded kindly, and had called for the services of the best physician in town. He was a kindly old man, but it was soon evident that his skills and title were honorary more than anything else. He had administered doses of this, prescribed so much of that, and so much of this, but none of it helped. He had bled Thomas Morgan on more than one occasion, and the last time the young lad ended up faint and weak. Morgan had protested further attempts to bleed him, and Pierce, never in favor of that particular medical practice, had ordered it stopped.

He knocked lightly at the door. There was no answer, so he opened the door gently and stepped in. The room was warm, nearly hot, the air stagnant with the odor of sickness and infection about it. Pierce instinctively gasped for breath.

"Captain, that you?" Morgan's voice was small and far-away.

"Aye, Tom, it's me," answered Pierce quietly. "You missed a good dinner last night. For once I was glad to have attended." Pierce did not elaborate.

"I'd have gone, sir, surely, had my leg felt better. But these days it's sorer than when I was hit!"

Pierce drew up a chair and sat along the bed, accidentally bumping the frame. Morgan winced in pain, even though his stump had not been contacted. Pierce laid the back of his hand across Morgan's brow, feeling its damp hotness. The midshipman's face was flushed. He had not been shaved for several days and looked like the specter of death. If the doctors could not combat the infection now racing through his body, how much longer before that vision became reality?

"God, Tom, aren't you burning up in here?" he asked. "This room's a damn sight warmer than below decks when we crossed the line!"

"And as still as the morning we were becalmed. No wind at all, and we just baked, sir!" Morgan reminisced.

"Then by God, I shall open the window, Tom, and get you a breeze, and for myself as well." Pierce was nearly desperate for a breath of fresh air. The fetid heat in Morgan's room fast undid the benefits of his earlier coffee.

"I wouldn't do it, Edward," Morgan said feebly. "The doctors say cold air isn't good for my condition."

"Fuck 'em, lad! They haven't yet figured a way out of this fix. Can we trust 'em about the air?" Pierce went to the window. "I'll just crack it enough for the flow, more than for the cold. Ah, that's better already, should you ask me."

"Aye, I can feel it as well. Ed, I mean Captain...."

"We can dispense with formality, Tom."

"Could you lift these quilts? With the cooler air, I notice warmth under them even more."

"Of course."

Pierce turned back the covers to let the cooler air at Morgan's form. As he did, the stench increased noticeably and he nearly retched.

"Lord have mercy, Tom, but you are in a worse way than I had imagined. I'll ask Lord Sutherland to call someone else if possible. I'll not lose my senior midshipman and acting second lieutenant without giving it the best fight I can, Tom!"

"I'm not done yet, Captain!" Morgan lay back wearily. Then he sat up and reached for a glass of water.

"If I am called home, sir, I'd like it not to be here. This place is all right, truly it is. But we are really prisoners. If I go on that final voyage, please God that it will be from our schooner at least! That or the island, if not in our own world, or even England!" He choked slightly and Pierce could see uncertainty, perhaps fear, and a touch of moisture in his friend's eye.

"But, Tom, I'm no doctor, so I can't say as to the seriousness. We are not yet at an end point."

"I do feel great strength within, and I shall fight with all that strength until, until...."

"Until you recover and mend fully!"

"Aye, Ed. Aye!"

"I'll be aboard for a while this morning. I'll see the surgeon, unless he is here with you, and I'll tell Mr. Hotchkiss to look in on you."

"I would appreciate that, sir."

"Here is a book you might find interesting. I borrowed it from Major Howard, planning to read it. However, I find I don't have the time or the interest at present."

"Thank you! Most kind, sir. Just lying here is nearly the worst of it."

At the pier, Pierce brusquely acknowledged the Vespican militia sergeant's salute. There was a small detail of militia adjacent to the schooner to prevent any theft or damage. He went up the gangway and his salute to the quarterdeck was returned by Steadman, officer of the watch. He also acknowledged the salutes of the Tritonish marines stationed onboard, who served to prevent the entire crew from being aboard at any one time.

Steadman said, "Welcome aboard, sir. Hands busy caulking the lower deck. Carpenter and his mates at that shot hole forward. Hands pooled their shipyard wages and bought some scraps lying about. It'll replace what was destroyed by shot, sir. Light work with how this barky's built."

"It should do nicely. Carry on and keep the hands busy that you can! I'll be below."

"Aye aye, sir!"

"Mr. Steadman!"

"Aye, sir?"

"Should you find a lack of work for the hands, look at setting up the backstays again."

"Aye aye, sir!"

"I'm not satisfied with their present condition."

"Aye, sir."

Pierce entered his cabin and shut the door. He made the usual entries in the ship's log. He noted the day and date, the position of the schooner, and that once again he was permitted aboard. Then he added details about the past two days from notes and rough logs left by Hotchkiss and Andrews.

That done, he carefully and quietly moved his chair and expertly pried up one of the deck planks. He had hidden papers there that he did not want the Tritonish to find. They detailed the precise route that *Island Expedition* had followed to reach this world. Smythe had suggested that he hide such things before the schooner sailed to explore this new world.

This world referenced a different Prime Meridian, but the degrees of latitude were the same. With elementary mathematics, longitude could be translated from one world's variation to the other. He did not want anyone in this world to know the route he had sailed to get here. More importantly, he did not want them to know the way back to the other world. When Smythe finalized those figures, they would be guarded even more closely.

Pierce yawned mightily. He was still tired. His head ached a little, and it seemed that everything in the world -- both worlds -- was going by the boards. He sat unmoving at the table which, along with his cot, took up most of the cabin. He was done with what he considered his duties for the day, and it wasn't even noon.

How he would keep himself busy the rest of the day? How would he or Steadman keep the hands busy? One third of the crew was aboard, and he wanted some productive work out of them. But what?

He did not want them ashore and in the taverns, bars, and brothels. They had enough time for that, enough that the sharpness built up over the last weeks at sea was fast wearing away.

Pierce leaned forward with his head in his hands. His elbows braced against the tabletop. What a mess he had made of his first independent command! He had sailed halfway around the world and had crossed an immeasurable chasm to another one. But now he, his ship, and his crew were stranded, suspected, and at times barely tolerated.

They had reached the island, their original destination, without a single loss of life amongst either the crew or the passengers they carried. Then he had fought a battle that should not have been fought. Several good hands, shipmates, and friends had died as a result. Others had been wounded. Most of the injuries were relatively minor, but a couple had been serious.

Simmons was better, healing rapidly from the splinter wound in his abdomen. Morgan had lost his leg, and for a while seemed to be on the mend. But he had been taken aback and grew worse every day. Lord, what a mess Pierce had made of it!

Sad and melancholy, Pierce wanted desperately to be a child again. He wanted to tell someone how awful he felt. He wanted to be held and told that everything was all right. His deep and lasting friendship with Isaac Hotchkiss would not answer. Even between them there was a certain distance, an image, and a false dignity that had to be maintained.

There were recesses in his soul he would open to only a select few. He could allow his parents in some areas, and perhaps his brothers in others. Perhaps he could let Evangeline know his deepest fears and disappointments. They had grown close enough before the voyage that he felt he could share his weaknesses as well as his strengths with her. He could expound upon his dreams and hopes as well as his nightmares and fears. Should he tell her his deepest thoughts, he knew she would not ridicule or demean them. She would understand, comfort, and show him a way out of the dismal abyss into which he continued to sink. If only she were here!

But as it was, he could not leave this place and return to her, whether for the joy of togetherness or to comfort and be comforted. Nor could any of those with him return, and all had reasons to return. That they couldn't was his fault, and the blame stained his hands like a victim's blood marked the killer. They would remain in this world, in New Guernsey, in Vespica, until they died. They would all die here, and he would be their killer.

Pierce's thoughts drifted to the more recent past. He had enjoyed the previous evening with Leona Jackson. Surprisingly, he felt very little guilt over their night together, although he thought he should on Evangeline's behalf. His feelings for her were true and would not be compromised by any chance physical enjoyment.

This far from home, this far from her, and in the state he was in, he needed an escape. Leona Jackson provided it, and he was not sorry to have taken advantage.

But he could not allow her to know his innermost fears and failings. He did not see her in his future. She was simply the *now* of what life had dealt him. Lately life had dealt a rather nasty hand, and this new diversion was a rare face card.

The joker was that she was married. Aiding her in being unfaithful to her husband troubled him, but he recollected the callous brutality with which Lowell Jackson disciplined his crew. Perhaps this was revenge for the scarred backs and constant terror amongst the hands of HRMS *Furious.* She had told him that Jackson forgot his own marriage vows whenever his ship sailed and he found himself in another port. Pierce wondered that if no man was married once at sea, perhaps no woman was married with her husband gone?

He excused his recent activities with those thoughts. He could explain Leona Jackson's activities with them as well, and could even find reason for Lowell Jackson's reputed escapades. But what about Evangeline? Pierce recalled the mental struggles he had endured when he imagined her not waiting for him. He remembered imagining her courted by others and perhaps bedded and wed by one of them. He had often worked himself into such a state of worry that he could not sleep. The thought of her being with another had been almost more than he could bear. Now he saw the possibility with a different focus.

Despite the night spent with Leona Jackson, he did not love her. He could grow fond of her, but he could not picture them as a couple throughout the years. It was Evangeline Smythe that had his heart. He had promised to return to her -- and by God, he would. But with the length and complexities of the voyage, he realized that he might take a detour or two. Waiting for him, should she encounter a few diversions too ... that was as it was.

Eight bells sounded. Pierce had dozed off. The chimes of the time, noon, ceased aboard *Island Expedition*, but fainter and less distinct, he heard it from the many ships in Brunswick Harbor. Timekeeping by a sand glass was notoriously inaccurate, and that inaccuracy was amplified when many ships were assembled. He checked his watch, set earlier to the chronometer, and knew it was as close to right as could be. It was nearly ten minutes past when Pierce no longer heard ships' bells announcing the hour.

He heard shouts, hails, and good-natured banter and bartering alongside. Bumboats approached from seaward, and vendors and their carts appeared on the pier. Even though the galley was fired up and a simple dinner being prepared by Franklin, many crewmen would spend their hard-earned but rather abundant cash for a procured tidbit or a meal. He thought to have Steadman chase the sellers off and require that the hands eat the meal being prepared for them.

But when Steadman arrived in time to avoid a reprimand for tardiness, and reported the bumboats and venders, Pierce merely said. "No more than three at a time to the pier, Mr. Steadman. And see they don't keep their shipmates waiting!"

"Aye aye, sir!"

"And no one from the boats allowed aboard!"

"Aye aye, sir!" Steadman turned to go, but within seconds turned back and asked, "Shall I fetch you anything, sir, from the pier, or the boats? Perhaps, sir, something from the galley?"

Pierce alleged that he wasn't hungry, and as Steadman left a second time, Pierce added, "Unless you have specific tasks for the hands this afternoon, you may put them to make and mend. Let them get personal gear sorted and repaired."

"Aye, sir," replied Steadman. "There's not much that can be done aboard, other than what has already been done twice already. Much of that, sir, and they'll get testy."

"True. At four bells you may let the most deserving knock off and go ashore!"

"Aye aye, sir!"

"We'll toss a coin and see which of us stays full on to eight bells." Pierce now wanted nothing more than to be ashore. As captain, it was his right to simply announce he was going ashore. But it did not set well with him to arbitrarily require the midshipman to remain aboard. Perhaps Steadman hoped to hit the beach early as well. He did not want to simply override the desires of his subordinate and go himself. By tossing a coin, he could leave it to chance. Should the junior win, Pierce could remain aboard and not appear to have yielded to the less senior man.

"Why thank you, sir! Thank you!"

"Do remember, you may not win. Report back prior to four bells and we'll see what lady luck holds for us!"

"Aye aye, sir"

At four bells Pierce saluted and stepped ashore. He had won the toss, even after trying to be as fair as possible. When he had won the initial toss, he had, in a conciliatory mood, suggested they go two of three. Steadman had won the second, but the third confirmed that luck was with Pierce that day. He went ashore knowing that he had done his best for one of his officers and had given him as much of a chance at an early secure as possible.

On the pier, Pierce had no idea of what to do or where to go. In a rare instance, he simply did not want to be aboard ship. He considered returning to the consulate to try to make up the sleep he had missed the night before. As he strode slowly in that direction, he passed by the Frosty Anchor, where he and others had lately spent a great deal of time. He didn't have a thirst, especially for beer or any stronger spirits, but he opened the door and went in.

"Welcome, Commander!" said Humphrey. "Beer or something stronger?"

"No, I think not," he responded. "But if it's fresh, I'll trouble you for a piping hot cup of coffee!"

"Certainly, sir. I'll have it momentarily."

"Thank you." He moved to a table along the back wall and sat down. The place was quiet. In the middle of the afternoon, not many had a chance to be out and in places of entertainment. Pierce noticed eight or nine others scattered about. Most sat alone while quietly sipping their beer. Two sat at a table and carried on a low and restrained conversation. Humphrey moved easily about, removing an empty mug here and bringing a full mug there. He kept up a friendly and casual banter with his customers. It was what one would expect to hear in such a place: the weather, ships newly arrived in port, or ships set to depart. With those who cared not to engage in even that level of conversation, the tavern keeper did his duties with long- practiced silent politeness.

Humphrey brought a large steaming mug of coffee. Pierce nodded his thanks and contemplated a while before he took his first sip. It was hot, freshly brewed, and much better than what was available on *Island Expedition*. It was even better than the coffee at the Tritonish consulate. He took another sip. The coffee was good enough that he would most certainly stay, have a second and perhaps a third cup. As he wished, Humphrey left him alone with his thoughts.

He had hoped to see Dr. Matheson to discuss Morgan's condition and to insist that more be done. But the doctor was gone, this being his day of liberty. If he had been aboard or at the consulate, Pierce had missed him. Possibly he was caring for another patient.

Morosely, he blamed himself for the lives lost over the past weeks. Some had been killed outright in the battle with *Hawke*. Others had later died of their wounds, and a few were still at risk.

Pierce mourned not only the loss of his own men, but also the deaths aboard his one-time foe. They had suffered a much greater loss than had the British schooner. He even felt that Whitcomb's death, flogged unmercifully by Jackson, was his fault. There had been too many deaths lately, all of them somehow connected to his actions and decisions.

Now the possibility of one more death loomed over him. He worried about Morgan and wondered if he could stomach the death of even one more of his crew. Morgan was not only *Island Expedition's* acting second lieutenant, but had been a shipmate and friend for many years.

He finished the coffee. Humphrey took the empty mug and returned it full, hot, and steaming. Pierce sat, still in deep brooding thought as he absentmindedly sipped his way through that cup as well. When that was gone, Pierce sighed and looked about him. Business in the Frosty Anchor was at its nadir. No one else was there.

In the distance, Pierce heard ship's bells toll the hour. Nearer, a church bell rang three times. He checked his watch. Yes, six bells, three o'clock, just as he would have expected, having sat and slowly consumed two cups of the hot beverage. Humphrey came to claim the empty mug, clean it, and refill it.

When the tavern keeper returned, he carried two mugs of coffee. He set Pierce's before him. "Could I join you in a cup, Commander?" he asked, almost hesitantly. "This might be my only chance for the evening. We'll have a crowd afore long."

"No doubt." Pierce's answer was noncommittal and perhaps uninviting as well. "But sit here if you choose. I am not the best companion at the moment, but I'll not let a man drink alone unless he chooses."

"Thank you." Humphrey sat and took a sip of his own steaming mug. He sat silently, drank his coffee, and Pierce was grateful for his quietness.

At length the tavern owner said, "I don't mean to intrude, Commander, but you seem not quite yourself."

Pierce looked and thought a moment. "Went to a dinner last night, and as usual ate and drank too much. Today I pay for it."

"A condition that I've experienced before."

"And I worry about the health of one of my men," said Pierce, now that the silence had been broken.

Humphrey looked at him inquiringly.

"You've met Mr. Morgan, I believe?" said Pierce. "Lost his leg against *Hawke*?"

"Aye, he's come a time or two with you or other shipmates. I've not seen him these past several days."

"He's gained an infection in his stump that now seems to have spread throughout his body. The surgeons and physicians can't seem to remedy it."

"That bodes no good, sir!"

"Aye! Matheson, our ship's surgeon, is at a loss with it. Dr. Blackburn, whom Lord Sutherland called in, is as well baffled."

"If I might offer, sir, I know a doctor who might be of aid."

"Please!" Pierce felt a little of the great weight and responsibility lift from him. He saw the faintest glimmer of hope. "Who would it be, sir? And how do I contact him?"

"I can send for him, sir. If roads are good, he could be here in a week, two at the most."

"Please do! I've had enough men die under my orders, and I'll not lose another if it can be helped. But who?"

"I'll tell you, Commander, but there is a tale that goes with it. First, though, I'll get a message on the way."

While the man was gone from the table, Pierce resumed his solitary thinking, but he wasn't as depressed as he had been. Whether or not this new doctor could reverse the infection eating away Morgan's being, the thought that another might try was hopeful.

He heard a horse gallop off on the cobblestone street. Humphrey returned, ruddy-cheeked, having most recently been out-of-doors.

"The message is on its way, even as we speak, sir!"

"My thanks, sir, and I am sure, the thanks of Mr. Morgan as well. But now, what of this doctor?"

"Right, sir! Let's clarify the world situation today, sir. The real world, this world -- not that imaginary world you always talk about."

"Go on."

"We are in New Guernsey, a former colony of Kentland. When I was a lad, we fought for our independence, and we won it, too!"

"I'm aware of that."

"Aye. But the Independent Lands of Vespica are just that. We bicker and fight amongst ourselves instead of uniting to fight the common foe."

"I have heard that that is so."

"The Tritonish, the Gallicians, and even the Cordobians play upon that disunity to their own advantage. They are at war, and yet they all apparently respect Vespican neutrality. But do they? Each of them tries to drive a wedge between the various Lands. They also try to drive a wedge between each Land and their opponent in this war. No battles are fought here, but believe me: the war is being waged intensely as can be."

"To what purpose?" Pierce asked.

"Each hopes we will grow tired of the others and expel them from our Lands. The survivor would have a monopoly on trade and, most importantly, access to the resources of this continent. We may have what it takes for one side or the other to finally win the war."

"Please continue, sir! But how does this doctor of yours fit?"

"I'll get to that, sir. I'll get to that. But first, more coffee?"

"I'm afraid I'm near full. I'll pass this time. But please, fetch more for yourself."

Humphrey returned, a full mug of coffee in hand. He sat, had a short drink, and continued.

"These foreigners try to keep the Lands of Vespica from working together as one nation. They want to keep us weak, lest we grow tired of their meddling presence and oust the lot of them.

"There are men from across Vespica that believe we should not only be independent, but that we should be united. They want just what the Kentish and the Gallicians fear -- that we'll drive all of them out, rather than just their opponent."

"I see," remarked Pierce. Much of what Humphrey had told him he already knew or had surmised. However, news of a group pushing for true unity was new to him.

"The Unity Congress is meeting in Bostwick, New Sussex this very week. The doctor is a member of that congress, and will, I pray, upon receipt of my message, excuse himself for a few days and journey here to look at Mr. Morgan."

"And your connection, may I ask, sir?"

"Well, sir, it's not something I freely say. But you and your shipmates, Commander, have always done me right. You've brought me a lot of business and for the most part haven't caused any trouble. Especially, sir, you and yours don't have that air of superiority that many of the Kentish or the Gallicians have. Well, sir, it's more like you were the same as us, Vespican, New Guernsey men."

"I consider that a compliment, Mr. Humphrey."

"The Unity Congress has three or four members from every Land. They devise plans to put before the Joint Council of Lands that will hopefully achieve our aims. But there are many more of us with the same interests who work behind the scenes for the same cause."

"And the doctor represents New Guernsey in the Congress?"

"Oh no, Commander. He stands for Charlenia, to the north. On his journeys for the cause, he has often come here, and I have had the fortune to meet him."

"Is he a doctor of medicine, or does the title reflect his level of education?"

"Both, I would say. But his first claim is as a man of medicine."

"I ask because Dr. Blackburn was recommended as the best, and I find his talents are not what his reputation implies."

"I don't know that any doctor is infallible. But I believe Dr. Robertson has a better chance of success than many others."

"I pray that your confidence in his abilities will be realized."

"As do I. But I must point out one thing more, sir."

"That is?"

"I don't know your take on it, Commander, or Mr. Morgan's. But Dr. Robertson is part Rig'nie, and a lot of white folks don't care to have him treat them."

"I am concerned only with his abilities, sir. I believe Mr. Morgan will feel the same. Indeed by the time he arrives, Morgan may not be able to protest, regardless."

"Then let us hope he arrives soonest."

"Aye, and if I could trouble you, I'll have another cup at your convenience."

Pierce felt much better the next morning. He had eaten more sensibly and had gone to bed at a sensible and civilized hour. He had gotten a decent night's sleep, despite a stealthy midnight visit from Leona Jackson.

He had gone to see Morgan soon after arising, and had found the midshipman's condition the same, if not slightly worse than before. The room had been cooler and the fetid smell of infection had dissipated some. Pierce had been grateful that the doctors had not returned to close the windows and bundle poor Morgan into a feverish sweat-soaked cocoon. At the same time, that they hadn't returned irked him. It was inexcusable that they would not spend even a few minutes to see to a patient in such obvious need. But both of them had other patients, and perhaps situations with those had prevented their return. Or had both Matheson and Blackburn decided no hope existed for Morgan and simply avoided seeing him?

Pierce was in Major Howard's office later that morning, engaged in a lively discussion of how to prove his innocence. The major had done his utmost since their arrival, but Pierce was impatient with the progress. As the morning wore on, tempers sizzled and voices were raised.

Just before it turned into a full-scale argument, a marine knocked at the door.

"Yes?" said Major Howard.

"A gentleman to see Commander Pierce, sir!" shouted the marine through the door.

Pierce asked, loudly, "Does he have a name?"

"Aye, sir."

"Well what is it?" demanded Howard.

"Says it's 'Dr. Robertson,' sir."

"This is unbelievable!" said Pierce and a smile spread across his face. He leapt from his seat. "He could hardly have come so quickly! This is unbelievable!" Then to the marine at the door, he said, "Tell him that I will be there straight away! Major, I'll give you respite from my temper. This is unbelievable!"

Pierce found the doctor in the consulate's waiting room. "Dr. Robertson?" he inquired, although it could be no one else. "I am Master and Commander Edward Pierce."

"Most happy to meet you, Commander," said the doctor, extending his hand.

"And I, sir, you!" exclaimed Pierce as he took the proffered hand in a strong grasp and pumped it vigorously. "You are here so quickly? I did not expect you until next week at the earliest!"

"You were expecting me?" asked Robertson.

The doctor was younger than Pierce had imagined, his first guess being that the two were close to the same age. The doctor was an inch or two shorter and had a thicker and stockier build. His Native Vespican ancestry was apparent.

What caught Pierce's attention were the man's eyes. Dark brown, nearly black, they exuded warmth and humanity, fairly twinkling with good-natured kindness. There was a familiarity about the man that Pierce could not fathom.

"Lord, yes! Humphrey, at the Frosty Anchor, sent the messenger only yesterday! I was told four or five days or more for you to journey from Bostwick!"

"Then it is answered, sir! I was not in Bostwick."

"You are not here for Midshipman Morgan and his amputation gone awry?"

"I have not been told of a Mr. Morgan. But as I am here, I will look into the matter."

"Thank you, sir!" said Pierce. Beside himself with relief, he grasped the doctor's hand and shook it strongly once more. "But if you have not come regarding Morgan?"

"I come about you and your men. When my father returned from his visit to your colony on Stone Island...."

"Your father?"

"Shostolamie."

"Shostolamie is your father?" Pierce knew why the man's eyes were familiar.

"Yes. When he returned to the mainland, he had me organize a shipment of supplies to take to the island. I went along with the hope that I could explain things more clearly than he did. He thinks he speaks Kentish so very well, but his thoughts are Kalish and often get lost in translation."

"I often have the same difficulty, even though I think and speak in the same tongue."

"A common failing," continued Dr. Robertson. "As I was saying, I journeyed to the island, met with Mr. Smythe and others. I was told you had left some three weeks earlier to explore and map the surrounding waters. I made a second trip recently, and there was great concern because you had not returned. Upon my return to the mainland, I heard stories of a Galway Rebel taken by the Tritonish Navy. The tales mentioned he claimed himself innocent and to be from a different world."

"You knew then that it must be me?"

"A simple matter of deduction, Commander."

"But, why didn't Humphrey fathom it? Is he not connected with the Unity movement?"

"He is, sir. But only a few know the significance of your arrival. He had no idea."

"I see," said Pierce, relieved that no one had withheld information on his and *Island Expedition's* behalf. "And now what do we do?"

"I'll see about Mr. Morgan, sir. Then I will go to Bostwick. If the Congress acts, perhaps it can convince the Joint Council to press for your release."

"I am most grateful, sir, for whatever effort you make on our behalf. A drink to mark this momentous occasion? Or coffee?"

"Coffee would be fine, sir," replied Dr. Robertson. "My father told me of your affinity for it. No doubt you noticed his as well. I do not share the affectation to the same extent, but I do enjoy it. And then I must see Mr. Morgan. I should not want you thinking me unresponsive to my first calling, that of healing and saving life."

Chapter Twenty-Four

A Ray of Hope

Immediately after the doctor's arrival, he and Pierce enjoyed a cup of coffee to celebrate their meeting, and then went to see Mr. Morgan.

Robertson was most professional as he examined the patient and commented on the efforts of the previous medical attendants. "While I cannot agree with all that has been attempted," he said, "I know standard procedures and practice call for it. Nonetheless, we shall follow a different course to set this to rights."

"How so?" Pierce asked.

"All that can be accomplished with Baltican medicinal disciplines has been done. With your permission, and indeed yours, Mr. Morgan, I would apply the knowledge and wisdom of my Kalish ancestors."

"I don't quite follow you, sir."

"Nor I," Morgan enjoined weakly.

"To put it plainly, I have the advantage of two cultures. I studied in Kentland and other Baltican nations to learn all I could of those medicinal disciplines. I also lived with my father's people and learned ways that have served them as long as have the ways of the Balticans.

"The Baltican mind sees Original People as unlearned and ignorant, but they have a lore and an understanding of things that so-called 'civilization' will not accept. There are medicines, herbs, drugs, and procedures available from the primitive side that can have wondrous effects. I think that for Mr. Morgan to recover, we must explore that side of the medicinal street."

"I'll stand for it, providing Mr. Morgan does as well," Pierce said.

"Aye," Morgan added. "I am at the place, sir, where I would try anything to feel better."

"But first, we must make you comfortable. It is good that you have kept the windows open. Many medicos disapprove, but I believe cool fresh air helps." Dr. Robertson searched through his kit and extracted a small vial. He was about to open it when he suddenly stopped short. "Commander, could we have hot water and towels?"

"Of course, but may I ask why?"

"I don't know the reason, but I have found cleanliness helps. Too often it seems, problems in the medical world result from unclean conditions or foreign objects and substances entering the body."

"That stands to reason, Doctor. I'll call for them."

"Mr. Morgan," the doctor continued. "Once I wash, you'll have a dose of this. While I am gone you will take the same each day, once each morning and once again at night." Morgan looked at the doctor inquisitively.

"No, this is not of the wisdom and lore of the Kalish people. It is something to ease your discomfort a little. I must go into the countryside, into the wilderness to find what I need to effect a full cure."

The next day, the doctor and Pierce set off. Pierce had cited his need to muster daily with the consulate staff, but the doctor said, "I'm sure Sutherland will grant you leave, Commander, for this expedition. If not, perhaps he will release you to my custody. Despite my Rig'nie heritage, I possess certain influence amongst the Kentish and Vespicans."

As predicted, Lord Sutherland readily granted Pierce permission to accompany the doctor. Robertson arrived very early at the consulate and brought clothing and equipment suitable for their trip. He provided horses: two to ride, and a third to carry their gear. Ever the thoughtful and forward-looking individual, he provided clothing for Pierce. The doctor assumed that a seaman would lack skill with horses and gave Pierce a mild-tempered, older mare that would cause him no trouble.

"You needn't have bothered, sir, with such a gentle beast. I grew up with horses. My father is a coachman, and I ride quite well," Pierce said as they departed.

He felt strange, not being in uniform or in well-tailored civilian clothes. Now he dressed as a man of the frontier: buckskins, furs, moccasins, a large knife instead of his sword, and a hat that was not cocked or pinned or shaped in any way. The hat had a large floppy round brim and a band of once-bright cloth with a nondescript feather in it.

Doctor Robertson dressed much the same. He wore no hat or cap, but had two feathers tucked into his untied hair. Anyone who saw him that morning would never know that he was an honored graduate of the most prestigious Baltican colleges.

"I am sorry, Commander, to have underestimated your equestrian abilities. Many seamen are totally inept at the horse. I did not take the individual into consideration. Yet I think you will be pleased with the animal. She has good wind, and will keep up. Indeed, my poor horse may have to keep up with her."

"Quite all right, Doctor. Shall we be off?"

They left the consulate courtyard at a walk, the hooves resounding loudly on the stone paving. They rode side by side through the streets and alleys of Brunswick. The doctor also led the packhorse. Outside town, the doctor urged his mount into a trot, and Pierce found his own animal ready and eager for the faster pace.

Pierce enjoyed the journey outside the city. In the open countryside, he found exhilaration and a freedom akin to being at sea. Despite the protests of his backside, unused to the saddle, he drank in the pleasures of being away from the city.

But they were not yet in the real wilderness. The road they followed was manmade and well traveled, and they often met others traveling the same route. Early in the afternoon, Doctor Robertson called a halt. They rested, gave the horses a blow, and ate a little of the dried and spiced beef the doctor had brought along. That evening they stopped at a small frontier inn, supped, and slept in the small room that Pierce paid for.

"Tomorrow, Commander, unless I find what I seek, and we return here, we shall encamp out-of-doors," Robertson said, just before he drifted into a deep and restful sleep. "I hope that you will not be discomforted to do so."

"I think not. I've often slept in less-than-perfect places," Pierce replied, remembering times curled up in the cable tier.

As the pair rode eastward the next day, the road became narrower and narrower. Finally it ceased to be a road and was merely a trail. There were still many signs of Baltican civilization about. Tracks of previous travelers were discernable, and many were prints of boots, shoes, or shod horses.

"I am amazed, Doctor," Pierce said, "that you fit so well into two cultures. It must be trying to find which you prefer or feel most comfortable with."

"It can be an advantage. I prefer one or the other, based on what I seek from it, what it has to offer, and what I can offer in return."

"I imagine many might see it differently."

"Many see only half of each culture and resent the half they do not favor."

"Perhaps, Doctor, it is the manner in which you were brought up?"

"I am most fortunate in that. You have met my father, Shostolamie, and I hope you saw his wisdom and intelligence, despite his primitive appearance and bearing."

"A most remarkable man of any culture or heritage," Pierce declared.

"My mother is much the same. They each gently insisted, but did not force me to learn and absorb each of their cultures. Paramount was respect for the other culture."

"A sentiment we often overlook. We think our ways are best, and look at others as imperfect. We tend to think of those with other ways as something less."

Doctor Robertson nodded silently, and the two rode on in silence.

Finally, Pierce's curiosity could not be reined in, and he spoke again. "Pray tell, Doctor, how did your parents come together? It seems odd that an English, excuse me, Kentish woman would marry a person of native blood."

"It is unusual, but also a beautiful and wondrous story, if all I have been told can be believed. It is also a story of pain because members of both families and cultures were much opposed to the union."

"That is understandable."

"Mother's people were missionaries who journeyed into the frontier to enlighten the so-called heathen savage. It could be said they took their lives in their hands. Only a few years prior to their arrival, Kalish and other Rig'nies had been on the war trail.

"Father's people resented the increasing number of white men, the loss of traditional lands and hunting grounds. They fought and slew many, trying to preserve their way of life.

"When her family arrived, there was peace. It was not for any great purpose, other than that the Kalish were tired of fighting. Too many warriors were dead, and too many lodges held widows and orphans. They had seen the ever-increasing number of white men and realized it was a hopeless matter.

"My grandfather, who was then Dream Chief, said that it was time to stop fighting and join with the strangers to find a better way for all."

"Wisdom flows from father to son," Pierce suggested. "Will you be Dream Chief in your turn?"

"I think not, sir. My younger brother seems more in tune with that calling."

"I see."

"The missionaries built a small meeting house halfway between their settlement and the Kalish Village. They invited the Kalish to join them and hear the Word of their God. The Kalish listened, but were unhappy that they could no longer believe all they had believed for generations. Once again the Kalish held hard feelings regarding the white strangers.

"But there were some fine feasts at the little church, and many Kalish went gladly. Shostolamie went once simply out of curiosity, having heard of the delicious and bountiful food served. Alice Madison was there as well. It was her first time to attend, as normally her parents kept her away from the Kalish.

"I have heard many times that from the moment they first saw each other, a bond existed between them. Each had been led to believe that the other was of repugnant and disputed quality. No Kalish warrior would take a weak and pale white woman to his lodge. No gentle Baltican woman would even think of intimacy with a savage heathen male.

"But there are tales of virtuous and lonely white women dreaming of seduction by powerful and sinewy red devil heathens." The doctor chuckled good-naturedly. "Indeed, Kalish warriors may have entertained similar thoughts about the untouchable Kentish women that increasingly populated the land.

"From the moment they saw each other, there was magic between them. Her parents forbade it, and his people strongly discouraged it. But it was love in the truest sense, and would not be denied."

"They say 'love conquers all,' but there must have been some strong demands upon them to gain its full measure."

"She left her parents' house to be with him. They shut her out and forbade her to return. She lived with his people, and although they were not fond of her at first, they treated her correctly, as is the custom. Gradually they accepted and then cherished her, as my father did. As my father does!"

"She must be a remarkable lady, sir!"

"She won Kalish acceptance by respecting their ways. She did not condemn what she did not understand, and tried hard to comprehend it. Her family's faith allowed no other beliefs to exist, despising anything else. However she managed to find many similarities between that faith and the beliefs of the Kalish.

"Shostolamie was much the same. He saw the sameness in many aspects of both faiths and in daily customs and traditions."

"Such a shame she was barred from her own family!"

"I put that banishment to an end, sir!"

"Pray tell, how?"

"A most simple matter. A grandmother wished to see her grandson. She softened in her anger, which had never been as strong as her husband's. Over time and with the presence of a grandson, even he softened in his opposition to her marital choice."

"As they say, Doctor, a 'happy ending'!"

"Or a beginning?"

"How so?"

"I was raised in two cultures. For a part of each year, we lived with the Kalish. I learned the language and the ways of my father's people. During the rest of the year we lived in the settlement. I went to school, learned to read and write, and to follow the faith of those people. Like my parents, I tried to add each side of my heritage into something greater than the two parts. Modestly, Commander, I believe I succeeded."

"Indeed, you have, sir!"

"My thanks! I went to college in Kentland and other Baltican nations as the result of an experiment. A Vespican official theorized that a Rig'nie or even a half-n-half such as I could do as well as a white man. I was one of a small number of Kalish and other Original Peoples selected for the white man's idea of higher education."

"How did the others fare?"

"Not as well, I'm afraid. They did not lack intelligence, but without basic schooling and instruction, they could not fully comprehend and advance. It was quite a step to read signs of game one day and the works of Krakenberg the next. But could the Kentish that were in our classes come here, even where we are now, and know what I know of this place?"

"I would be hard pressed to know the finer aspects of siege warfare. Yet, those generals who are expert at it would not know port from starboard."

"My point exactly! Oh! Look there, Commander!" The doctor stopped suddenly and peered into the deep woods that lined the trail. "We have found some of what we need!"

Four days later the two returned to Brunswick and the Tritonish consulate. In woodsman's and native garb, and with a week's growth of beard, the guards didn't recognize them. At first they were denied entry. It was only when Pierce spoke, and the sentry recognized his voice, that they were admitted.

They hurried to Morgan's room and found him as well as could be expected. The medicine that Doctor Robertson had left had done as it should, and he had remained stable, neither improving nor deteriorating beyond what he had been.

Assured that the patient was doing well, they retired, each to his own quarters, bathed, shaved, and dressed more to what was expected. After a small meal, Doctor Robertson began to prepare the harvest and turn it into the medicines he hoped would speed Morgan's recovery.

He was given the use of one side of the consulate kitchen. Over the next day, he chopped, ground, pounded, mixed, boiled, cooled, and boiled again, the special ingredients that he had retrieved from the wilderness. When he finished, and left the last to cool, he ate his first full meal in over a day's time.

Pierce spent much of that time aiding the doctor as he could. He also received permission to visit the schooner, even though it was not his scheduled day. He updated the log and his personal diary, and added details of his journey to the edge of the Vespican frontier. He had a long talk with Hotchkiss about the trip and the outlook on their situation.

That night, exhaustion, and his excitement regarding Morgan's possible recovery relegated nocturnal activities with Leona Jackson to a lower priority. For the first time since meeting, their late-night encounter consisted of conversation only.

Two days after they returned, a haggard but recently refreshed Doctor Robertson appeared before Pierce, who sat reading in the consulate study. "Commander," the doctor said. "I believe it is ready. Will you accompany me to Mr. Morgan?"

"I would, yes," Pierce answered. He carefully marked his place and returned the book to the shelf.

Morgan was well-rested and relatively pain-free when they arrived. The doctor had already called for hot water. When it arrived, he washed thoroughly, not only his hands, but Morgan's swollen and infected stump. The midshipman gasped at the gentle contact, even though he tried to disregard the pain.

"We must move him to the other bed," the doctor stated. "It has fresh clean linen, which will aid his recovery. The staff can burn this. Do you think we can move him?"

"Certainly!"

"If you would support and balance me, I will hobble on my own," Morgan interjected.

When Morgan was in the other bed, the one with clean and crisp new linens that smelled fresh and inviting, the doctor uncovered the pots and crocks of Kalish medicinal concoctions. However, before he applied or administered any of it, he took a small native pipe from his bag. He charged it with tobacco and other dried herbs, and lit it with an ember from the fire burning low in the fireplace. He drew a couple of deep breaths through the stem and inhaled the smoke deep into his lungs. He passed it to Pierce, who, attempting to emulate the doctor, choked and coughed slightly. The doctor held it so Morgan could also draw in some of the purifying smoke.

After the three shared the pipe, Doctor Robertson offered it to the four cardinal directions, water, the earth, the sky, and of the most importance, the Great Creator and Healer Spirit.

"I don't know if the ritual is needed for the medicines to work. It is a part of Kalish medicine, and I would not risk losing the power by bypassing these steps," he explained.

"Understandable," Pierce replied. "The rite may offer all some comfort."

"Aye!" Morgan added.

Doctor Robertson gently lifted Morgan's shortened limb and slid a small square of cloth under it. He reached into the smallest pot, and coated the stump with a thick tar-like mixture. When the stump was thoroughly coated, and Morgan had recovered sufficiently from the discomfort, the doctor folded the smaller cloth over the end of the limb. He tied it into place with strips of cloth, and coated the exterior with more of the same salve.

Three more times he applied the salve, each time adding another layer of cloth and another coating of the balm. He applied two final layers of linen without the medicinal ointment, and over all he tied a canvas boot to protect the bedclothes from seepage of salve or fluids.

Contact and manipulation of his painfully sore stump exhausted Morgan. The young midshipman was drained and pale when the procedure was complete. The doctor let him rest a few moments, and then insisted he drink some broth warmed over the fire. Morgan made a face of disgust as the first sips passed his lips. Soon, however, the midshipman had the taste of it and sipped with a certain relish.

The doctor said, "The salve will draw the infection out, and the broth will strengthen him. When the stump is free of infection, I will remake it and hopefully find what causes the infection. I dare not do so now. It would drive the infection deeper into his body."

Morgan was nearly asleep, at rest from the soothing effects of the broth and from the fatigue brought on by treatment of his infection.

"It feels better already, sir. It doesn't ache so much."

"Very good! I have managed to prepare things properly. There should be some immediate relief, although it will take several days and several applications of the salve to achieve any real results. And several servings of broth as well.

"Indeed, Mr. Morgan, you should also eat or drink whatever you may desire. Your body will tell you what it needs, if you listen to it. It will also tell you what it doesn't want. Again, you must listen to it."

When Pierce glanced at Morgan after the doctor's short discourse, the midshipman's eyes were gently closed and he breathed in a slow relaxed manner.

"Resting comfortably," Pierce whispered as he and the doctor left the room.

That evening, Pierce and the doctor ate in the study, and now sat, each with a glass of wine. Pierce thought it an excellent Port, but here it was known as something different. "Tomorrow, sir," the doctor said. "I'll show you and Mr. Hotchkiss how to apply the salve and bandages. Now that we have done the first application, you need not do the ancient rituals of purification. The actual treatment is all that is required. Perhaps we should have Mr. Andrews trained as well."

"But surely, Doctor, you can do it yourself? Do you seek others to do your work?"

"I do not shrink from my duties, sir."

"I meant no affront, Doctor."

"I took none. Tomorrow I journey to fetch my assistant and protégé. When I am certain that one schooled in Kalish medicine is here, I must go to Bostwick and work for the release of you and your ship."

"Why -- bless you, Doctor. I have become so caught up in Mr. Morgan's condition that I have quite forgotten our overall situation."

"You appear quite exhausted, Commander. Tonight, I suggest you sleep well and for the entire night. Refrain from strenuous activities, no matter how pleasurable! A full night's rest will be most beneficial."

"Indeed," Pierce answered. He had not hidden his nocturnal adventures as well as he had hoped.

"I will insert no message of morality into what I say. But you must realize her husband can be dangerous. While he has the reputation of a rake and a rambler, she also has a certain sordid history. Each knows the faults, failings, and wanderings of the other. She seems not to mind his, and always welcomes him back. On the other hand, he can be extremely possessive and jealous."

"As many a man would be, I would think."

"He has ruined many men, even if only suspected of involvement with his wife. If he has not challenged them, he has caused them financial, social, political, or service ruin."

"You think I'm unaware of possible consequences, if what you imply is occurring?"

"I mean no offense, Commander. I say it as someone I hope you regard as a friend. I know you have been discreet, but such liaisons do make themselves known. I warn you for your safety. I do not seek to save your soul."

"I am grateful, Doctor. Perhaps it never should have begun. But there are factors that influence our decisions, and...."

"We are all human, sir, and we sometimes yield to temptation. But use caution should it continue. Be aware of Jackson seeking redress for real or imagined wrongs."

"I shall keep that in mind sir," Pierce replied, astonished to have just discussed with another what he had thought secret. It was something he had sworn never to do. He had not discussed it even with Isaac Hotchkiss, his boyhood friend and second-in-command. Perhaps that Hotchkiss was second-in-command was why Pierce never discussed it with him. Doctor Robertson was not under his command, and Pierce could regard him as being of equal stature. As the doctor had hoped, he did consider him a friend.

The next day the doctor showed Pierce, Hotchkiss, and Andrews how to change the bandages and salves.

When the doctor returned a week later, he brought with him a young, attractive Kalish maiden, and an older woman who glared menacingly at any man looking twice at the younger.

"This is my cousin's daughter, Cecilia, my protégée and assistant," he said as they gathered in Morgan's room.

The older woman coughed and turned her intense glare upon the doctor. "This is her mother, Bessie. Her one aim is to protect her child from men: young, old, white, red, or a little of both. Her Kentish is not as good as even my father's, but she will make her thoughts known." The older woman smiled briefly and resumed her glare at the men gathered round.

"I am most pleased to meet all of you," the younger lady said. "I do hope you are not shocked to find one of my gender and tender years as his assistant?"

"It is a bit of a surprise," Pierce began, "but as the doctor has confidence in your abilities, I do as well."

"Thank you, sir. You must be Commander Pierce."

"I am, ma'am."

"I have introduced the ladies but have forgotten to mention your identities. Forgive me, gentlemen?" begged the doctor.

The doctor continued and introduced Pierce once again, and Hotchkiss, Andrews, and of course the patient, Morgan.

"Mr. Morgan," said the doctor when he completed the introductions, "you have already allowed a half-Rig'nie doctor treat you. Do you object to the care of this young Kalish woman? You can all rest assured that her skill and knowledge are far beyond her years."

As the doctor spoke, Cecilia drew a chair to Morgan's bedside. She sat next to him, and reached out to touch his brow and check that he was not feverish. From the look on Morgan's face, Pierce wondered if she had some power or magic in her touch. The midshipman's eyes shone with admiration, a smile had played upon his lips, and he plainly but quietly whispered, "No objection, sir."

She renewed the salve and bandages that day. When the bandages were off and the end of the amputated leg exposed, Doctor Robertson examined it closely.

"Within a week I shall clean it out and remake it. If we are lucky, we will find a foreign substance or object that causes the infection."

Morgan paled at this announcement, as it meant that he would once again be under the knife and subject to the pain and horror of surgery. Pierce saw the reaction and understood it well. He also saw the young woman grasp his hand and squeeze it gently. Morgan relaxed and his face resumed a look of serenity. Later she fed him some of the broth and a little soft bread, which he devoured hungrily and asked for more.

Five days later Doctor Robertson opened up the partially healed stump. Pierce, Hotchkiss, and Andrews were there, both to aid as they could, and to support to their comrade as he faced the trauma of a second surgery. Pierce had seen such operations before, and he was amazed at the delicacy of the doctor's work. He was also astounded at the competency of the young lady who assisted.

Before they began, both washed thoroughly with the hottest water they could tolerate, and a cleansing agent the doctor provided from his kit. Morgan was given a double ration of rum, and that was followed by the most laudanum the doctor would allow. With the midshipman well into his cups, the doctor made a minute incision in the very end of the stump. It bled very little. Cecilia instantly rubbed a powder, also from the doctor's kit, into the wound. A few minutes later, Robertson suddenly jabbed the stump with a small knife. Morgan did not react.

"It deadens the nerves. He will feel nothing, or very little, and we can proceed now," the doctor said. He worked slowly and intently and scanned every square inch of flesh and bone as he opened up the half-healed previous surgery. When he was sure he had examined all that had been exposed before, he had made a final examination. The young lady held a candle close, and the doctor used a reading glass to see in finer detail. Finally he gave a small grunt of satisfaction, and with forceps removed the smallest piece of old cloth.

Morgan gritted his teeth. Cecilia alertly dusted more powder over the wound.

Doctor Robertson held the small fragment up for all to see. "It appears a small piece of clothing carried in during the initial injury or surgery. Perhaps something remained on Matheson's instruments from a previous operation. With it removed and the wound cleaned thoroughly, he has an excellent chance at recovery."

Pierce was in a wonderfully good mood as he sat in his cabin aboard *Island Expedition*. He had been in a great frame of mind for some weeks now. He did not growl menacingly at the consulate servants. He was no longer cross-tempered with Major Howard or even Lord Sutherland. He could not remember when he had answered one of his men in short fashion.

Pierce had put some order in his life. He attended dinners and other social events, but did so sparingly. When he did attend he watched how much he ate, and his weight returned to what he regarded as normal. Most evenings he went to bed at a regular time and slept well and undisturbed. He had taken to walking, glad to be out in the rapidly warming weather and burning off the excess bulk he had acquired.

The days grew longer as the calendar moved through August and into September. At times Pierce needed to remember that this was the southern hemisphere and that summer approached, rather than winter.

Morgan had begun again to heal, and this time there were no setbacks. His progress was rapid, and a week ago, the doctor's assistant had allowed him out of bed. The carpenter had fashioned a crutch, and Morgan began to extend his short walks.

Now the carpenter was making a substitute leg for the young man.

It would be a while until the stump was healed enough to take his weight, but it was to the point that preliminary fitting could be done. Morgan was on course to full recovery, and very soon would have a good portion of his former mobility.

Pierce wondered if it was the doctor's skill, the patient's constitution, or the care provided by the doctor's assistant. Perhaps it was attributable to all sources, plus a little faith and prayer by them all.

He noticed that a bond had developed between Tom Morgan and Cecilia. Was it concern for the welfare of her patient? Was it gratitude for kindness offered and treatment rendered? Pierce wasn't sure. He did see a certain light burn bright in Morgan's eyes whenever the young Kalish woman was in the room. If it were more, he certainly did not fault the midshipman. If not for Evangeline, he certainly could take an interest in Cecilia. His thoughts darkened as he remembered Evangeline and his current relationship with Leona Jackson. He did not need to complicate his life with a third woman. Nor would he allow himself to interfere with an old shipmate's happiness.

Following the surgery on Morgan's stump, Doctor Robertson had remained for a week, ensuring all was going well. Then he journeyed to Bostwick, where he belabored the Unity Congress to act regarding *Island Expedition's* detention. His latest report had been received yesterday. Progress was slow, but in a week or two, the Congress would begin work on a resolution to present to the Joint Council. Perhaps then, that volatile assembly would act regarding the schooner and its crew.

Morgan was healing and the Unity Congress was discussing their plight. He credited both to Doctor Robertson. Pierce also noted that his dreary, dismal, and self-loathing mood had all but disappeared since the doctor's arrival.

Pierce yawned, stretched, and went topside. "Mr. Steadman, do you have plans for this afternoon?"

"None, sir, not until eight bells."

"Very well. I shall be at the Frosty Anchor. You and any others that wish may join me when secured. I'll leave it to you, if any are to knock off early. If some would go and see to Mr. Morgan's transport, I'm sure he would be happy to join us."

"Aye aye, sir!"

Pierce saluted the colors, saluted the quarterdeck, and walked down the gangway to the pier. As he walked along on the sunny and warm afternoon, there was a certain bounce and lightness to his step.

Momentarily, a small shadow of doubt darkened his day. He wondered, for a brief instant, whether this new-found euphoria would last until *Island Expedition* would be allowed to sail.